I write fun, flirty fiction v  edge.
Writing romance is cool because I get to wear  stead
of wellies. I live in a mountain kingdom in Derbyshire, where
my family and pets are kind enough to ignore the domestic chaos.
Happily, we're in walking distance of a supermarket. I love hearts,
flowers, happy endings, all things vintage, most things French.
When I'm not on Facebook and can't find an excuse for shopping, I'll be walking or gardening. On days when I want to be
really scared, I ride a tandem.

You can follow me on Twitter @janelinfoot.

PRAISE FOR JANE LINFOOT

Cupcakes & Confetti

The Little Wedding Shop by the Sea

JANE LINFOOT

A division of HarperCollins*Publishers*
www.harpercollins.co.uk

Harper*Impulse* an imprint of
HarperCollins*Publishers*
1 London Bridge Street
London SE1 9GF

www.harpercollins.co.uk

A Paperback Original 2016

First published in Great Britain in ebook format by Harper*Impulse* 2016

A catalogue record for this book
is available from the British Library

ISBN: 9780008197094

Set in Minion by Palimpsest Book Production Ltd, Falkirk, Stirlingshire

Printed and bound in Great Britain

MIX
Paper from
responsible sources
FSC C007454

FSC™ is a non-profit international organisation established to promote
the responsible management of the world's forests. Products carrying the
FSC label are independently certified to assure consumers that they come
from forests that are managed to meet the social, economic and
ecological needs of present and future generations,
and other controlled sources.

Find out more about HarperCollins and the environment at
www.harpercollins.co.uk/green

For Anna, Jamie, Indi, Richard,
Max, Caroline, M and Phil xx

The best thing to hold on to in life is each other.

Audrey Hepburn

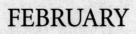

FEBRUARY

1

In my flat at Brides by the Sea: White letters and net curtains

LOVE YOU, LOVE CHOCOLATE MORE...

I can't help smiling at the message the client has ordered to put on top of the cake as I stamp the letters out of the thinly rolled icing. White words on a mocha background, and all going on top of a dark chocolate sponge. It's just out of the oven, steaming on the wire cooling rack next to the tiny table where I'm working, and filling the kitchen with a heady mix of vanilla and cocoa. I lean forward to crank open the little porthole window to let in some air, and catch a glimpse of the sea, turquoise and glistening in the February sun. When I lived with Brett, his penthouse had seaward facing balconies and floor to ceiling ocean vistas, but this last six months I've come to love my jewel sized view from this borrowed crow's nest flat. A tiny corner of an attic over a wedding shop might not be everyone's first choice, but it's home for me.

'Poppy, Poppy, come down quick.' If Jess's shriek hadn't come echoing up the stairwell, I could have filled you in on the gory details of how I came to be here. As it is I need to go, and fast, because it's also part of the deal that I help in the shop whenever I'm called. Which is why I'm clattering down the stairs two at a time, instead of giving you back story.

Bridal shops are emotional places, but Jess the shop owner is usually the one holding the mayhem together and mopping up the tears, not the one screaming like a banshee. This must be big news. I wind my way downwards through the shop, past the dark blue of Groomswear, through the shell pink Bridesmaids Beach Hut. I hurry through the Shoe Room with its shelves of exquisite heels, zoom through Cakes, then Flowers, before I finally find Jess in the ground floor White Room, flapping her hands and all breathless next to the rail of wedding dresses.

'And?' I skid to a halt on the white painted boards, hurriedly wiping the icing sugar off my hands with my apron. You'd think I'd get blasé seeing acres of gorgeous lace and satin every day, but a cascade of tulle still makes my heart beat faster. But why the hell is Jess *this* excited?

'You've heard of Josie Redman…THE Josie Redman?'

'You mean the reality TV star featured in every issue of *Closer*, *Heat*, *OK!* and *Hello?*' I ask. I can't quite remember what she did to be famous, but I know the one. 'Dark hair, swallow tattoo up her leg?' Don't worry, it's a lot classier than it sounds. 'The one who was too famous for Celebrity Big Brother?'

Jess nods madly and it might be worth pointing out here that Jess doesn't do crazy. Anyone who could build up her shop, Brides by the Sea, from nothing has to be super serious. She began with wedding flowers in one room on the ground floor, and now she has the whole building, and a wedding emporium that attracts brides from the whole of Devon and Cornwall, and beyond. Believe me, it came from hours of hard labour, coupled with some equally hard headed business savvy.

'It came up on the Celeb-News app on my phone, and it's all over twitter so it's definitely true.' Jess gasps. 'Sera's up in the

4

studio, talking to Josie's PA now, sorting out details.' As the words tumble out of her mouth, she's flapping her hands harder than ever.

'Details of what, tell me what's happened Jess?'

For a moment I think Jess is going to have a mother-of-the-bride-breaks-down moment. I'm scouring the velvet sofas and gilded side tables for tissues, when first Sera's distressed boots, and then her long legs, come into view on the stairs from the studio.

'Here she is, she can tell you herself.' Jess gives another breathless squeak.

Sera's coming down the stairs as if she's an extra from a zombie movie. As she slides off the bottom step and does a slow motion collapse into the nearest carved armchair I swear her face is several shades paler than her bleached blonde hair.

'Sera?'

Given that she's clutching the hem of her shorts, and opening and closing her mouth with no sound coming out, I turn back to Jess.

'Josie Redman has chosen Seraphina East...' Jess's squeak slides to her usual baritone mid-sentence. 'To design her wedding dress.'

The words take a few seconds to sink in. In my head I'm silently mouthing O-M-G in slow motion, because this is huge. HUGE with the caps lock on. That would be Seraphina East, a.k.a. Sera, the local girl who touted her dress designs round to Jess's newly opened wedding shop in her cut off shorts when she was fresh out of college. She's still wearing the ragged shorts, but the rest has moved on a long way. That was around the same time I gave up my proper job in London and came back to move in with Brett, and popped in to ask if Jess would be interested in show casing my wedding cakes. Since then Jess has encouraged, nurtured, and supported both Sera and me all the way. But whereas my cake baking was a sideline I squeezed in alongside Brett and his starry career, Sera threw everything and more into her dress designs.

Sera now has her studio on the top floor, just below my attic room, and the shop has been the exclusive stockist for her collections in the seven years since she came. And now all her hard work, not to mention Jess's considerable financial backing, is paying off. Because they're hitting the big time here with paparazzi darling, Josie Redman.

'Oooooooo…' I can hear I'm doing that embarrassing howl that comes out all on its own whenever I'm over excited. 'That's sooooo amazing Sera…' And it's going to be equally amazing for Jess and Brides by the Sea too. Brides from across the country will come flocking here now to get a wedding dress like their favourite celeb. It's the stuff of dreams. 'Well done…both of you…' As I grapple Sera into a hug her cheek is wet with tears.

I'm about to track down a tissue for her when the phone in the next room begins to ring. Jess and I exchange glances.

'There you go, I bet that's the first booking coming in now,' I say, not quite believing it. Josie Redman chooses Seraphina East, and an army of brides follow hot on the trail. 'Who'd have thought it would be this fast?'

But it is. For the next two hours we field non-stop calls. By the time we turn the phone off every booking for the next six weeks has been taken, and it's dark in the street outside.

'We're going to have to set up another dressing room…not every fitting will transfer into an order…' Jess is thinking aloud as she lowers herself into the nearest armchair and kicks off her loafers.

Sera's zombie state is beginning to wear off, because she turns to me. 'How the hell am I going to do this?' Her strangled shriek is ten per cent desperation, ninety percent pure panic.

'We'll be here to help,' I promise, hoping for Sera's sake that we will. Poor Sera is amazing at selling anyone else's designs, but when it comes to her own she withers.

She lets out a desperate moan. 'I freeze when I meet customers at the best of times, what am I going to say to a celebrity?'

'Whatever the gossip columns say about Josie, I'm sure she's not that much of a diva…' I begin, realising my mistake too late.

'What?' Sera lets out a shriek of horror.

Damn. Sometimes she seems so sheltered from the real world, I wonder if she gets out at all, other than to the beach. 'I'm sure Josie will turn out to be lovely,' I say, hoping I'm right.

Jess carries on, apparently oblivious to Sera's nervous breakdown. 'So long as we can produce the volume of dresses, Sera, we'll need a room dedicated to your collection.'

At least we have space. The building rambles over four floors. That's the whole reason Jess was able to come to my rescue, and offer me my place here in the attic when Brett and I broke up.

Jess gives me a meaningful stare. 'Be an angel please Poppy, and grab us all a drink.'

Bridal boutiques favour white fizz because it gives you a lift and doesn't stain. 'Prosecco?' I suggest. There's always a fridge full. As Jess says, bubbly brides are happy brides, and happy brides buy.

'Hell no, we need something stronger,' Jess waves me away. 'Get us some stiff G&Ts, there's Hendricks in the desk drawer. I'll have mine supersized, like the cocktails at that place in town, Jaggers.'

Sera and I raise our eye brows at each other. 'When did you go to Jaggers, Jess?' I have to ask. It's strictly for under twenty surfers, and Jess is double that and more. If my voice is high, it's because I can't believe this either.

'Oliver and I often drop in on our terminally single Friday night bar crawls,' Jess says, as nonchalantly as if she'd been a fag hag all her life. 'It's so much more fun going out once you give up trying to pull.'

Sorry about the cliché, but Oliver is gay and in charge of Groomswear. And this is the first I've heard about his celibacy vow, or these racy Friday nights. I admit I've had my head under the duvet these last six months, but this is ridiculous. If this is her way of taking Sera's mind off her immediate problems, it's certainly working.

'You could come too?' Jess adds brightly. 'Much better than hiding away, babysitting in the country, or whatever it is you do. Or working nonstop like Sera.' Although Jess seems to be overlooking that Sera's work ethic is turning to gold for both of them.

My Friday evenings at my best friend Cate's house, helping her look after her dogs and four kids, have become a bit of a ritual for me. I know I'm not ready to start dating again after Brett, but I'm still reeling a bit at being included for a night out with self-confessed 'terminally single' people. As for Sera, I suspect she might be married to her job. I side step the invitation by dashing to the fridge for ice and mixers. By the time I get back Jess is already on to the next thing. As I hand her a clinking pint glass, she motions me to sit down.

'So this is no bad news for you either, Poppy.' Jess stares at me over the top of her Prada reading specs which are still balanced half way down her nose. Probably left there from when she was scribbling in the appointment book. She might hang out in trendy cocktail bars, and have the latest apps on her phone, but she hasn't quite got her appointments on screen yet.

'Sorry?' There's no point pretending. My sinking stomach knows exactly what she's coming to. I just wish she wasn't.

'That dress of yours. The one we don't talk about...' She swirls the ice in her drink.

I know exactly the dress she means. Of course I do. It's the dress I bought when Sera had a very exclusive private sample sale in The Studio a few months ago. I popped in for a teensy peep before it all began. And ended up buying the wedding dress of my dreams.

In my defence, I've been aching to be a bride my whole life. It goes right back to the time when my besties, Cate and Immie, used to dress me up in net curtains when we were kids, and I'd parade around the garden in my Barbie tiara. That was before

8

we went to infants' school. I wonder now if my lifelong wedding obsession had something to do with me not having a dad around. But whatever, I'd waited *so* long to be a bride, no-one could blame me for getting ahead of myself. Brett and I seemed so secure. I had no clue my life was going to come crashing down as it did. One minute I thought my wedding was definitely on the very near horizon, the next the groom was…Well, maybe best not to go there. Enough to say, Brett and I didn't get married.

My main excuse is that on the day I fell in love with the dress, I really did believe it was about to be my turn. I'd waited so many years for Brett to propose. And that week, although he hadn't exactly got down on one knee, for the first time ever, he had said we should be thinking about getting married. When I came across the perfect dress only hours later, it felt as though it was meant to be. As if all my planets were suddenly colliding in a spectacular piece of auspiciousness, or coincidence or whatever it's called.

And although it cost a mind boggling amount, it was a sample dress, so it was amazing value for money. And because I sold my cakes though the shop Sera gave me a special deal. Obviously back then, I didn't live here, because I was still living with Brett.

I scrunch up my face, silently praying that Jess isn't about to whisk my wild impulse purchase out of the storage room. Wild as in wildly expensive, wild as in wildly misjudged, wild as in wildly over optimistic. Wild as in wildly wide of the mark in every way possible, given what came after. And a very well-kept secret, that only Jess, Sera and I know about.

'What about my dress?' I suddenly wish I'd sloshed more gin in my drink. It's hard to compare the giddy rush of the day I bought it with the troughs that came after.

Jess and Sera understood at the time that it was very early days for me and my wedding plans. It wasn't as if I'd even had time to share the news with anyone. We hadn't even got as far as the engagement ring. Luckily we're known for our discretion at Brides by the Sea. To give Jess credit, the day I bought the dress she said it would stay between the three of us. And Jess and Sera have both kept their word on that one. My best friends, Cate and Immie, don't even know about it. And Jess kept the dress safe, hanging in the dress store, all this time. Fully insured too.

'Your dress is one of the most beautiful dresses Sera has ever made.' Jess purses her lips, and out of the corner of my eye I take in Sera's echoing nod.

'It is a totally beautiful dress,' I agree. If you saw it, I promise you'd completely understand. Silk cut on the bias, simple yet with the most exquisite lace detail, it flowed over my curves as if I was barely there. 'But I can't even bear to look at it.' It's a relief to get that confession out. I sometimes wonder how one dress could have had so many tears cried over it.

'I know that dress is very emotionally charged.' Jess knocks back another slug of gin as she makes that understatement. 'But when Sera hits the spotlight, you'll see a good return on your investment.'

Sera sends me a nod of solidarity over the top of the mint sprig I stuffed in her G&T.

I take it Jess is referring to the financial kind of investment. Ever the good businesswoman, she usually sees things in terms of the bottom line, and she grins and rolls her eyes when I wince at the word. I sometimes wonder how someone who does such beautiful things with flowers can be so financially minded, but Jess has been around the block. She insists that going to hell and back with her ex-husband was what toughened her up. Believe me, she must have been playing hard ball to extract a building like this out of her divorce settlement. Freehold, mortgage free. Just don't tell anyone I told you that.

'Wait until Josie's had her celebrity wedding and then sell. You'll make a killing,' she goes on.

'B-b-b-but...' The word 'sell' sends a chill through my chest. 'I'm not sure I'm ready.' I'm not sure I can even bear to sell it at all. I mean I'm hardly going to get another one am I?

'You'll have at least a couple of months to get used to the idea.' She pats my hand gently. 'What else can you do? That dress is spoiled for you, you'll never use it.'

I have no idea how she can sound so matter of fact about something that wraps my stomach into knots.

I pull a face at Sera, who's gnawing at her thumb nail. 'I don't want to turn into the woman in the attic wearing my abandoned wedding dress.' I let out a half laugh. After the way Brett let me down, that's the only way I'll ever get to wear a wedding dress now. I won't be getting involved with a guy again any time soon, that's for sure. 'I know you're right, Jess, it just hurts.'

Jess tilts her head. 'Think of it as your nest egg. It's always good to have one.'

I gawp at her middle aged thinking. 'I'm thirty two, I'm way too young to think about stuff like that.' My squeal of protest fades as I remember exactly where the dress came from. Bought with the money my mum gave me just before she died. 'A nest egg' was exactly how she put it too. I swallow back the lump in my throat. My mum would have loved to see me marry in that dress. In any dress for that matter. I squeeze my arms around my chest as I take a reality check. No family. No Brett. I'm completely on my own. If it wasn't for Jess and her attic I'd be homeless and jobless. I support myself entirely by baking cakes and helping in the shop. I can't afford to shy away from this.

Jess drains her glass. 'Our scars make us who we are. Wear them proudly, and move forward.' Her smile acknowledges that she's said that same line to me more times than I can count in the last six months, then she narrows one eye. 'Moving forward being the important thing now.' She waggles her glass at me. 'As soon as you've got me a refill that is.'

As I rush off for another pint of gin, deep inside I know she's right.

2

In Rose Cross village: Ice breakers and a handful of hounds

'Bolly, Brioche stop pulling!'

The wind whooshes away my wail as I stagger after two lurching honey-coloured bottoms and wagging tails. Dog walking is never like this on the IAMS adverts.

'Brioche, Bolly, heel pleeeeeeease!'

I'm doing my best to be in control, but channelling my inner dog-charming goddess is impossible this early in the morning. The extra early start is because Cate, Immie and I have a big shopping day ahead of us. They don't come much bigger than shopping for bridesmaids' dresses, especially when we're shopping for eight. And if you think eight bridesmaids sounds excessive, you should see the rest of Cate's plans. Her wedding is shaping up to be *the* Cornish country wedding of the decade.

As an in control dog walker, I score an epic fail every time. You'd hardly think I'd been doing this most Saturdays for six months, which is how long it is since I decided to dedicate my scarily empty Friday evenings to a babysitting sleepover, so my bestie, Cate, and her soon-to-be husband, Liam, can have a weekly night out together.

With four kids, two lively labradoodles and full-time jobs, they find it hard to spend any quality time together. Although sometimes when I'm tucked up on their sofa with little George, and the three older kids, it's more as if they're the ones looking after me.

As a cake maker I like to match people with their perfect cake. Cate's cake is a delicious Moroccan orange sponge, with a covering of perfectly piped buttercream, and crystallised orange trimmings. Cool, yet sophisticated. Sometimes I still think of Cate as she was when we were six, when we were at Dancing Jillie's tap class in the village hall. Cate was the one who could do all the steps, not a blonde curl out of place, tapping away like she could give Ginger Rogers a run for her money, while I was the one getting my legs in the arm-holes of my lycra all-in-one, and losing my shoes. But Cate's luck ran out at twenty five when her husband ran off with a woman from the reprographics department. Left with three kids under four, she grappled her way through the next few years. Now she's finally found the guy she deserves, and had another baby, I couldn't be happier for her.

Back to the labradoodles, I swear we crossed the last three fields without my feet touching the ground. Although today fast is good. When I get back, Cate will have finished giving George his breakfast. And then we'll meet up with Immie, whose signature cake is either a donut or a double chocolate muffin. She's had the same stocky build and no-nonsense short hair since we were kids, and however much we try to persuade her into other outfits, she always wears jeans and a sweatshirt. We're heading to Brides by the Sea, which is where we all know Cate's going to buy the bridesmaid dresses. It helps I get mates' rates.

My feet finally make contact with land again as we come to a stile. The dogs bound over into a muddy puddle the size of St Aidan Bay, making tidal waves as they leap. As I follow them Bolly does a double bounce that soaks me, then yanks me off the hillock I'm balanced on.

'Nooooo Bolly…'

I let out a wail as my left Ugg plunges deep under water. Blinking, I scrape the mud splat out of my eye with my fist, and let out a deep sigh as cold oozes round my toes.

Whereas a mud pedi on a Tuesday morning in a salon in St Aidan would be bliss – not that I can afford them these days – I could do without a DIY Cornwall countryside version. The same goes for the leopard print pattern of mud, dappled all the way up my jeans. We'll all be in line for a hose down from Cate when we get back home. It's completely my own fault. If I'd taken a removal van instead of a flight bag when I left Brett in a hurry, I'd be wearing my beloved purple festival wellies, and my feet would be dry now.

As we work our way back along the lane towards the village, Rose Cross, the dogs are beginning to flag, but the cluster of house roofs peeping over the hedges, and the promise of some civilisation perks me up no end. This is the village where Cate, Immie and I grew up. But whereas they love the countryside, I think of it as wilderness. At eighteen I couldn't wait to leave for London. Even coming out here from St Aidan on a Friday night gives me a culture shock, and not in a good way.

Taking advantage of the slack leads, I slide out my phone to check I'm not running late. Then, as we round a bend, we come across a grey Land Rover Defender parked on the verge ahead. Impressed by my car knowledge? All gathered when I had to make a Land Rover fortieth cake for a 4x4 obsessive, with full detail and chocolate mud splatters. I inherited the cake baking gene from my mum, picking it up because she did so much of it when I was little. My earliest memory is standing on a chair in our cosy kitchen, licking out cake mix bowls, and drawing shapes with my finger in the dusting of icing sugar on the kitchen table. Give me a sponge and some icing and I can work wonders Whether it's fairy castles, dumper trucks for birthdays, or the multi-tiered wedding cakes I make so many of now, they come easily. Sadly, if icing isn't involved, I have a great talent for stuffing up.

I'm in my own world, thinking about mum as a guy in faded jeans saunters from behind the Land Rover. Two words pop into my mind.

Perfect ten.

Talking about the guy here, not the car, obviously. Although that's definitely not a compliment. More of a warning to myself to avoid at all costs. When they have it on a plate like that, they rarely learn to be nice.

My gaze slides past a cashmere sweater, and comes to rest on what has to be one of the most cross looking mouths in the south west. This guy might be a straight ten, but he looks way too bad tempered to be working those good looks. Yes, Immie, who's studying psychology at university, would have a lot to say about me honing in on the lips, but in this case I'm only reading the situation. I don't need a degree to recognise obstinate when I see it.

A sharp tug from Bolly and Brioche jolts me back to reality, knocks my phone out of my hand, and as it skids across the dirt track I see why they're pulling.

Somehow I've failed to notice the guy has a dog with him. It's huge and black, and it's bounding towards us now. Before I can scramble to reach for my phone, I'm in mid-air as the dogs lunge. Whereas Bolly and Brioche are careful where they put their gigantic paws in the house, when they're in midflight they don't give a damn.

'Look out!' I shout, but my warning comes too late. They collide with Land Rover Hunk, who staggers, waves his arms, and topples backwards onto the verge.

Man down! Literally. There's no time to wince at the thought of cashmere hitting mud, because the dogs bound on.

As the dogs all come face to face, there's a blur of dog limbs, and excited yelps. They tumble and roll, thump into me at knee height, and I slither sideways. As the barking subsides, I come to a soggy and chilling halt in the gully below the hedge.

'Bolly, Brioche…' It's hard to sound masterful when I'm on my back, bum deep in the ditch. More icy water, this time seeping up my spine. On the plus side I'm actually pretty proud that I'm still hanging on to the leads.

A stream of angry swear words comes from the guy as he scrambles to his feet.

'No need to panic, they're only playing.' Mr Land Rover is hauling Black Dog out of the heap by the collar. He shoulders the dog back into the car. 'They're wagging their tails, see? But seriously, you need to get those dogs of yours better trained. It's completely irresponsible to let dogs run wild in the countryside.'

Excuse me? I'm the one who kept hold of the leads here.

'At least they haven't killed each other.' I mutter. 'It might have helped if yours had been on a lead.'

He ignores that and is looming over me now, holding out his hand expectantly.

Shit. Introductions. I remember my manners and stick out my spare hand. 'Pleased to meet you too…' I realise I'm mumbling as well as lying. And why the hell am I rubbing the mud off my face with my sleeve and trying for a smile?

He lets out a low laugh. 'It's not an introduction, I thought I could pull you out. Unless you'd rather stay there?'

Anywhere else I might have shrivelled at my mistake, but when you're soaking wet in a hedge bottom there's not much point. A moment later, he's yanked on my arm, and I'm back on my feet by the roadside, dripping for England. I'm not sure my festival wellies would have saved me here either.

'Your phone…' He hands it to me. 'You're very wet…'

This guy goes in for stating the obvious. As he passes over the phone I'm distracted by how his rugged hand doesn't fit with his expensive jumper.

'Although if you go rampaging around with two mad hounds, hurling yourself into ditches, you can hardly expect to stay dry. I'd offer you a lift, but…' He trails off awkwardly.

The way he's screwing up his face, we both understand. 'But' is the meaningful part of that sentence. No way is he inviting me and two sopping dogs into his precious Land Rover. He needn't worry. Even if I did accept lifts from total strangers, I'm not about to ruin his up-market seat covers with puddles and labra-doodle splatters.

'I'm so sorry…don't worry…it's completely fine…we don't have far to go…' I'm doing it again. Babbling. And apologising. Both things that Immie's trying to train me not to do. Anyone else but me would have managed to laugh it off by now with a witty quip about mud wrestling.

'It's no-one's fault.' He shrugs as he reaches for the car door. 'Sorry all the same. I bet you didn't plan on mud wrestling when you set out?'

There you go. Why couldn't I do that?

As he moves back to the car his expression softens. 'I guess I'll see you around then.'

If he's glad to see the back of us, the feeling's mutual. 'See you.' I say this airily, safe in the knowledge that I absolutely won't. Ever.

I know I should be over being embarrassed about stuff like falling into a ditch. And I'm working on it, okay? As long as the clean up doesn't delay the shopping trip, the girls will most likely wet themselves laughing about it.

'C'mon dogs.' Two furry faces instantly turn to me. Mud up to their ears, but still looking like butter wouldn't melt. 'Hurry up, there are dresses to try on…' As we set off, my wet jeans are stiff, and the water in my Uggs sloshes with every step, but for some reason my mouth still curls into a broad smile.

Land Rover Guy might have avoided me and the dogs muddying up his Landy, but from the mud slick on the back of his jeans, I'd say he's going to leave a pretty good bum impression on the driver's seat.

3

At Brides by the Sea: Dimples and Saturday girls

Saturday is the busiest day at Brides by the Sea. As Cate and I push through the door on the dot of nine, the shop is already buzzing. We manage to pass the chaise lounge and the shoe cabinet without getting waylaid by any rampaging bridezillas. Then just as we reach the stairs Jess comes hurtling towards us, a dress in a cover in one hand, and a tiara and veil in the other.

'Cate, lovely to see you.' As Jess flies past she tosses us air kisses. 'I'll be with you as soon as I've sorted this pick-up.'

Cate, phone in hand, looks doubtful. 'Sorry, it's only me at the moment, apparently Immie's running late.'

When she's not studying for her psychology degree, Immie works at the local farm, running the gorgeous barn conversion holiday cottages. We know she's delegated most of her jobs for today so she can come to the fitting so this must mean she's tied up with her family. Immie has a shed-load of brothers who she hauls of trouble. Saturday mornings at the police station are a regular thing.

Dodging a large display of freesias, I call over my shoulder. 'We'll grab a coffee upstairs while we wait for Immie.'

Jess calls back through a cloud of tulle. 'No worries. Come down to the Bridesmaids' Beach Hut as soon as she arrives and we'll go through the dresses.'

As we finally finish our climb to my attic, I drop my bag in the flat hallway, and lead the way to my kitchen. 'Are you hungry?'

One look at Cate's pained face, and I turn on the oven.

She groans. 'I'm ravenous, more so now I'm up here with the permanent smell of baking.' She's still battling to lose the baby weight from George in time for her wedding, although the curves really suit her. She gazes up at the shelves groaning under the weight of mixing bowls and wooden spoons and cake stands and recipe books.

'I know it isn't a tenth of the size of Brett's place' I say, assuming she's making the comparison. 'But I don't miss getting the cake mix splatters off his expensive, polished surfaces.' My baking things were the one thing I brought with me when I left.

Cate pulls up a stool. 'This kitchen suits you way better.' She leans to sniffs the daffodils in the red tin jug. 'I love it because it feels so like your mum's. When I think of all the wonderful cakes that have come out of your kitchens over the years, I'm drooling.'

'How about I make pancakes while we wait for Immie? Or better still, muffins.' I grab a bowl from the stack on the shelf, and I've cracked the eggs and added the oil and milk before she can argue.

Cate, Immie and I grew up together, breathing in the delicious smell of my mum's baking. Cate's mum worked at the bank and paid my mum to look after Cate from when she was a baby. Immie and her brothers all piled into the cottage next door where their gran lived, but from the day Immie learned toddle, she invariably ended up at ours. Not that my mum minded. She was on her own with me, so two extra made us more of a family.

'Chocolate or blueberry?' I ask, knowing Cate takes her five-a-day very seriously. She'll always go for the healthy choice. As I whisk in the sugar, the batter begins to turn creamy.

Cate leans forward to sneak a finger into the mixture. 'Pops, are you sure you're okay with all my wedding stuff?'

As I tap my hand on the side of the sieve, the flour lands in a dimpled pile on the batter. 'I work with brides every day, I can hear the word wedding without getting break-up wobbles.' The funny thing is, when weddings do give me that lump in my throat it's more because my mum isn't here, than because Brett and I broke up. 'It's not as if Brett and I were even engaged,' I say, to emphasise the point.

'You may not have had the ring, but you were together a long time.' Cate's pats my hand on the way in for another dip. I'd have banned her from the kitchen for putting her fingers in the mixture if I were baking for a customer, but this morning I look the other way.

'The trouble with the break up was when Brett went, my whole life went with him.'

I push a couple of baking trays and a stack of muffin wraps towards Cate. She knows how it feels to get dumped, so she goes out of her way not to flaunt the deliriously happy bride thing. Even though she had her heart truly trampled back in the day, she never gave up on love. Now she's found Liam, who's truly her Mr Right, she deserves a wonderful day. Cate has booked her dream wedding at Daisy Hill Farm just outside Rose Cross, where Immie looks after the holiday cottages. When they started doing weddings last year Cate was first to book. Believe me, she's going to need acres for the size of wedding she has in mind.

'Blueberry then?' I grab a handful from the fridge.

'How did you guess?' She passes me the tins.

I spoon the mixture into the cases, then there's a rush of hot air from the oven as I open the door, and push in the muffins. 'Twenty five minutes, then we're good.'

Her eyes light up expectantly. 'Can I lick the bowl out?'

'One condition.' I grin. 'No pink bridesmaids dresses. When you've got orange hair like mine you have to be very careful what you put it next to.' Taking the scissors to my blonde ponytail was my way of rebelling after the break up. But I still get palpitations every time I catch sight of my spiky pixie cut. As for the home colouring, it's nothing like as easy as it looks on TV. Last time I missed pillar box, and ended up vermillion. Seriously, Johnny Rotten in the butter advert was *not* the look I was aiming for.

Cate tugs her fingers through her layered bob as she ponders. 'Pink dresses would look fab in a hay meadow, but there again…' She grabs the mixing bowl. 'Okay, you've got a deal.'

Cate's still scraping her spoon around the bowl five minutes later when there's a clattering on the stairs, and Immie bursts in.

'Dean, drunk and disorderly, no charges, enough said.' She throws her bag onto the table. 'Sorry I'm late…can I smell muffins?'

'Blueberry ones, they'll be ready in twenty minutes.'

'Okay, so where are these dresses then?' She's already got her 'disgusted of Rose Cross' face on. 'With my short legs and my beer gut, I know I'll look like a duck's arse in most of them.' She gives a determined jut of her chin. 'Although Freda from the Goose and Duck says I'll be fine so long as we stick with navy.'

'Right.' Cate purses her lips. 'Blue is out because the boys have nabbed that.'

Immie gives a groan, and I'm ashamed to say I'm doing silent cheers. Navy's not really my colour.

'Actually there's something I need to tell you before we get onto dresses.' Immie's frown lines deepen. 'I'm so sorry, Cate, you might want to sit down. The word at Daisy Hill Farm is that Carrie the wedding planner has quit.' Immie leans back against the work top, hands on her hips, to let the news sink in.

'No.' Cate's face falls.

Immie's looking grave. 'It gets worse. Big boss Rafe is talking about pulling out of weddings altogether…as of now.'

Under her blusher Cate's cheeks have gone three shades lighter. 'He can't…can he? We've already paid the deposit?! The wedding's barely seven months away.'

Immie shrugs. 'Who knows? The wedding planner went back to London for Christmas, and she's decided not to come back.'

'She took her time, it's February now.' Cate lets out a moan.

Immie carries on. 'Rafe's tried to replace her, but there aren't many bookings, and the hours are erratic. Not to mention he's not the easiest person to work with. Anyone decent runs a mile.'

Cate's sigh is long. 'Right. I'm not giving up on this. This is my wedding day.' Her mouth hardens into a determined line. 'I need to find someone to save the day and fast. I need a wedding coordinator.' She turns on Immie and me. 'Who do we know?'

This is why Cate has zoomed up the ladder at the council in her day job. She won't take no for an answer, and when the going gets tough, she fights.

I screw up my face and think. Who could take over the wedding coordination at the farm? Jess would be amazing but she's got her hands full with the shop. I come up with zilch. As I open my eyes again, Immie and Cate are both staring at me.

'It's obvious.' Cate says.

'It bloody is,' agrees Immie.

I blink at them. 'Am I missing something here?'

Immie rounds on me. 'You're the perfect person for the job.'

What? It's a moment before I take in what she's saying. 'But why me?'

Cate jumps in now. 'I need the help, please Poppy. I work a fifty hour week in a highly stressful job at the council, and I've got a house and four kids to look after. And Liam, and the dogs too.' She looks desperate. 'This is my wedding day at stake.'

I turn to Immie. 'Well you're at the farm now anyway, managing the cottages, why can't you just add in weddings too?'

You know those no-can-do stares that builders have? That's what Immie rolls out here. 'No way.' She folds her arms. 'I love you Cate, and I want your wedding to be perfect, but Morgan's running wild now he's fourteen. If I'm not around he'll be balls deep in trouble in no time. Then there's my degree. Final year is full on. I've got all the holiday cottages to manage and clean. Plus my stand-in shifts at The Goose and Duck. Weddings would be the last straw.'

I try once more. 'Your final year at uni isn't until next year.'

She dismisses that. 'I've still got assignments coming out of my ears.'

As I look from Cate to Immie, I can't help feeling they're ganging up on me.

'Whatever.' Immie shrugs. 'You know you'd be awesome at this, Pops. You've always loved weddings.'

'And you've had so much experience with the brides at the shop.' At least Cate has the grace to look guilty about pushing me into this. 'Not just with your cakes either. You know the wedding business inside out. It could be the perfect career move.'

Immie chimes in again. 'Out of all of us, you're the one who could nail this.'

When they put it like that, I need to go on the defensive.

'I can't organise weddings. I'll end up ruining them!' There's a squeal of panic in my protest. 'I left my London job years ago.' Once upon a time I was a food designer, working in food development. Remember hedgehog flavour crisps? They were my baby. And my salmon en croute for a certain famous supermarket scooped all the awards. As did one extra special luxury Christmas pudding, with almonds and Cointreau. And my Huggie Bear Birthday Cake was a huge best seller. But that was another life. Since I moved back to Cornwall all I've done is run around after Brett and play at making cakes.

Immie jumps in. 'You could easily fit the Daisy Hill job around your cakes, and the extra cash would come in handy.' As a single

23

mum at uni, Immie knows all about juggling jobs to make ends meet. And she's not wrong about the money either. I'm ashamed to admit how much I'd come to rely on a well-paid boyfriend.

'Seriously, Poppy, you could do this in your sleep. You deal with brides all the time.' Cate's tone is persuasive. 'It's only until the autumn. And I need you.'

My mind flashes back to the fields in Rose Cross, and the mud. A job on a farm would be my worst nightmare, even if it did involve weddings.

'But I've got no *actual* experience.' I might as well point it out.

Cate brushes that aside. 'If we're going to save my wedding you're damn well going to have to blag it.' Her cheeks are flushed now. 'You've had the insiders view from so many brides, you're practically an expert already.' She gives a triumphant shake of her fist.

'Exactly.' Immie is cheering her all the way. 'And I'll be there for back up, if it all goes tits up.'

'Tits up?' I echo. If I had any sense, this is the moment I should have run. But Cate is my best friend, and she needs me.

The look Cate flashes Immie for the tits up mention is filthy. 'We're talking a few tiny weddings here. There won't be any problems.' Her voice is soothing. 'Please Poppy, give it a go, just for me?'

Cate's been like a big sister to me all my life. The last few months she's really looked after me, and this is one way I can show how truly grateful I am. I need to man up, and save the day for Cate.

4

At Daisy Hill Farm: Nothing personal

'I can't believe I've been working up here all this time and you haven't visited before.' Immie is hurrying across the cobbled courtyard of Daisy Hill Farm to meet me, as I clamber out of my car next morning. She's arranged an interview for me with the owner of the farm, Rafe.

'Maybe it's because I avoid farms like the plague.' I point out. 'Fields and cows and windy days are why I live in town, remember?'

Immie and Cate weren't going to hang about. They abandoned all thoughts of bridesmaids' dresses yesterday, and got straight onto beautifying my CV. But whoever heard of an interview on a Sunday?

Immie flashes me a grin. 'So don't mind Rafe, he's like a bear with a sore head, but it's nothing personal.'

'What?' If she'd leaked this information any earlier I might have had an excuse to resist. She's hurrying me past a faded Georgian farmhouse, with rows of dusty sash windows, towards a range of stone out-buildings.

'He doesn't do charming, but don't let it bother you.' Immie, telling it straight again. 'No need for nerves, you're going to walk this.'

I give a shrug. Even though I'm going to give this my best shot, I'm not worried. I know I don't stand a cat in hell's chance here. However much they tarted up my CV before they emailed it over to this grumpy Rafe person, it's obvious that icing is the only thing I'm qualified to smooth over.

'The office is in here…' Immie pauses outside a grey painted plank door. 'Play your cards right, and he'll probably offer you a cottage to live in too.' She raises an eyebrow, clicks the latch, and pushes me into a warm, white-washed room. 'Rafe, this is Poppy, I'll leave you two to it, have fun.'

She sweeps out, and as the door slams shut behind her I take in a desk that looks like a recycling skip got tipped out on it, a guy in a grey jumper standing by the filing cabinet, and a black dog lying in the corner, giving gentle wags of its tail. My heart beat is louder than the wagging thumps as I wait by the desk. As the guy whips around and holds out his hand I choke.

Oh.

'Poppy, great to…' His voice grinds to a halt. From the way the guy from yesterday's ditch is suddenly lost for words, I'm guessing we're both equally gob smacked to see each other again. When he said 'see you around', I'm sure he didn't intend it to be this soon.

I dig deep. Actually I've nothing to lose here. There's no need to give a damn at all. I simply have to spend a few minutes not getting this job, and I can be off.

'Hi again.' I jump forward, and grasp his hand. 'No mud wrestling today for me.' I get that in early and throw out a tentative smile, hoping my smartest black jeans and the white shirt Immie lent me will cut it. With Cate's borrowed wellies to show I mean business, now I've got this far I might as well go for broke. 'And I left the labradoodles at home too.'

Hopefully he won't recognise the Barbour jacket is Immie's too.

I turn my full beam smile onto him, and try to put the brakes on any babbling. 'Brill, shall we get on with it then?'

He takes back his hand, rubs his chin and gives a deep sigh. 'Remind me again why you're here?'

The dark circles under his eyes suggest he's as tired as he sounds. *Probably knackered from having sex all night.* Not that it's anything to do with me. I shove that thought away, and try to pick up my bounce where I left off.

'The wedding coordinator job…Immie sorted the interview…' Given he isn't reacting at all, I recklessly go on. 'Immie emailed you my fabulous CV yesterday?' My 'tada' arm flourish wilts as he fails to react, although it does get a raised eyebrow from the dog.

'Weddings…right.' He shakes his head. 'Sorry, I've been in the barn all night with a difficult calving.'

Fine. So now we know there wasn't any hot sex.

'And how did that go?' I toss in another smile.

Land Rover Guy exhales again loudly, and drops into his swivel chair. 'We lost the calf.'

I carry on smiling, determined to see the positive side here. 'Great. Or at least it will be when you find it again.'

'Lost, as in died. The calf died.' He says, as if on remote control, and leans back and taps on his keyboard. Finally getting round to reading my application.

I kick myself for that blunder. 'Sorry.'

He clears his throat, but doesn't look up from the screen. 'It happens. There's a big vet's bill, but at least we saved the mother.' If he's reading my CV, I take it from the way the corners of his mouth are turning down that he's spectacularly unimpressed.

He looks up momentarily. 'Okay, you're hired. Welcome to the team.'

'What?' If my voice has gone all high, it's because I'm aston-ished. Even the dog has pricked up his ears in shock.

27

'Start tomorrow...' He's already focusing back on the screen in front of him. 'How does nine sound?'

Talk about bish bash bosh. 'This isn't how you interview people.' I have to tell him, I can't let this go. 'Excuse me for asking, but what part of my background and experience makes you think I'm qualified to be a wedding coordinator...on a farm of all places?'

'Your background?' He stares vaguely, then looks at his computer screen and his lips twitch into some twisted kind of sardonic grimace. 'I'm not reading about you here. I don't even know where your CV is.'

Worse and worse. 'So how do you know I can do the job?'

He finally bothers to turn his attention to me. 'To be honest, I don't.' He rests his chin on his knuckles, and pauses long enough for that blinder to sink in. 'But Immie thinks you can, and I trust her.' He sits back, locks his fingers behind his head. 'And to be brutally honest a second time, you'd have to be a complete imbecile to make a bigger mess of the weddings here than they are in already.'

I take in the way his voice resonates over the word trust. Those hazel flecked eyes. And that scar on his right cheek bone. Then I move on swiftly, and focus instead on a gaze that is as direct as any I've ever met. My breath catches.

'Thanks for coming.' With one swoop he's on his feet and grasping my hand again. 'But I have to rush. I'll deal with contracts and questions in the morning, although from what you've said I doubt if you'll be in any position to bargain, given your lack of experience.'

If he wasn't already out of the door, I'd shut my gaping mouth and call him on that. As it stands I'll have to wait until tomorrow. He's still shouting as he disappears across the yard.

'Oh, and don't look at this as long term, it's strictly temporary and it definitely won't develop into anything more permanent.'

And that's fine by me. The sooner it's over the better. I just hope Cate appreciates what I'm doing for her here.

5

In the office at Daisy Hill Farm: Comfy chairs and neat freaks

'So the previous wedding coordinator, Carrie, didn't have an office, and she shared the desk and computer with you?' Despite me swivelling in Rafe's swanky up-market chair, and him perching on the inferior – folding Ikea, in case you're wondering – chair opposite, by the end of the first morning I'm beginning to see every reason why the wedding business is in trouble.

Rafe frowns. 'I'm rarely here, and this way you can cover the phone too. Think of it as hot desking.'

Hot desking? If he'd said that with the tiniest bit of humour, I'd have laughed. As it is his morose expression hasn't cracked once, although every time I mention Carrie, his scowl gets worse. Whatever Immie's psychology books say about body language, I'm picking up tension over the absent Carrie.

Lunchtime has arrived without me noticing, and as my stomach rumbles I finally take a slurp of cold tea and a bite of the carrot cake I got out for elevenses. 'As for hot desking...' I'm spluttering through my crumbs. 'We're in rural Cornwall, not central London.' Pointing out the obvious here, but sometimes you have to. And space is definitely not at a premium, given there are out buildings as far as the eye can see. 'And hot desking only works if you follow strict rules.' I scowl at the paperwork piles collapsing across the table. 'Like tidying up, for example.'

He's straight in there, snapping my head off. 'Well you're the one dropping cake. Eating is taboo at a shared desks unless you clean up afterwards.'

How did I imagine farmers were relaxed? Just my luck to meet one the only one in the world who's anal about crumbs.

'Sorry, would you like some cake? It's carrot with almonds in.' I offer, kicking myself for letting my hunger get ahead of my manners. 'Trial baking is the up-side of being a cake maker.'

Only when he looks bemused do I realise that he hasn't got the foggiest idea about what I do when I'm not here. He still hasn't bothered to read my CV.

He shakes his head. 'Thanks, but I'm not big on cake.'

Sorry for being judgmental, but that explains a lot.

'I'm only scratching the surface with the paperwork.' I begin tentatively, not wanting to drop Carrie in it. 'But the record keeping seems pretty chaotic.'

This is the nice way of saying there's no diary, no list of book-ings, no client details, and as yet, no record of transactions. All I have to work with is a carrier bag of scribbles on scraps of paper. As for Cate's booking, so far there's no trace at all.

He gives a dismissive shrug. 'Nothing more or less than I expected.'

Despite my fears about fighting for desk space, something tells me that bad mood bear Rafe might not be around that often. If we're seriously doing questions and answers, this might be my only chance to go for it. 'So last year was your first round of weddings.' I take in his slow nod. 'How many did you do?'

He grunts. 'Three…maybe four.'

'And how did they work out?' I'm pushing now.

He narrows his eyes. 'They were chaos.' For the first time

there's a hint of ironic humour behind his morose mask. 'But apparently people still enjoyed themselves, despite the mess ups.'

I can't help myself – the next bit spills out before I can stop it. 'You make it sound more like Daisy Hill Disasters than an aspirational wedding venue. If you have no interest, why the hell are you carrying on for another year?'

He drums his fingers on the table. 'Good question.' He stretches his legs out in front of him and leans back in his chair. 'Let me give you the back story. Farming is currently in the shit, we need to diversify to survive. Personally I'd have chosen a wind farm every time, but in response to local opinion, I agreed to try weddings first.'

'Okay.' I nod.

'We also have holiday cottages, which are thankfully running smoothly and bringing in a decent income. As for why I'm carrying on with the weddings – if I don't I'll lose my holiday cottage manager, and I can't afford to do that.'

My eyes widen as I take that in. 'Immie's holding you to ransom, to secure Cate's wedding? And you're going along with it?'

He looks me straight in the eye. 'We choose our battles Poppy. Seriously, would you want to fight Immie?'

An image of Immie flashes into my mind. She's seven, she's standing square in the playground with her feet apart, and her face scrunched up, and she's ready to take on all the big boys who've been pulling my hair and making me cry because I haven't got a dad. One look at that intimidating scowl of hers, and those bullies melted away. And she hasn't changed since. She's fiercely loyal, and she battles tooth and nail on behalf of all her friends, and Morgan, her son, and her brothers, a lot of whom don't actually deserve it.

'No.' I have to admit. 'I couldn't take on Immie. Have you seen the way she bunches up her mouth like she'll fight to the death?'

He nods again. 'So the upshot is, I'm stuck with weddings, and you're stuck with hot desking, until this Cate has her big day.' He slaps his hands on his thighs, as he gets up. 'And then we can shut it all down and I can get back to running my farm without any interruptions. Any other questions?'

Shit, he's going. There are still a million things I don't know. I begin to blurt. 'Where are the weddings held? What about the electricity? What shall I say to enquiries?'

'I'll show you round, sometime soon.' He's doing that thing again, talking as he walks out the door, and it's already annoying the hell out of me. 'I just hope this Cate's worth it.'

'Oh she is,' I say, but a gust of wind has already caught the door and slammed it shut.

6

At Brides by the Sea: Dashes and dots

The up side of having different jobs is the variety. Yesterday I was sorting out the chaos in the farm office. Whereas today I'm putting the finishing touches to the icing on some cupcakes for a Vintage Tea Dance themed wedding, when I'm called down to the shop to help Sera with a hem.

Right now Sera's on her knees, working her way around a bride in a gorgeous lace sweetheart-neckline dress with a very full skirt. And while Sera's sorting out the final length of the exceedingly long hem and train, I'm handing her the pins, and making sure the bride doesn't pass out by chatting to her. We've been going half an hour, and Sera's nearly back to where she began when Jess appears.

'Almost done? Not too stiff from standing, I hope?' Jess beams at the bride, then turns to me. 'Poppy, I'll take over here, Immie's come for a quick word. I sent her up to your attic.'

Knowing Immie has a soft spot for cake, I don't hang around. I make a dash for the stairs and reach the kitchen just in time.

'Cupcakes, my favourite.' Immie's leaning over the table, drooling.

'Hands off!' I whisk the cakes across to the work surface, counting the pastel coloured tops waiting for final decoration. I heave a sigh of relief when I see they're still all there. 'Put the kettle on, there's a new chocolate mocha cake I'd love you to test.' Hopefully this will more than make up for the disappearing cupcakes. 'You can have some with your tea.'

'Sounds like a deal.' Immie squeezes behind the table, heading for the sink.

I take it this is a social call, although Immie normally prefers to socialise over beer rather than tea.

'And while I finish icing these cakes…' Cath Kidston themed, in blues and pinks, with polka dots, bunting and roses, in case you're wondering. There's a three tier wedding cake to match the cupcakes, and they're being collected later, which is why I'm pushing on now. '…you can tell me what I'm going to do about Rafe.'

Immie frowns. 'Rafe? What's the matter with Rafe?' Something tells me she's faking the surprise.

'Where shall I begin?' I pick up my icing pipe and a cupcake, and begin to add white polka dots to the duck egg blue butter-cream topping I spread earlier. 'He hates weddings, he doesn't smile, and he doesn't like cake, which is the worst thing I've ever heard. If he's not snapping, he's totally disinterested.' I'm ticking the points off on my fingers as I go. 'He walks away when I'm talking to him. And although he objects to my crumbs on *his* desk, his tidy obsession doesn't extend to the rubbish he leaves on *my* desk.' I spent the whole of yesterday battling with Rafe's towers of papers. 'There has to be some way to bring him into line. I'll never make it through to October if I can't bribe him with sugar.'

I break off to get Immie's cake. As I open the tin and cut a huge wedge, her eyes light up.

'You're a woman with wiles.' She wiggles her eyebrows at me. 'I'm sure you'll find some other way to manage Rafe. Playing the damsel in distress in a ditch didn't do you any harm did it? I mean it landed you the job. You're the heroine who came out from under the hedge and saved Cate's wedding. It almost has a Cinderella ring to it'

If that's what she thinks, I'll let her carry on. If I tell her saving the wedding was all down to her being intimidating, it might go to her head.

'Count my feminine powers out of this one.' I put a pink sugar rose in the centre of the cupcake, and move on to the next. 'If I have to resort to persuasion with Rafe, I'll be using savoury flans not sex. I'd rather flash a broccoli and tomato quiche than my assets any day.'

Immie chortles as she drops tea bags into the cups. 'And cooking isn't feminine manipulation?' She gives a burst of her throaty laugh, watching as I arrange pea sized icing circles onto a cupcake covered in bright pink buttercream.

'So what are you doing in town then?' I'm concentrating on the bunting string of icing I'm piping across the next cupcake.

'I've been clearing Carrie's cottage all day. I came into town to post her the stuff she left.'

'What?' My icing string wiggles to an abrupt halt as my head jerks up. 'Are you sure she wants you to do that?'

'If I had Agent Provocateur undies, I'd want them sent on. Especially the thongs with rubies on.'

I'm impressed that Immie, with her throwaway attitude to men, even knows what Agent Provocateur is.

'I'd have thought she left her things here so she had an excuse to come back?' It slips out before I can stop it.

A slow smile spreads across Immie's face. 'And are you speaking for yourself here Pops, or for Carrie? You still haven't picked your things up from Brett's, have you?'

This is typical Immie. She's always reading the subtext. As for

Brett and I, we're well and truly over, whatever she's implying.

'Sorry but you're wrong there, Mrs Freud.' I move things on. 'Actually I wish someone *would* send me my stuff.' I say that in the hope it'll shut her up, although in reality I'm not sure I even want it any more. 'No wonder Rafe's grumpy though, if Carrie dumped him.'

Immie's voice rises in surprise. 'Carrie and Rafe were never an item, what made you think that?'

I shrug. 'Maybe the way Rafe has smoke coming out of his ears whenever she's mentioned?' Although now I come to think of it, I seem to have that effect on him too.

Immie gives an eye roll. 'Carrie was Rafe's mum's latest attempt at matchmaking. Carrie planned to make herself indispensable doing weddings, and grab herself some landed gentry into the bargain.'

'Rafe is landed gentry?' I've temporarily stopped picking up icing triangles for my cupcake bunting.

'He's not short of a few acres. That was good enough for Carrie.'

'You don't sound as if you like her much?'

'I know Rafe's a grumpy bugger.' Immie gave a rueful grin. 'But taking an all-round view, I reckon he deserved better.'

I'm trying to work out if this is Immie 'seeing things as they truly are', or if, underneath her gruffness, she's hiding a soft spot for her boss.

'I'm not sure which he hated most,' she says, 'bridal parties processing all over his best grazing fields, or Carrie with her Knightsbridge ideas and her red lipstick.'

I try to sound neutral. 'It's no fun having a meddling mother when you're his age, even if she does choose you women with jewels on their knickers.'

'His mum was only trying to help,' Immie goes on. 'Rafe used to live with a nice girl called Helen, but she dumped him and married his best friend.'

'That's tough.' At least I got cheated on, then did the dumping, although when you've sunk to ranking getting left, it's pretty sad.

'It was years ago, she left because Rafe refused to get married. It's time he manned up and moved on.' Immie gives the tea bags a last vigorous dunking and pushes a mug towards me.

Given the tea is the colour of tar, I go back to my bunting instead. Picking up some triangles, I line them up along my icing line.

'Which reminds me…' Immie grins at me over her mug. 'Rafe said he'll throw in a cottage as part of your employment package.'

The shock of that makes me push my last flag into completely the wrong place. If I splodge this cupcake any more I'll have to give it to Immie.

'I told you he would.' Ignoring my reaction, she takes another bite of cake. She's enjoying a free tenancy in one of Rafe's cottages down in the village. And she's determined I should do the same.

I sigh, pick up two more cupcakes and pop a sugar rose on each of them. Then I go back to dots.

'Thanks, but I really don't want a cottage.' Jess came to my rescue by offering me the flat above the shop when I left Brett. My attic may be little more than a cupboard, but I pick up a lot of orders by being on the spot at Brides by the Sea. What's more, I'm finally beginning to feel settled. 'Even if it's bigger than here, who'd want a cottage in the middle of nowhere, tied to a temporary job?'

'Whatever.' Her disgusted sniff suggests she disagrees. 'Anyway Rafe said tomorrow's good for the grand tour.'

'What?' I look up blankly from the spots I'm arranging.

Immie laughs. 'Keep up Mrs. The tour of the farm he's supposed to give you – the wedding area, the cows, remember?'

Cows. My favourite. Not. 'Couldn't you show me round instead?' It's a plea.

She shakes her head. 'Rafe's adamant. He said be there for two, and wrap up warm.'

Another afternoon with the world's most joyless farmer and I might just lose the will to live. 'I'm not going to get out of this?'

'No point trying.' She laughs. 'But the good news is this mocha cake is delicious. Is there any more?'

If only I'd stuck to cake making.

7

A Tour of Daisy Hill Farm: Do cows eat cake?

First things first. Please don't look at what I'm wearing or I might just die of shame.

'You can't go out in a flimsy little thing like that to see a farm,' Rafe says, pointing to my thickest warmest fur-lined winter parka, as I arrive in the yard the next day. 'I'll find you a Barbour.'

The way he says the B word, he makes it resonate, as if it's full of spiritual significance, and then he rushes off to the house. 'Great,' I say, remembering the short almost on-trend jacket Immie lent me on Sunday. Except what he brings back isn't anything related to that at all. It might go by the same name, but it's definitely not the same species. Somewhere along the line it's mutated, which is why I'm currently doing an impression of a yurt on legs.

'Thanks.' I'm not wanting to sound ungrateful, but a marquee would have fitted better. Although I have to admit there's something immediately addictive about the smell of the wax oiled fabric.

If news on the style front is disastrous, as long as you ignore that we are not travelling by car, we are not even travelling by Landy, we are actually travelling by tractor – and that is the kind with four wheels all approximately the size of the London eye, where you practically need a ladder to get on board – the rest is better.

An hour later, my brain is popping with information on feed prices and milk quotas, not to mention every fun fact there is to know about organic farming methods, past and present. What's more mind boggling still, it seems that Rafe's family collect land and farms at approximately the same rate I collect Kate Moss dresses from eBay. But on the plus side I've discovered that the way to soften up Rafe is by talking cows not cake. We're standing in a drafty barn, but the good part is there's bouncy yellow straw on the floor, and we're watching some very cute black and white calves with wobbly legs, skittering around.

'The last time I saw straw like this was in a nativity play when I was at infant school.' This is the extent of my conversation on the subject of straw, I just hope the man appreciates it.

'Come over here…' Rafe's voice is low.

A calf is sticking its nose through the railings, and is nuzzling his hand.

'If you put your finger in its mouth, it'll suck,' he says.

I shudder, and not in a good way. 'Thanks, but I don't think so.'

'You might find you like it. People do…' Rafe is rubbing the calf, tickling the tufty hair between its ears

Cow slobber? I steel myself, and creep towards them. The next thing, there's a slimy wet nose pushing against the palm of my hand.

'Oh my.' Waxed jackets were obviously designed with slobber in mind. I'm just totally relieved this isn't happening to the front of my best parka.

'Not so bad is it?' Rafe's letting out the nearest thing to a laugh I've heard, but then I realise he's talking to the calf, not to me.

'Awww…his eyes are blue…and look at his lashes…' I might sound besotted, but it's always the eyes that get you with babies. According to Immie we're biologically programmed to react to them, and kick into care and protect mode.

'Here.' Rafe takes my hand and gently guides my fingers into the calf's mouth.

Its tongue is raspy and sticky, warm on my hand. As it begins to suck I let out a gasp.

'We don't do this too often, or they give up drinking from the bucket,' he says. 'But it's a good way of making the humans less nervous.'

How the hell did his voice get this chocolatey without eating any brownies?

'You might want to visit at tea time, they knock you over to get to their milk.' His lips twitch into a semi smile. 'Not all farming is this cosy, but it's a good place to start.'

Everything I had to say about weddings has gone. Which is a pity, because while Rafe is all relaxed and chatty, it might be an ideal opportunity to run a few things past him.

'Daisy Hill Farm needs a website you know.' I blurt out the first item from my list of priorities as it pops into my head.

A second calf is sniffing now, and before I know, Rafe grasps my other hand, and what do you know, I've got two calves sucking on my fingers.

'Set one up then.' He says not even bothering to look in my direction. Blunt as that.

'Me?' Now I'm warmer and out of the wind, I can smell a hint of delicious aftershave wafting up from the corduroy collar of my borrowed coat. I try to block out that it might be his.

'You're the one that wanted the job. It's down to you. Do whatever you have to.'

'Great.' This should be easy, so why is he making it sound hard?

'One condition –' this time he does look at me, and it's almost

41

a glare '– don't bother me with it, because I don't want to know.'

'Right.' So what about the other hundred items on my list that all need answers?

'If that's clear, when you can bear to drag yourself away, I'll take you to see the wedding field.'

I'm strangely reluctant to detach myself from the snuffly noses, but I do. Slowly.

After a long goodbye, he hands me a towel, which is good because I've never known slime like it. I'm still wiping my hands on the back of my jeans as the barn door clangs shut behind us.

'As for your contract, Wedding Coordinator doesn't adequately describe the responsibility you'll be taking here. You won't just be planning, you'll be the one everyone turns to on the day. The one in total charge. In other words, it's your head on the block.' He's ushering me towards the tractor, and shouting over the roar of the wind. 'You'd better change your job title to Events Manager.'

Immie was so right when she said this guy has no idea.

8

A Tour of Daisy Hill Farm Continued:
Red boots and spring rain

'So if you were having a birthday cake, I think either a tractor, or a cow would suit you.' I'm musing here. Allocating cake designs to people? It's a thing I like to do as soon as I get to know a little about someone. Even if they are blowing hot and cold.

We're bowling along rutted tracks back to the main farm, and to be honest there's simply no space left in my head for another fact about cows or sheep or fertilizer or slurry. Slurry? It's the most disgusting thing out. Take it from me, you DO NOT want to know details. And don't write me off as an air head, but my brain is officially rammed. There's enough agricultural information in there to last at least two lifetimes, which is why I decided I have to fill the space as we drive back to the farm with a conversation about normal stuff.

'Why the hell would I want a birthday cake?' Rafe sends me another of his disbelieving sideways glances. I've noticed he resorts to these a lot when it's me doing the talking not him.

I'm torn between frustration at him being so unreceptive, and a horrible pang of sympathy for someone who obviously hasn't blown out any candles in a very long time. How can a guy be so out of touch with the fun side of life?

'When did you last have one?' This is less rude than it sounds, I'm only trying to keep the conversation on topic. And asking questions will save me from what Immie calls my nervous splurging.

'How do I know? Probably when I was about five.'

Probably not true at all. Isn't it a typical guy thing to dismiss what doesn't interest them?

'My mum made the most awesome birthday cakes,' I say. It's out before I can stop myself, because usually I'd rather not talk about my mum, especially not with strangers, so I move on swiftly. 'For my fifth birthday I had the most amazing merry-go-round cake, with prancing horses and barley sugar twists holding up the roof.' Growing up in a kitchen with the table covered in icing bowls and piping bags definitely rubbed off on me, but there's no point sharing that with a cake hater.

'So I grew up with cows and tractors, you grew up with cake. That explains a lot.' He gives a sarcastic laugh. 'It's always the kids who have easy childhoods who grow up to be annoyingly happy adults.'

Two side swipes in one breath. I doubt that my mum bringing me up on her own counted as easy for her, not that I'm going to tell Rafe that. My dad died when I was too young to remember, we never had much money or owned a home, but my mum made up for it in every other way. Our home might have been tiny, but it was filled with warmth and love and colour. If those digs were meant to shut me up, I'm not letting him get away with it.

'Whereas you had so much, and still turned out moody and bad tempered,' I snap back. That came out more harshly than I intended, but maybe someone needs to tell him.

He comes straight back at me. 'Well, sorry I don't go round

44

wearing spotty wellies and thinking the whole world should be made of sugar, but some people have responsibilities.'

I had no idea he'd even noticed Cate's red boots. What kind of guy takes offence at wellies?

He gives a snort. 'And just so you know, in-your-face red hair might match your name, and it might be fine if you want to scream "happy hippy", but I'm not sure it sends out the right message for a Wedding Coordinator.'

I'm wearing borrowed wellies, have go-wild-after-break-up hair, and I've been thrown into the job. I take a minute to collect myself in the face of that attack.

'Actually, I'm not a Wedding Coordinator, I'm an Events Manager according to you.' I throw that at him for starters. And whereas I might have been thinking along those lines myself about the hair a couple of weeks down the line, now he's been so rude, I'm damned if I'm going to tone it down. 'As for my name, I'm called after the blue poppy, not the red one.' My mum's favourite flower, our garden was bursting with them. 'Known as meconopsis.'

His only reply is to lean forward and flick on the stereo, and we roar up the lane back towards the farm. Oasis blasts away the silence, and the beat is loud enough to make my head throb. As we pass the farmhouse Immie is there waving her arms, and there's lucky respite as Rafe cuts the music and slides open the window.

'You two getting on okay? No more falling in ditches I hope?' She asks with a breezy laugh.

I'd say overall it's a big fat 'no' to both those questions, but she isn't waiting for an answer.

'By the way Rafe, Morgan texted, says he'll be round to help with the engine rebuild later,' she adds.

'Fine.' Another monosyllabic reply from Rafe.

Immie's fourteen year old son, Morgan, has morphed from a sweet boy to a monster overnight due to a testosterone rush.

That's Immie's description, not mine. But if Rafe is an example of Immie's choice of fun male role models to keep Morgan out of trouble, I feel sorry for poor Morgan.

'We're just off to see the venue field, I'll be back for him in a bit.' Rafe says, as he slams the window shut, and then we're bouncing off down the lane again.

As he turns through a gateway with an open five bar gate, I'm a) still fuming b) thinking we need some signage.

'So what would yours be then?' His question comes from nowhere as we skid down a field.

'Sorry?' I have no idea what he's talking about.

'Your birthday cake. What kind would you make for yourself?'

Who'd have thought he'd ask that?

'A summer garden, bursting with flowers.' Easy to answer. 'And I might not have a cake, I'd probably make a cupcake tower.'

Too much information there obviously, given he's shaking his head again, but then he pulls to a halt in front of an open barn, and my eyes go wide.

'This is it,' he says, with a 'take it or leave it' shrug. 'Ceremony in the building, marquees anywhere on the grass, and car parking in the next field beyond the trees. Nothing more to it than that.'

I know I shouldn't be gushing, but my surprise whooshes any remaining crossness away. 'It's so pretty.' Even on this grey winter's afternoon it's beautiful. With the carved wooden pillars across the front of the open barn and the ancient flag floor, I can imagine it festooned with garlands of summer flowers. As I take in the field rolling gently down past a fairy wood to a stream, I can suddenly see why Cate has set her heart on marrying here.

Rafe flings open the tractor door and jumps out, and cold air floods into the cab, along with the most disgusting stench.

I bury my nose in my sleeve as I clamber down after him. 'What the hell is that?'

'The smell?' His expression suggests amusement, but on second

46

glance it's more of a grimace than a smile. 'Muck spreading in the next field.' He folds his arms. 'Is there a problem?'

Obviously he doesn't think so, despite the stink being enough to make me retch. I peer over the hedge. The grass is covered with a thick brown mat of what looks like cow poo.

'You aren't going to…' My voice is coming out as a squeak. 'You aren't going to do that in this field are you?'

'It's next on the work sheet,' he says, as if it's the most matter of fact thing in the world.

'Are you mad? You can't have brides wading through…' I man up and say it. '…cow shit.'

He doesn't flinch. 'Don't worry, a bit of spring rain, and it'll soon soak into the ground.' Spoken like a farmer talking to a townie, not a wedding venue owner talking to his Events Manager.

My brain whirrs. This is another thing I needed to tell him. 'The first booking is at Easter.'

He looks unruffled.

'Which is the 25th of March.' As I count back in my head my hands go clammy. 'That's only five weeks away.' I might just be shrieking now. It's going to take a deluge of rain to clear this lot by then.

The way his mouth is set, he almost looks jubilant. 'As I said before, it's over to you now. That's your problem, not mine.'

Last week I might have let that go. Ten minutes ago I might have shied away. But thanks to the cow shit, something's shifted inside me. I shove my hands deep into the pockets of my Barbour and clench my teeth.

'Fine.' I stick out my chin, begin to take a deep breath, then think better of it and take a small sniff instead. 'If I'm in charge, I say, we won't be having muck spreading in this field, and we won't be having it in the surrounding fields either. Is that clear?'

I reel at how decisive I sound.

'I'll stop it then,' he mutters. 'But it won't be good for the soil in the long term.' With a loud sigh he turns away and gets out his phone.

'Soil isn't my problem,' I hiss.

No, my problems are way bigger. Like how to deal with the nightmare known as Rafe Barker. And how to prepare for a wedding, in only five weeks' time, when, thanks to the chaos left behind by Carrie, I don't have the first clue how to get in contact with the bride and groom.

9

In my flat at Brides by the Sea: Anyone like a cupcake?

After the shock of the news that her wedding venue was under threat, Cate didn't want to tempt fate and look at bridesmaids dresses last Saturday. But now her wedding's back on track, we've arranged to look at the bridesmaids' dresses after work today. And to put us in the country wedding mood, I'm making a last minute batch of cupcakes. So I'm in my cosy, pocket handkerchief size kitchen, sprinkling sugar daisies on top of swirls of lemon buttercream when Immie's text arrives.

I'm here, I'm early, are you in? xx

She's not kidding about early. I was counting on another half an hour to finish the cupcakes, and to get changed. Dragging off my apron, I clatter down four flights of stairs, and fling open the door to find Immie, legs bowing under the weight of a huge box.

I waft her into the hall with a couple of air kisses. 'I didn't know you were bringing dresses.'

'I'm not.' Her frown is uncertain. 'I have a feeling you're going to kill me for this, but I had a tutorial in Falmouth, so I've been round to see Brett.'

'What…?' I open and close my mouth, as I collapse quietly against the door frame, but nothing more comes out.

'After what you said about Carrie's stuff, I thought it was time you had yours.' Immie blows out her cheeks. 'Actually the car's rammed.'

What…? At least she has the decency to look slightly shame faced, which doesn't happen often with Immie.

'I'm sorry Pops, but someone had to do it.' She dumps the box by the stairs. 'Come on, the car won't unload itself.' Before I can open my mouth to protest, she grabs my arm, and the next thing I know we're shuttling up and down the cobbled mews behind the shop, with bags and boxes.

By five when Cate arrives, Immie and I are red and sweating, and my tiny top floor bedroom is piled high with bulging black sacks.

'Packing up to move to the farm already?' Cate takes off her Alice band and shakes out her hair. Then she slips off her mac, strides over a stray bag, and lays her coat on the bed.

'No, this lot is on its way in, from a certain penthouse.' Immie explains for Cate's benefit. 'I'm re-uniting Poppy with her festival wellies,' She gives me one of her tough love stares. 'It's time to accept that you and Brett are over, Poppy.'

'I see,' Cate sounds doubtful. She's left work early to do brides-maid shopping not a house move. It's Friday afternoon. After a hard week she's looking forward to a glass of prosecco, and a cosy session in the shop downstairs.

I twiddle with the edge of a black bag. 'I think leaving my things behind was a way of playing for time.' With my things here, the break up suddenly feels very concrete and final. And it's not about losing Brett, it's more about accepting that from now on, I'm on my own. And that's me on my own forever, because I'm done with relationships. 'It's hard to think I might never be part of a couple again. Or a family.'

Cate's arm lands round my shoulder. 'Move to the farm, and be nearer Immie and me. We're your family.'

Immie nods in agreement.

The thought of leaving my cosy attic in the heart of St Aidan is bad enough, but anywhere near Rafe Barker would be my worst nightmare at the moment. 'What? And live next door to the boss from hell?'

Cate scours my face for clues. 'You and Rafe aren't getting on?'

Immie laughs. 'Understatement of the decade. The good news is our meek mouse Poppy has finally found her inner lioness.'

'I'm so sorry, Pops, it's all my fault you're in this situation.' Then suddenly a beam spreads across Cate's face. 'But the lion bit sounds good, what happened?'

'Anyone like a cupcake?' I try to distract them. 'There's fizz in the fridge too.'

They don't move. When were they not bribed by the promise of prosecco?

'Come through, and I'll tell you while I open the bottle?' My last attempt works, and we all cram into the tiny kitchen as I pop the cork. I wait until the girls have wine in hand and mouths full of cake, so they can't interrupt too much, because between you and me, I've been asking myself the exact same question. Why am I jumping down Rafe's throat all of a sudden, when I can barely say boo to a goose?

'I'm winging it here,' I begin, not quite knowing what to say. I've inadvertently taken a bite of bun, and as I talk through my cake, the crumbs falling down my front remind me of Rafe picking me up about crumbs on the desk. And suddenly I know. 'I always bit my tongue with Brett because I didn't want him to dump me. I never told him what I thought, because I was scared I'd lose him.'

'So you concede you were a bit of a doormat then?' Immie is grinning. I'm not sure if it's the sugar, or the first wine of the day going to her head.

51

Immie's glass is already empty, so I top her up, ignoring the doormat bit. 'Brett acted like he was the boss, and that was fine because he *was* better than me.' I ignore Cate and Immie's matching appalled looks and blown out cheeks, and carry on. 'I gave up a good job to live with him, but once we were together here, he was the one with the big salary, the flat, the fast car. All I did was bake a few cakes.'

'I'll let that amazing piece of self-dismissal go...' Immie is shaking her head. 'But how come you tell Rafe exactly what you think?'

'Ha, that's easy.' I don't hesitate. 'To start with I was really angry that he nearly robbed you of your wedding, Cate. And fighting your corner is way easier than doing it for myself.'

'Go Poppy!' Cate cheers. 'Thanks for that.'

'The wedding side is in complete chaos.' I have to be careful here, because I don't want to alarm Cate. If she knew there was no trace of her booking she might just lose it. 'In confidence,' I meet eyes with Cate, 'to give you an idea, there's a wedding booked for a month's time, but I've got no clue at all who made the booking, and no way of getting in touch with them.'

Cate's eyes go wide. 'Oh crap...'

I go on. 'But then Rafe's not even apologetic, and he's so so rude all the time, and so damned annoying.' Even as I think about him the back of my neck begins to prickle. 'He's got it all – looks, a rich family, a great place to live. All that, and he can't even be bothered to be civil. So for the first time in years I didn't hold back when he pissed me off, I said exactly what I thought.'

'Bloody hell.' Immie sounds impressed.

Cate waves her glass in the air. 'Yay Poppy!'

I slosh out more wine all round. At this rate it'll be taxis home.

'And although we're having all-out war, for the first time in years I feel like I'm being true to myself.' I slug back my own wine so fast, the bubbles sting my nose. 'And you know what, I like saying what I think.' I glance at my watch. 'Sorry to rush you, but we'd better head down to the shop. Jess will be waiting. Take your glasses, I'll grab another bottle or two to take down with us.'

'It's nice to have our feisty Poppy back.' Cate grabs a last cupcake as she heads off down the white painted stairs. 'I'm going to need all the strength I can get if you're *both* saying it like it is. Have you got any hard hats in those bags of yours, because I have a feeling we might need them? Bridesmaid wars here we come.'

10

The Bridesmaids' Beach Hut is the upstairs shop area dedicated to bridesmaids, but you probably guessed that already. Jess recently gave it a beachy make-over, hence the name, and as we troop in across the artfully scuffed floorboards she's straightening the pink striped fitting room curtains.

'Wow.' Cate's eyes light up when she sees the love seat decked with fairy lights. But when she spots the long rail of dresses beyond, her beam stretches the width of the bay.

'Cate, Immie, come on in,' Jess purrs. 'You both know Sera don't you?'

Sera, her back jammed against the rough planks of the fitting room wall as she sketches, leans into view and gives a wave. 'I'm working on some designs for bridesmaids dresses now, so I hope it's okay if I give you guys a hand? Get a feel for what bridesmaids want?'

'Of course,' Cate flashes a momentary smile at Sera, then looks straight back to the dresses she's hovering next to. As she skims past the bright colours and comes to a halt next to the pastel, extra-floaty dresses, Immie groans and makes a silent throat cutting sign behind Cate's back.

Ignoring Immie, I grab some glasses from the tray on the pale pink dressing table, and pour Sera and Jess some wine. In my hurry to get this started, I've come down in my Uggs and jeans rather than the black pumps, black trousers and black top that Jess likes us assistants to wear when we're helping out in the shop. But given we're all friends, I doubt she'll mind this once. When I was at my worst after the break up, slurping about in my pyjamas all day, Jess thoughtfully provided me with a black pair, so I could wander round the shop without the customers realising I wasn't really dressed.

'So, make yourselves comfy.' Jess waves Cate and Immie to a couple of Louis XIV chairs with ice blue linen cushions and white rope tassels. 'I'll let Poppy show you the different dresses, and then you can decide which you'd like to try.'

'Great.' I tentatively flick through the dresses, wondering where to begin. 'So, we've got a selection of styles here, but all the dresses can be ordered in lots of different colour ways.' I'm trying to keep to the simple styles, given Cate's buying for eight here. As my hand comes to rest on a short plain silk one, Immie gives it the thumbs up by waving her wine so hard it sloshes onto her jeans.

'Definitely not.' Cate mops Immie with a tissue, and vetoes the dress with one determined head shake. 'In fact I can see the one I want from here.' She gets up and reaches towards the floaty chiffon.

'These are at the expensive end,' I say, turning to Jess for back up.

'We sell a lot more of these,' Jess says diplomatically, whisking out an almost identical, much cheaper dress. 'How about this one?'

'No way.' Immie gasps under her breath, and slumps down in her seat.

'The first one's definitely the one I want.' Cate sounds decided.

'Are you sure?' I ask. We bridesmaids had mentioned paying for our own dresses, but we couldn't afford these. She's picked the most expensive bridesmaid dress in the shop. 'Those are £595 each.' That's after the friends and family discount I've negotiated, too. 'Times eight,' I say, desperately trying to do the maths.

Jess holds up yet another dress, offering her an out. 'Here, this one's similar, but half the price. Not that I'm supposed to say it, but other dresses are just as well made for a lot less than the make you've picked out.'

'Nooo, I'll look like a pregnant fairy in all of these,' wails Immie.

'We'll try the first one,' Cate insists. 'I'm only doing this once, I'm damn well doing it with bridesmaids looking how I want them.' She reaches out, and smiles as she runs her hand over the fabric. 'Dreamy isn't it? I haven't finally decided if I want them in cream or nude. It'll depend which wedding dress I finally go for.'

Which reminds me, we haven't even started on Cate's dress, but that's a whole other story. I pretend not to notice that Immie's miming being sick over the arm of her chair.

Jess turns to Sera, who's blinking at what she's witnessing, and whispers, 'Brides with firm ideas are a dream to work with, Sera. When you try to please all the bridesmaids everyone ends up compromising. It's fabulous when a bride decides to please herself.'

Cate sends Immie a firm frown, then turns back to me. 'This dress was in the wedding magazine I bought the morning Liam proposed.' She folds her arms decidedly. 'I've known all along those are the ones I'm having.'

What's she talking about? She got engaged months ago. 'So why are we even looking at others?' I ask. What's worse, I'm going through my own agonies here. My blotchy orange hair is going to look so cheap and trashy beside this upmarket dress.

Cate gives another grin. 'It was to show Liam that we'd explored every option before we settled on this one.'

Immie's aghast. 'Times eight, and I've run out of fingers. I hope you've got something spectacular up your sleeve for when Liam finally does his calculations and finds out how much this is costing, Cate.' Immie's given up on her glass and she's drowning her bridesmaid sorrows straight from the bottle.

'I'm the accountant in the family. If Liam ever does the sums, he's in for the dirtiest night of his life.' Cate laughs. 'Although this is nothing compared to the other thing I splurged on this week.'

Immie and I both squint at her. When did careful Cate turn into a cash splasher?

'The marquee company got in touch with a special offer on the most gorgeous open sided tents. I couldn't resist so I ordered two.'

'What, instead of the main marquee?' I'm not sure 'open' is a good idea, as for two...

From Cate's airy waft of her hand, she might have been talking about tenner-a-go pop up tents, not three grand a time event venues. 'No, I've ordered these as well, I thought they'd make a nice extra.'

I'm still picking my jaw up off the floor, but Immie's covered it. 'Liam's going to be up to his boxers in filthy sex when this shit hits the fan.' Eloquent as ever, she takes another swig.

Jess looks at her watch. 'Time to try on then?'

She's got a bride coming in for a final fitting at six, so she'll have to go downstairs for that. Given Immie's stroppy scowl from behind the prosecco bottle it may be no bad thing.

'You go to your bride,' I say to Jess. 'Sera and I can carry on here.'

I knew I should have given Immie twice as much fizz before we started. With Immie the line between making her compliant and keeping her standing is indiscernible. She goes from saying no to falling over, with barely a second to catch her saying yes.

As Jess slips away, Immie's starting to rant.

'Do I look like I'm ready to be transformed into a trifle?'

To be fair, she's a committed jeans and sweatshirt girl, so I'm not sure how this is going to go. The last time she wore a skirt out of school was probably when she was a carnival rosebud, thirty years ago. I don't have to dig too deep to come up with the kind of bribe she'll go for.

'You try on the dress, Immie, and we'll send Sera for another bottle of fizz.'

Sera grins at me and heads for the stairs.

Immie rolls her eyes, and sighs, but she gets up. As soon as she's on her feet I shoulder her into the fitting room, shove the dress in with her, and whisk the curtain closed.

Cate and I take deep breaths as we retire to a safe distance.

Cate frowns and turns to me. 'I've been thinking, you can't struggle with a man as difficult as Rafe from now until September.' She runs her fingers through her hair. 'There must be something we can do to soften him up.'

I shrug. 'He doesn't respond to cake.'

Cate sniffs. 'He probably needs a good roll in the hay, we'll have to find him a woman.'

After Immie's rundown on the history of his nonexistent love life, I grin. 'Good luck with that one.'

'There is one person he doesn't object to.' Cate's lips are flickering. 'Immie has him eating out of her hand. That has to mean something.'

I'm not sure I agree with Cate here. 'It means she scares the bejesus out of him.'

'But he spends a lot of time with Morgan,' Cate observes.

She's right about that. Morgan's always dragging what I assume to be bits of broken tractor round the farmyard after Rafe.

'Rafe wouldn't take an interest in Morgan if he wasn't interested in Immie, would he?' Cate leans in, and she's whispering.

'In the interest of smoothing the way for *my wedding*…' She says those two last words very close and very loudly. 'I think you might need to sprinkle some cupid dust on Rafe and Immie, okay?'

I reel. Cate's not usually this forceful. 'Hold it there Bridezilla, how exactly am I supposed to do that?'

'Organise a Daisy Hill Farm night out, and we'll work on it together.'

'Night out?' I query, as I sink onto a stripy director's chair. 'What did you have in mind?'

'Cocktails here in town might be good?' Cate gives a satisfied nod, as if it's already in the bag. 'You'll thank me for this. It'll make the run up to the wedding easier for all of us.'

Cate's wiggling her eyebrows excitedly. 'We could start at Jaggers.'

'You go to Jaggers too? So does Jess.' If I hadn't already sunk into a chair, I would do now.

'We often call in there on Fridays, they do great mojitos, you should try them.' She shakes her head at me. 'You need to get out more, Poppy. Starting this week. I've been too easy on you, giving you the excuse of babysitting for me. I shouldn't be taking advantage. You need a life too.'

And here's me thinking that Cate and Liam barely get further than the village pub. Has the whole world gone mad while I've been hiding under my duvet?

'Everything going okay here?' Jess breezes through the doorway that leads to the shoe department, a pair of rhinestone stilettos balanced on each hand.

'Immie's currently trying the Miranda, in blush,' I tell her. Every dress in the shop is allocated a different girls name, and that's how we refer to them.

'Well done, we don't often get bridesmaids as reluctant as Immie,' Jess raises her eyebrows. 'There's good news from downstairs too, Poppy.'

'Celebrity gossip?' Given the fall out after last week's Josie Redman Twitter storm and Sera's huge spike in popularity, I'm not sure I can cope with more.

'No, no much closer to home…I think I've found your lost couple.' Jess flashes a triumphant beam. 'My six o'clock bride just mentioned she's getting married at Daisy Hill Farm the week before Easter. I'll give you her number later.' Jess gazes doubtfully at the shoes in her hands. 'I'm not sure these will mix with mud though. If you're going to be putting on lots of weddings in fields we'll need to order in some sparkly wellies.'

Before I have time to tell Jess that any weddings in fields will be strictly short term she's sped off back to her bride, and Immie is pushing her way out of the fitting room, face like a stormy sea.

'Great news, we've found our missing Easter bride.' I say it brightly to take her mind off what she's wearing.

Immie's talking through gritted teeth. 'Well my news is, I'd rather wear the curtains than this dress.' She's wading through waves of chiffon.

As Cate and I stand back to assess, I'm ready for the worst.

We both hold our breath.

'It is a bit long,' I say, 'but actually you've got curves for the first time since…forever.' It's surprising to think Immie's been hiding that hour glass figure under her baggy T-shirts. 'You have to admit, you're looking pretty sassy.' Despite her cropped hair, the pretty dress suits her.

Immie's holding her hand in front of her chest, screwing up her face. 'You know I hate fitting rooms,' she protests. 'I refuse to look, it's too humiliating.'

Cate bites her lip. 'If you lose the anger, and have a yard chopped off the bottom, you'll look amazing. Maybe with a little tiara too…'

Immie lets out a yowl. 'I'm not wearing a fucking…'

Cate laughs. 'Okay, no tiaras.' She bites back a grin. 'How about floral crowns made from daisies?'

'Worse and worse.' Immie's pulling her vomit face again.

'There's no such thing as a happy bridesmaid,' I say to Sera. Given she's brought up three bottles of prosecco, I'd say she's catching on fast.

'Okay, my turn next.' I grab a Miranda in cream, and head into the empty fitting room.

I've helped with enough bridesmaid fittings this last few months to know the majority of bridesmaids walk down the aisle in a dress they would prefer not to be wearing. But they all love their brides too much to argue. I'm already cringing at how the scoop back is going to show off my muffin tops. But that's a minor worry when I think that next week I'm going to have to make contact with a bride and groom to plan their special day and admit I know nothing about it. And somehow I have to persuade the worst tempered guy in Cornwall to come out for cocktails. Cate might think throwing Immie and Rafe together is the recipe for true love and an easy year, but from what I know of both of them, tiaras or no tiaras, it's more likely to cause World War Three.

11

In the office at Daisy Hill Farm:
Monday blues and craggy trees

Things to do first thing Monday…

*Chase up the missing Bride and Groom, who've had their phone
off all weekend*
Tackle Rafe about sharing office with chickens!!!!
Chase up Portaloo company
Organise work trip to Jaggers
Sort out Daisy Hill Website
Daisy Hill Farm Weddings Facebook Page??? :(

'Morning Pops!' Immie dashes into the office, trips over a chicken,
and sends us both into a spin as she saves herself by grabbing
onto the padded arm of my executive swivel chair. As she comes
to a halt, she's practically sitting in my lap. 'Oh my god, you're
on Facebook…' Her squawk echoes in my ear, as her chin bumps
against my shoulder.

So this is me with my self-imposed Facebook embargo, caught

red handed. It's the first time I've logged on since the morning I had the second most horrible shock of my life – being faced with Brett, tagged right left and centre in a friend's stag night photos, his mouth surgically attached to some bimbo. It wasn't as if it was just the once. This tonsil hockey was on a tournament scale, and they looked like they were playing for England. And enjoying it. Even thinking about it now brings the sick into my throat. Two days later we'd broken up, and I've stayed away from Facebook since.

'Happy Monday to you too.' I take a slurp of the coffee I made when I arrived half an hour earlier, and try to change the subject. 'Drink?' Brett was full of excuses, but with thirty odd guys all posting their take on the party, his cheating was covered from every angle. I scoured the photos frame by frame. I pieced the whole sordid evening together before you could say 'hangover'. There's nowhere to hide when a thousand people around the world have seen the pictures.

'No time for tea, I've got lots of cottages to sort after weekend checkouts.' Immie slides back to standing, addressing me, then the bird. 'Sorry for squashing you, Pops. Sorry for kicking you, Henrietta.'

We'll have words about her talking to the poultry later, not to mention the whole 'hens in the office' issue. As for Brett, in the end he put the blame on me, and at the time I went with that, because I wasn't in the habit of disagreeing with him.

'So why Facebook? After all this time?' Immie screws up her face as she puzzles. You have to give her full marks for persistence. 'You vowed you'd never go on again.'

I sigh. 'The farm needs a Facebook presence.' We both know that's true. 'And when I looked down today's work list, making a Facebook page for the wedding venue was the easiest job.' I've rushed the page together, using a picture of calves from my phone, from last week's farm tour, and added in some dreamy half focused photos of lace and sparkles I took in the shop yesterday. Somehow using Facebook for work is okay. The last thing I'm going to do is stalk Brett. 'The rest of my jobs for today are worse, believe me.' Explaining to the bride that we'd lost her details is bad enough. Reassuring her that she can trust us with her wedding is something else.

'Nice photos.' Immie nods as she scrolls down the screen looking at the new Facebook page. 'I think you should call the page Weddings at Daisy Hill Farm though.'

'Brilliant idea,' I say. 'I wanted to get the page up and running, to catch people who might have fallen through the holes in Carrie's booking net. If we get everyone we know to share the page, I can offer a gift for every couple with a booking who get in touch via the page.'

There's a flurry of wings and feathers and squawks in the corner, as Henrietta flies onto the top of the filing cabinet.

'Good thinking Mrs.' Immie scratches Henrietta's head as she settles herself down next to the broken document shredder.

I'm cringing at the thought of touching feathers, when there's a knock, and the door pushes open. Immie and I turn. As a guy in a soft grey parka walks in, muffled against the cold with a bright stripey scarf, our mouths open in a silent, but collective, 'wow'.

There aren't that many guys around here who look like they've escaped from some high fashion magazine, complete with the expensive clothes. True, there are some good looking surfer types at the beach, but none of them go in for the kind of grooming we've got here.

'Hi.' He shakes his perfectly cut, artfully messy, nut brown hair, and holds out his hand. 'I'm Jules, I'm here for the photo shoot. Rafe said to come on in.' His gaze is a startling topaz blue. 'I take it that's okay?' As his coat slips open to reveal a chunky knit that might have walked off the pages of Telegraph Living, there's a delicious waft of expensive aftershave.

He has to keep on talking, because Immie and I are still

gawping. We're halfway between being lost for words, and convulsing in giggles.

No surprise that Immie recovers first. 'Fine, come on in.' Immie leaps forward and grabs his hand which looks clean and buffed. 'I'm not sure you're at the right place though,' she adds doubtfully 'Definitely haven't seen any cameras or lights anywhere round here this morning.'

That makes him smile, and when he smiles his cheeks crack into deep lines. You know those long ironic dimples you get on guys like Johnny Depp? The ones that make your legs dissolve? That's what I'm talking here. And from the way Immie has sprawled against the desk, I'm guessing in her case, dissolving is fully complete.

Then he gives a long low laugh that bounces off the white-washed office walls and leaves me helpless too.

'No, I'm bringing the cameras, I'm the photographer.' The smile he flashes is luminous enough to suggest he's on great terms with his dental hygienist.

'Remind me what you're taking pictures of?' Immie's doing well here, given her legs are all floppy, and she hasn't got a clue what he's talking about.

'The engagement shoot for Lara and Ben's wedding…back in December we booked to have it here this afternoon…?' Those blue eyes are full of hope as they search our faces.

I struggle to make my expression less blank as he goes on.

'I say engagement shoot, it's really just to get the happy couple relaxed in front of the camera before the big day. Some people do their engagement shots in New York or Paris or somewhere exotic, but these two went for Cornwall in February. I came early to check out the best shots. Let's hope the weather's improved for the real thing at Easter…it's only four weeks away now.'

And finally the penny drops. He's a wedding photographer. And the couple he's talking about are the bride and groom I've been trying to get hold of all weekend, and they're coming here this afternoon. If ever I wanted a fairy godmother moment, this is it. Not only has a hunk of a guy been delivered to my office – not lusting, just admiring here, you understand – but my most dreaded task of the morning just melted away.

'Of course, I'm so sorry,' I begin. 'We've had staff changes, you're down in the book for later.' Shhhh, I know it's a porky, but he's not to know there isn't a book yet. 'It's absolutely fine for you to be here now.' I can tell Immie thinks I'm gushing, but I'm so damned relieved. 'I'm Poppy Pickering, Events Manager, tell me what you'd like me to do, and I'm all yours.'

I grab Jules' hand and give it a vigorous shake, ignoring Immie, smirking behind her fingers.

'I'm in my 4x4,' Jules voice is half purr, half growl. 'If you could possibly spare the time to show me a few locations…? With the weather as it is, we'll be working to big up the rugged side. I'm on the lookout for five bar gates, craggy trees, backdrops of sky, picturesque barn doors, stuff like that.'

'No problem.' Immie is straight in there. 'I know this farm like the back of my…'

Whatever happened to those pressing weekend check outs she was off to? Not to mention her disdain for men in general. No doubt if she stopped to think about it with her uni head on, she'd have a lot to say about how her reproductive instincts are completely over-riding her sensible brain, when she's faced with this vision of genetic male perfection. I'm guessing Jules' resemblance to an over-sized puppy probably swung it for the animal lover in Immie too.

I jump in before she has me sidelined completely. 'It's fine, I know you're busy Immie, I'll handle Jules.' Wincing a bit at the word choice there, but I've been to so many weddings, and poured longingly over the pictures afterwards, wishing it were me, that I know exactly what he's wanting. And this is my first real taste of my new job. 'Promise I'll shout if I need you Immie.' I sweep across the office to grab my jacket, noting that the fairy dust hasn't extended as far as the yurt coat. With luck and a following wind Jules might read my over-sized Barbour as extreme boho chic. 'Shall we go?' I'm suddenly tingling with excitement at the thought. And it's nothing to do with any hot guy hormone rush, it's all about getting Daisy Hill Farm Weddings up and running.

12

On Location, at Daisy Hill Farm: Step ladders and panda bears

As the day goes on, Jules proves to be a lot more than a pretty face. He's scarily organised, meticulous about his work, and he's brilliant at putting people at their ease. And I don't only mean the happy couple, Ben and Lara here, I also mean me. Somehow the morning disappeared as we whizzed around finding suitable gateways and hilltops for the shoot. And the next thing I knew, I was agreeing to swap my afternoon plans to work on the website for Daisy Hill Farm, and go and be a photographer's assistant instead.

'It'll be a great way of getting to know Lara and Ben,' Jules promised. 'And in return, I'll help with that website you seem so stressy about.' Given he offered to provide me with an unending supply of wedding pictures, in return for credits, and that I'm shooting in the dark as far as websites go, the only answer was 'yes'.

I also took my notebook, and jotted as we chatted. So I now know that there will be forty guests in the day and a hundred in the evening. At night they'll be dining on hot dogs, served from a retro burger van. The ceremony is booked for midday at the church, which means I don't have to deal with registrars this time, and they'd love Morgan to help with the parking. I also got the names of the marquee company, the caterers, the florists, the stylists, and the furniture hire people, not forgetting the band. All of whom will be arriving to set up.

The downside for me was the twang in my chest as Lara and Ben chatted about their excitement, and all the details for the day. At Brides by the Sea, when I'm discussing cake orders or helping with dress fittings, I see brides with their friends, or their mums, and that's fine. But being so involved in helping a couple realise their wedding dreams is something else. Ben dropping devoted kisses onto the top of Lara's head, untangling the hair on her forehead, gently twisting her engagement ring round so the camera would catch it. Lara digging her elbow in his ribs and teasing him about his wedding spreadsheet. All the coupley love I've lost is being paraded under my nose. Whereas in normal life if I see it I can simply look the other way, here it's part of my job. There isn't a Wedding Coordinator in the world who wouldn't get involved. Yet when I see the easy way his arm flops over her shoulder, as they put their heads together and share a joke about for better or for worse, I'm there thinking how close I came to doing the same. That this was *almost* me.

'Let's just do it.' Those were Brett's exact words, the last time we talked about us getting married. If someone said that to you, you'd think it was happening wouldn't you? You would feel safe to build up those expectations you'd held in check so carefully for so many years. And a week later he'd stuffed it all up.

I hadn't expected being a firsthand spectator in someone else's wedding build-up to hurt quite this much. And in the next few months I'm going to be faced with couple after couple, all about to tie the knot, and every time it's going to make me feel like shit.

'Are you okay over there, Pops?' It's Jules calling, and he's already fast forwarded to Immie's nickname for me. More scarily, he's also picked up that I've dropped out of the game momentarily. 'Any chance you could bring the steps over?'

Judging by the pictures Jules has been flashing at me on the screen of his camera as we've worked our way around the picturesque places on the farm, he's a hot shot photographer.

'So, for this one last picture, how about you both climb up onto the wall.' Jules yells to be heard above the wind.

I whisk the step ladder in place right on cue, help Lara and Ben into position, then whip the steps out of shot. As Ben and Lara shuffle uncomfortably on top of the wall, I pull my woolly hat over my eyes, and haul up my coat collar.

'We're going for wild here, sit facing each other, let your jackets flop open, and let the wind blow you.' Jules leaps around, his movements fluid and easy, snapping from all angles, constantly checking his shots. 'Camera bag please, Poppy, I've a feeling the sun's about to break through those clouds.'

I lug the holdall across to him, and he swaps cameras, and seamlessly swoops to take more shots of the couple laughing amidst chaotic strands of windswept hair, silhouetted against the sudden brightness of the sky behind. He's been like this all afternoon – exhausting, yet exhilarating to watch, working with what was there, seizing every opportunity, catching Lara's surprise when a flurry of rooks rose from the trees. The moment when Lara fell off the gate and Ben instinctively dived to catch her in his arms.

'Okay, got you. Everyone into the car, we'll head back to the farm.'

His voice is throaty, as he swigs from a bottle of water as he jumps into the driving seat, and throws a flask of coffee to Ben and Lara in the back seat. 'Here, warm up with that, you've both been stars out there.' His nonstop praise has definitely kept Lara going when she looked like she was flagging.

'Phew, I'm exhausted, and all I've done is watch.' I heave

myself into the car, and flop into the passenger seat beside him. It's been amazing to watch how this guy took this inhospitable afternoon, and somehow managed to warm up and coax these freezing cold lovers into beautiful moments he could capture. 'Hardly ideal weather for a photo shoot either.'

As Jules turns on the engine, the music starts too. I forgot to mention the whole afternoon has been played out against the most romantic soundtrack in the world ever. Earlier we were bouncing down the lanes to Hozier's *Take Me To Church*, and right now *Nothing Compares 2U* is coming and going in the background. I deliberately don't listen too hard to the words, or I'll have to swallow back the tears.

'You've done a whole lot more than watch. I certainly asked the right person to help.' Jules gives a low laugh. 'And actually the weather's perfect – extreme conditions make the most interesting pictures.'

It may be unfair to make comparisons, but I can't help think of Jules with his can-do attitude, and easy coaxing manner, beside grumpy Rafe, and his tractor load of negativity. As if to underline the impression, Jules flashes me a wide, warm smile.

'Is that the last stop?' I ask with a sigh. Even though it's exciting to see Jules at work, after three hours I could kill for a mug of sweet tea and a chunk of chocolate shortcake.

'I think we'll call it a day at that,' Jules confirms to all of us. 'I'm confident I've got some pictures you'll like.' He shoots a satisfied beam over his shoulder to Lara and Ben in the back.

In my head I'm already putting the kettle on and opening the biscuit tin.

'Ohhhh.' A groan of disappointment comes from Lara.

This far I hadn't got her down as whiney.

'What's wrong, Panda?'

And this is something I forgot to mention earlier. Panda Bear is Ben's slightly annoying pet name for Lara. Whoever thinks I only mind because I'm jealous is totally wrong. As I'm basically only meeting them for a day after this, I don't need to stress about it, but to be honest, if someone started calling Immie Panda Bear in public, Cate and I would have to put a stop to it. Immediately. With physical force if necessary.

'I was hoping to have just one picture in the dress I was wearing the day we met.'

I wonder if Jules has picked up the same winsome note in Lara's voice that I have.

Ben grunts. 'For chrissakes, Pand, we met in Greece, it was forty eight degrees, and you were only wearing a thong, that's why I noticed you.'

Panda's hiss is indignant. 'I had my dress *with* me, one picture is all I'm asking for.'

Jules raises his eyebrows. As he steers into the farm courtyard, and the car swoops to a halt Rafe marches out of the office, and stomps over to the car. If I had a hard hat with me, I'd reach for it now.

'Great shoot.' Jules' electric window slides downwards. 'Thanks for some amazing locations.'

'Any time.' Rafe backs away with a shrug. Two words and he's reached the limit of his engagement.

'I don't suppose…' Jules is trying his luck here. 'You wouldn't happen to have an inside space we could borrow for ten minutes?' Seemingly oblivious to Rafe's dismissal, Jules switches his gaze pointedly to the farmhouse.

As Rafe pauses, a pained look passes across his face. 'The house won't be suitable, it's empty and mostly falling apart.'

Jules is straight in there. 'It sounds perfect, thanks, we won't bother you for long I promise. Come on guys.' He's already out of the car, grabbing his cameras, and striding past a stormy-faced Rafe, towards the front door. Rafe shakes his head, but all the same he goes to open up from inside.

Why didn't I think of acting like an over enthusiastic dog to get Rafe to roll over?

'In we go…' Jules loses no time, ushering us all into the hall the moment Rafe opens the front door a crack.

Beneath the glow of a bare bulb, it takes a second for my eyes to get used to the gloom as I step in out of the wind. Despite the shredded wallpaper, and bare floorboards, it's the broad staircase with its beautiful swooping handrail that has us all gazing. It could have come straight from a shabby chic magazine, which is probably why Jules' grin has turned from triumphant to ecstatic.

'Great stuff, we can definitely work with this…' Dust rises, as Jules drops his bag and turns to Rafe. 'Is there anywhere Lara can go to slip her dress on?'

I'm holding my breath. This free pass into Rafe's private domain is an unexpected bonus. I'd imagined him climbing into a king sized bed with a smart new painted brass bedstead, but that doesn't fit with the patina. Shocked that I've imagined his bedroom? Me too, to be honest, but cake icing can be a repetitive business. There's plenty of time for your mind wander to places you had no intention of visiting. There's nothing more to it than that.

'Sure, she can change in here.' Rafe sighs loudly, pushing on the nearest door, and clicking a bank of switches. 'You can take pictures here too, if you must.'

We follow him into a big empty room, where the floor is flecked with flakes of distemper that has fallen off the walls. There's a clatter as he moves down the room, opening shutters as he goes, letting the last of the afternoon light seep in through four tall, small-paned sash windows.

'What a fantastic fireplace.' Jules breaks the stunned silence, and says what we're all thinking. 'And a fabulous room.' And he's seriously understating it here. The fireplace is huge and square with the most intricate carvings in the pale stone surround. My head is doing a quick reshuffle, and flashing up images of Rafe's huge Jacobean four poster.

Rafe gives a grunt, and breaks the dream. 'It's a bit big for a farmhouse, my Georgian ancestors obviously had delusions of grandeur.'

'And delightfully empty…' More positive spin from Jules, overlooking the dust sheet covered piles around the room.

Before we have time to take it in, Rafe has pushed through some double doors in the central wall which open into yet another room. Tentatively we follow him into an ancient conservatory, with glass so misted and cobweb covered, it's hard to see through.

'This is the orangerie, which like the rest has seen better days. It opens onto a walled garden behind the house.' Rafe says, with a nod towards the glass structure. 'Not sure how many oranges it's seen, certainly none in my time.'

'A truly fabulous place to live.' Jules is gushing now. Not surprising given the locations Rafe has just handed him.

In the interests of fairness, and to prove there's no favouritism going on, I force myself to picture Jules' bedroom. Definitely in a loft apartment, with chunky wood hewn furniture. I hastily add in a massive wardrobe, and a bright coloured quilt with a chunky knit throw.

Then, back in the farmhouse again, I shove my hands deeper into my coat pockets as I suppress a shiver. Lara's going to be almost as cold in here as outside, but they'll get some great shots. Let's hope they're quick.

'This is no place for me on my own, and anyway, I prefer modern. I keep to the end wing, hence the cobwebs here.' Rafe shrugs again, as he backs away towards the hall. 'Okay, I'll leave you to it, knock yourselves out. Give me a shout when you're done.'

Which leaves the Rafe in my head bouncing on a retro fifties ash bed from Habitat, while he shouts about ancestors and house wings. I mean, what planet does this guy live on? Certainly not the same one as the rest of us.

'Bloody hell…' Ben is shaking his head, gazing up at the sagging ceiling.

My thoughts exactly.

Jules rubs his hands together, and they're slightly less pristine than earlier. 'Right Lara, pop next door and get your dress on. Five minutes of freezing at most, I promise the pictures will be fab.' He turns his smile on me. 'Poppy, tea would be awesome, biscuits or cake would be a big bonus, we'll be with you before the kettle boils.'

I'm reeling at the way he tells it as he wants it, but the way he half closes one eye softens the dazzle of his smile to something much more personal and intimate. Anyone in a more susceptible place than me might have swooned on the spot. As it is, when I rush to fill the kettle in the office kitchen and catch sight of myself in the mirror on the door, there's a distinct red patch on each of my cheeks. Almost like I'm burning up, not freezing cold.

I just hope Immie doesn't walk in and spot the afterglow.

Meanwhile, I'm whizzing around the office waiting for the kettle to heat up, still in my tent coat, grabbing mugs from the shelves, and sneaking a cheeky chocolate shortbread out of my drawer when I come face to face with Henrietta. Or more aptly, beady eye to beady eye with Henrietta. If hens roosting on the filing cabinet was beyond the pale, a chicken sitting on the biscuit barrel and snuggling up next to the clean cups is a million miles off the scale of what's acceptable. And sorry to disappoint Jules, but cake's off today.

Which reminds me that somehow I've got to get down off my cloud, and address my Monday list. Much more pressing than the problem of unwelcome livestock in the office, there's my biggest burning question of the week.

How the hell am I going to get Rafe on a work night out?

13

In the office at Daisy Hill Farm:
Light bulbs and snowballs in hell

I'm not sure this hot desking idea of Rafe's is working. As I walk
into the farm office the desk is stacked so high with Farming
magazines, I can barely see the man himself behind them.

'What are you doing here?' Rafe looks up from the letter he's
reading, making what sounds more like a complaint than a
welcome.

'Delivery in the next village,' I explain. Taking in his glazed
stare, on balance I decide not to tell him about the three tier
silver-wedding cake I've been slaving over. Or that it's left my
fingers tingling from hours of squeezing icing out of piping bags.

'I thought I'd pop in and put some text together for the website
as I was passing.' Good thing I have too, another day out of the
office and I get the feeling I might have been re-located into the
yard.

Rafe carries on flicking through the pages of the letter he's
reading. It's only as he reaches behind the stack of magazines for
a pen that a flash of russet coloured feathers makes me gasp.

'Omigod, is that Henrietta sitting on the bloody desk?' I hear myself shrieking.

He looks up slowly, with a pained expression. 'Sorry, do you have a problem with that?' It's not an apologetic kind of sorry. It's more the 'don't have a clue what you're going on about' kind of sorry.

'Livestock in the office.' It's certainly on my list of issues to tackle this week, I just wasn't fully prepared to do it right now. 'It just isn't right.' Even I know that was lame, so I blurt out the next thing that comes into my head. 'Anyway, shouldn't you be out milking cows or something?' I'm surprised how fast I'm learning to talk like a farm person. 'For a farmer you spend a remarkable amount of time indoors.'

He gives an exasperated sigh and slams the letter down on the desk. 'Haven't you got a wedding to go to?' then with a bad tempered snarl, he scoops up Henrietta. Two flaps later he deposits her on top of the filing cabinet, then turns to me with a sneer. 'Happy now?'

As the letter hits the table, I glimpse the edge of a bank logo. No doubt he's been counting up his millions again. I might have been happier if he'd opened the door and put the hen outside. I'm trying to think of a stinging verbal comeback that covers health and safety, office tidiness, bad temper in the work place, and male territoriality when my phone beeps.

I momentarily suspend the argument, to open a text from Cate.

Immie and I both free 2nite. Bring Rafe to Jaggers for 7.
Operation #HappyFarmer is live! ;) xx

Damn. If the text had come five minutes earlier, I'd have been less snarky. Although looking at Rafe's stormy frown, even a Strawberry Daiquiri wouldn't sweeten that to happy. As for getting him to Jaggers, I'm thinking of snowballs in hell. Not a chance. My phone beeps. Cate again.

This has taken a LOT of organising, it's the only way forward for an easy year for ALL of us!!! Think of my wedding, get Rafe here ASAP! DO NOT BAIL ON ME!!! ;) xx

So like Cate to send a second message, just to be sure. If you ask me, she's been on too many motivational courses. I grit my teeth, which is exactly what she meant me to do. As for her wedding, it's come from nowhere, and now it's ruling my life. Somehow I've got to do this, I just don't know how. It's pointless making comparisons, but if Rafe had even a tenth of Jules' charm and positivity, this would be a walk over. And suddenly, remembering Jules, I have a light bulb moment. Jules didn't have any problem making Rafe do what he wanted. Maybe I need to be more like him?

14

At the Goose and Duck, Rose Cross Village:
Pointers and pork scratchings

'Works drinks with Rafe? How did you manage this then?'

Immie's unwinding her scarf as she marches down the bar towards me. I shrug, and hope that the mention of Jules isn't going to put her off the main objective. I don't want her swooning at the thought of that 'photographer from heaven' – her words – when we're here to get her together with Rafe. Not that we've told her that part.

'So I took a few pointers from Jules.' I admit. 'I didn't ask Rafe or suggest, I simply told him. "Drinks down the pub. Get in the car. Now"' I can't believe how well it worked, although to be fair, Rafe was pretty short of excuses. It all happened in a bit of a rush. 'My main tactic was surprise. With the implied threat of force thrown in too.'

The Goose and Duck has been given a makeover since Brett and I last came here with Cate and Liam and the kids for Sunday lunch. As I take in the wall to wall checked taupe decor, I can't remember when I was last in a bar. Drinking and falling off stools might be the perfect antidote to heartbreak for some people, but I never quite reached the wild nights out, drowning my sorrows under the table stage.

'Rafe hasn't exactly got a lot going on in his life.' Immie points out. 'Apart from the odd cow giving birth, he's completely uncommitted.' Good point well made. She plumps up a grey tartan cushion, and settles into a substantial oak chair. 'Remind me why we're doing this again?'

Now I'm the one who's short of excuses. 'Cate thought it would be a nice if we all got together.' I'm bluffing here. 'Smoothing the way for her wedding…' One mention of the 'w' word, and Immie gets it.

'So this is a first.' Immie beams at Rafe incredulously as he delivers her pint of lager, and two cokes. I'm wishing she'd cut back on her 'what-the-hell?' stare. This is only part one of the plan. Starting down the village pub is the easy bit. The hard part is going to be making the move to Jaggers. I'm already shifting in my tweed arm chair, psyching myself up for that part.

'Am I the only one drinking?' Immie downs half her pint with the first gulp.

Take it from me, this woman could drink for England.

'I'm designated driver,' I say, although Rafe has no idea we're about to whisk him to St Aidan for a drinking fest at Jaggers. Cate's plan is that if Immie and Rafe down enough cocktails, they'll fall drunkenly into each other's arms. Job done.

Rafe lifts up his coke. 'And I'm driving too.' Despite Gav the barman's jokey banter, and the free pork scratchings by the till, Rafe still hasn't cracked a smile.

'That's a very nice jumper you're wearing,' I say to Rafe. Given he has more cashmere sweaters than anyone I've come across, and that he also keeps sheep, I reckon wool's a good subject to start with. And it works, because his mouth twitches into an almost smile.

'A present from my mother.' His embarrassed shrug softens him. 'She's always turning up with them.'

'Trying to make you presentable no doubt, so you'll catch that elusive woman she's so desperate for you to meet.' Immie laughs, and gives him a surprisingly free and friendly pat on the knee.

'Does she live nearby?' I ask. Somehow, despite Immie talking about her, I can't imagine Rafe having a mum.

'We built her a bungalow at my brother's farm, but right now she's travelling in the States.' From the grimaces he and Immie exchange, it looks like a relief all round.

'She loves country music,' Immie chimes in. 'At least it gives you a couple of months off from her matchmaking.' She follows that with a loud guffaw as she sinks the rest of her drink, and adds a matey dig in the ribs for Rafe. 'Anyone for another?' She raises her glass, gets up and sets her sights on the bar. So far so good. Immie and Rafe are surprisingly relaxed with each other, and it looks like Immie's hell bent on drinking enough for both of them.

I glance at my phone, knowing we should be moving this into town.

'The next one's on me.' I jump to my feet. 'And I promised to meet Cate.' I rack my brains, imagining how Jules might put it if he wanted everyone to drive ten miles to the next drink. The knack is to say it like there's no alternative. 'We're having the next round at Jaggers.' Despite my inner doubts, I manage a big grin, and it comes out pretty damned forceful. 'I hope you like mojitos.' Whoop, I'm on a roll here.

No idea if this is going to work, but I don't wait for them to argue. Immie's banter is getting a great response from Rafe. Cate's right, if we can pour enough cocktails down him, he'll soon feel the friends to lovers vibe.

'Jaggers it is then!' Without a looking back, I pick up my coat and head for the door.

15

In Jaggers Bar: Lost property

'Great evening then, thanks a lot for dragging me along.' Rafe's cheek is almost rubbing on mine as he puts his mouth up to my ear, and he still has to yell for me to hear him over the shouting and the techno music.

Thursday night's Cocktail Happy Hour was in full flow when we got here, and the place was heaving. I have no idea about the hour, because it already seems to have lasted forever. As for the cocktails, they're strong enough to make your head spin with the first slug. Then you man up. Unlike everyone else in the place, I'm just having the one. But you know those times when the more you drink, the more you want?

'Quick, grab those seats!' Rafe's grip is tight on my shoulder as he steers me through the crush of bodies, and shoves me up onto a purple plastic bar stool.

I take it he's being ironic when he says about a great evening. No-one could actually be enjoying this mayhem.

At some point he's stripped off his jumper, and now I'm sitting beside him, I can see that under his ragged T-shirt, he's pretty ripped. I squint as I try to make out the logo on the fabric folds.

'If found return to the farm,' Rafe says helpfully, then sighs. 'Not what I'd usually wear out, I wasn't expecting anyone to even see it, it's supposed to be a joke.' Which is so funny for someone as un-funny as Rafe that it sends me into a fit of giggles.

I know what he means though. I wasn't expecting anyone to see my skimpy vest either, but it's so damned hot in here, it was a choice between stripping down and showing off half my bra, or expiring.

'Top up of margarita?' Cate squeezes in from behind with a jug as I put down my glass. One slosh later, my glass is full again.

So much for not drinking. The last thing I remember eating is a banana at breakfast time, which is probably why I'm feeling a bit light headed now. 'Last one.' I yell, as Cate whirls out of view. As for Rafe getting legless, he hasn't actually started drinking yet.

'That has to be the sixth time you've said that.' Rafe's lips twist into a smile. 'Don't worry, I'll carry you home.'

'No.' That really doesn't sound right. Seven cocktails? Maybe that's why the neon signs around the walls are beginning to blur. I lean over a little unsteadily to Rafe, and end up grabbing his arm to get my balance. 'You're supposed to be carrying Immie home, not me.' As I release my grip on his biceps, it's the most natural thing in the world to share this with him. I grab his knee, as I push myself back into position on my stool, and stage whisper. 'You know, you two are supposed to be an item,' I confide.

For some reason, instead of taking me seriously, he cracks up at that. I had no idea the man could actually laugh at all, so his deep seated roar takes me by surprise.

'So I'm going to have to fight the surfie guy?' Rafe says. He's suddenly serious now.

'Fight who?'

He nods over his shoulder. 'The guy she's with over there.'

I follow his glance. 'Shit.' Behind us Immie's all over a blond guy in torn denim, who between you and me can't be much older than Morgan. As she catches my eye she gives an enthusiastic wave of her glass, empties half the contents over the guy's bulging biceps, then goes straight in for a head-lock snog. Looks like she's skipping courtship, and going straight to mating.

Rafe raises an eyebrow and shakes his head.

'Sorry, I might have a witty logo on my T-shirt, but I can't compete with jeans like that,' he laughs. 'Although aren't drop crotch very 2013?'

I'm glad someone finds it funny. That's our whole evening wasted, not to mention our only hope for making Rafe half way human. I need another drink.

'Damn.' I study Immie carefully as she stretches up, peels off the guy's headband, and puts it on herself. 'From the way she's staggering, I'd say she's pity prissed.' I'm vaguely aware of mixing up my words. 'Pity pissed I mean.' I try again. 'Pretty prissed.'

'You don't say.' Rafe rubs his chin.

'Is there any more drink in that jug down there?' I ask, and then I see Cate coming over. Great, with any luck she'll be bringing more cocktails.

As I wave frantically at Cate, my foot slips, and I lurch forward, but before my head hits the bar, someone catches me, and pushes me back onto my stool.

Wow, near miss there. These stools are way too slippery. 'I need more mojitos,' I call as I re-orientate myself on my seat. As Cate arrives at my elbow I update her.

'Immie's rilly rilly prissed.' I say, knowing it isn't coming out quite right, but not knowing how to correct it. 'She's pitty much trying to dev…dev…eat that guy back there whole. Where've you put the mojitos? She's supposed to be snogging R…'

Cate's hand lands on mine before I say the name Rafe, but her smile sails over my head. 'I was coming to say, is it time we made a move?'

How the hell is she still work-perfect, in her shirt and suit skirt after all this booze? And why's she talking to Rafe not me?

'Still okay to do what we said before?' Cate's still ignoring me. 'I'll do the honours with Immie, and you take Poppy?'

Sensing they're talking transport here, I rack my brain about mine. 'I need my car,' I say, 'I need my car tomorrow.' That much I know, the rest is hazy. There's something about nine o'clock too. 'Where's my car? It's only an old one, I had to give my new one back to Brett, I can't lose this one.' I'm working up to a wail as I slide off my stool, knowing I have to find my car. But as my foot hits the floor it slips, and the next thing I know, the room is tipping.

'Poppy…' Rafe's shout is loud and urgent, and he's not laughing any more.

Then there's a jolt as my head smashes backwards and hits the ground.

16

In Rafe's Kitchen: Possibly even purple

'Coffee, Poppy?'

When I stir next morning, the voice coming through the fog in my brain is Rafe's, and I assume I must still be a) asleep and b) dreaming. I mean when did Rafe ever offer me hot drinks? As I shift on the pillow my head pounds, but I open my eye a crack, enough to see an unfamiliar checked quilt covering me. Where the hell am I? I'm face down, my feet are pushing against the end of a sofa, and I'm looking down on a stone flag floor. If someone embedded an axe in my skull while I was sleeping my brain couldn't hurt any more than it does now. I have a vague recollection of bumping my head yesterday. I dare to open my eyes a bit wider and some legs in jeans come into focus.

'Milk no sugar, right?'

So it must be Rafe in the jeans. Flashes of what happened at Jaggers yesterday evening are coming back to me. Somehow he avoided drinking the whole night, was last man standing in charge of a Land Rover, and he brought me back to his. Presumably to sleep on the sofa in his kitchen.

I let out a long groan, and not only because of my sore head. I don't even remember drinking much. As I push up to sitting, I see there's a bucket next to the pillow. Oh shit. Surely I can't have?

'Tell me, what's with the bucket? I wasn't, I didn't?' I search Rafe's face for clues, appalled.

He shuffles and passes me the coffee. 'I'm afraid you did, but it's not a problem.'

Worse and worse. My stomach clenches with shame as I take the mug. My first night out for six months, and I end up legless enough to fall over, then I'm sick. How embarrassing is that?

'I'm a farmer don't forget, I've seen a lot worse. I spread muck on a daily basis.' He's shrugging it off by talking in T-shirt slogans. 'Good thing you weren't in the best guest room. Much easier to check you were okay down here.'

Across the room, I notice a rug and a pillow draped over an armchair. 'You stayed up all night?'

'No problem, I do it all the time with the stock.' He's playing it down. 'You were pretty out of it though.'

I already gathered that much thanks. 'I never used to be this much of a lightweight before…' I stop before I say too much. There's no way I want to whine about Brett. But this guy just stayed up all night watching over me like some wounded animal, I owe him some explanation. 'I just mean my alcohol tolerance used to be way higher. I had a break up, and I haven't been out much since.' Hopefully that keeps it to a minimum.

'I seriously doubt many people could have drunk what you did, and still be standing. Although those jugs are deceptive.' Note the way he's harshly, horribly realistic, but builds in a last minute excuse. 'And I'm guessing you're probably better off without whoever it was you were talking about last night.'

'I mentioned Brett?' Excuse me for my high pitched panic. If throwing up was mortifying, this is so much worse.

'Once or twice,' he says, which tells me absolutely bloody

87

nothing at all. 'Take it from me, being on your own has a lot to recommend it,' he goes on. 'Pleasing yourself is great, once you get the knack.'

'Spoken like a dedicated loner,' I say. If he's being coldly observational, I can be too. That would be the loner who we were trying to pair off with Immie. From the way he's talking now, yesterday evening was doomed before it began. Except for the getting totally off my face part, which I managed like a pro.

'Whereas Immie could do with the right guy in her life,' he says, as he picks up a neatly folded pile of clothes from the table. I'm vaguely surprised that Rafe's table is so designer. I'd expected country farmhouse, not hewn wood and steel.

Rafe considering Immie's private life comes as a shock too. 'Surf boy from last night wasn't right.' I sigh. As the rest of the huge room pulls into focus, I take in a seriously stylish kitchen. I'm not sure if the mechanical parts scattered around the work-tops are part of the decor, or more of Rafe's chaos.

'But, just to be clear, I'm not that guy either.' His eyes are boring into my face, as he checks I've taken that on board.

Pretty clear where he stands on that one. 'Right. Got that now.' I take my eyes off what looks like a tractor engine next to the black Aga, and try for a weak smile. If my brain was working better I'd revisit that Country Living article about what the colour of your Aga says about your personality. Pretty obvious Rafe would go for black. Whereas Jules might go for cloud grey, or possibly even purple.

Rafe pushes the clothes towards me, nodding at a plank door in the corner of the kitchen. 'Here's a sweater and T-shirt of mine for you to borrow. The shower's through the hall.' He glances at the big clock on the trendy brickwork wall beyond the island unit. 'If you go now you should be ready in time.'

In time…'For what?' My head spins as I try to catch up.

'That's why you stayed over,' he says as if it's the most obvious thing in the world, not that it makes it any clearer to me. 'You were convinced you had a desperately important appointment you couldn't miss.' There's a mocking sneer in his tone.

I wish he'd get on and tell me. 'And?'

'I checked the book and you're expecting Jules at nine.' By the way Rafe's spits that out, he's not impressed. 'By the way, do you want breakfast? Bacon, eggs, tomatoes, toast?'

But the word breakfast makes my stomach wrench so hard I have to make a dive for the bathroom.

17

In the office at Daisy Hill Farm:
Paper mountains and flash photography

On the dot of nine, Jules is pulling up a chair next to mine, and slipping off his parka.

'So, I see Rafe's still working through his paper mountain.' He laughs as he pushes back a pile of magazines on the desk. As he opens his laptop, Adele breaks into song.

'Your wedding mix again?' I ask.

'To help us get in the mood.' He sends me a wink, which I take it is meant to be funny this early in the day. 'I'll let you have my Spotify playlists.'

Jules did a small wedding here last year, which I assume is why he knows all about Rafe's filing pile.

'Fab.' I wince as the scent of his body spray hits my nose. It's spicy, and a lot more in my face than I can cope with this morning. Luckily, this far he doesn't appear to have noticed I'm looking like the undead.

'So, for the website, I've sorted out some pictures you might like to use.' He tilts his screen, and signals for me to lean in. 'I suggest you keep it simple, and keep it lovely,' he turns, and waits for my reaction.

I kick my brain into gear. 'A website's great as a first point of contact for customers.' I'm quoting Jess here, desperately trying to sound on top of my game. I'm so grateful Jules is helping, because I haven't got the first idea how to do this website on my own.

'Not everyone books weddings years ahead.' Jules sounds like he knows what he's talking about, which is exactly what I'm banking on here. 'A good website should bring in last minute business too.'

'That's exactly what I thought.' I try to sound like I knew that all along, and move in for a better view of the bride on screen, but I wasn't counting on him moving in too. My cheek is pretty much rammed against his polo shirt here. 'Although I'm not sure Rafe is keen on adding in any more bookings.' I reckon this is putting it mildly. 'He's desperate to move onto wind farms.'

Jules tuts. 'Wind farms are last year's thing, whereas weddings are booming. Most farmers I know would kill to have somewhere this picturesque to open up as a venue. Handled well, it could bring in a lot of income. That farmhouse is pure gold.'

If I'm not entirely comfortable with Jules being so close I can see the pores on his eyebrows, I'm even less comfortable discussing Rafe's finances. But I need Jules to understand the context. This website is for a limited time only. It needs to be good, but not amazing.

'Rafe's got farms coming out of his ears, I doubt he needs the money from this.' I'm sure his holiday cottages will more than see him through.

'With all the tax they had to pay when his old man died, and then building a new place for his mother, Rafe needs to be milking this to the max, excuse the pun.' Jules sounds very sure of his facts as he flicks up an amazing shot of a bridal couple in front

91

of a huge tipi. 'See, all you need are a few shots to inspire people, these ideas could all be recreated at Daisy Hill…'

'Wow…' I lean in closer as the most beautiful pictures of weddings Jules has covered flash in front of me. Open sided marquees in full summer, grooms in boaters and striped waist-coats, bridesmaids dancing around maypoles, vintage camping fests with camper vans, a field full of tiny tents with ragged bunting flapping in the breeze, a huge marquee with flowers garlanding the entrance. And some of the most gorgeous brides winding through summer meadows, laughing as they climbed trees, wading across streams. 'Idyllic…' I breathe.

Jules turns to me with a grin, and gives my arm a squeeze. 'That's the idea. We want this website to sell the dream.'

If I wasn't so wobbly, I might be enjoying this more. As it is, instead of giggling and flashing my smile about, and doing flirty flicks of what's left of my hair, I'm strangely rigid.

We both jump as the door latch rattles, and when the door swings open a second later, I've pulled as far away from Jules as I can. If this is Immie I know I'm dead meat, so it's a relief to see Rafe's gigantic Hunter boot appearing round the door edge. But when he marches into the office his frown is so dark, I'd rather have faced Immie after all.

'Sorry, I wasn't aware I'd be interrupting.' From the disgust on Rafe's face, he's not joking.

Jules is straight back at him with an unrepentant grin. 'If you provide a Do Not Disturb sign, we'll be sure to put it up in future.'

Rafe lets out a snort, and clears a duck out of his path with his boot. 'What's with the awful girly music?'

Jules opens his mouth to answer, but seeing as this is my office, I get in first. 'I'm playing love songs at a wedding venue, Rafe. If you have a problem with that you'll have to man up.' My fighting talk wilts as a duck waddles around to my side of the desk and I shrink back in my chair. 'Can you put the duck outside please, it's not…' I tail off. I'm not in the best place to give lectures to Rafe about hygiene this morning.

'There are worse things to clean up after than ducks,' Rafe says pointedly.

Damn it. I walked right into that one.

He balances the edge of the tray he's carrying on the desk. 'If you could possibly suspend your love fest, I could do with some help here.' As he begins to clear a space, papers fly in all directions.

'Let me…' As I go around the desk, Rafe's expression lightens a shade. 'What's this anyway?' I take in three mugs, a pot of coffee, and a plate piled high with bacon sandwiches.

'I thought you might be wanting food…' Rafe narrows his eyes, but it's Jules he's watching for a reaction. 'Given you turned down breakfast when you woke up.' He throws that in like a hand grenade, and his face breaks into a satisfied smile as Jules' eyes practically pop out of their sockets.

'Right. Matching jumpers. I should have realised.' Jules says.

It's the first time I've seen him deflated. My heart sinks as I take in what he says. My eyes lock on Rafe's jumper. The exact twin of the borrowed sloppy charcoal sweater I dragged on top of my denim skirt this morning. I'm just relieved my borrowed T-shirt isn't on show. *My tractor's sexy, that's how I got a hot girlfriend* is not a message I want to show the world. Whatever standoff is going on here, I want no part of it. They've obviously got some silly practical farmer versus arty photographer thing going on. But seeing as Jules is helping with the website for Rafe's damned venue, the least I can do is to clear this up.

'I ended up spending the night here…on the sofa…' I linger on the word sofa. 'After a cocktail or two too many at Jaggers last night.' I ignore Rafe's cough of disbelief. 'That's all.'

The grin that spreads across Jules face exposes every perfect tooth. 'Jaggers Happy Hour claims a lot of victims.' His nostalgic sigh turns to a chortle. 'Some of us are dropping in there tonight actually. There's a Sex on the Beach three for two offer, if you're up for it, Poppy?'

More cocktails? I give a silent shudder, but before I can get out a reply, Rafe cuts in.

'Are you damned well blind?' He's glaring at Jules with a disbelieving stare. 'The woman's a walking hangover, of course she won't be coming out tonight. She won't be out for the rest of the weekend, and if I know Poppy, she probably won't be out for the rest of the year.'

My mouth drops open, and I'm too stunned to close it again.

Rafe pulls himself up to his full six two, with a satisfied sniff. 'Help yourself to coffee, Jules.' Then he turns to me. 'Poppy, for chrissakes, eat something, now, or you're going to feel like death all day.' He scoops up a pile of papers from the desk, and strides across to the book case. 'So knock yourselves out. Anything you want, I'll be here all morning. I'm going to catch up on my filing.'

MARCH

18

In My Kitchen at Brides by the Sea: The extra mile

'So, when we've checked through the text again the website can go live?'

Two weeks later, I'm at my kitchen table with Jules, putting the finishing touches to the Weddings at Daisy Hill Farm website. You're completely right, it's ridiculous. I'd half hoped Jules might suggest using the loft apartment I imagine he lives in, but he didn't. So instead we're crammed in here, perched on stools, with barely enough room to lift a cup of coffee. But compared to refereeing the standoffs and running battles between Jules and Rafe at the farm, it's a piece of cake. On the up side, thanks to Rafe refusing to leave the office if Jules was there working with me, there's not a paper out of place, and the desk is clear, probably for the first time in living memory. As for the down side, Jules is a lot closer than is comfortable in my kitchen built for one, but for one last afternoon, I'll work with that. After today, I'll probably only see him if he's working at a wedding.

'And once the website's up and running, we're kind of done

aren't we?' I didn't mean it to come out sounding as if I'm pushing for more, because I'm not.

'Which is exactly why I keep asking you to come for a drink.' He turns and looks me full in the face. When you're in a room that measures six feet across including work surfaces, there's nowhere to hide.

Today his eyes are the same colour as the sea we enthused about earlier when we peeped out of my porthole. I hold his deep blue gaze for a second, then look away. 'My answer's still the same,' I sigh. And it's nothing to do with not facing cocktails. 'When you lose the person you thought you were meant to be with, it takes a while to adjust.' I'm gently reminding Jules what I've told him before. The idea of another relationship leaves me cold.

Jules runs his fingers through his hair, and flops it back into place. 'Fine, I'm happy to wait.' He sits back, and folds his arms. 'We'll be friends for now.' His finger dances over the track pad of his lap top. 'Although if that's the case, I warn you, this website won't ever be officially finished. I'll be round to see you with constant suggestions to improve it.' Something in his steady gaze tells me he isn't joking. 'And that person you were with can't really have been "the one", or you'd still be with him wouldn't you?'

I take a deep breath. There are times when you have to ignore Jules' forward-thrusting statements.

'Thanks for the stalker alert anyway.' I decide against a wink, and instead give his foot a kick, as he brings up the Weddings at Daisy Hill Farm home page. I know he felt it, because he pushes back on my ankle, just a little.

'I'm really pleased with the font we chose,' he says. 'It's kind of stylish, yet relaxed, with that all important vintage vibe.'

Thank Christmas he's decided to move the conversation on. 'Your pictures are what make it,' I say, as we flick through, yet again. 'You really do get the most amazing shots.'

In a way it's sad to think these long afternoons poring over a laptop with Jules have come to an end. I still can't quite get over how he transforms the flat. It's not just that he's incredibly decorative, with his long legs, easy humour, and stylish clothes. The sheer force of his personality sends energy pulsing through the place, and I don't just mean the soundtrack he takes with him wherever he goes.

'Those pictures have to be good, they're my job,' he muses. 'In one freeze frame, I have to pin down all the love between a couple. And if it's their wedding day, it's likely one of those shots will become an iconic image they'll look at every day for the rest of their lives.'

'No pressure then.' I laugh, and pass him another cupcake. Made specially. His latest request was for bitter coffee sponge, topped with coffee icing, sprinkled with toasted almonds. Believe me, after miserable no-cake Rafe, Jules is a pleasure to bake for. He peels back the paper case of his cupcake, half closing his eyes as he takes a bite. It's strange, because I can't actually remember a time when I was ever fascinated watching Brett biting into food, yet here I am, mesmerised.

'I don't know how you do it.' I say, wishing I could hold my wedding day nerve like he does. 'I'm already beside myself worrying about Ben and Lara's wedding, and I'm just the coordinator.' It's true, I'm waking every night, in a cold sweat, imagining I've forgotten something vital.

'I'll be there to help you, don't forget.' Jules rests his hand on mine in what I take as a supportive gesture.

And here we go again, with the whole Rafe comparison. Whereas Rafe constantly says stuff's not his problem, Jules is just so damned helpful. He'll go that extra mile. Even when it's nothing to do with him.

'The secret of a successful wedding is a good photographer.' He sends another wink, presumably to show he's not bragging. That's the second this afternoon. 'A good photographer drives and directs the whole day. I've been at the centre of so many weddings, I instinctively know when disasters are about to happen, and how to avert them. I'm there, invisible, yet completely in control. You have no idea how many times my quick thinking has saved the day.' If he sounds like he's boasting, I'm sure it's justified.

'It's good to know you'll have my back.' He has no idea how grateful I am for this, or how much I'll be relying on him. 'Making you coffee cupcakes paid off then?' Given we're winking this afternoon, I finally dare to send him a wink of my own, to show him I'm joking. Although I hope he's not counting up my winks like I'm counting his. And I'm not actually certain I'm joking – there are times when the right choice of baking pays big dividends, and I sense this might be one of them.

'Remember, I'm always here. Anything you need, just call me.' He neatly collects the cake crumbs from the corner of his mouth, and licks them off his finger. 'Whatever kind of help you need, I promise I'll come to your rescue. Every time. Great nuts by the way, they make all the difference.' We get wink number three here.

'Thanks, that's so great to…'

'Poppy…?' There's a clatter of feet on the stairs, and Jess runs into the room gasping. 'I know you're busy, but we've got an emergency, could you possibly…'

Her pink cheeks and panting tells me I'm needed right away. Jess might yell up for me from time to time, but I've rarely seen her this flustered.

'I think we've probably done as much as we need to, haven't we?' I say to Jules. If not, I doubt he'll mind having an excuse to drop in again. I give his knee an appreciative squeeze as I get off my stool.

'Unless you'd like a walk on the beach later?' Jules' puppy dog eyes would melt the hardest heart, and he's working them to the max.

Jess is hopping from foot to foot. 'This may take a while.' She drops her voice to a whisper. 'Josie Redman just arrived unannounced. Sera's pouring bubbly for the entourage as we speak, and at the same time trying to hide the fact she's hyperventilating so hard she can't do anything. Quick…' She grabs my sleeve and tugs hard. 'We need you NOW!'

In the light of that news, I'm guessing we're forgetting Jess's all in black rule for today. Rafe's sweater and my old jeans will have to do for now. Okay, I know I haven't given it back yet, but it's comfortable.

'Sorry to be running out on you, Jules.' I'm backing out of the kitchen, waving as I speak. 'Let me know if you think of anything else.' I'm confident that he will. 'And take the cupcakes… and the box…' Confident he'll do that too.

Jess and I scurry down stairs, bumping the banisters as we go.

'That one's a keeper if ever I saw one,' Jess pants, as we dash through Groomswear. 'His wedding pics are to die for. And he drinks in Jaggers.' Only Jess would waste oxygen discussing men. 'I heard him offer to rescue you…Robbie Williams singing in the background too…you've landed on your feet with him.'

Worse and worse. All I can hope is that the excitement of the next hour will bring on a bout of her busy-person forgetfulness.

19

In Brides by the Sea: Detoxes and perfect complexions

'I'm so sorry to be putting you on the spot...' Josie keeps repeating.

If she's trying her best to make up for the tidal wave of panic that's raging through the shop, she's failing hugely. But far from the larger-than-life character she's portrayed as in the tabloids, within moments it's obvious that Josie's sweet and considerate. She's surprisingly small, and way prettier than any of her pictures in *Hello*. And despite her reputation as a drinks thrower, within minutes Jess decides prosecco is the only way forward, and trusts her with a glass. As for the flying visit on the way to Bristol, Josie's three friends have tossed their huge studded handbags in a multi-coloured pile, settled into the sofas, crossed their very long legs, and are flicking their spikey heels about as if they're here for the evening.

'Anyone for cake?' I ask. I've forgotten to bring down my emergency supply, but it doesn't matter, as there's a mass shaking of perfectly mussed heads, a smoothing of slender thighs, and a loud muttering of the word detox.

'Luckily white wine's allowed.' Josie laughs, but as she waggles her glass about, I feel Jess tensing slightly. 'The thing is,' Josie begins hesitantly, 'I wanted to pop in to see the dresses, so I'm prepared for our design meeting next week.' Josie sends Sera a beguiling smile. 'I'm worried I'm going to get all indecisive, and this way I'll be less of a pain in the bum.' As she puts her glass down again, Jess relaxes visibly.

'So Sera you could begin by showing Josie your ready to wear dresses?' Jess is prompting here, because Sera is shrinking behind a folding screen, one foot hooked behind her knee, still paralysed by shock. 'And then you can bring some things down from the studio later.'

Sera, dodging out of the customers' view, catches my eye, and gives a two second mime of someone having their throat slit. Showing off and selling her dresses is the part of being a designer she finds hardest, and to be fair, Jess has always handled that side of things for her. I know Sera's going to have to talk to Josie about designs later on, but for now I take pity on her. She's only in pieces because Josie appeared out of the blue when Sera wasn't prepared for her. Who wouldn't be, when there's so much at stake?

Grabbing Sera by the hand, I coax her onto the nearest Louis Quatorze chair. 'Or, maybe you and Jess can show Josie the dresses, Sera, while I bring down the rest from the studio?' I suggest, and select the first dress I come to on the rail. 'Okay, this is one of Sera's most popular designs this season, she called it Bali after one of her favourite places.'

'That's so cool, I love beaches too.' Josie's already enthusiastic.

'Even on the hanger you can see Sera's signature flowing lines make her dresses super flattering, and fabulously easy to wear,' I explain, trying not to gabble. 'And the lace detail is just so pretty and unusual.' I hesitate, thinking of my own dress. As I pass the dress to Jess, the silk floats as if it's almost lighter than air. Josie's friends look on, their long varnished nails fluttering to their lips.

'Completely gorgeous,' Josie breathes. 'Just what I want.' She turns to her friends. 'And so different from the jewelled meringue that the media are expecting me to wear. See now why I need Sera to make my dress for me?'

Sera is chewing her finger nail, but I think she might be smiling too. As I head for the stairs that lead up to her studio, I flash her a thumbs up. 'I'll grab anything suitable, are you okay with that?' I hiss as I pass her, and she gives me a thumbs up in return. 'Don't worry, you look lovely, and so do your dresses.' Poor Sera was planning to have at least a professional make up session before Josie saw her.

One of the amazing things about wedding dresses is the way they unite the women in a room when they start to look at them. There's no better ice breaker than a totally beautiful wedding dress, and in Brides by the Sea's newly arranged Seraphina East room, every dress is stunning. The appreciative hum from below drifts up to the studio as I carefully search through Sera's works in progress. As the prosecco flows and everyone relaxes, the applause gets louder. When I finally wind my way back down and hand Jess Sera's dresses from the studio, they're greeted with more excited squeals.

'This one's so new it hasn't even got a name yet,' Sera admits, still shy.

Jess deftly flips out the soft tulle skirt, and fingers the delicate lace clinging to the most slender straps 'Again there's that same combination of lightness and simplicity mixed with exquisite detail.'

Josie's friend with a halo of backcombed hair leans across and touches Josie's arm. 'It's all very well letting one of us model the dresses for you. You sure you aren't going to try any on?'

Josie scrunches her face. 'I'll work up to that next time. For today I just wanted to see how they looked in reality rather than in pictures.'

Secretly thinking of my own dress here, I chip in. 'When you do put on one of Sera's dresses, you'll get this strange feeling that you couldn't possibly be any more beautiful or amazing. They have this kind of magic that you don't feel in other dresses.' Not in any of the ones I tried on anyway.

Sera, now standing again, with her foot propped on the wall behind her, joins in. 'I think that's pretty much my entire collection at the moment.'

Jess holds up a hand. 'There's one other dress I'd love you to see…it's very special, and we'd have to get the owner's permission…' Everyone stops talking.

Sera gives a puzzled frown. 'Isn't this everything?'

Sera might be in the dark, but I know it's my dress Jess is wanting Josie to see.

Jess turns to me. 'What do you think, Poppy?'

Ignoring that my stomach has just done a triple vault, I try for a brilliant smile, but it comes out like a watery sun. This is Sera's big break, however much it hurts I need to man up.

'If you get the dress, Jess, I'll make a call and check it's okay,' I say, in a voice that's much more wobbly than mine.

Jess claps her hands. 'Great, give us a moment.' Before I know it Jess is steering me through the shop, towards the dress store. My legs are acting as if they belong to someone else, and my stomach's churning. As we come into the White Room, instead of heading for the room where the dresses waiting for collection are kept, Jess detours to her desk.

'Are you sure you're okay with this?' she asks in an urgent whisper.

I swallow, trying desperately to keep my lunch down. It's only a bloody dress after all, it shouldn't be this hard.

'I'm sorry to do this to you, and it's fine to say no.' She fumbles in the drawer as she whispers to me. 'Josie seems nice enough, but these celebrities are horrendously fickle, and I want to make sure they see enough to make them come back. If they decided not to go ahead and we hadn't shown them yours, I'd never forgive myself.'

I get her point. 'There's no way I can handle them asking about my wedding.' I'm blurting now, talking softly and fast, to cover ground. 'Seeing the dress again will be awful, but so long as they don't realise it's mine, I'll do it for Sera.' I'm convincing myself here, because my chest feels as if it might be about to implode, but suddenly I know it's the least I can do. 'Do it happily.' I add, as I hug my arms around my ribs.

Jess scours my face doubtfully, then slams a bottle of Hendricks onto the desk. A moment later, she pushes a shot glass half full of neat gin into my hand. 'Here, drink this while I get the dress. Knock it straight back, I promise it'll help.' She gives a worried grimace as she disappears.

I brace myself, then do exactly as she says. By the time the empty glass is on the desk Jess is back.

'Good girl.' She pats my arm with one hand, holding my dress aloft in her other. 'Don't look at the dress, forget it has anything to do with you at all.' She drags in a deep breath. 'Right. Let's do this.'

I'm not sure if it's down to the rapid intake of the gin, but as I scurry after Jess to join the others, I have no need for the tissue box I've grabbed in anticipation of a flood of tears. So much for the dread, instead of breaking down, within seconds I'm gritting my teeth, pretending this dress belongs to someone else entirely. I make sure I keep my eyes averted, and next thing I know I'm sighing and gasping and clapping along with everyone except for Josie. The noise fades as we turn to watch her.

Josie's opening and closing her mouth, flapping her hands in front of her face. Under her luminous foundation, her cheeks turn very pink then very pale again. After what seems like forever, a strange whimper comes from her throat. 'I loved the other dresses, but this one is even more what I'd hoped for, without actually knowing what I wanted, if you know what I mean?'

Judging by the line of empty bottles on the corsage table, her friends look like they've had so much prosecco they probably don't give a damn if they can understand her or not, but they all nod anyway. Not that I have any room to talk, having knocked back neat gin, but I wonder how they'll make it out of the shop when they put their six inch heels back on.

Josie's biting her lip, welling up. 'I don't even need to put it on,' she murmurs. 'It's just like everyone said it would be, I already know, if there was a dress like this that didn't belong to someone else, it would be "the one".'

For the first time Sera's broad face lights up. 'I can change the details so yours will be completely special for you. Jess is right,' she says ruefully. 'This is one of the most beautiful dresses I've ever made.'

'That would be lovely.' Josie sniffs, and I rush forward, turn my back to the dress and offer her the tissue box.

20

In Brides by the Sea: Hot dates and brave decisions

'I thought gin was supposed to make you weepy,' I muse later, as I help Jess with the final tidying.

'That's when it's sipped gently,' Jess says, as she puts the last chair back into place. 'Inhaled it's more of an anaesthetic.'

Which seemed to work, although I was helped by Jess who whisked my dress out of sight afterwards as fast as she'd found it.

'Are you sure you aren't coming out tonight?' Jess says, cloth in hand, as she dips down and checks the table tops for wine rings. 'You can't possibly hide in the attic on a Friday night with a gem like Jules hot on your trail.'

Jules the Gem? That's a good one. However uninvolved I am, after what Jess saw earlier there's no point in denials. 'I've got a hot date with a guy in Rose Cross.' I slip it out casually.

'What?' She's across the shop in a second.

That worked well. 'He's called George.' I can't help enjoy Jess's widening eyes. 'Although I admit he's mostly snoozes through our dates.'

'You kept that quiet, but he sounds a long way short of Jules. Who the hell is he?'

I laugh as I put her out of her misery. 'George is Cate's son, he's three in October.'

Jess's exasperated eye roll turns into a thoughtful frown. 'I was just thinking earlier, given that Jules is a wedding photographer, who would you get to take the pictures if you two actually got married?'

'Now you're being ridiculous.'

She shakes her head. 'Valid question, given the way he was looking at you.'

'Now we've finished the website, I doubt I'll see him again until the first Daisy Hill wedding.' My pulse is racing even as I think about it. The wedding, I mean, not Jules.

'Which is when exactly?' Jess is straight back at me. The trouble with Jess is her brain never stops.

'Just before Easter.' Two weeks. Only two short weeks and it's all got to be ready.

'Take it from me, you'll see him before then.' Jess gives a grin, before her brow furrows again. 'Brave couple doing an outdoor wedding in March. Not only a risk with the weather, but it's going to be dark so early.'

'Dark?' I say, and that's when I have my light bulb moment. 'Omigod, outdoor lighting! I've never even thought about it. Shit!' I knock my fist on my head. How the hell could I have overlooked something so obvious? 'Thanks Jess!' I cry as I make a run for it. More to the point, what else have I forgotten? Adrenalin is coursing through me as I fly upstairs two steps at a time, desperate to get to the lists on my laptop.

When I arrive, breathless, in my kitchen, I find Jules' multi coloured scarf draped over the table.

21

At Daisy Hill Farm: The day before

'That damned photographer would save us all a lot of time and effort if he surgically attached that bloody scarf of his.'

This is Rafe, as he storms out of the courtyard, literally tearing at his hair. And yes, he's ranting about Jules. Again.

Although he's making a good point about how careless Jules is with his scarf, the rest of Rafe's attacks on Jules are less justifiable. To save time and pain, I'll cut to the chase, and give you the figures from the past two weeks.

Number of times Jules has left his scarf behind (various locations): 8

Number of run-ins between Jules and Rafe, started by Rafe: 15

Number of arguments between me and Rafe about Jules: 17

Number of other major disagreements between me and Rafe: 24

Minor disagreements between me and Rafe: lost count.

Get the idea?

Immie shakes her head, muttering under her breath as Rafe stomps off. 'Give me strength.'

I'm pleased it's not only me. These guys are driving everyone round the bend. The way it works is, if Jules is around Rafe is invariably there, picking fights right, left and centre. The minute Jules leaves, Rafe is nowhere to be found, which to be honest is not ideal, given I have a hundred things an hour to check with him.

'Come on.' Immie heads for the driver's door of the farm jeep. 'Let's go and get these lanterns into position, then you can cross that off your list.'

Remember that light bulb moment I had? The good news is, lighting is under control. Apparently we have a dedicated technical team a.k.a. Geoff and Bob the farmworkers, who are in charge of the generators, outdoor flood lighting and other techie issues. And there's also a whole load of pretty storm lanterns, which Immie and I are about to put out along the path from the wedding field to the parking area. As for Immie, she's totally got my back here, even if her Land Rover driving does leave a lot to be desired.

'That blue and white striped marquee looks so beautiful doesn't it?' My knuckles are white from clinging onto the door handle as we roar up the lane, and she does a handbrake turn through the gateway, and the vehicle skids sideways into the wedding field. I know what you're thinking, but if I tell her to slow down, it'll only make her worse. Instead I give a little cough and a reminder.

'We're trying not to mess up the grass, remember?'

Immie ignores that, and instead throws the door open. She leaps to the ground, mallet in hand. 'Right, I'll bang in the stakes, you secure the lanterns.' She gives a nod towards the marquee, where people are running in and out to cars and vans parked nearby. 'You see, there was no need to worry, I told you it would all appear like magic, and it has.'

Magic? Two days of hard graft by the marquee guys more like, but at least it's here, along with a luxury tow-along toilet block that's nestling discretely behind the hedge. Would you believe, it's got marble clad cubicles, and real flowers next to the wash basins? And right now there's an army of people hurrying in and out of the marquee, carrying boxes from the cars and vans clustered near the entrance.

'The tables and chairs all went in this morning, and now Lara and Ben are doing their own flowers and styling,' I'm giving a running commentary, although Immie probably knows this already, given that she's been here a lot.

'Lots of friends to help I see, some of them damned good looking too.' Immie grins, as a hunk in a vest strides past, balancing a substantial tree in a large pot on one muscular forearm. She turns, mesmerised, as he eases the branches decked with lemon ribbons past the awning supports, then she gives an appreciative nod. 'That's my kind of removal man.'

Maybe Rafe is right when he says Immie is ready for a guy.

She's peering after this one, as he disappears into the marquee. 'I'm seeing lots of twigs and daffodils and bunting, is there a spring theme?'

'The bridesmaids are in yellow,' I say, knowing how Immie will react to this.

She grimaces. 'Jeez, poor girls, yellow's even worse than peach.' Even now she still hasn't grasped the concept of nude as a colour.

'But the theme's more Easter Bunny, because Lara's house rabbits are coming too,' I add. It's the first time I heard of a wedding with bunnies, but it sounds fun.

'Plenty of hay bales to keep the rabbits happy.' Immie says absently, obviously concentrating on the tree man.

At least when it came to hay, Rafe didn't hold back, and using bales as seats has saved Ben and Lara a fortune too.

Immie gives a shiver, frowning as she pulls her jacket zip higher. 'It's a bit cold for an outdoor wedding though.'

'It's tropical in there with the blower heaters. The muscle men haven't just stripped off for your benefit.' I send her a wink, and glance at my watch. 'If you can tear yourself away from talent spotting, shall we get on?'

Reluctantly she turns. 'Great to hear you make a joke at last.' As she pats me on the back, and she grabs an armful of stakes she gives me a hard stare. 'I was worried the stress was getting to you?'

She's not wrong about that. I've been waking earlier and earlier, my brain buzzing with lists.

'I've been scared for weeks, but now it's happening I'm shitting myself.' I drag in a deep breath. 'Being responsible for something as important as a wedding is huge.' A whole wedding is so much more than just a cake, which is what I'm used to delivering. As it is, I'm starting to understand why Rafe might not want to do weddings. It's fine if things go well, but the potential for disaster is immense. It would be so horrible to disappoint people on their special day. A couple only get married once, the day is so major, and there's no such thing as a second chance. I'm clenching my teeth, and my arms are going rigid as I think about it.

'Hey, lighten up.' Immie gives me a nudge. 'This time tomorrow it'll almost be over.'

'No, this time tomorrow, it'll have barely begun,' I wail.

'You've done brilliantly so far, and we'll all have your back.' Immie doesn't do soothing, but she's making a good job of it now. 'Even Cate's taking a day off to help.' She gives a chuckle. 'Which is only right, seeing as she's the one who landed you in this shit.'

'Right.' When did my voice get this small and weedy?

'And anyway, what's the worst that can happen?' Immie's pushing me here.

'Collapsing marquee, flooding, stampeding cows…' None of which will be down to me. But that's the whole thing about

113

disasters – you can never predict what's going to go wrong.

'The sky falling in?' Immie helpfully adds the one thing I hadn't thought of. 'As soon as it's over you'll wonder what you were so worried about,' she adds breezily. 'In the meantime, grab some lanterns. And for chrissakes…'

'What?' I grin at her, but only because I already know what she's going to say.

'Man up!'

22

In the Office at Daisy Hill Farm:
Guard dogs and sparkle cleans

'Rain's still holding off.' It's Rafe, and if he's poking his head around the office door to discuss the weather, he needs to remember that an hour from now some of us have a wedding to organise.

'Great,' I say, meaning anything but. I put down the insurance certificate I'm reading through for the twenty fifth time, and dive onto my laptop to turn down the music. True, I wouldn't usually be so obliging with the volume, but right now I'm not up for another argument about *Bat Out Of Hell* being too loud.

'Forecast is awful for later, we might get as much as an inch,' Rafe says, still shouting over the non-existent music. 'Are you sure you're okay, Poppy?'

'I'm fine,' I lie, and throw in a beam for good measure.

'It's just you're looking a bit…' Rafe tilts his head, and screws up his nose.

I brace myself for whatever insult he's selecting. Rough, ill,

115

tired, stressed, green? Like I'm in the middle of a silent nervous breakdown? Any of those would fit.

'Errrr…prickly…perhaps?' He says tentatively.

'What?' Seriously, I have no idea what he's talking about.

He tries again. 'Spikey maybe?'

Oh shit. In the excitement I'd momentarily forgotten yesterday's hair disaster. Chopping off the straggly bits of my growing out pixie cut before I went to bed, after another medicinal dose of Jess's Hendricks, was definitely a mistake. How the hell could I have thought it would make me look more sophisticated?

'And possibly a bit on edge?' He's doing a strange wiggle as he holds the door open for whatever animals are following him.

Luckily it's only Jet the dog he's bringing in. No way can I cope with hens and ducks today. Actually, I couldn't be more jittery if it were me getting married, but I'm not going to share that thought with him.

'My wellies have had a sparkle clean,' I say, desperately trying to pat down the most unruly bits of my hair. 'I've got Immie's best Barbour, I'm good to go.' Or at least I am now I've run around the desk, punching the air, singing along to *Don't Stop Me Now*. Thank Christmas Rafe didn't walk in five minutes earlier and catch me doing the actions.

My Spotify playlist, *Five Tracks to Fight the Fear (It's only a wedding dammit!)*, as suggested by Jules, is proving to be a total life saver, although right now a blast of easy confidence from the man himself would go a long way. There's no chance of that, given he's capturing the bridal party getting ready, the groomsmen at the pub, and then will be heading straight to the village church. Instead I'm stuck with Mr Moody droning on about rainfall figures and my hideous hair.

'Fancy a sandwich?' Rafe's crossed to the desk now, and he's putting down a tray with the nearest thing I've seen to a smile for days. 'I assume you haven't eaten, given you've been here since four?'

'Damn, I'm sorry, did I wake you?' So much for sneaking in under the radar. As for breakfast, I might be chewing my fist, but I'm never hungry when I'm this anxious.

'I didn't hear you arrive, but Jet did.' Rafe nods at the dog. 'He's good like that.'

Jet, standing next to Rafe, lifts an eyebrow in appreciation of the mention, and thumps his tail against the desk. As the scent of fresh coffee wafts past my laptop screen, my mouth begins to water.

As I spot the plate piled high, and a ketchup bottle I can't resist asking. 'Are those bacon sandwiches there?'

'Yep. You need to put away your spreadsheet and eat. You'll be far too busy running around later to think about food.'

As Rafe pushes the tray towards me, a warm glow spreads through my chest. Who'd have thought he'd be so considerate and understanding. Maybe he's not so bad as a boss after all.

'Thanks.' As I grab a crusty cob and take a bite, my empty stomach growls in anticipation. No way am I admitting I've been to the marquee and back six times already.

Rafe clears his throat, and drums his fingers on the filing cabinet which he's now leaning against. 'Another small thing…' The way he hesitates is ominous. 'I…err, just wanted to confirm you won't be drinking later?'

'Sorry?' I stop in mid chew as my mouth drops open in surprise.

'There'll be lots of alcohol around, it doesn't look good if the staff get drunk.' He's saying staff, but this is directed entirely at me. 'You have the responsibility, you need to stay sober.' The stare he's giving me is hard enough to rival Immie's.

As if I didn't know that. The back of my neck prickles with indignation. 'I wouldn't dream of getting drunk.' My voice has gone all squeaky and high. 'Definitely not at work,' I add, blinking away the image of Jess's gin.

'You made a pretty good job of it a couple of weeks back.'

His forehead wrinkles into a frown. 'Unless you've forgotten?' He's looking right down his nose at me now. 'Alcohol can cause memory blackouts.'

Shit. He's got me there. Although accidentally getting legless on a night out is another scenario entirely, but I'm not about to argue the point. Whatever I said before about an understanding boss, I take it all back. He obviously doesn't have the first idea.

'Right, well this time I'll *remember* not to knock back every bottle of wine I come across.' If I'm sending him a mocking sneer, it's only because he deserves it. 'And you make sure your locked up cows don't stampede through the wedding.' Hopefully neither is likely to happen, but if he's got the point I'm making, he's not reacting.

'If we've cleared that up, it's over to you,' he says, his face impassive as he backs towards the door. 'Have a good day.'

That's it? A food delivery masquerading as a lecture on alcohol abuse, and now he's off.

'Thanks,' I say airily, as he steps out into the yard, making it clear I don't give a damn that he's walking out on this. I'm just muttering, 'thanks for bloody nothing,' when his head appears around the door edge again.

'By the way…'

He can stuff his 'By the ways' up his…

'If something important crops up…' He's drumming his fingers on the door, annoyingly.

If he was the last man on a desert island, I wouldn't be asking for his help. 'There won't be anything the team can't handle.' I stick my chin in the air. 'And if I fall over drunk I'm sure someone will call you.'

'Whatever.' He rolls his eyes, and his long sigh leaves me in no doubt how much he's hating every minute of this. 'I'll be in the office or the kitchen all day.'

23

In the office at Daisy Hill Farm: Disco rabbits

'So that went well.' Immie's beaming at me, leaning back in the office chair. Feet on the desk, a lop-eared rabbit cradled on her lap. 'See, I told you there was nothing to worry about.' At least she's taken her boots off.

'It isn't over yet,' I remind her, as I slam the door against the wind, and shove my dripping umbrella into the bucket, which someone – probably Cate – has thoughtfully provided. 'There's still another half hour to go.' Although I'm only here for a moment I ease down my jacket zip. 'How are the bunnies anyway?' Okay, it's confession time. When the heavens finally opened at ten, I gave up on vanity, and took refuge in the yurt coat. It might not look great, but who cares if it keeps you dry in a downpour like we're having now.

Immie took over rabbit care when Cate finally gave up on looking for ideas for her own wedding and went home. Who'd have thought Cate would have overlooked a chocolate fountain? She remedied that by putting in an order straight away, except – no surprise – hers will be super-sized. The doting way Immie is tickling the bunny's head reminds me how she used to make us sit through back to back screenings of my mum's *Watership Down* video when we were nine. 'The bunnies have been fine since we brought them up here.'

'I'm counting myself lucky, rabbits almost having heart attacks because of the disco is the worst thing that's happened today,' I say. 'That and Rafe assuming I was going to get paralytic.' I give that the eye roll it deserves. This is the first opportunity I've had to mention it.

Immie pat's her rabbit's back. 'You might need to forgive him for that.' She gives a rueful smile. 'He probably didn't want to say, but Carrie got rat-arsed at every wedding.' Her smile turned to a grimace. 'And she usually made a lunge for the best man at some point too.'

'That explains a lot.' If I'd known that I'd have saved myself a day of fuming. At least he spared me the lecture about jumping the guests. 'So,' I go on, sliding back into organiser mode, 'Lara's mum is picking the bunnies up on her way home, which should be in about half an hour. Where's the other one anyway?' I glance around the floor nervously. 'A lost bunny is all I need.'

'Keep your hair on,' Immie chides. 'He's only under the book-case, he's having a great time making a nest out of paper.'

I let the hair reference go. 'Paper?' I'm puzzled. 'There isn't any paper, not since Rafe had his filing fest.'

When I stoop under the bookcase to investigate, sure enough there's a fur ball of a bunny, surrounded by scrunched up paper scraps. As I pick one up, and smooth it out, my heart gives a lurch. 'Oh shit.' I pick up the next piece and let out a long groan.

'Problem?' Immie looks up from twisting her bunny's ear.

'These look like wedding notes.' I fish out the rest of the papers, and spread the bundle out on the desk. 'I think our nesting bunny just found the rest of Carrie's filing system.' Opening the drawer, I ram them in. 'There's no time for this now, the taxis will be here any minute, I need to direct them to the parking area.'

Grabbing my umbrella, I'm about to make a run for it, when the door opens and Rafe saunters in. When you're racing around like a mad thing, there's nothing more annoying than someone all laid back and nonchalant, blocking your way.

He scratches his head, oblivious, and peers at Immie's knee. 'Rabbit?' he asks slowly. 'I saw the *No Dogs, Due To Loose Livestock* notice on the door.' He's acting like he's just woken up from a snooze, although he's fully kitted out in all weather gear, which seems a bit extreme as he's only walked from the house to the office.

'Two actually.' Immie gives a laugh.

'Nice one.' The corners of his mouth pull downwards, as he leans forwards and tweaks the bunny's ear. 'I see our Wedding Planner's relaxed her rules about livestock in the office then?'

I haven't got time for this. 'I'm your Event Coordinator,' I snap, immediately regretting saying 'your'. 'And if you don't mind moving, I need to go to meet the taxis.' I put my hands on my hips, to show him I mean business.

'Taxis? Here's me talking about rabbits, and I should be telling you about taxis.' He rubs his chin but doesn't move. 'Morgan just rang me to say there are ten taxis, all in the bottom field.'

My stomach plummets. 'But they're early.' And in completely the wrong place. Even as I wail, I know this is my fault, because I was supposed to show them where to go. 'And they're supposed to be in the top field.' The bottom field was already a quagmire this afternoon, and that was before the rain.

'The taxis always arrive at least half an hour ahead of time for wedding pickups.'

I can't help snapping. 'It might have helped if you'd told me that.'

He shrugs off my complaint as if I hadn't spoken. 'What matters more is that they're currently stuck fast, up to their axles in mud.'

Shit. Worse and worse. I grab my shrinking stomach, because

I think I'm going to be sick. 'What the hell am I going to do now? The guests will be stuck here all night, it's my worst nightmare, a wedding that never ends.' I hear my voice getting higher and higher. This is the ultimate cock up, and it's all down to me.

'Keep your hair on, Poppy, it's only a few bogged down taxis.' From the way the corners of Rafe's lips are twitching, I suspect he might be enjoying this. 'The tractor's outside ready, we'll pull them out in no time.' His face splits into a full blown grin. 'Hop in, I'll give you a lift back to the front line.'

As we bounce through the darkness towards the cosy glow of the marquee, the rain is hammering down on the tractor cab, and the strings of lights around the field are swinging wildly, in the gale.

'I hope the bride's brought her wellies.' Rafe says, as he swings the tractor into the wedding field. 'I knew she was going to need them.'

Don't you just hate know-it-alls? Especially when they're right. Even more when they're filling the space with the smell of really nice aftershave, which by rights, given the stubble on their chin, they shouldn't be using at all.

'Lara chose to get married in a field in March, she was completely prepared for mud,' I bluff through gritted teeth, because I can't bear him gloating. Now I know Lara and Ben better, I'm even more desperate for them to have an awesome day.

'More fool her,' he sniffs, and even though it's dark, I know he's rolling his eyes.

'Let's hope she's had a brilliant day,' I say, a lot more brightly than I feel. Right now I'll just be glad when the taxis have all been pulled free, and everyone's driven away. Thank goodness they're all from the village, so no-one's staying over in the cottages.

'You've certainly gone the extra mile for her,' he grunts, as he pulls up by the marquee entrance. 'I hope they damn well appreciate it.'

Excuse me? Was that Rafe handing out a compliment, albeit a back handed and grouchy one?

'I'm sure they do,' I assure him hurriedly, when I finally pick my jaw up off the floor.

Rafe pulls up by the burger van outside the marquee. As he reaches across me and opens the tractor door to let me out, a figure in a sodden parka springs into the headlight beam. There's a flash of a camera lens, and a glimpse of familiar stripy scarf, and suddenly, I'm smiling.

'David bloody Bailey's still here then?' This is Rafe, signing off the day, as 'disgusted of Daisy Hill Farm'. 'Do me a favour, and tell that tosser it's past his bed time, he needs to go home.'

'Thanks for the lift,' I call, ignoring the insults. Gingerly I climb down from the tractor, knowing I owe Rafe for a whole lot more than that. I'm deep in the shit here, and this is the guy who's saving me.

Rafe is still blustering about Jules. 'On second thoughts, tell him…'

Except I don't hear what he has to say, because there's a throng of guests under the marquee awning, clutching umbrellas and armfuls of daffodils, who rush towards me, all asking where their transport is.

APRIL

24

In Brides by the Sea: Something for the walls

The down-side to having a bright yellow car is it makes it diffi-cult to hide, and as I only go to two places anyway, I'm not hard to find. If I'm not at Daisy Hill Farm, I'll be at Brides by the Sea. Which is probably why, yet again, Jules is outside on the pave-ment, waving past the gauzy wonders of Sera's bestselling dresses in the window and making 'I'm coming in right now' gestures. Okay, I might be making this more complicated than it sounds. He's putting up two thumbs, bouncing in the direction of the shop door, and giving me his broadest, most enthusiastic, puppy dog smile. In fact it's so broad, I'm not the only one who catches it.

'Jules? Again?'

I can tell by the little purr Jess gives, that despite her one raised eyebrow, and the fact that I'm supposedly working for her, not for me today, she doesn't mind at all.

'I wonder...' She gives another purr. 'Is he bringing us some pictures at last?'

Given he just put up two thumbs, I'm guessing he's here empty handed, at least for today. But Jess is putting on the pressure big time, trying to persuade him to let her have some fabulous shots for her walls, in return for what she calls 'invaluable wedding shop exposure' and 'downstream marketing'. We all know what she's actually angling for is for him to rent some exhibition wall space from her, but this far, he's holding out. No mean achievement. When Jess puts the screws on, she's very hard to stand up to.

'I'm sorry he's always crashing in here,' I say to Jess, 'I'd much rather he invited me to his loft apartment, just so I can have a look.'

Jess is onto me in a second. 'And who said he lived in an apartment?' She peers at me over her specs.

'I can't remember,' I admit, 'A loft goes with his lifestyle somehow.'

Jess gives a laugh. 'Jaggers is a great place for gathering information. Sorry to disillusion you, but Jules lives in a bungalow.'

'Really?' This doesn't fit with my image of him at all, unless it's one of those super swish places.

'With his mum.' She adds, grinning at my shock, as she brings the final hammer crashing down on my illusions.

'Surely not?' I gawp at her. I'm supposedly cleaning surfaces for an hour while my cakes cool, but my feather duster is hanging limp in my hand.

She crosses the shop, to hiss in my ear. 'How else do you think he affords that car of his? Not to mention all those super expensive clothes? He's fully subsidised by the Bank of Mother.'

'OMG,' I mouth silently, half appalled that I got him so wrong, half of me thinking that it doesn't matter at all. I don't even want him, but if I did, I'm not completely shallow and materialistic. Although I'm not sure I'd be up for a mother-comes-too package.

'Think about it, Poppy.' Jess is still talking under her breath. 'He doesn't do that many weddings, he's pretty much always either here or traipsing after you, up at the farm.'

As the door pings open, I flash Jess a look, warning her to

back off, and fast. She's a great source of information, but sometimes it's too much.

'Afternoon, Jules.' I hope the smile I send him is sincere enough to make up for Jess just blowing his credibility out of the water.

Jess is doing the big smile thing too, in fact she's looking so guilty, I'm half expecting her to offer him prosecco.

'We were hoping you'd brought us something for the walls?' As she sidles up to him, and slips her hand on his shoulder, I'm getting an unwelcome insider-view of the male-persuasion tactics she boasts about.

'Sorry to disappoint you, Jess.' As he takes her hand in his, and gives it a squeeze, something tells me she's met her match, and not in the dating way. 'Today I'm trading ideas.' He gives her the full benefit of the smile that shows all his teeth.

Trading ideas? The phrase is a teensy bit cringey. As for whether Jules is brilliant, or a total fake, I reckon I'm still on the fence about that one.

'Although my first suggestion is more for Poppy than for you.' There he goes, with all the teeth again. He's completely disarming simply because he's so direct.

'Lucky Poppy,' Jess says, but she's saying it totally without rancour, and what's more she's simpering, so I'm guessing she's still putty in Jules' hands.

'And?' I cock an expectant eyebrow at Jules. Not that I'm pushy myself, but some of his directness is definitely rubbing off on me.

As he turns his full attention my way again, I falter in the face of those startling blue eyes. 'Now you've got the first Daisy Hill wedding under your belt, I think the next important step is to have a photo shoot, up at the farm.'

'Okay.' This far I'm following.

'I'd like to set up a fake wedding shoot. We choose a perfect day, we provide everything, and we get the run of the venue, without the inconvenience of a wedding to get in the way.'

It sounds intriguing. 'Go on,' I say.

'If we get wonderful shots of all the picturesque places around the farm, it will not only showcase the venue on the website, but it will also inspire brides to book, because they'll know they can have those same gorgeous locations in their very own wedding albums.'

'Fabulous ideas, and so very, very bankable.' Jess chimes in, more involved in the conversation than I'd expected. 'I'm impressed.'

Bankable, whatever it means, being the highest praise Jess gives. Preceded by two 'very's, it's off the scale.

'But why would you do this for Rafe?' He's hardly been sucking up to Jules. Quite the reverse in fact.

'You did such a great job with Lara and Ben's day,' he says.

'I'm not sure guests with mud all over their tuxes and Phase Eight dresses counts as great,' I squirm. 'And what about the rabbits having nervous breakdowns?'

'Stop putting yourself down,' he says sharply, then directs one of his soft winks he does, straight at Jess. 'Jess and I both know a great formula when we see one, don't we love? Put it this way – we're backing a winner here, and this way we get a piece of the action.'

When the hell did these two get so pally? Although I'm not sure how Jess will react to being called 'love'.

Jules turns back to me. 'You'll be our bride, Poppy.' He hesitates for effect, then adds, in a tremulously deep tone, 'Obviously.'

Crap, crap, crap. 'Obviously' my butt. I can't pretend to be a fucking bride. Not a fake one.

'Absolutely out of the question.' Jess has swooped in from nowhere, uninvited, to save the day again, bless her interfering ass. 'Categorical "no" to that. Sorry, you'll have to choose someone else, Jules.'

Firm and direct – that same winning combination. I'm definitely watching and learning here.

Jules opens and closes his mouth. 'Okay,' he drawls, scrunching up his face.

Thinking on his feet here, he's suddenly changed from a gorgeous Spaniel puppy into an ugly French Bulldog. Good for us ordinary mortals to know there are times when even he's not a hundred percent stunning.

'Your friend Cate's gorgeous, and very photogenic.' Jess is straight on the case. 'Cate can do it. She damn well owes you, this is all because of her anyway.'

This makes me smile. There's definitely some divine justice in Cate being our fake bride. She'll love the practice anyway.

'And then you and Immie can be our bridesmaids.' Jess is beaming at me.

I hesitate. 'I don't know about Immie.'

'What she lacks in height she makes up for with bone struc-ture,' Jess says, 'and it's definitely good to have bridesmaids that look real, rather than everyone looking like models.'

As for doubts about Immie, I was thinking temperament not bones, but whatever. But there again, a dry run might soften her up for the real wedding.

'Excellent, that's all settled then.' Jules is flying. 'And I'll provide the groom.'

He said that so enthusiastically, I wonder, not for the first time, if, despite the time and attention he's lavishing on me, he's actually gay. But aside from these bi-curious musings, I can't believe these two have missed out the most crucial item. 'All brilliant, but what on earth are we going to wear?'

'I'm coming to that,' Jules turns his blue gaze straight onto Jess. If he was asking her to walk into the ocean fully clothed, I think she'd be about to follow him.

Then she lets out the biggest purr I've yet heard. 'I can't believe you're asking that, Poppy.' She's practically squealing with excite-ment. In the walking into the sea scenario, she's kicked off her loafers, and she's happily diving into the waves. 'Brides by the

131

Sea will provide the outfits, of course we will, it's a no brainer Jules.' Her beam stretches from one crystal drop earring to the other.

'Fabulous, fantastic, amazing, totally awesome.' Jules grins at Jess as the superlatives gush out of him. 'I just knew you wouldn't be able to resist.'

Jess's cheeks might be pink, but her voice is back to normal. 'Great,' she says, as she brings him nicely back to heel. 'We'll need to be credited, of course.'

25

In Rafe's kitchen at Daisy Hill Farm:
Fuchsia lips and a bit of a problem

'I can't believe we've had to wait until the end of April for a warm sunny day for the photo shoot. And it's so good of Jules to agree to do it, even though it's his birthday.' Yes, it's me, showing Jess into Rafe's kitchen the morning of the shoot. 'We're almost ready to put on the dresses.' I tell her.

'A great omen that everyone could drop everything and come at a moment's notice,' Jess says, as she picks her way through the mayhem. She lowers her voice to a whisper. 'Did you manage to sort out a cake? It's lucky Jules mentioned needing to finish in time for the birthday dinner with his mum, or we wouldn't have known.'

I nod. 'It's not my best.' Thrown together late last night, and just my luck for my industrial size stocks of cocoa to run out. 'I went for a plain sponge with piped chocolate buttercream sides and filling, with caramelised sugar toffee on top.' An old favourite of my mum's. The toffee is sometimes hard to cut, but the mix of soft sponge and chocolate and crackling toffee is delectable.

'And I improvised for the decorations.' At least Jules' early dinner date with his mum means there's no time for birthday drinks. Perfect for an anti-social person like me, although I feel mean thinking it.

'Good girl.' Jess pats my shoulder. 'Let's have the cake now, while everyone's here. Give me the nod as soon as he comes back in.' With a groan Jess throws first her giant bag, then herself onto Rafe's kitchen sofa, and settles down to watch the preparations.

It seems so long ago since I woke up on that same sofa. Looking back, breakfast on a tray that day was the high point in my working relationship with Rafe. Despite us battering our way into his kitchen today, he's still less than helpful about anything to do with weddings, and totally black about life in general. But given the shoot is indirectly for his benefit, he could hardly refuse today could he?

'Brilliant that you could get us a whole beauty team too, Jess. Prosecco?' I beam, as I whoosh across the room the width of a dance-floor to hand Jess a glass of fizz. 'We decided wine would help get us in the mood, and the cake will soak it up once Jules comes back.' Fingers crossed Jess will decide it's way too early for the Hendricks I know she'll have in that cavernous bag of hers.

How the hell Jess blagged four hair and make-up artists at twelve hours' notice is anyone's guess. But they arrived on the dot of seven, and they've been hard at work ever since, their fold out boxes and stand up mirrors spread along the length of Rafe's chunky kitchen table. Cate and Immie and two other friends of Jess's, who have come along to fill out the bridesmaid party, are lined up on chairs.

'Gorgeous hair.' I catch Cate's eye, as the make-up lady moves in to spray on her foundation.

Cate runs her hand over the braids and curls entwined on back of her head. 'It's lovely to have a dummy run. I'm definitely booking this team for mine.' She does a sitting down dance in time to The Supremes singing *Baby Love*.

I'll give you one guess whose iPod we're listening to. Locating Rafe's iPod dock was the first thing Jules did when he arrived, straight after kissing everyone on both cheeks. In case you're wondering, this is his *Up-Tempo Romantic* list.

In the next seat along, Immie's frown deepens as her make-up lady moves in with the lip brush. 'Give me pink fucking lips, and I won't be responsible for my actions,' she hisses through gritted teeth.

Cate and I exchange glances. Swooping in with more sugar is the only way to diffuse the situation. 'Don't worry Immie, it looks pink, but it comes out paler,' I promise. I'm completely bluffing here. Hopefully Jules will appear soon so I can sweeten her up with a huge piece of birthday cake, because in less than five minutes from now somehow we have to persuade her to put on a floral bridesmaid's dress.

And right on cue Jules appears, camera in hand.

'Okay, hold it there, I'll just get a few "getting ready" shots.' Somewhere along the line, Jules seems to have entirely forgotten that this isn't for real.

Talking of cues, I take this as mine. Skipping across to where I've left the birthday cake on the side by the Aga, I catch Jess's eye.

'No, actually Jules, *you* hold it there.' I'm using my most commanding voice, and catch the astonishment on his face as I clap my hands.

Jess gets to her feet, and as someone turns down the volume on the music the room goes quiet. She gives a husky cough then she turns to the room. 'Okay everybody. Jules is the brains behind this fabulous – we hope – wedding shoot.' She pauses for the ripple of laughter. 'And he is extra fabulous, because he's come to do it on his birthday. So before we start, we'd like to sing Happy Birthday and give him his cake…'

Taking this as my second cue, I whip the cake out of its box. 'Jules, this is for you.' There's a gasp around the room, then a round of applause, which is a lot more than I deserve given how fast I threw it together. Happily everyone overlooks the less than perfect piping, and is wowed by the toffee and the decorations – a stripy icing scarf knotted on the top, and an icing camera on a tripod made from barbecue sticks.

I put the cake down, then reach over to Jules. His usual stunning smile has stretched to a dazed, yet delighted, grin. There's something else different about him today, but in the excitement I can't put my finger on what it is.

'Happy birthday, Jules.' After a quick hug and a peck I dip away. As I light the candles on the cake, the queue for birthday kisses with Jules is already long.

Somehow Jess has crossed from the sofa to the front of the line. No surprise there then. As soon as she's had her hug – which between us went on for way longer than necessary – she moves on to lead the singing. Once the Happy Birthday chorus is done, Jules manages to break off from hugs for long enough to blow out the candles, and pose for a picture. Then I chop up the cake and send it round the room in serviettes. Maybe lashings of soft chocolate icing wasn't the best idea, given that everyone ends up with it smeared across their cheeks. Even though I say it myself, that cake is so delicious it's worth every calorie. Eventually someone turns the music back on again, and Jules dusts the crumbs off his lips and picks up his camera.

'Thanks Poppy, for a wonderful cake, and thanks everyone for the birthday wishes.' He's back to his picture perfect grin, and all eyes are on him. 'We need to get back to work now. So I know you're still in your dressing gowns ladies, but big smiles all round please.' He swoops in and begins to snap. I'm just hoping he doesn't insist on bridesmaids in lingerie shots, or he might catch a right hook from Immie.

'And now we need a smile from Poppy too.' Jules spins his lens towards me. Note the way he's telling, not asking. 'You are already looking amazing, sweetie.'

Sweetie? When did he start calling me that? I wrinkle my nose into a grin, because he might just be right about me looking great. I was beautified first, probably because my no-hope hair was so quick to do, but the make-up they're using is translucent, yet luminous. People talk about make-over transformations, but I've never felt more fabulous.

'Sweetie, can I have a word?' Jules is artfully steering me into a corner. 'Outside,' he murmurs pointedly, and the next minute he shoulders me through the door into the hallway.

'Is something the matter?' And then it hits me. It's the first time I've seen Jules without his scarf. That's why he looks different. My eyes lock onto the downy chestnut hairs poking up at the open neck of his dusky blue Ralph Lauren polo shirt. For a fleeting moment I'm worried that he's about to come in for a full blown birthday snog.

But his hands are rammed into the pockets of his safari jacket, and his voice is urgent. 'We're a man down, Poppy.'

'Man what?' I'm not sure I get what he means. At least I've escaped the snog.

'The damned groom's let me down. I thought he was running late, but he's just sent a text to say he's not coming at all.'

'Oh, bugger.' Nightmare scenario. Grooms who don't turn up are bad news all round, although I'm secretly thanking my lucky stars this isn't a real wedding. At least today we can replace him. 'That's a bummer, especially given we're almost good to go in the kitchen. What are you going to do?'

Jules ruffles his fingers through his hair, and his waves fall back into perfect place. 'You're going to have to find someone else.'

'Me?' I look at him, open mouthed. Fleetingly I wonder if my hair would fall perfectly if I raked my fingers through it and left it to flop, but I decide his haircut probably cost an arm and a leg more than mine. 'Why me?'

'Basically, because you're the problem solver round here.' His

137

flash of the full tooth smile, fades as fast as it appeared. 'Actually I've racked my brains to think of a stand-in and come up with diddly squat.' He's looking suitably shamefaced as he squeezes out the last word. 'Sorry.'

Looks like it's over to me then, dammit. My mind races. First things first. 'What size was the groom anyway?'

Jules purses his lips. 'Probably about Rafe's size.' He says sheepishly.

Something tells me he had Rafe in mind all along. 'You have to be joking, we can't use him.' These two have the worst relationship of any two men I know, though I still haven't worked out why. 'But the other guys who work on the farm are all stockier, so they won't do either.' I'm thinking aloud. Talk about grab a husband.

'It can't be just anyone, we need looks too,' Jules reminds me. 'Which is another reason why Rafe would work.' He definitely has thought this through. 'Much as I hate to hand out compliments, he's got a great jaw, and cheekbones to die for. He'll have to step in.'

I can't say I've noticed those details myself. But maybe Jules is desperate to get this show on the road.

Jules claps his hands. 'Great, that's settled then. If Rafe stops scowling long enough to put on a suit, I reckon he'll be dreamboat material.' He's back to the many-toothed smile. 'Be a good girl, go and ask him.'

I'm wincing at how patronising Jules sounds, but at the same time not wanting to let everyone else down. 'I would, but I have absolutely no idea where he is.' That's the whole truth, and the perfect excuse. Lately Rafe's taken to disappearing for hours at a time. We'll have to find someone else.

'It must be our lucky day. Talk of the devil,' Jules says, peering out of the window. 'Guess who's crossing the yard now? '

'Great,' I say, really not meaning it. Immie and Rafe? I doubt there could be two less cooperative models in the entire world. Jules has no idea what he'd be letting himself in for.

'So, what are you waiting for?' Jules is steering me again, this time towards the door to the yard. 'Off you go! Grab us a groom!'

26

In the feed store at Daisy Hill Farm: Grabbing a groom

'Rafe?' By the time I catch up with him, he's already in the feed store, and I'm flailing to find the right words. How the hell do you ask a guy to be a groom for a day? It's embarrassingly close to proposing.

As Rafe walks into a beam of light that's slicing across the gloom, for the first time I get the full benefit of his sculpted cheekbones. My stomach clenches, but it's probably just nerves for what I'm about to ask. Who'd have thought I could have missed those all this time? And luckily for us, he's still clean. He could put the groom's suit straight on.

'You looking for me?' He hoists a sack up onto his shoulder, and the muscles of his back ripple through his ragged T-shirt. As he turns, his mouth stretches into an unfamiliar grin. 'Bit late for pyjamas isn't it?' he laughs. 'What's with the pink horses, I thought you didn't like animals?'

Sniggering at my *My Little Pony* dressing gown is low. I decide not to retaliate about the slogan on his T-shirt, telling me that

Farmers Do It In Wellies, because I need to concentrate on the job I'm here for.

'Yes, I am looking for you.' The breath I drag in goes on forever. I grit my teeth, try to ignore that I'm standing here in my slippers with him towering over me, and brace myself. 'You're needed in the kitchen. Like, right now.'

He narrows his eyes. 'I'm just feeding the chickens…' He's going to need a much better excuse than that to wriggle out of this one.

Despite feeling like I'm jumping off a cliff, I launch in. 'We're short of a guy in a suit for the shoot. No arguments, you have to step in…step up…whatever…' To show him I mean business I put my hands on my hips. Big mistake, as my dressing gown gapes, exposing most of my strapless bra, plus a fair amount of the cake I was eating earlier. The plus side is, the view leaves Rafe speechless, so at least he can't protest.

Brushing the crumbs off my boobs as best I can whilst being gawped at by a burly farmer, I take a moment to adjust my belt, then carry on. 'Obviously you'll need to get someone to cover for you out here.' If I've learned one thing about farming, it's that animals, like men, need their meals regularly. My attempt at one of Jules wide smiles ends up as a grimace, but I carry on regardless. 'This is going to take all day. Make your way to the kitchen, I'll follow you.'

27

Out and about at Daisy Hill Farm: Going downhill fast

'Bloody hell, I wish your mother was here to witness this Rafe.'
Immie's shaking her head, and laughing as Cate and Rafe run
hand in hand down the hill, in what Jules calls a 'background
horizon' shot.

'Okay, got that,' Jules shouts, as he scrambles up from his
prone position. Some shots can only be accessed while lying down
apparently.

'It's a shame the grass isn't longer,' Jules says. 'I'm not really
getting the deep-meadow effect I was after.'

'If he wanted long grass, he should have come in June.' Rafe
snorts, as he comes to a breathless standstill next to us bridesmaids, and lets go of Cate's fingers. 'Don't get any ideas, this is
a one off, I'm definitely not doing this again.'

Cate laughs. 'I just hope the sky is this blue when I'm marrying
Liam. If he scrubs up half as well as my groom today, I'll be
happy.'

Cate's got a point. You know how sometimes a suit transforms
a guy? When Rafe stomped through the kitchen wearing his jeans

and a scowl, people barely noticed him. Three minutes later, when he came back in a snowy white shirt and sharp navy suit, rubbing that stubble of his, and fiddling with his belt, the girls' jaws dropped. I'm not exaggerating, the oestrogen surge in that kitchen was like a bloody tidal wave. When Jess suggested he needed help straightening his tie, there was practically a stampede. And let's face it, if she hadn't been holding five bouquets and the props box at the time, she'd have definitely been over there, doing it herself.

Rafe gives Cate a nudge. 'Make sure you get your first choice of groom, not a stand-in like today.'

That's another thing. Sure, we had to jolly Rafe along at first. If it hadn't been for Immie joking around in the first hour, I'm sure we'd have lost him. But once he stopped taking himself so seriously and began to relax he's been much less of a pain in the bum. At times he's even been funny, and he's been constantly considerate to Cate. A couple of times back there, when Jules was going for blurry togetherness shots, a teensy bit of me wished I'd gone with what Jules suggested, and been the bride myself. I mean, who wouldn't want to see how it felt to have strong hands like those on their shoulders? Especially when it's all fake anyway.

Jess's dulcet tones crash through my day dream. 'Okay, time for a wine break.' She's thrown rugs down on the grass, and now she's diving into her hamper for fizz and plastic champagne flutes. 'There's pasties and strawberries too.'

Being good bridesmaids, Immie and I help Cate down onto her own rug, shroud her in serviettes, then deliver her refreshments on a tray, at a safe distance. As we go off to the other rugs, she takes a bite of pasty, and settles back in the sun.

'This is such a gorgeous dress,' she sighs, as she runs her hands from her tiny nipped in waist and down over the gathers of her full skirt. 'I didn't know tulle could be this soft.'

Jess and I both know it's one of Sera's designs, which Jess brought not only because the size was right, but because it photographs so well. We also know Cate is set on buying from a much bigger name for herself, so we are keeping quiet here.

Cate examines the delicate lace edging on her wrist. 'I'd never have thought of anything long sleeved either, but this lace is so light it's barely there.'

'It's a good choice for a spring wedding,' Jess says casually, as she passes out the wine, 'or a September one come to that.' The woman is such a pro.

'So do you have many more shots in mind?' Cate stops Jules on his way past her rug.

Given she's been photographed on top of practically every wall and every gate on the farm, with every kind of animal, run either up or down every field and hollow, frolicked by the stream, and climbed on the trees, and been snapped doing all that from every possible angle imaginable to man, with and without bridesmaids, I can't see how there's much left to do.

'I'd like to go back to the farm again,' Jules answers, whisking his wine out of Jess's hand. 'Just to capture the textures of the buildings around the courtyard, now the sun's changed position.'

Jules is such a perfectionist. Not only that, but he's also making a bee line for our rug. But a second before he gets here there's a thud on the ground behind me. Next thing I know, Rafe's delicious aftershave drifts past my nose, and Jules is glowering down at Rafe who is apparently sitting right beside me. If he didn't have his hand full of pasty, Rafe's black expression suggests he'd leap up and run Jules off the farm.

Jess is straight on top of the situation. 'No fighting over seats, boys. Come over here Jules, there's plenty of room for the birthday boy to snuggle next to me.'

Rafe cuts in. 'Jules taking every excuse to hang around for longer, how does that sound familiar?' He gives a sniff, then goes on jubilantly. 'Can't leave his scarf today though, because he's not wearing it.'

I could say, 'Rafe taking every opportunity to snipe about

Jules, how is that familiar?' but I don't. Instead, in an effort to ignore that Rafe's blue suited legs are appearing on the left of mine, I begin to examine my dress. 'This flowery bridesmaid dress print works so well in grey and white and lemon doesn't it? It's kind of vintage country, yet sophisticated isn't it? And a long dress lets you wear wellies underneath if you need to. It goes so well…'

A sharp dig in my right ribs stops me in mid flow. Thank you, Immie.

'Shut up, you're babbling,' she hisses. 'Embarrassing yourself in front of both your bo…'

Holy crap. I say anything to cut Immie off, because I'm certain the next word she's about to say is 'boyfriends'.

'Don't the dresses look lovely with the white daisies in the posies?' I grin round at everyone like a crazy lady, and pray for someone to pick up the conversation and say something sensible.

The delicious smell of Rafe is suddenly much closer, and the next moment his blue suited sleeve is clamped up against the bare flesh of my arm.

'The dress is definitely a big improvement on your horsey dressing gown.' Rafe gives a low laugh. 'Although what do I know?'

As the pressure on my arm eases, and he moves away, I gasp. Shit. That was just a nudge then. A nudge and a stupid fucking joke, about my *My Little Pony* dressing gown. It wasn't even funny. Why the hell am I all dizzy because of a nudge? Talk about oestrogen rushes, and the power of a suit.

I'm just getting my breath back, when the scent is back, but this time it's his temple that's tilting against mine. 'Cut all the jokes about scrubbing up, truly, you do look lovely, Poppy.' He stays there for long enough to make my heart bang like a hammer drill, and my cheeks to go puce, dammit, and then he pulls away. Next thing you know, he's smiling at the girls on the next rug, and lifting his glass. 'A toast to all the bridesmaids, really, you *all* look fabulous today.'

Talk about a smooth operator. Whatever happened to bad mood bear Rafe? Where did he go?

Never one to be missed out, Immie is reaching across me. 'Nice one, Rafie,' she says, patting him firmly on the knee. 'You can tell me I look fabulous whenever you like.'

When the hell did Immie start calling him Rafie? Rafie's almost as bad as Ben calling Lara Panda.

Jules is on his feet again, glowering in front of us, waving his wine glass around. Whoever thought wine would be a good idea needs to think again.

'A toast to the bridesmaids.' As he wafts his glass in an expansive arc a shower of wine drops shine like diamonds as the sun catches them. He goes on. 'And to today's lovely, and most obliging and beautiful bride Cate.' His glass goes in another arc, and a second slurp of prosecco splashes across the grass.

If he carries on like this he'll have spilled most of his fizz. As for Jess's motto, 'fizz makes happy brides'. From the sneer on Jules face, it seems to have made this photographer pretty unhappy.

He lifts his glass again. 'As for the groom, it looks like this one's hell bent on acting like a proverbial best man, and getting off with the head bridesmaid.'

If Brett had made a remark like that, I'd have ignored it. If someone else had made a remark like that when I was with Brett, I wouldn't have liked it, but I'd probably have let it go too. But for some reason, the Poppy that comes to Daisy Hill Farm doesn't let things go. And I'm not happy to sit here, and stay silent. Jules is way out of line here, and even if it is his birthday, I've got to tell him. Jess is standing up and coming over, but I've already sprung to my feet.

'Jules, you've done amazing work all day, for which we're very grateful,' I'm sending him one of his own big smiles, but I'm growling with anger at the same time. 'But you are way out of line here.'

I turn to Rafe. 'Thank you for stepping in Rafe. We are all very grateful to you.' I raise my head to everyone. 'Thank you to everyone, for fabulous work, and a fabulous day. We'll call that a wrap. Now let's all go back to the farm, it's time to go home.'

MAY

28

At Brides by the Sea: Bumpy roads and amnesia

'So, that's my moving boxes finally sorted. I just dropped the last load off at the charity shop.' I give a silent cheer as I hurry into the shop, and find Jess, flicking through the appointments book, waiting for her next bride.

'You've been keeping the Cat Rescue shop going single-handedly. How many bags did you take them in the end?' Jess asks. She always likes to quantify everything.

'Probably about a hundred,' I laugh. It's an exaggeration, but I can't help grinning. The sun's out, I've got that light, walking-on-air feeling, that you can only get after a good de-clutter. Especially one that somehow symbolises throwing away my old life, which also implies I'm ready for a fresh start. Better still, after two months of climbing over mountains of stuff every time I wanted to sit on the sofa, I can see my living room floor again.

Jess walks across to the window, and glances out at the street. 'No sign of my eleven o'clock, but Ella, from your next wedding, is here for you.' Absently, she tweaks the satin bow on the back of the display dress. 'She had her first fitting for her Madelaine yesterday.'

Madelaine's a gorgeous empire line dress, with cascades of soft lace, perfect for pregnant brides. 'How's Ella's bump?' I ask.

'Neat, but growing. I'm pleased we ordered the fourteen not the twelve.' Jess says. 'Is the dark good-looking one her fiancé?'

I have to smile at Jess's man antennae. 'Ella's brought Jack to show him the final cake designs,' I explain, as I open the door, welcoming them in, and lead them through to my cake display table. 'And I'm guessing any groom who comes to talk cakes will be interested in a taste?'

'Got it in one,' laughs Ella, as I cut them two generous slices of a small icing sugar covered sponge I baked this morning.

'The real one will be much bigger and taller of course, more like the picture here.' As Ella and Jack bite into their sponge, I point to a mouthwatering photo of a towering four tier cake. 'One I made earlier,' I smile.

'Wow, and wow.' Jack mumbles, nodding first at the picture and then at the cake in his hand, his voice thick with raspberry jam and vanilla butter cream filling.

'And for the decoration around each tier, Ella decided on a mix of real pink roses, and strawberries.' I point to a water-colour sketch I've done of the finished design. 'And it'll be presented on a platter which is basically a slice of tree trunk.'

'A tree trunk? That's cool.' Jack licks his fingers.

'It goes so well with the Daisy Hill venue.'

Ella and Jack are my second wedding couple at the farm. But for me their wedding is worse than the last one, because they're having the ceremony there as well as the reception, and have booked out the cottages too.

Ella turns to Jack. 'Is that all okay for you?'

'Perfect.' He grins, then hesitates. 'Except…'

'Yes?' I say, aware of Ella rolling her eyes behind him.

Jack gives a guilty shrug. 'I love raspberries. Could we possibly have some raspberries on there too?'

I look to Ella for confirmation. It took her weeks to decide on strawberries and roses.

She smooths the crumbs off her bump, and gives a reluctant sigh. 'Okay then, let's have raspberries too.'

'Not long now,' I smile, trying to crush the fear that's making my stomach clench.

'No,' Jack gives a huge sigh, and pats Ella's tummy. 'Six weeks from now I'll be a dad.'

Ella laughs, and shakes her head. 'Poppy doesn't mean the baby, Jack, she's talking about the tiny thing that's happening first…your wedding.'

Oh my. I'm guessing for a guy it's maybe natural that becoming a parent is such a huge and terrifying life event, that it could easily make you forget your own wedding.

'So two weeks today,' I say, beaming at Ella to hide that my heart is already hammering. This must be the human flight response Immie goes on about. My subconscious brain thinks I should be running away as fast as I can, and I'm pretty much in agreement.

'It sounds really close.' Ella hugs herself, brushes her blond bob out of her eyes, and gives a shiver that I hope is excitement. 'So long as Jack remembers to turn up, that is.' She gives a nervous giggle.

'I might just.' He gives Ella a playful nudge. 'I'd never forget something this huge, it's going be mega.'

'A whole tipi village clustered around a mother tent, and the oldies in the cottages, it should work well.' Ella counts them off on her fingers. She's remarkably calm, considering. 'And then there's all the camper vans and extra tents too.'

Shit. I keep my smile in place. I knew this was a humdinger of a wedding, but this is the first I've heard of camper vans. I'll have to check we have a space for them later.

'And, of course, the biggest cake in the universe.' Jack gives me a nod.

'With raspberries, and strawberries.' I say, 'but definitely no blueberries?'

'No!' They shout. 'We both hate blueberries.' Despite Jack accidentally overlooking the small matter of their wedding, these two are heart-warmingly together.

'So that's it, unless…' I see Jack eying the cake longingly. 'Anyone for another slice?'

29

In the fields at Daisy Hill Farm: One sceptical eyebrow

A week later, I'm in my shorts and my festival wellies, running up hill, panting hard enough for my lungs to burst. Talk about feel the burn, I'm so hot I might just spontaneously combust. Don't worry, I haven't gone on a fitness kick. Jeez, you know I'd never do that. I'm currently on a mission to hunt down Rafe, who's been A.W.O.L. from the office for so long that I can't put this off any more. And thanks to important intelligence about his soft spots, discovered accidentally the day of the photo shoot, I'm armed with a powerful new weapon – a Cornish pasty.

There's a tractor parked at the top of the next field, which is a sure sign that Rafe won't be far away. Squinting into the sun, I scan the field edge, and spot a figure, moving by the wall. He's heaving rocks around, and crap, just my bad luck, he's stripped to the waist. I take a deep breath, scramble over the wall from the lane, and dash towards him.

'Rafe, Rafe…' If I arrive at the speed of light, waving and yelling, I might just be able to pretend I haven't noticed that broad back, gleaming in the sun.

I'm twenty yards away from him when he turns, and his face is like thunder.

'Did you just climb over the wall down there?' he snaps.

I'm getting the feeling this was the worst thing to do. 'Yes,' I shrug, baffled. 'How else was I going to get into the field?' I'm kicking myself for the bad start, because I'm desperate for this to go smoothly.

'You could have come through the gate.' Rafe gives a snort. 'Or was that too obvious?'

'The gate?' I'm open mouthed. 'If you mean the gate that's about a mile along the lane...' I nod my head in the direction of the opening, which is so far away it's practically a spec on the horizon. 'Well that's fine for people like you who travel everywhere by tractor, but not so fine for people like me who are on foot.'

'Thoughtless, ignorant people like you climb walls and knock them down,' he scowls, 'then I have to slog my guts out re-building them.'

I reel at suddenly being branded as thoughtless and ignorant, when the worst I've been up to today is an annoying pain in the butt. 'I'm sorry, I didn't know.'

'And why should you, you're just a townie.'

He says it in a disparaging way, which is funny, because I'm damned proud to be a townie. That would go well on one of those crappy slogan T-shirts he's so fond of wearing. To be honest I'd hate to be anything else.

'Great that you've got the time to waft around and enjoy a country walk,' he says, with a sarcastic sneer, 'but some of us have to work.'

Excuse me? 'Enjoy and country aren't words I'd ever put in the same sentence.' There's no point hiding how much I hate it here. As for me stopping to rub the cows' heads as they looked over the fence on the way up here, that was a definite one off. 'In any case, this is a professional visit.'

Rafe lifts one sceptical eyebrow. As he rubs his hand along a tanned bicep, I battle to keep my eyes on his face. Those abs of his are disgustingly well honed, and a glimpse of his battered jeans sliding low on his hips fills my tummy with a sudden storm of butterflies. I lock my eyes on a dandelion, and drive my brain elsewhere. In fact, since I've been sorting out weddings as well as my cakes, I've been working long hours. But let's face it, Rafe might only be driving round his acres on a tractor, or talking to cows, or complaining about the cost of feed, but he never switches off. Maybe that's why he's so grumpy.

'You might sound less bitter if you got out more,' I say, because, frankly, someone needs to tell him.

The way he narrows his eyes, maybe I should have kept my mouth shut.

He picks up a rock from the pile on the grass, and heaves it onto the half-built wall. 'If you're asking me…'

I jump in to make myself clear. 'No I'm damn well not.'

Rubbing his thumb across his jaw, he turns. 'Good, because I was about to say I'm really not up for any more fall-over Fridays.'

Bringing that up is low, *and* he's wrong. 'Actually, it was a Thursday.' I stick out my chin, happy for a small victory.

'Whatever.' As he sneers, and jams another rock into place I close my eyes to shut out his rippling back.

Ridiculous of me to think a savoury snack could make anything better here, but I pull it out anyway. 'I brought you a pasty.' I pass him the paper bag. 'There's a can of ginger beer too.'

'Okay, thanks,' he says slowly. The corners of his lips twitch as he pulls the pasty out of the bag. 'Is there a catch?' Those dark brown eyes bore into me.

I may as well come clean. 'There's no such thing as a free lunch,' I laugh. I cram a piece of my own pasty into my mouth, because I'm ravenous after the walk. 'There are things you need to know,' I mumble, brushing the crumbs off my T-shirt as I chew. On balance I decide to miss out the word 'important'.

There's no point scaring him off when I'm this close. I've been chasing him round for weeks, and tried everything, but this one won't go away.

'You've got five minutes.' He says, glancing at his phone. 'Go on.'

It's always best to get the worst over first. 'Some more paperwork came to light,' I begin tentatively. There's no need to admit it was found by the rabbit the night of the wedding, or that I've been trying to sort the problem ever since. 'The good news is, it means more bookings, but unfortunately two weddings have been scheduled for the same day.' I'm skimming over the details here, talking fast so I can hold his attention. Pulling out the calendar, I point to the dreaded day in August. In the wedding business, a double booking is the worst crime there is. With the paperwork in the state it was in, we're lucky there aren't more. 'I've checked, and neither couple is willing to change their date.' Not surprising, really.

Rafe swallows, and pops open his can. 'It's not a problem,' he says, then he takes a swig. 'The guests can all park in the middle field, and we'll have a wedding either side.'

Proving again that he really has no idea. 'It's not some rock festival,' I almost shout. If I'm shrieking, it's because I'm so appalled. 'These couples have chosen an exclusive-use venue for the most important day of their lives. They don't want to get married in a row of marquees, to the sound of next door's disco.'

He takes another swig of drink as he takes in that thought. 'So, what's the alternative?'

I take a deep breath, knowing he's going to hate what I'm about to say. 'One of the parties is fairly small. We could keep everything separate if we let them use the garden behind the house.' It's the only solution, but it could save the day for everyone, us included.

'Absolutely not.' He's straight back at me faster than I expect. 'It's bad enough having drunken revellers down in the field. I refuse to have them crawling around the house too.'

He's entitled to his opinion, but somewhere down the line he's got to take responsibility. There's no alternative. This is a total mess, but it exists, and it has to be sorted out.

'Take some time to think it over,' I say. It's hard to sound reasonable when I'd like to wring his neck. It's not as if he ever uses his garden anyway.

'You'll have to come up with something better than that.' He snorts. 'Is that it?'

If he's hoping I'm finished, he's going to be disappointed. I've barely started. At least he's provided me with an opening. I brace myself, and pull another piece of paper out of my rucksack. 'In the light of the new bookings, I've pulled a few figures together.' I flourish the paper under his nose. 'The income from weddings is good, but when you add in the extra holiday cottage rentals, it's too spectacular to ignore.'

With a reluctant sigh, he takes the paper. 'And your point is?'

My point is, why the hell won't he take his stubborn head out of the sand, make the most of a damned good source of income, and stop fighting the weddings? Everyone knows farmers are having a hard time.

I carry on. 'We're having loads of hits on the website, since we put up the new pictures.' I can only tell him, I can't force him. 'With a little extra push, we could really make the wedding side fly.'

'Much as I appreciate the picnic, you can't just come up here, whipping props out of your bag like a magician, expecting me to change into someone I'm not.' He pushes the last piece of pasty into his mouth. 'Read my T-shirt, I'm a farmer, not an event promoter. I deal with animals and crops, not frivolity and party goers.'

That would be the T-shirt that's crumpled on the ground then. If you ask me, a T-shirt saying 'awkward sod' would suit him a whole lot better. I decide to try a different approach.

'Take that view…' I wave my hand towards a group of buildings nestling into the next hill. That's one of the pictures that looks amazing on the website. 'Weddings simply let you make the most of what's here.'

Rafe's jaw tenses and he lets out a bitter laugh. 'Great choice. Do you know that's the farm where my ex lives?' His tone is bleak.

Shit. 'I'm sorry, I didn't know, I didn't mean to upset you…' Damn for jumping in with both feet.

'It's fine,' he says, less bitterly. 'It was a long time ago. Local rumour might say differently, but I wish Helen well.'

It spills out before I can stop it. 'I'm a long way from thinking happy thoughts about Brett.'

Rafe's voice is quietly reassuring. 'You will do, one day.'

'When someone you're close to lets you down that badly, it's hard to imagine letting anyone in again.' I sigh, and bite my lip.

He narrows his eyes. 'That photographer's certainly doing his damnedest to help you move on.'

'Jules?' It's more of a confirmation that a question. Not surprisingly, Rafe hasn't bothered to name him. I sigh. Jules couldn't be more helpful or attentive, and Immie and Jess swoon over him, but his sexy side passes me by completely. It has to be because I'm not up for another relationship. 'Being on my own is teaching me to rely on myself,' I try to explain. It's true, I'm changing every day. 'But even when I'm strong, I can't see myself trusting anyone again. Moving on for me won't mean another relationship.'

'Thanks for lunch, anyway.' As Rafe crumples the empty bag into his back pocket, his mouth stretches into a grin. 'It's good to get the facts straight.'

My point exactly, and having traipsed two miles uphill, I'm reluctant to leave things hanging. 'So you'll think about the suggestions then?'

But he's already turning back to the wall. 'You've obviously forgotten how I feel about weddings.' he says. His mouth has already returned to a grim line, as he slams another stone into position. 'Two words to remind you: Not interested.'

30

In the tipi at Daisy Hill Farm: Orange glows and rounders bats

'That cake is truly awesome.' Immie's licking her lips as she gazes. 'It's such a perfect combination of delicious and pretty, I'm actually drooling.'

Ella and Jack have had their cake cutting moment captured by Jules, and now Immie's come down to help me slice up the cake whilst the guests are outside, enjoying the sunset.

'It's been great.' I admit, as I pass Immie a clean apron, and tie up my own. 'I've been so busy making the cake, in the end I barely had time to worry about the wedding.'

'Which has all gone without a hitch, thanks to your careful planning,' Immie sends me a wink. 'Just as I predicted it would.'

'They couldn't have had a sunnier day,' I muse.

'I told you I'd order one of those too.' Immie laughs.

'They're here until tomorrow lunchtime, so there's still plenty of time for things to go wrong.'

'The hardest part's over,' Immie says. 'Once it's dark, the whole place will look magical, with the orange glow from the tents and the strings of lights.'

Beyond the poles on the open side of the tipi, a huddle of children are making daisy chains. Further away, the guests are spread across the field, enjoying an impromptu game of rounders. A roar goes up, as Ella, barefoot and poised, bat in hand, slams the ball into the distance. She hurls the bat to the ground, picks up her skirts and waddles around the bases.

'Amazing.' Immie shakes her head. 'How's she still going?'

There's another roar, and shouts of 'Rounder!' resound across the grass.

I shrug. 'She's determined to dance the night away too.'

'Definitely got her nesting instinct,' Immie says, explaining when I look at her blankly. 'It's this sudden burst of energy you get just before labour. Most women clean the house from top to bottom, but Ella's obviously using hers to party. I wish I'd thought of that when I had Morgan.'

So far, apart from watching One Born Every Minute, the whole baby experience has passed me by, and it's right off my agenda now.

'Talking of kids, Jules got some lovely shots of the little ones with the calves earlier,' Immie goes on. 'Baby animals are yet another selling point for Daisy Hill Farm. He said he'd already uploaded some to the website. He really goes the extra mile for you.'

I undo the wrapping, and lay out a pile of serviettes to go with the cake. 'It's true, Jules has been brilliant with his pictures.' I have to admit, he does seem exceptionally eager to please. 'I don't think he's ever refused to do anything I asked.' If I was looking for reliable, he'd be ticking every box so far.

'And you still won't go on a date with him, poor man.' Immie chides, giving me one of her hard stares. 'But the more you tell him "no", the more he bounces back.'

'I hope people don't think I'm using him.' I don't ask him to do any of the things he does, but he's endlessly enthusiastic, and thoughtful too.

'How long will it be before Prince Jules proves himself worthy of Princess Poppy?' Immie laughs. 'You do know he's staying in the yard in a camper van tonight too, so he can be on hand early for pictures in the morning.' She sends me yet another wink. 'Just saying. In case tonight might be the night.'

'It definitely won't be.' I begin to ease the flowers off the middle ledge of the cake.

Immie snorts. 'Poppy Pickering, sometimes I don't believe you.' She might be talking through gritted teeth, but she still holds out the plate for the rose buds. 'If that man had the hots for me half the way he does for you, I'd have had him against the barn wall months ago.'

I jump as I hear a familiar voice behind me.

'So what kind of a cake do you call this then?'

Rafe's the last person I expected to meet in the wedding tipi.

'Nude, rustic, rose and berry.' I say, as I stoop to pick up the rose I dropped. 'Take your choice.'

'Monumental suits it better.' he says.

'Created by Poppy.' Immie chimes in.

'You actually made it?' Rafe's eyes widen. 'It's practically the size of The Shard.'

Who'd have thought he'd compare it to anything other than a cow? I'm shocked he even knows what The Shard is, seeing as he never goes out of the village, let alone to London. 'All my own work,' I say with a grin, 'although three feet tall is a pretty standard size.' I can't help asking. 'What are you doing here anyway?'

'I was being a good farmer, checking no-one's going to get stuck in the mud, and I came inside when I spotted you. What's your excuse?'

'We're making ourselves useful.' I lift off the top layer of cake and slide it into a box for safe keeping, then ease the cake slice under the next layer, lift it down, and begin to slice it.

Rafe watches me in silence. He has to be the only guy I know who wouldn't clamour for a taste. 'There's one other thing before I go…' His hesitation is ominous. 'There's a camper van parked in the yard. Is it anything to do with you?'

Immie and I exchange frowns over the butter cream and sponge. It's unbelievable, but probably not a coincidence, that Rafe has come all the way down from the farm to complain about Jules' van.

My chest tightens, as my knife flies in and out of the cake, scattering crumbs across the tablecloth. 'The van belongs to wedding staff.' I'm not going to be any more specific than that. I drag in a breath, to help me stay calm in the face of Rafe's extreme pettiness. 'It will be there over night, but you have my assurance it will be moved first thing in the morning. Okay?' Sticking my chin out, I challenge him to disagree.

Rafe sniffs. 'I suppose it'll have to be.'

'Good.' I reach for another large plate, and flash him a bright smile. 'So if that's everything, some of us need to get on.' Hopefully he'll take it as a hint to get the hell out of here before I have to chase him.

As Rafe turns and strides out into the evening sun, Immie hides her laughter in her sleeve.

'What are you two like?' she mutters. 'You're handling him like a pro though.' She narrows her eyes, and sends me one of her more piercing stares. 'It's all about marking territory. You do know, in dog terms, this is Rafe cocking his leg. On you.'

31

In the courtyard at Daisy Hill Farm: Backing off

It's funny how, on a normal night I'm yawning by midnight, but if there's a wedding I'm still running around at three in the morning. While I have to dismiss Immie's dog pee theories, I can see exactly what she means about adrenalin keeping you alert. Tonight, now I've finished every job and every check, it feels like I'm definitely the last person standing. The lights are all out down in the field, the distant cries have faded, and the sky is starting to bleach towards dawn as I tiptoe across the courtyard to the farm office.

As I hold my breath and move past the camper van, a click of a door makes my heart bang, and not in a good way. Next thing I know, Jules' head pops out from behind the stripy curtains.

'Poppy, over here.' His voice is little more than a low murmur.

I pull my cardigan closed as a breath of night air brings my arms out in goosebumps. A faint whiff of whisky wafts on the air as I cross the cobbles.

Jules gives his scalp a vigorous rub, re-tousling his waves as I approach. His irises are strangely flat and muddy in the low glimmer of the courtyard lights. 'Fancy a night cap?' Sure enough, he pulls out a bottle.

Much as I love camper vans, climbing into one with Jules in the middle of the night is definitely making the wrong kind of statement. 'Sorry, I'm driving.' Even as I make the excuse, I know that's why I planned it this way. 'I'm off home now, and I'll be back first thing.'

'You'll need to get up before you go to bed.' He's twinkling at me now, but something isn't working at all.

'What's the matter with your eyes? Has the strain of peering through a view finder for the last eighteen hours taken its toll?' I'm thinking detached retinas here, cataracts, macular degeneration.

'My eyes?' he whispers, wrinkling his nose. 'Sorry, I didn't think you'd notice. I usually wear blue tinted contact lenses, but I've taken them out.'

'Right.' Jeez, so much for Mr Blue Eyes. And how shallow that I can't keep the disappointment out of my voice.

Stepping outside, he puts his mouth close to my hair. 'They're not prescription lenses, they're purely for professional reasons.' From the way he's hissing straight into my ear, it's obviously crucial no-one else finds out. 'If you don't mind, I'd rather you didn't tell anyone.'

There you go.

'Professional how?' I murmur into the half-light, intrigued.

He backs off a little. Even if his eyes aren't real, under the alcohol he still smells expensive. 'They give great results. It's easier to hold people's attention for pictures when your eyes are really blue.' He turns his full face smile onto me, but even in the half-light, minus the startling eyes, it's mainly teeth. 'That's the only reason I wear them.'

That's the only reason my arse. Doubtless they also have a useful side effect in that they help to make susceptible women… well…susceptible. And from Jess and Immie's reactions, I'd say they're working. Big time.

'I'm glad everything's okay, anyway.' I'm backing away. Not that I'm feeling cheated, but it feels like the right time to make a run for it. 'I'm off now.'

'But...but...how about a drink, or...'

Ignoring his protests, I take a tip from the man himself, and say it like there's no other way. 'I'll see you in the morning.'

Two minutes later, I haven't looked back, and I'm at the office, feeling strangely empowered. I'm fumbling to find my key when I hear a voice, over by the cottages.

'Poppy, Poppy...'

As a figure in sweat pants jogs towards me, I recognise the groom, Jack.

'Jeez, am I glad to see someone who's not pissed. Everyone else is off their faces.' He's panting, pushing back his spikey hair, holding his hands to his face. 'It's Ella, she's having cramps.'

'Would you like me to come and see her?' Although I'm not sure what help I'll be, we run, push through the open door of the cottage and find Ella hunched on the sofa.

'So much for our wedding night,' she says with a gasp. As her bath robe falls away from the bump of her tummy, she brushes the damp straggles of her fringe out of her eyes. 'My waters broke when I got up for a pee an hour ago and...' She breaks off as her face contorts, and she grabs her stomach, groaning. 'Since then it's like all hell broke loose.'

Shit. This looks scarily similar to One Born Every Minute. 'I think they're maybe contractions rather than cramps. How often are you getting them?' Not that I'm broody, but six months on the sofa means I've seen every episode. At least three times.

'She's been getting them on and off since earlier this evening, but she didn't think they were real.' Jack is hugging his head with his hands, as he watches Ella sink back on the sofa. 'It can't be that, the baby's not due for another month or more.'

Babies don't always wait for their due date, but I don't say that. 'Would you be more comfy on the bed?' I ask, knowing the bedroom's on the ground floor.

'I'm not sure I can move.' As Ella jack-knifes again, she lets out a moan. 'Whatever they are, they're coming wave after wave.'

Not that I want to cause panic, but there are times when labour happens very fast. I pull Jack into the kitchen. 'I think we should call an ambulance. Just to be on the safe side.'

He tugs on his hair. 'The midwife at the classes said not to rush to the hospital, there's always plenty of time.'

And in rare cases, there isn't. A split second later I make the decision for him. Pulling my phone out of my pocket, I dial nine-nine-nine, and push the phone into Jack's hand. 'Answer their questions. You're at Daisy Hill Farm, Daisy Hill Lane, Rose Cross. Say she's having strong, continuous contractions, and I'll be back in a second.' Thank god Jules is still awake.

As I sprint across the yard I literally bump into Jules before I reach the camper.

'Everything okay, Pops? Did I hear someone calling you?' At least he's looking out for me here, and it's good he's half way to the cottage already.

'Ella's in labour, Jack's in denial, please can you come and help?' I'm flapping my hands as I blurt out the words. I've been poised to deal with disaster all day, but this is something else.

'Holy shit.' The groan Jules lets out is as loud as Ella's. 'There's no way I can do child birth, I pass out if I prick my finger… Sorry, but…'

Crap. I don't have time to argue with wimps, who aren't going to be any use in any case. There's nothing else for it. I spin, and head for the dimly lit windows of the farmhouse. In a nanosecond I'm at Rafe's kitchen door, hammering hard enough to make my knuckles bleed, praying he's a light sleeper. As the door swings open a moment later, I practically tumble over the threshold with relief.

'Welcome to the Wide Awake Club.' Rafe rubs his hand on his threadbare jeans, propping himself against the door frame as nonchalantly as if it were midafternoon. 'Anything I can do for you?'

His T-shirt tells me he'd rather be tractor driving, and for once I'm with him on that.

At least I've got an excuse to gabble. 'Ella's having her baby, we've phoned for the ambulance and…'

As I tail off, Rafe breaks in. 'The ambulance will take at least twenty minutes to get here.' He rubs his chin. 'How close is she?'

The goosebumps prickle up my spine. 'Very close.' My voice is a squeak. 'I think.' I'm no expert, I'm going on instinct, and pure fear.

Rafe calls over his shoulder as he bolts into the house. 'Let me grab some towels, and I'll be with you.' A second later he's shepherding me across the yard, where Jules is still hovering in the shadows by the camper. Rafe shouts across to him. 'Go down to the road, and when the ambulance comes, send them up to the cottages.' He turns to me as we creep into Ella and Jack's cottage. 'I take it he can manage that?'

As we slide through to the living room, Jack meets us, phone to his ear, his eyes wild, talking a million words a minute. 'The head's crowning, I've seen it, they're talking me through, we've got to stay calm…'

Rafe puts a hand on his shoulder to steady him. 'Don't worry mate, it'll all be okay, I'm Rafe by the way.' He smiles down at Ella, who's on all fours on the floor, blowing and panting. 'Great way to spend your wedding night, but the honeymoon suite is well sound-proofed. No need to keep the noise down, just go for it.' He turns to me, passing an armful of towels. 'Spread these out under Ella, I'll keep a couple to wrap the baby.'

My chest lurches at the word. In all the lurid worst case scenarios I've imagined, I've never considered this.

'Jack, I'm scared.' Ella's shuddering and writhing on the striped rug, while Jack hangs onto one of her hands and grimaces at us over her head.

'Keep blowing.' Rafe puts a reassuring hand on her shoulder. 'No need to be scared, everything's going to be fine, we're here now, we've got this under control.'

I can't believe how calming he sounds. I'm praying I can believe him.

'Hold on Ells,' Jack pleads. 'They'll be here soon, I promise.'

Ella lets out a wail. 'I can't wait, I've got to push.'

Rafe stuffs a towel into my hand. 'Mop her forehead,' he says, as he grabs a towel of his own. 'Everything's fine Jack, you stay there, I've got this.'

As I struggle to find Ella's face, all I can see beside me are Jack's eyes, wide enough to pop out of his head, and his mouth, which is twisted in a silent scream. Ella gives a huge groan, a yell, then another heart stopping groan.

'Here it comes,' Rafe soothes, as he safely delivers the crying newborn.

As Ella sinks to the floor, and Jack stoops to help her, the baby begins to howl. With a few deft movements Rafe wipes the squirming baby, then gently wraps it like a parcel, carefully avoiding the umbilical cord.

'Here you go Ella, one lovely baby girl.'

I swallow back a mouthful of saliva. 'Lovely…amazing…a girl…wow…congratulations.' I make myself shut up at that point. If I wasn't already kneeling on the floor, I think I might have fallen, from the sheer relief bursting through me.

As Rafe leans and places the bundled baby onto Ella's chest, there's the sound of an engine, and flashes of blue light begin to circle around the room.

'The ambulance is here,' I say, even though we all know that already. 'I'll go and bring them in.' It's the least I can do.

As I scramble to my feet, Rafe stops wiping his hands, and leans towards me. 'Well done.' His low voice resonates in my ear, and his breath is warm on my cheek as I pause on my way past him. 'You did brilliantly.'

'Back at you,' I say, knowing I should be hurrying, but just for a minute my gratitude gets the better of me. Next thing I know, I've flung my arms around Rafe, my face is scrunched up against his T-shirt, and I'm drinking in the scent of fabric conditioner, and…and…It takes a second to sink in. Hot, delicious man. That's it. For one delirious moment I think I'd like to hold on to him forever, then I remember what the hell I'm doing, and prise myself away. 'Thanks.' I give his arm a passing squeeze. 'You saved all of us here.' And I make a dash for the door.

It's only as I look back over my shoulder that I see he's wiping away tears.

32

In Rafe's kitchen at Daisy Hill Farm: Milk and sugar

There are times when what you'd like to happen next, and what actually happens, are a million miles apart. And tonight was one of them. As I showed the paramedics into Jack and Ella's cottage, somehow I imagined Rafe and I stealing away, to snatch a quiet cup of tea and have a pull-myself-together debrief in his kitchen. Then maybe he'd take me down to see whatever cow he'd been up looking after, and as a pink dawn broke over the barn we could share our hopes and fears, and then he'd offer me his spare room, where I'd curl up cosily, until he woke me with breakfast – full English, obviously, with real fried bread – just in time to wave the guests off.

But in reality, the blue light wakes the light sleepers in the nearby cottages, who all get up and wake the heavy sleepers, and in the end, as Jack and Ella finally leave in the ambulance for the hospital, everyone from the cottages pours back into the farm kitchen for tea after waving them off.

'Milk, sugar, tea, coffee, mugs.' Rafe zooms around the kitchen pointing out the essentials to me. 'The kettle's on the Aga, are you sure you don't mind doing this?'

'Of course not.' And I'm not lying. Rafe opening his kitchen to wedding guests is such an unexpected and major breakthrough, I'd have happily do cartwheels to entertain them too, if I was a more athletic person.

'I'll check on the cow, and be back up as soon as I can, depending how it goes.'

Cow labour, like human labour, varies. That much I've learned the last couple of months. It could be ten minutes, or he still might not be back tomorrow afternoon. Somewhere along the line, he's changed into a very tattered T-shirt that says *Sexy Farmer and I Know It*. Definitely the worst choice yet, because even though it's four thirty in the morning, and even though the words are barely legible, for the first time possibly ever, I find myself agreeing with him.

'Great,' I say, as I re arrange the mugs on the side, and pull out a chair for Ella's grandmother.

'Help yourself to the guest room if you finish here, and I'm not back,' he says, picking up his keys, and stepping aside to let Jack's parents in, as he goes out.

In the end I take him up on the offer of a bed. At least that part of my wish that came true. But by the time I get up to help Immie with the cottages the next morning, and to welcome in the tipi dismantlers and the mobile toilet company, Rafe's gone off somewhere else entirely.

JUNE

33

At White White White Weddings in Bristol:
Blinis and guffawing like a donkey

'I know there's a cluster of weddings coming up, but once you've had a bride giving birth, you can give up worrying.' Cate smiles, and waggles her glass of bubbly at me. 'Nothing will ever be more traumatic than that.' She leans back on her white leather bar stool, takes in the single rail of wedding dresses hanging against the bare brick walls, and gives a satisfied sigh. In these high end places, less is inevitably more, and despite the industrial decor, today we're pretty damned close to the pinnacle of wedding dress establishments.

If you're thinking, all these people ever do is sit in wedding shops knocking back Prosecco, you're close to the truth. Although I'm not drinking today, because I'm designated driver, and as I've just driven all the way from Cornwall to Bristol, you can give me a break. And as Cate's a bride who's taken an overtime day to come wedding dress shopping, she's got a good excuse too. In fact she's drinking pink champagne, because the shop we're in is super posh. Whereas Immie, who's bunking off lectures, on her third glass, and doesn't even know that blush is a colour, deserves every bit of your judgement.

'Poor Ella, the birth was so fast and fierce, she didn't know what had hit her,' I say, taking a sip of my freshly squeezed mango and passion fruit juice. It still makes me shudder to think about it, two weeks later.

'At least she didn't really get time to swear at the dad.' Cate grins. 'When I had George, I was cursing Liam so much I'm surprised he ever asked me to marry him afterwards.'

'It did take him a couple of years to get round to it.' Immie laughs. 'Maybe that's why?'

Cate skilfully skirts Immie's dig. 'So Rafe's gone up in your estimation, Poppy?' Cate grins.

'He was spectacular in that particular crisis.' I have to give him that. 'They're calling the baby Rafaella.' I pause to roll my eyes for effect. 'It's gone straight to his head, and he's bloody insufferable, so we're back to square one.' Which isn't strictly true. Since that night things between us have shifted. For a start, I truly appreciate that those dusky brown eyes are all his own.

'It's a bit of a shame about Jules though,' Cate muses, glancing at her watch. She's a stickler for time, and all the champagne in the world isn't going to make her overlook that this appointment's running late.

'It's not Jules' fault that he's more into personal style than home births.' Immie's still leaping to his defence, but then she didn't see him without his blue contacts. 'His mum was a model, he's had facials since he was little. He's bound to be a bit precious. It's only like your mum's cake making rubbing off on you, Poppy.'

'Jules failing to come through was good in a way.' I say. 'It reminded me not to rely on *anyone*, even if they're helpful a lot of the time. It'll help to remember that when I plan my future.'

Cate nibbles on a smoked salmon canapé. 'You're not thinking of making changes are you?'

'Yours will be the last wedding at Daisy Hill, and I can't expect

Jess to put me up indefinitely,' I say. 'I might have to pick up what I was doing, before I moved back to be with Brett.' Sooner or later I'm going to have to face it – if I'm on my own long term, it makes sense to go back to my food technology career. It pays a lot better than cake making.

'Surely you wouldn't move away from your support?' Her voice is full of concern.

'It was great living on my own in London before.' It seems like a long time ago. I wave my hand towards the people out on the pavement beyond the wide shop window, and the queue of cars. 'Let's face it, the city vibe is much more "me" than fields of bloody cows.'

'We'll see about that.' Cate fluffs out her chest under her smart Karen Millen blouse, the way she does when she's building up for a fight. I'm spared the argument when an assistant with a dark tan and towering block heels clatters across the roughhewn floor, and whisks Cate away.

'Thank jeez she's only trying on one dress.' Immie scoops up the remaining blinis, and washes them down with a slug of champers. 'We'd be in serious danger of missing lunch otherwise.'

I can't quite believe how long it takes Ms Stompy to get one small bride into one not so tiny dress. It seems like hours later when Cate re-appears, looking a lot less triumphant or triumphal than I'd anticipated.

'So what do you think?' Cate stands, waiting expectantly for our reaction.

Admittedly, in wedding terms, she's leaving her dress decision very late, and this dress is both top-flight designer, and available for September. But given the price tag she whispered in the car had a nine in it, at the beginning, not at the end, I have to admit, I'm seriously underwhelmed. The chiffon's shiny, the beading's OTT, as for the saggy cut, "expectant" is the word that fits. So how do you tell your bestie that the wedding dress she's set her heart on looks less than perfect?

'Bloody expensive canapés,' Immie mutters. Nicely put.

'Well...' I've no idea what to say, but I draw in a long breath and brace myself.

'Poppy...it is you isn't it?'

I'm momentarily saved from giving my opinion when some cut glass vowels slice through the air. Only one person I've ever met speaks like that, and I suspect it's completely put on. I turn, and sure enough, Nicole, one of our August double-booked brides is dashing towards me, her outstretched arms sagging under the considerable weight of designer carrier bags. I narrowly miss having my bare upper arms lacerated by a flurry of acrylic nails, and instead end up in a cloud of air kisses, and enough Yves St Laurent Black Opium to knock out an army at ten paces.

'Nicole, great to see you.' I know I'm gushing, although obviously no-one here knows quite how great it is, or that her timing is impeccable. 'What are you doing here?' I'm hoping she's going to give an endless answer.

'Isn't it funny that we both shop locally? I'm here to pick up my wedding shoes,' she says.

The fact she thinks three hours in the car is local gives a good illustration of the woman.

'And what an amazing shop, isn't it?' I'm playing for time, because I've an idea she's about to get out the shoes in question. I give a silent cheer as she drops her bags to the floor.

'Do let me show you.' As she dips into a bag, she looks up at Cate, then suspends her unwrapping. 'You look very familiar too, where do I know you from?'

'Sorry.' Cate smiles patiently. 'I don't think we've met – unless you work in government finance?'

Nicole blanks that last comment and narrowly misses poking her own eye out, as she lifts her fingers to her forehead, in an exaggerated mime of concentration. 'Got it!' One russet acrylic square end nail points straight at Cate. 'Daisy Hill Farm Weddings – you're all over the website.'

I rush in. 'Cate models,' I say. It's not a complete lie. 'She took part in our recent photo-shoot.'

'God, that dress you're wearing on there is heaven,' Nicole says. 'If I hadn't bought mine already, I'd have had to go for that one.'

'Cate's actually getting married at Daisy Hill Farm in the autumn,' I explain. 'She's here trying on dresses now.'

Nicole stands back, thrusts her hands on her hips, and looks Cate up and down critically. 'No, take it from me, that one does nothing for you at all. Not unless you're going for the sack of potatoes with sequins look.' The peal of tinkling laughter she lets out develops into a loud braying, and finally ends in a snort.

'Fucking hell, that's a bit harsh.' Immie says into her fist.

'Off you go, take it off, I'll get out my shoes while you change into the next one.' Nicole begins to rummage again.

From across the shop, Cate studies herself in the monumental mirror, bunching up the fabric at the waist. 'It's actually a lot less fitted than it looked in the pictures,' she says. 'And it doesn't skim my bulges, it accentuates them.'

Nicole's straight in there. 'They pin the dresses to make them look good on the shoots,' she says, as if she's party to insider information. 'But as a model you'll know that Cate. Albeit a model with a lot of bulges.' This time her laugh goes straight to the bray.

Under cover of Nicole's donkey guffawing, Immie and I exchange appalled glances.

As soon as Nicole's got past her end snort, she's pulling out a shoe box with a flourish. 'Ta-da! Now unlike that dress you've got on Cate, these beauties *are* the business. And a snip at six hundred.'

'Oh my, I'm not sure I've ever seen so many gems on one shoe.' I'm desperate to keep Nicole on side, whilst not condoning her bitchier asides. 'And that overlay of blooms down the heel is very unusual.'

'Exquisite isn't it?' Nicole strokes her finger down the shiny silver heel, which is home to a giant liana of beaded flowers.

'Might be an idea to get some sparkly wellies too,' Immie adds, flashing me a 'what is this woman on?' frown. 'Just in case.'

In case of what, Immie? A visit from the taste police?

It doesn't matter because Nicole carries on as if Immie hadn't spoken. The Gucci handbag Nicole dives into next is almost large enough to contain her whole body. After some time she emerges with her phone. 'Seeing as we're all brides together,' she pauses to give a sickly wink, 'I'll give you a teensy peek at my dress.'

That will be whether we want to see it or not, I presume. I ignore that Immie's cheeks are blowing out as they do when she's about to literally explode with laughter.

'It's a Seraphina East, but not a ready to wear one, it's custom made, hugely expensive and immensely special,' Nicole says, which really, should have prepared me, but it didn't.

As Nicole flashes round the photo of herself in her dress, I practically swallow my tongue with shock. The dress I'm staring at is stunningly like mine. Peering in closer I notice a lot more beading and decoration than on mine, but the damage is done. As I choke on my constricting throat, I go hot enough to send a river of sweat trickles down the hollow of my back, then I turn icy cold.

'Blini crumb' I gasp, grabbing a tissue, wiping my eyes and blowing my nose. 'Went down the wrong way.'

'Get it up, woman.' Immie, glad of something to distract her from her giggles, thumps me on the back with a lot more gusto that I need.

She and Cate have no idea why I've gone puce, then deathly white. They don't even know my dress exists. If Nicole were more likeable, it might be easier to come to terms with watching her get married in a dress very like mine. As she is – and I'm thinking hideous, outspoken, self-centred, and insensitive here, and that's just for starters – it's a bloody nightmare. What's more, I just know she's going to be shoving the pictures in my face at every turn.

'Great dress,' says Cate to Nicole flatly. After Nicole's quip about Cate's bulges, you can tell Cate's thought balloon adds *for a bitch*.

Sensing she's lost her audience, Nicole has slipped her shoes and phone away, and is sliding her bag handles onto her arms like slinky bracelets. The watch that she glances at is diamond encrusted. 'Well, I can see you guys desperately need my styling flair, but I'm already late for lunch with someone more important, so I'll have to dash.' She gives us an airy wave as she totters across the shop. 'Chow. I'll catch you soon Poppy, I need a word about those awful cottages.'

As the shop door clicks closed, Immie blows upwards hard enough to make her tiny fringe stand out from her head. 'Holy fucking crap, what was she like?'

Cate's still pulling faces at herself in the mirror, 'She was right about this dress though, I can't think why you two didn't say as soon as I came out of the fitting room.' Cate drags the fabric backwards and forwards around her body. 'It really doesn't suit me at all.' She gives a sigh. 'I don't know how I got this so wrong. I'm sorry for dragging you two so far to see a complete blunder.'

From where I stand it's a result that she hasn't blown nine grand on an awful dress, but I can't come out with that. 'All in a day's work for your dedicated bridesmaids,' I say instead. 'It's always good to rule things in. Or out.'

Immie scratches her head. 'What I want to know, is who the hell would want to marry someone like Nicole?'

'A rich masochist, with a fetish for multi-coloured shoes?' I laugh, trying to block out the image of Nicole in her wedding dress, which seems to be burned onto my retinas. 'I hate to reinforce the stereotype of Bridezilla and the easy-going groom, but when I talked to Nicole's fiancé he sounded like a nice guy. Chas, I think it was.'

183

'Nice name,' Immie says, airily. 'Thank jeez we've seen the last of her, anyway.'

'Wrong, Immie.' I bite my lip, because instinct tells me today was just a warm up session. 'I suspect we're going to see many more sides of Nicole before her wedding is over.'

'And talking of cottages,' Immie goes on, somewhat randomly. 'That reminds me. Rafe's been asking when you're moving into yours.'

34

In the office at Daisy Hill Farm: Don't count your chickens

'So how are the eggs?'

It's the kind of hot June day when you leave the door open and hide in the shade to work, because otherwise you'd expire. Which is why Rafe is in the doorway, asking his question, before I notice he's here.

'Eggs?' I look up from the list of wedding guests and cottages that I'm trying to untangle. 'You need to be more specific. Easter? Cream?' What other kinds are there?

'The eggs Henrietta is sitting on?' Rafe rubs the stubble on his chin, absently.

'I fail to see where eggs come into this, Henrietta is sitting on the waste paper basket.' I may as well say it like it is. 'And refusing to move. Like she has been for the last month. End of.' Rafe already knows my thoughts on this, because I've told him repeatedly, but he's too stubborn to acknowledge my feelings on the matter. Things around here are rarely straight forward, I'm currently putting rubbish in a Sainsbury's bag on the filing cabinet by the kettle, but there you go.

'Strictly speaking, Henrietta's sitting *in* the waste paper basket, *on* my second best cashmere jumper, so it's a good thing my mother's still away.' Rafe lets a grin go. So long as his mother's well out of range, he seems to enjoy getting one over on her.

'If it's all the same to you, I'm a bit busy for a discussion on semantics,' I say, sad that I have to point it out. 'The same goes for chatting about eggs.' Especially non-existent ones.

'Come over here,' Rafe says. He's squatting on the floor next to Henrietta, stroking her head the way he does, the corners of his lips twitching.

As I go over and kneel down beside him, I can't help notice the deep tan of his forearm next to my own pale freckles.

'Give me your hand.' He doesn't wait, but takes it anyway. Next thing I know, horror of horrors, he's sliding my hand under Henrietta's bum.

'Waaaahhh…' I pull back, and not just at the thought of touching a hen's bottom. 'Isn't she going to peck me?'

He has a firm grip on my hand. 'She's been sharing an office with you for months, she trusts you. I promise she won't peck.' He slides my hand under the feathers. 'Now what can you feel?' His face is so close I can practically count his eyelashes. As he stares at me quizzically, he's holding back a smile.

Oh, shit, so this is what he's going on about. The silky warmth on my hand makes me momentarily suspend my disgust and push deeper. 'Eggs. She's sitting on eggs.' Who'd have thought?

'Rest your hand on a shell.' He's talking softly, still holding my wrist, but it's still an order. 'Can you feel anything?'

I try to ignore that my head is rammed against his T-shirt sleeve, and that I'm breathing in the scent of sun on skin, with a distinct overtone of warm guy. Once I forget that, I feel a weird vibration where my fingertips are resting on an eggshell. 'There's a tapping…on the egg.' Jules perfume-counter haze never made me dizzy like this. On balance, it would be a whole lot easier if Rafe came in smelling of farmyard.

186

'There is a tapping.' He's biting his lip. 'And if you listen hard, what can you hear?'

When I close my eyes, and black out the view of his folded thigh, bursting through the threadbare denim, it's easier. Sure enough, there's a noise – faint, yet high pitched. 'Is that squeaking?'

He draws my hand out, and dips his own back under Henrietta. When he brings it out he's cupping something in his palm. 'Look, here, just for a moment...'

As I lean in, I jump as I hear a loud cheep, then I make out a bundle of grey fluff in his hand. 'Omigod, it's a baby chick.' As I reach out a finger and touch the downy scrap, my stomach squelches, and not in a good way.

The grin he's been holding back breaks, lighting up his whole face. 'It's Henrietta's party piece, she hatches a brood of chicks in the office every year. She's been incubating the eggs for three weeks, and they started to hatch this morning.' His voice is bursting with pride. Deftly, he slides the baby bird back under Henrietta. 'No doubt you'll meet them soon enough. There should be a dozen or so, they'll be following her round the office in a day or so, I'll put up a barrier later so they don't get lost.'

I'm not sure whether I want to say ahhhhhh...Or arghhhhh-hhhhhhhh! One desk-top hen was bad enough, but thirteen? Even if they're cute and cheeping, it's a big ask.

Rafe gets to his feet, rubbing his hands on his hips. 'Right, that's enough poultry for today, don't you think?'

Not that we usually agree on anything, but I'm probably with him on that one.

He's straight in, firing the next question. 'So, when are you moving into the cottage, Poppy?'

Crap. Where did that come from? 'Err...I'm sorry?' I'm kicking myself for being caught on the hop when Immie warned me this was coming.

'You moving up here, I was under the impression it was part

of the deal.' The way he's putting it, he's making it sound non-negotiable.

I purse my lips. 'Hmmm…it's a bit complicated.'

He lets out a sniff. 'Nothing new there then, it's never straight forward with you.'

On balance, I decide to let that go. 'Have you read my CV yet?'

He pulls a face. 'No. And to be brutally honest I'm not going to.'

Four months on, and other than seeing me cutting Ella and Jack's cake, he still hasn't got a clue what I do. 'My main job is making wedding cakes, and I live above the shop where I find a lot of my customers. I also work in the shop. As I'm there a lot more than I am here, it doesn't make sense to move.' Firm, and simply put.

'I see.' As he props an elbow on the filing cabinet, his frown says he might understand, but he doesn't like it. 'I was under the impression you'd be here full time, that's all.'

And we all know how much that would thrill him, having me in his hair twenty four seven. As for me, I get panicky if I'm out of town overnight. If I was here full time I'd be climbing the walls after a weekend. When I was growing up in the village, I couldn't wait to get away. London was my dream location, which I only gave up to move in with what I thought was my dream guy. I was wrong there, but whatever. Living on an isolated farm has always been my worst nightmare.

'Moving here full time isn't an option,' I say, remembering the trick of saying it as if there's no other way. 'Especially as you're not carrying on the wedding business after the end of the season,' I add, as an inspired afterthought.

Rafe's jaw clenches, 'There are a lot of weddings coming up.' He narrows his eyes and drums his fingers on the filing cabinet. 'I've been looking at the calendar.'

'Well that's a first.' I can't hide my astonishment that he's taken that much interest.

He screws up his face. 'It's obviously best for you to stay over when there's a wedding.' He hesitates. 'Especially bearing in mind what happened at the last one.'

Suddenly I get where he's coming from. He'd rather not have me crashing in his spare room. Shit. And suddenly it's obvious he's thought this through already. 'So what are you suggesting?' I send him a cool, professional smile, to make it clear I'm definitely keeping my distance.

'The cottage is there, use it whenever you need to.' He makes it sound simple.

So long as he understands it's only occasional. 'Thanks, that's very…useful.' If he wants to waste a cottage, that's up to him. 'But I'm not moving in. You do understand that?'

'Fine.' He sighs, gives Henrietta a last tickle, and sidles towards the door. 'I don't like to think of you driving back to town late at night. So long as we avoid that.'

What is this? 'I'm a big girl,' I point out. And he's suddenly treating me as if I'm not. 'I can look after myself.'

'I know you can,' he says, swinging out of the door. 'But it doesn't hurt for other people to look out for you too.' The smile he sends me from the threshold suggests he thinks he's won the argument. 'Immie will give you the keys, you can bring your stuff as soon as you want, come on Jet.'

Jet, who's been sitting patiently on the step, gets up, and his tail thumps on the door.

I sink back down onto my chair, trying to remember what the argument was. What the hell just happened there?

A minute later, Rafe's back. A hand on either side of the door frame.

'One other thing.'

My heart sinks. I've had enough of Rafe's good ideas and input for one morning.

'About the wedding in the garden.'

I manage to catch my dropping jaw and grind it into gear

enough to croak. That would be the one in August he's previously categorically refused to contemplate. The one that's had me tearing my hair out with anxiety at two in the morning for weeks.

'We need to get on it and make sure the venue is ready.' He's saying it as if I'm the one that's dragging my heels here. 'You'd better have a look around the house and see what you think. Is Thursday morning any good for you?'

I'm speechless.

35

In the courtyard at Daisy Hill Farm:
Hot tubs and a fireman's lift

'Oh my giddy aunt, I don't believe what's coming.' Immie's groaning as she peeps out of the tiny window next to the office door, as Bridezilla Nicole and her poor fiancé Chas pick their way across the courtyard. They rang for an appointment to look around, just as Nicole promised they would. And now we're bracing ourselves for whatever's coming.

'We might as well go and meet them,' I say, waving at them enthusiastically from the office doorway. 'If we wait for Nicole to check every cobble for dirt before she puts her foot on it, we're going to be here all day.'

'What she going to be like when she gets down to the meadow?' Immie gives a groan. 'Has anyone told her fields are made of mud?'

'How did she book in the first place? And on the same day as someone else too.' I mutter. 'Judging by that pencil skirt and those strappy sandals, she's hardly rocking the boho farm wedding chic thing, is she?' As for the double booking, Nicole's wedding is so big, it's the other smaller one I'm trying to move.

'I think she was one of Carrie's mates from Surf and Turf Dating, who got lucky and fast forwarded to a wedding.' Immie's derisive tone turns to a soft sigh. 'Whereas Chas on the other hand…' She lingers over his name, as she looks him up and down and soaks up the faded chinos, and open neck polo shirt, not to mention a few well-toned muscles. And then does the same all over again. 'Now he looks *right* at home here.'

I get where Immie's coming from. Whereas Nicole is all dark gloss and brittle nerves, Chas is your classic blond hunk, and laid back with it. Ignoring that Immie has melted into a hormone puddle next to me, I carry on. 'Nicole, Chas, great to see you, I'm Poppy, and this is Immie.' By going straight in for handshakes, we by-pass the hugs and get away with a smattering of Lady Million air kisses, and the odd bash from another huge Gucci bag that appears to be glued to Nicole's shoulder.

Nicole, thanks largely to her seven inch heels, is looking down on all of us. 'We might as well get to the point, I'm here to inspect the accommodation.' If her vowels were a bit la-di-dah last time we met her in Bristol, today she's channelling her inner Royal. 'The Bridal Suite's what matters, so we'll go straight there.'

'Fine,' I say, 'if you'd like to follow Immie…' As I give Immie the nod, I'm wishing I'd chosen something more refined for refreshments. I'm not sure a lemon drizzle cake, made at top speed before I left the shop, is going to come up to Princess Nicole's expectations, even if I have brought matching yellow serviettes.

'Buttercup Cottage is where most of our couples spend their wedding night, due to the spacious layout,' Immie explains. As she shows us straight through to the bedroom, I can tell she's on her best behaviour too. I mean, when does Immie ever use the word spacious?

One glimpse of the four poster with its gauzy muslin drapes is usually enough to have couples clamouring for it, but today we're not so lucky. I can already see Nicole's nose is wrinkling.

'It seems a bit pokey.' Ignoring the acres of floor and the four substantial posts, instead she gives the quilt a doubtful prod. 'Checked bed linen is so very eighties, don't you think?' Without waiting for an answer, her attention turns to the walls. 'It's all so rustic and dreary, Chas, I'd hoped for a foil paper at the very least.'

'Annie Sloan's chalk paint lime wash is very now,' I say. No idea if these particular walls are painted with it, but whatever.

'Really Chas,' she hisses, 'I've seen better thread counts at Premier Inn.'

Chas turns to me with a bemused stare and an apologetic shrug.

Personally I'm gob smacked she got beyond the car park of anywhere so down market. 'Why not see what you think of the bathroom?' I suggest, thinking she might be impressed by tiles from Fired Earth.

Without even looking, Nicole's straight back at me. 'Is it en-suite?'

Crap. She's got me there. 'It's immediately adjoining,' I offer, knowing I'm trying my hardest and failing.

'Technically it's *á coté*,' Immie says, sniggering behind her hand.

When did she get good at French?'

'You could say it's more of a *cul-de-sac* location,' Chas adds, with a big grin.

It's not that funny, but he and Immie both fall about giggling. It's amazing what nerves can do to people.

Nicole dismisses that with a sniff, and resumes her quick fire assassination. 'Hot tub on the patio?' She peers out of the window with a grimace, completely overlooking the pretty table and chairs.

'Currently no hot tub or jacuzzi, I'm afraid.' I sigh.

'American fridge?'

I ignore Immie mouthing fucking hell at me. 'There wasn't one the last time I looked.'

'Wouldn't fit through the door, so we sent it back' Immie adds, unhelpfully.

'Complimentary drinks?'

At last I have something to smile about. 'Champagne on ice.' In my head I punch the air because I've finally got something right.

Wrong. Nicole's face crumples. 'Champers is so very last year,' she says with a disgusted eye roll. 'Everyone knows that cocktails are the new Bollinger. As for hideous cartoon animal pictures…'

And finally she's made a good point. I'm with her on that one. The decor is down to Rafe's mum, and the pictures in question are truly awful. 'We could definitely take those down,' I offer, then think again. 'Actually, some of our more refined couples do choose to move on to hotel accommodation for their wedding night, have you considered that?'

For the first time Chas jumps in. 'No way am I going to a hotel.' He sounds adamant. 'All our friends are camping in the field, if I had my way we'd be down there too. We'd booked our own luxury tipi, are you sure you won't reconsider that option Nic?'

'Those big tipis with furniture are *so* romantic.' Immie gives a sigh that's a lot too dreamy for her own good.

'How many times do I have to tell you…?' Nicole's snap turns to a bellow. 'Don't call me Nic!'

Putting the perfect event together can be very stressful, a bit of pre-wedding friction is inevitable. And with every passing wedding, I'm having my idealistic impressions of true love blown right out of the water.

'Anyone for tea and cake in the office?' I say, in an effort to take the pressure off.

The look Chas sends me could not be more grateful. 'Brilliant suggestion,' he beams, then sends us a wink as he links arms with Nicole. 'If we set off now, we might be there by morning.'

Thanks to Chas powering Nicole along, we make good time

crossing the courtyard, but as we change direction there's a sudden shriek from Nicole.

'There, that's it!' Happily when she's yelling very loud she sounds a lot less like royalty and a lot more normal. Her long silver nails are flapping around so fast, she could be a body double for Edward Scissorhands.

'What's what?' Chas says, patiently, pulling out of range of her nails with a swift twist of his torso that has Immie's eyes out on stalks. Living with Nicole, this guy must have to channel his inner saint for a large proportion of every day.

'That's the cottage where I want to spend my wedding night,' Nicole says, one determined square-end nail pointing straight at the farmhouse.

Chas blows upwards so hard his fringe flips into mid-air. 'That's not a rental cottage, it's the big house where the farmer lives.'

'Which sadly is little more than a shell,' I explain, hurriedly, trying to blank that I'm currently trying desperately to relocate the other half of their double booking to the garden area. There's no way their big camping wedding would squeeze in up here. 'It might look amazing from the outside, but inside I promise it wouldn't tick any of your boxes, Nicole. There's no jacuzzi or wallpaper or furniture, there's only flaking paint and lots of dirty rooms.'

'But I've set my heart on it,' Nicole wails. That would be all of five seconds ago. 'It so looks like my kind of place, it's the sort of location everyone at work stays on their wedding nights.' Her voice rises to a wail. 'And you want me to stay in a tent...'

As Nicole's bottom lip comes, out Chas swoops in to kiss her. 'I know it doesn't happen often, but this time it really is a "no" to the big house, which is why the cottage is a great compromise.' Chas pauses, perhaps because compromise is an alien concept for Nicole. 'So let's go and get this tea and cake.'

In an effort to keep things light the rest of the way to the office, I begin to talk them through the lemon drizzle recipe, but

195

I've only got as far as grating the lemon zest when a shout goes up from Immie.

'Crap Poppy, Henrietta's out.'

Sure enough, the board Rafe had propped across the doorway is flat on the floor in front of the open door, and Henrietta is strutting towards the farm house, followed by more cheeping chicks than I can count.

'Head her off, Immie, send her back towards us.' I'm yelling instructions, even though I know diddly squat about chickens.

'Keep calm, I'm a fireman!' Chas leaps forwards. 'I've got this…' As he dashes down the yard, carefully circling around Henrietta, there's an angry squawk from Nicole.

'Hey Chas, you can't take my Gucci!' But she's too late, it's already gone.

Before we can say Angry Bird, Chas has reached the escapees, Gucci bag waving wildly. In a flash he's got the bag unzipped, and he's dropping in chicks. Next thing he's striding back towards us, beaming triumphantly, complete with Henrietta wedged in the crook of his elbow, a startled look in her beady eyes.

'In here I presume?' he says, heading for the office. Two seconds later, the board's back across the doorway, and he gently deposits Henrietta, then the chicks, on the floor. 'There you go, job done, no panic necessary.' Standing behind Nicole, he slides her bag back onto her arm, and gives her a squeeze. 'Thanks for the loan of the bag, you're a star, Nico.'

As Nicole tugs away from his caress, she elbows him hard in the ribs. 'How many times do I have to tell you…my name's Nicole…' she bellows.

Her perfectly pencilled brows have turned into Z bends across her forehead, and she's snarling through her teeth now. 'We'll talk about my ruined bag later…' She turns and begins to power away. '…in the car.'

Immie, Chas and I watch in silence as she stamps towards Chas's 4x4.

'Let's do the tea another time,' I suggest, trying to smooth things over.

Chas blows. 'Phew, I'm sorry, you'll have to excuse Nic, she's under a lot of pressure.' He swipes his fingers across his brow. 'She's a beautiful person, but sometimes she sees things completely differently from everyone else I know.'

Immie gives Chas a friendly pat on the back. 'Don't worry, she'll be fine when it's all over, weddings are well known for making sensible people wappy,' she says, reassuringly. She sends me a secret grin from somewhere behind his shoulder. 'It could be a lot worse. Our best friend's just ordered a complete fairground for her Daisy Hill wedding, imagine that.'

I can't help shrieking. 'Cate's done what?' Surely she hasn't.

'Yep, she rang this morning.' Immie gives a shrug. 'Helter skelter, big wheel, roundabouts, the lot.'

I shake my head. 'Crazy.' I wonder if she's told Liam yet. I have an inkling that this may finally send Cate's long suffering and sensible husband-to-be over the edge.

'Completely mad.' Immie agrees.

Chas frowns. 'There isn't much danger of a fairground, a helter skelter wouldn't be Nic's thing at all, she hates heights. We met on a St Aidan Singles walk when she had a panic attack on the bridge across the creek going into Padstowe.'

'But that bridge isn't high,' Immie points out, with a dismissive nose wrinkle she really shouldn't be using with clients.

'I know, but that's exactly why I'm such a lucky guy,' Chas says happily. 'Talking Nic onto dry land that day was the best thing to happen to me in ages.' As the slamming of his distant car door echoes between the buildings, he gives a grimace, and hurriedly holds out his hand to say goodbye. 'I'd better go, but thanks for today, it went better than I expected. I'll chat to Nic and be in touch.'

Immie and I stand waving as Chas winds his way back to the car, and Nicole.

'That went better than expected?' Immie gives an appalled eye roll. 'How the hell does he stay so chilled in the face of *that*?' she asks, biting her thumbnail as she inclines her head to Chas's car. Immie's making no attempt to hide that her eyes are glued to his bum as he leaves.

'Firemen are trained to deal with worst case scenarios and crises' I say. 'Plus the guy's completely besotted, there's no hiding it, he's head-over-heels in love.' It must be amazing to have someone who adores you that much. When I think back, I can't ever remember a time Brett was half that crazy about me. Even when he asked me to leave London and live with him, it was all to do with train timetables and heavy weekend traffic. It was never because he specially wanted to be with me.

'If you ask me, Fireman Chas is going to get more than his fingers burned there,' Immie sniffs, disapprovingly.

'No-one did ask you, Immie,' I point out, because someone has to tell her. 'It's definitely not our job to be judgmental.' As for admiring the pants off a groom, I'll have a stern word about that later, when she's less flushed.

'In heat terms, he needs to get the hell out of that particular kitchen, and fast.' Immie says, completely ignoring me. 'In psychological terms, he's temporarily blinded by the happiness chemicals linked to infatuation. What's going to happen when he comes out on the other side of happy-land and finds out he's married the bitch queen from hell?'

'Not our problem, Immie. Really, really, not our problem,' I say, firmly.

Nicole might be dishing it like a diva, and I might be a teensy bit touchy that she's getting married in a dress that reminds me of mine. Yes, it's irrational to think 'that should have been me', and getting that sour feeling in my stomach isn't helpful either. But seeing the cottage through her eyes has made me wake up to the fact that there's a lot more that could be done with the rentals. With a small amount of input those cottages could appeal to a more up-market clientele, which would, in turn, bring in a lot more income. But that's for another day entirely, and that's probably not my problem either. There's another much more pressing problem, which I'm sure will immediately take Immie's mind off firemen. 'So what's this about Cate wanting a fairground?'

JULY

36

At Brides by the Sea: Cupcake towers and helter skelters

Even though it's amazing by the sea in summer, the magical glisten of the waves, and the fabulous surf rolling over hot sand don't always transfer to the inside of the shop. Today has been the kind of baking hot day where you have to peel the dresses off the brides, and we've had every disaster cliché in the wedding shop book. Bride's mums in floods of tears, bridesmaids coming to blows, and the worst, worst, worst of all, a bride who's changed her mind on the dress. Rather than being a day when the fizz flowed, and laughter echoed, I've been handing out endless cups of strong sweet tea and giant sized slices of comforting iced walnut cake.

'What a bloody afternoon,' Jess says as she rubs the sweat off her brow with her fist, then piles the last lot of plates and cups onto a tray. 'Many more like that, and I'd give up.'

'Thank Christmas for sugar.' I say, wafting the hem of my black blouse in an attempt to get some tepid air to my tummy.

'There's something here that might make our day end on a high.' Her lips are twitching as she draws her phone from her pocket. 'A text from Sera just came in…'

'Wow,' I breathe, because this is big. Sera's in London making the final final final adjustments to Josie Redman's dress, before her mega celebrity wedding next week.

Jess looks as if she's about to burst. 'And there's a photo…' Squeaking really isn't Jess's style, but she's making an exception here. 'Top top top secret, obviously,' she says, sliding the screen towards me. 'Sera knows if it wasn't for you and me saving her that first day when Josie came in unexpectedly, she wouldn't have pulled this off.'

'Of course,' I mutter, as I lean in. As my eyes lock on the photo, I gulp down so much air that I immediately cough it back. Talk about déjà vu. This is like a re-run of Nicole's reveal, but this time Josie's head has been carefully left out of shot, so seeing her in a dress that's could almost be mine is slightly less jarring. 'Gorgeous.' I manage to splutter. 'It's very like…'

Jess's face is close to mine and her hot breath hits my cheek. 'Like yours?' She's straight on my case. 'It is. And how do you feel about that?' Her hand lands on my shoulder.

Maybe because I've been through this all before in Bristol, the urge to bring up my walnut cake is less urgent. Although when I squint more closely, Josie's dress has less all-over lace, so it's more like mine than Nicole's. 'I guess from Josie's reaction when she tried my dress, I knew she'd be going for something similar.' It's true. This is less of a kick in the guts than with Nicole.

Jess pulls a tissue from a nearby box, and pushes it into my hand. 'Lucky you, it's the last one.'

We've never run out of tissues before, and although I sniff into it to show I'm grateful, I haven't got any tears to mop up. It's as if all my dress emotion was used up last time. Although I'm dreading Nicole and Chas's actual wedding, for now, so long as I don't see my own dress again in the flesh, I just feel numb.

'We'll talk about this later.' Jess's phone is back in her pocket. 'Your five thirty's here.' She nods to the door.

It's not strictly an appointment. Liam's popping in to talk

cakes, which I suspect is Cate's ploy to take his mind off those controversial fairground rides.

'So, cakes…' I say, once I've shoved Liam well out of eye shot of Jess, and sat him down on a squishy sofa with the last piece of walnut cake, and a bottle of the Fentimans Rose lemonade we usually keep for brides' mums who don't like alcohol. 'Cate thought it would be great if I found out about your cakey likes and dislikes.' If I'm hedging round the subject, it's because we're both aware that in reality Cate would *never* delegate *anything* to do with the design of her wedding cake.

'This is delicious.' As Liam lifts up his cake I notice there are dark circles under his eyes.

'Thanks, wait 'til you see these, they'll make your mouth water too.' I spread out a few pictures of cupcake towers on the table in front of him. 'Some people have cupcakes as well as the main cake.' Let's face it, a cupcake tower is the only outlet Liam's likely to get for his ideas, with Cate behaving like an autocrat. 'So I need to find out your favourite kind of cake, and what kinds of icing you like.'

Liam gives a long sigh. 'To be honest Poppy, I think it might be better if I cancel the cake altogether.' Under his tan his skin is almost grey.

'What?' I shout. 'Why the hell would you want to do that?' I didn't see this coming.

He gives a grimace. 'The way things are going, I'm not sure we'll be able to pay for it.'

Oh crap. The way Cate's been carrying on, the budget was bound to blow at some point. It could be worse. At least he isn't getting cold feet.

'As far as the wedding cake goes, it's my gift to you two, and you can have whatever design you want.' I say, suddenly thinking that maybe I should be listening more to Liam, and not only to Cate. 'No size limit either,' I add, remembering the guest list, as I flop down on the sofa next to him. 'Do you want to talk about the rest? I know Cate's been thinking...big...' To put it mildly.

Liam leans forward and puts his plate on the table. 'Cate's the accountant, she earns way more than me, so I left it to her. Until today...' He leans forward and puts his chin in his hands. '... when I accidentally opened the invoice for the balance on the marquee hire.' His eyebrows hit the ceiling at this point, and he lets out a long low whistle.

'Ahhh...The marquees...' All four of them.

Liam blows out his lips. 'Then I went and looked at the paper-work on the desk, and I'm sure that's not all of it.' He's shaking his head. 'She's got completely carried away. I need you to help me make her see reason. We can't afford the deposits, let alone the balances. And she's ordering more stuff every day. This week she's booked a petting zoo, an outdoor cinema and a gypsy caravan.'

'Shit,' I say, truthfully. 'I didn't know about those.' The fair-ground paperwork obviously hasn't made it onto the desk yet.

'It's funny' he says, leaning back and drumming his fingers on the sofa arm. 'You think you know someone, you have a child together, and then something like this happens, and you realise you didn't have a clue.'

It makes my chest ache to hear him sound so bleak. 'I'm sure you and Cate will be able to work this out.' I give his hand a squeeze. 'Cate's not the first bride to have got carried away with her wedding plans. All she wants is for everyone to have an amazing day, but the numbers are so big they start to lose all meaning.' Liam's left Cate to get on with it, which was what she wanted, but even with Immie and me, she's thrown out every suggestion to rein things in. I'm thinking back to the five thou-sand pounds worth of bridesmaids' dresses, which thankfully she hasn't ordered yet, but only because she hasn't been able to get all eight bridesmaids in for a fitting. It's only down to Nicole that Cate didn't splurge nine grand on a dress.

'There are so many zeros we'll need a second mortgage.' Liam's laugh is perturbingly bitter. 'I've put my car up on AutoTrader. I can get an older one, but it's still not going to cover it.'

'I'd just assumed Cate had a handle on it.' I bite my lip, kicking myself, because I feel partly responsible for the mess. Immie and I should have challenged Cate earlier, or at least checked that Liam knew the situation.

'I trusted her, and she's messed up big time.' Liam's tugging at his hair.

This is not what I want to hear from my best friend's soul mate. 'There are lots of areas where you can cut back and make big savings.' I say. 'But *you* need to take responsibility too. You need to stand up to Cate, and work out something more realistic.' I look into his eyes. 'Together. As a couple.'

'Right,' he says, a lot more doubtfully than I'd like. With any luck he won't ever need to know about the fairground.

'Immie and I will back you up, I promise. You'll still have a wonderful day.' If I chew on my thumb any more, I'll draw blood. I've changed my life to make this wedding happen. Hell, I've already endured six months of Rafe and his black moods in order for Cate to get her fabulous day.

And I'm not about to give up on it now.

37

In the garden at Daisy Hill Farm: Rose thorns and thick fog

'Immie was telling me that a groom-to-be caught Henrietta's chicks in a handbag.' Rafe says, as he marches around the side of the farmhouse. 'She was impressed enough to mention it twice.'

I'm psyching myself up for my tour of the grounds behind Rafe's house. First I have to check that the smaller double-booked wedding will actually fit into whatever space is there. And then, if the space is suitable, I'll be faced with the huge task of persuading Rafe to actually let it happen.

'Immie only mentioned it twice?' I say, amazed. We should be concentrating on Cate's wedding cut backs, but Immie refuses to move on from chickens. And IMHO as they say on Facebook, it wasn't the method of chicken capture or the end result that made an impact, it was the person doing it. And as he couldn't be more spoken for, she needs to shut the frig up about him and get a life of her own. I mean, whatever happened to surfer boy from Jaggers? 'It's summer, he left to go surfing' is no kind of answer.

As I follow Rafe towards a door in a high stone wall, I pull my notebook out of my bag so I have all the information to hand, and send a silent mantra to the god of double bookings to do his best for us. When Rafe opens the door to the garden, for a moment I'm too nervous to look. As I slowly open my eyes and see the view beyond Rafe's faded T-shirt, my heart misses a beat. I'm opening and closing my mouth, but no sound comes out, which doesn't matter, as Rafe is in full flow.

'The ceremony's in the local church, so we don't have to worry about that.' He waves an arm to the area beyond the garden. 'Parking would be on the field, accessed from the lane, guests would come straight into the garden from there. We'll take the fence down, obviously.' He crosses an extensive terrace made of old bricks, and steps out onto wide lawns. 'I've checked and an open sided marquee for forty will fit on the grass on the left.' He turns to me. 'And…?'

'Gr…eat,' I say, glancing at my now redundant notebook. Sounds like he's covered everything, but how the hell he's done that, I don't know. 'You found the details then?' Part of me wants to be cross, but all I can see is the flower border running the length of the wall. It's a mass of pinks and blues and reds clashing in the sunlight. Cornflowers and poppies are tangled with rampant jasmine, holly hocks entwine with climbing roses, and the scent of honeysuckle hangs in the warm air.

'I started with the bookings calendar, and after that it was easy.' He grins. 'Your filing system is remarkably clear and accessible. Well done with that, it's a remarkable turnaround.'

'Great…' I murmur again, wandering towards the flowers because that's the only way my feet will go. As I reach the border I lean forwards and trail my fingers across a swathe of pink roses. There's something softly familiar about the scent of the blooms. I stoop closer and breathe in deeply and before I know it, my eyes are pricking.

'So what do you think?' he says.

Grabbing a tissue from the pocket of my jeans I scape away

the tears. 'Sorry…' I blow my nose loudly, and swallow a mouthful of saliva.

'Is something wrong?' He's walking towards me, frowning.

I sniff into my hanky. 'It's the garden…' I gulp, biting my lip to force back the tears. 'The border's so like the one my mum had.' I'm not sure why that would make me cry.

He pads across the grass, and stops in front of me. 'No blue poppies though.' Putting a hand on each of my shoulders, he stares down at me.

'Are those Albertine roses?' I ask, trying to divert his attention away from my out-of-control weeping.

'Yep, planted by my grandmother.' He smiles down at me. 'She loved her garden too. The farm guys and I try our best, but it gets away from us a bit, especially in wet summers.'

Maybe it's the heat, maybe the tangle of plants, but for a minute I'm right back in the garden behind my mum's rented cottage in the village. I can't ever bear to think what happened to the garden afterwards, when the new tenants moved in.

'My mum died quite a few years ago.' If I stare very hard at the swallows sitting up on the telegraph wire I can keep my voice steady. 'The strangest things bring it back, I'm sorry, it's very unprofessional of me…'

'Bollocks to professional. Come here.'

The next moment, my face crashes against his T-shirt, and my nose fills with the scent of warm skin, as his arms close round my back. Clamping my eyes shut, all I can think about is the thud of his heartbeat against my cheekbone, the strength of his back muscles under my fingers, and how amazingly safe I feel. I have no idea how long I've been clinging on for when I force myself to push away.

'She had breast cancer, but she hid it from me. I only knew the last few weeks, and by then there was no time left for anything.' It comes out in a rush, to fill the gaping space that's suddenly there between us. I twiddle with the pink twist of ribbon pinned on the strap of my bag. 'She was trying to protect me by not telling me, but in the end the shock was…' Horrific. Awful. Mind blowing. I don't remember much. Being too numb to cry. Cate and Immie helping me talk to the undertaker. And being so confused I wore my black coat for the funeral, even though I know my mum would rather I'd worn red instead. How there were snowdrops in the churchyard. And Brett being tied up in Dubai on a month long sales initiative, and then finally flying back, and missing the funeral because of fog over Zurich.

'However it happens, it's tough.' Rafe reaches out, snaps off a rosebud, and gently winds it through the strap of my bag. 'My dad collapsed haymaking in the bottom meadow. Bad enough, but it's easier when there's family all around to help. Thank you for sharing that with me.'

'Back at you.' I say, and when I look up into his face, his hard lines have softened. 'Thanks for the hug,' I say, because it seems polite, given we're saying thank you, but then I'm floundering. 'I didn't have you down as a huggy person.'

His face creases in amusement. 'Me neither.' Then his smile fades. 'I didn't mean to cross boundaries. You just looked very vulnerable…and alone.'

Which is exactly how things are. And how they're going to be. Which is absolutely fine.

'So you've nailed the wedding plans then,' I say, swallowing, because we might as well get on with what we're here for. 'All your suggestions would work brilliantly to keep the two weddings separate. Although how would you feel about…' I'm thinking on my feet, which is not always a good idea.

He's straight back at me. 'About what?'

I twist one foot behind my ankle. Getting carried away because Rafe suddenly looks all approachable is only going to lead to disappointment. 'Thinking of ways to sell this to the double booked bride so she really won't refuse the offer.' I hesitate,

211

because there's a possibility this will send Rafe straight into one of his rages, and we'll be back to square one.

'And?'

'Is there any chance of offering a small room in the house for the bridal party to freshen up?' I stare at the swallows, this time because I can't bear to see his face go all black and thunderous again.

'Good thinking.' His voice is level and collected, and horribly sexy.

'Sorry?' I can't believe what I just heard. As for the sexy part, scrub that. If Immie were here, she'd have some psychological explanation about falling for the person who rescues you. Which I'm totally not, obviously.

'No idea which room, but I agree, it could be a good sweetener.'

My mind is suddenly racing, as I look along the terrace to the beautiful, cobweb draped orangerie. If Rafe's in a good mood, we might as well make the most of it. 'If we offered a downstairs reception room and the orangerie for use in case it rains, then they really wouldn't say "no".' When I notice that Rafe's eyebrows haven't furrowed like a ploughed field, I push on. 'Immie and I could all help to clean the rooms, and you know how wet this summer has been. This way you'd save churning up the lawn if it rained.'

I watch his face crumple as he agonises for what seems like forever. Then suddenly he relaxes. 'Okay, let's go for it. So long as the insurers will run with it, offer the bridal party the lot.'

I feel like I'm a champagne bottle and my cork just popped. 'Thanks Rafe, that's bloody brilliant.' Next thing I know, I can't help it, I've flung my arms around him, because I'm so damned happy, and I'm hugging him like a demon, until I accidentally lose my flip flop, and almost fall over.

He stands and laughs as I stagger backwards, then he slides me a sideways grin. 'I didn't actually have *you* down as a huggy person either.'

'I'm *definitely* not huggy,' I say. Unless Nicole is making such a bee line for me I can't avoid her. 'But it's not every day someone makes a turn around like yours.' On balance, I decide to miss out the word crucial. Not that I'm suspicious, but I have to ask. 'Any particular reason for the change?' I try to make the question as light as I can.

He rakes his fingers through his hair, and blows out his cheeks. 'Before Jack and Ella, I was very opposed to weddings, full stop.' Pausing, as if he can't quite believe the change either. 'But the night the baby arrived I stopped seeing the brides and grooms as cardboard cut outs I'd rather keep off the farm, and began to see them as real people.'

'Nice one Rafe,' I say, even though I'm ever so slightly appalled by his admission. Although it would be hard to live through the trauma and relief of Ella's labour and feel no after effects.

'The day they brought Rafaella round to see us, I realised how happy Daisy Hill Farm can make people. It's down to us to make every couple's day the best it can be.'

And finally. 'Exactly,' I say. Immie and I are still cursing that we weren't here for that baby visit, not because we like babies, but just because we missed seeing Rafe cooing over his namesake.

'So shall we take a look in the orangerie?' He's sounding dangerously enthusiastic about this.

As I scoop up my notebook from the grass where it fell, I get a full frontal view of the slogan on his raggy T-shirt – *Cornish Farmer, A Rare Breed*. 'Good thinking, Rafe,' I grin. 'Welcome to the Wedding Team.'

38

At Brides by the Sea: Déjà vu?

Women in wedding shops, drinking prosecco? Again? Well, yes…
and no.

Like the other time we were all here, it's after hours. It seems
like a lifetime ago that Cate, Immie and I were last in Brides by
the Sea, shrieking and groaning over bridesmaids' dresses, and
today's atmosphere is as different from that as it could be. Cate's
slashed budget, not to mention her big show down with Liam
when he finally confronted her about her spending, has taken the
edge off her delirious bride mood. But I've changed a lot too. All
those months ago, I was taking my first shaky steps towards making
a life on my own, and hating every minute. Being forced to go
and work at Daisy Hill Farm, not having the first clue what I was
letting myself in for was hard. Arriving and finding the chaos was
worse. As for the first few weddings, I've never been more terrified.
But I lived through the fear, and thanks to the help and support
of all my friends, I've come out the other side with more confidence. Weddings at the farm are happening regularly, and I'm
sailing through them. If there are hitches we work through them

together, as a team, and even Rafe's mellowed. So whereas Cate is temporarily in a worse place than she was, I couldn't be better. And it's Cate we've come to the shop for today.

We've been called here as part of a joint intervention by Sera and Jess. In honour of the gravity of the occasion, Jess has added gin and elderflower cordial to the usual prosecco. So we're all sitting in our summer florals, sipping her version of English Garden cocktails, waiting to see what the hell she has to say.

You can always count on Immie to break the ice. 'We love the window displays,' she says, waving her frosted tumbler around, and prodding at her mint sprig. She's talking about the explosion of lace and photographs in every opening on the shop's perimeter, celebrating that earlier this week Josie Redman said 'I do', wearing Sera's gorgeous dress. Immie and Cate have no inkling of how I had to scrunch up my eyes every time I came home to see so many versions of Josie, all looking like I once dreamed I would.

'Jules came through for us, with the pictures.' Jess's smile oozes pride and delight in equal measure. 'He played with the official publicity shots they sent through, then he did the prints for us.' At least a hundred, a fabulous mix of close ups, and distant views.

Once the photos were plastered all over the shop, they were impossible to miss. Somehow, the fiftieth time I came face to face with Josie wearing a dress so similar to mine, it was much less jarring than the first. Whereas once my own dress was all about spending the money my mum left me, and me marrying – or not marrying – Brett, somewhere down the line something's shifted. For so many years, deep down I was so desperate to become Mrs Brett King. But looking at those pictures of Josie in her dress made me realise that I've left Brett behind. Although I'm not sure when, or how I changed, what I do know is that me standing beside Brett in my dress isn't the picture that drifts into my head whenever I close my eyes. Better still, that isn't what I want to do any more.

Looking around the pictures of Josie's wedding now, I almost feel like I was there in person. The press went wild over her dress, all the more because of the surprise. They were poised to rip her apart for turning up in a white sequined boob tube, which had been accidentally-on-purpose leaked to the magazines, and instead she was so sophisticated and beautiful, the press couldn't do anything but praise her. There have been so many calls to the shop since, the phone has practically melted.

Jess stares at me pointedly. 'Jules might not be good at delivering babies, but he's certainly made up for it here. He's such a gifted boy.'

I'm feeling the need to issue a statement to show I've re-joined the Jules fan club. 'Jules did some lovely shots of bridesmaids and page boys playing with Henrietta's fluffy chicks at a wedding last week,' I say. Hopefully this will show that Jules and I are friends again. 'The chicks are getting a lot of love on the website, and I've got a blown up print hanging in the office.' Even if I'll never view Jules in quite the same way as before, we still work well together. It's not as if we were even close to being an item, because I never wanted that. And it's good to remember, if you ask too much of people, they can't come through for you. They'll let you down every time.

'So…' As Jess strides across the shop tapping her Swarovski crystal pen on her tumbler to get our attention, a hush falls over the sofa where we're lined up. 'Cate, we've asked you here today because Sera and I have a proposition. You did a fabulous job modelling Sera's dress on the Daisy Hill Farm shoot, and a lot of brides have come to us as a result of those pictures.'

'Hey, we told you how great you looked.' Immie grins and nudges Cate, who smiles as her cheeks turn pink.

Jess carries on. 'Poppy's told us about your…ahem…' Jess pauses as she searches to find a suitable word. 'Difficulties,' she says at last.

Difficulties is putting it mildly. To bring you up to speed, Cate and Liam's massive argument was followed by an equally massive wedding cull. They cancelled all but one marquee, they've shrunk the flower order, lost the fairground, the cinema and the zoo. But the invitations had already gone out, and their numbers are huge, so the catering budget is monstrous. And as Cate still has to buy dresses for herself and the bridesmaids, the final overspend hasn't yet been calculated.

Jess winces at the thought of the problems, and carries on. 'Because of your popularity as a bride Cate, Sera and I have a proposition. We're suggesting we provide you with a wedding dress and bridesmaid dresses from Sera's Country Collection for next year. And in return you could give us your real life wedding pictures, as taken by Jules, to use in our publicity. How does that sound?'

'Oh my…thank you so much…' Cate puts her drink down, sits back on the sofa and flaps her hands in front of her face. 'That s-ounds…' She stops and dabs a tissue to her eye. 'Amazing…I don't know how I'll ever repay you…'

'It's quite simple.' Jess cuts in brusquely, businesslike to the end. 'You'll be repaying us in full by giving us your pictures to use.' She pulls the ends of her mouth down. 'But being a realistic bridal shop owner, I know you might not find anything in the collection you want to wear. So let's try on some dresses.'

Cate laughs. 'If they're anything like the one I wore for the shoot, I'll love them. I felt truly beautiful that day.' She gives a sigh. 'It's a shame I can't wear that one, but everyone's seen it now.'

Jess moves across to the rail of wedding dresses. 'There are several to try, and selfishly I'm starting with the one that will look best on the pictures.' You have to love Jess for her honesty. 'This one has the nipped in waist that suits you so much.' She takes the first dress of the rail and leads the way to the changing room. 'Ready Cate?'

As Jess draws the curtain across the fitting area which spans

217

the room, Immie and I settle back into the cushions to wait.

'Bloody hell, lucky or what?' Immie says, smacking her lips as she knocks back her cocktail, and helps herself to a refill from the tall jug on the drinks tray.

'Mutually beneficial is how I'd put it,' I say. There's no such thing as a free lunch with Jess. And using a real live wedding for publicity shots is very original, and very 'now', and will get Sera's collection even more attention. It's also very in tune with the country wedding theme, which is why Jess wants Cate to have a dress from that collection. But you'd need a special bride to agree. And Cate is unique, not only because she knows Jules and Jess well enough to be comfortable with this, but also because she'll get the dresses for nothing when she's so desperately short of cash.

As Jess pulls back the curtain, Immie and I wriggle forwards to get a better view.

Cate swishes across the floor, and comes to a halt in front of us. 'So what do you think,' she says. 'And remember I want the truth this time,' she adds, but she can't hold her stern frown for long, because she's smiling so hard.

My nose begins to ache, and I scratch the dampness away from my bottom lashes. All I want to do is hug her, because she looks so lovely, and even better, so happy. But I can't risk getting running mascara all over the lace. I hear a loud sniff from Immie, and when she blows her nose, it's with the force of a gale. And then she sniffs again.

'So?' Cate laughs.

'Gorgeous,' I say. 'We're both in pieces here. What do you think?' I don't really have to ask, because her face says it all.

'I'm not sure I even want to try the others,' Cate says. 'I already know this is the one, because I cried in the fitting room as soon as I put it on.'

'So that's why you were so long.' Immie jokes. 'Any longer, I'd have been under the table.'

Cate stops by the full length mirror, and studies herself. 'I love the way the skirt's plain tulle, and yet the top's so pretty. And it's got those same really light sleeves as the other one.' She grins at Jess. 'Perfect for a September wedding, like you said the day of the shoot.'

Jess is watching from the other side of the shop, her lips in that pout she does when she's exceptionally satisfied. 'The others are here on the rail, if you want to flick through.'

Cate glides across the shop, holding the softly gathered skirt, and she and Jess examine the dresses. One by one Cate rejects them with a shake of her head, and then she turns to us.

'I can't believe it, I've found my dress. This is the one. How good is that?'

Immie lets out a low laugh. 'All in ten minutes flat, in less time than it took me to drink three cocktails. That's my kind of shopping.'

I decide not to point out that she's had way more than three, and instead I grab my phone and stagger to my feet. 'Shall we do a selfie to celebrate?'

'Great idea,' Cate cries, rushing over.

Jess picks up the cocktail jug. 'Then we'll have another drink and I'll call Sera down so we can sort the bridesmaids' dresses.'

39

At Brides by the Sea: My little pony and other stories

Choosing bridesmaids' dresses has a whole different feel this time around. With the new agreement with Cate underway, Jess is in total charge. Cate, Immie and I are back in a no-nonsense line on the sofa, sipping our refills, while Jess sorts the final details.

'Come on, Sera,' she says firmly, 'no hiding in the kitchen.'

Sera peeps around the corner at us, wrinkling her face. We wave at her as she sidles into view, thumbs shoved through the belt of her ripped denim shorts.

Cate widens her eyes at Sera's honey coloured legs. 'Is that tan real?'

'Yep,' Sera grins.

'Sera does all her design sketching on the beach,' I explain. 'Hence the sun burn on her nose and her knees.' It's hard to put into context the way Sera manages to avoid every box Jess tries to cram her into.

Sera tugs at a knot in her bleached blonde hair. 'I work best when I can smell the sea and hear the waves breaking on the beach.' She gives an apologetic shrug. 'Although I did go and sit in a meadow to work on my country designs.'

Despite years of effort, Jess has failed to tame Sera, and persuade her to work in the studio. She also shies away from dealing with clients, although she has consented to come down for the bridesmaids' part of this deal.

'So tell them about your bridesmaid designs, Sera,' Jess prompts.

Sera leans a shoulder against the wall, and hooks that telltale foot behind her leg. 'They're meant to have the same country feel as the bridal dresses. They're simple cotton, in different vintage styles, a range of plain and prints, designed to mix and match.'

As Jess wheels in a rail of brightly coloured dresses, I sense Cate's murmur of approval on one side of me, and Immie's slightly less enthusiastic grunt on the other.

'A bride chooses the prints and the styles, and then we'll have the dresses made up.' Jess says, as she plucks a red polka dot dress, and holds it next to a floral print one in pinks and reds.

'Yes!' Cate shouts.

She jumps up with a lurch that leaves Immie gawping at the splashes of English Garden she's spilled all over her jeans.

'The flowery fabric is just what I'd envisaged.' She takes hold of the pink and red one. 'That style. All the same. Short not long.' She looks almost as startled as we are at her decisiveness. 'It's perfect for my berry palette.'

This is the first I've heard of berry on her mood board, but whatever. They're a lot more 'Immie' than the nude chiffon Cate set her heart on last time we were here, which is something else we won't be mentioning either.

'Brill…' Sera twiddles with the strap of her crocheted over-vest. 'You can always add a petticoat, if you want something even more feminine.'

Immie hears the word petticoat and has an instant choking

fit. I'm busy slapping her on the back when I notice Jess disappearing towards the shop door. As she opens it I hear a man's voice, and a second later, Jess calls me.

'Poppy…' *Sotto voce* isn't usually Jess's thing, but for once she isn't shouting at the top of her voice. 'It's Rafe, he wants a quick word.'

Rafe? His name makes my stomach do a triple flip, but only because this is so unexpected. You know the kind of thing I mean? Like when you were little and your mum turned up in school time, and the surprise took your breath away. Because apart from that one foray to Jaggers, which I try never to talk about, the only place I ever see Rafe is at the farm. That's where he belongs. And him being anywhere else is plain-and-simple wrong. End of.

I slither to my feet, profoundly grateful that everyone is too busy to notice me tiptoeing away. As I reach the door Jess melts into the background, which believe me, is something she rarely does.

'Hi,' I say, willing my racing pulse to slow down, as I take in Rafe's open necked shirt and navy chinos. At least there isn't a farmer slogan to read today. 'Anything I can help with?' At the last minute I remember to add a shop girl smile.

'Not so much,' he says, holding something out to me. 'Your sandwich box, you left it in the office.'

'Thanks, I guess it's obvious it was mine,' I wince at the *My Little Pony* stickers, as I take the box from him, then decide not to be apologetic. 'Actually I like the unicorn one best. Cate's kids gave it to me for my birthday.'

Rafe's bemused head shake reminds me I'm gabbling.

'I was in town anyway,' he says, 'I thought you might need it.'

'Thanks,' I pop the box under my arm, ready to open the door to show him out. 'That's really thoughtful of you.' In what universe can you not get by without a sandwich box?

He narrows his eyes, and his lips twist. 'I'll be honest, I was curious to see where you were too. It's an amazing place isn't it?'

'Fabulous,' I laugh, satisfied he's admitted the interest. 'For a guy who hates weddings as much as you do, I'd say it's a nightmare shop.'

'It's pretty scary,' he laughs, 'especially all that screaming I can hear. Is someone murdering a bridesmaid?'

'Brides rarely choose dresses quietly.' I say, with a grin. 'Cate and Immie are in there, whooping it up as we speak. Are you coming in?' It's more of a dare then an invitation.

'You have to be joking,' he says.

Of course I am. 'Obviously.' Why the hell did I think he might want to sit on a sofa with banshees in the first place?

'I brought these too, I couldn't find any *My Little Pony* paper, so I used the Cornish Guardian.' He pushes a bundle of newspaper into my hands. 'Roses, from the garden, mind the thorns.'

The scent is unmistakeable, and as I peer in at the blooms I can't help smiling. 'Albertine?'

'Of course,' he says, 'they won't last, but I thought you'd like them anyway.' He makes a grab for the door latch. 'I'll let myself out, enjoy your party.'

As I hover by the door, watching him walk off and clutching my parcel, something inside me slowly deflates. Why would I be feeling disappointed? I make a detour to leave the roses and the sandwich box at the bottom of the stairs, then hurry back to the others.

'Where did you disappear to?' Cate asks. 'We're all sorted here, this has been the best hour ever.' She's back on the sofa, tapping furiously on her iPad. 'The bridesmaids need to be measured, that's all. And, thanks to today's arrangement, and a lot of cutting back, current calculations show I'm only committed to spending five grand more on this wedding than we originally intended.'

'Great,' I say, unsure if this is good news or bad. As for how happy (or otherwise) Liam will be with this, who knows?

40

At Brides by the Sea: Filling up the diary

'You have to admit, Rafe is wonderful groom material,' Jess says, as she puts the bridesmaids' dresses back onto the rail.

Luckily for me, when I come down to the shop again after putting my roses in water upstairs, I'm the only one left to hear this, so I pretend I haven't.

'He's single, sexy, he's got acres coming out of his ears,' she goes on.

I had a horrible feeling she wouldn't let this go.

'Know anyone who wants a grumpy workaholic farmer who wouldn't recognise fun if it hit him in the hay bales?' I say, to put a stop to it.

She ignores my input entirely. 'What's more Rafe's thoughtful enough to drive ten miles simply to return a forgotten sandwich box.' Her voice soars loud enough for people in the street to hear. 'You won't get better than that Poppy Pickering.'

If Jess hadn't just practically donated a wedding dress and eight bridesmaids' dresses to my best friend, I'd definitely have told her to eff off. Especially as she said something similar about Jules not so long ago.

But it's better not to fight Jess head on. 'The timing's not right,' I say, making my voice flat enough to close this down. 'Thanks for the heads up, but I'll pass on this one, because actually, I'm fine as I am.'

Even as I add the afterthought, my jaw is dropping as I hear myself say the words. They may have slipped out inadvertently, but I think I just accidentally implied that I'm happy with how things are in my life. There was a time last winter when I doubted I'd ever be okay again, but somehow feeling better snuck up on me while I was looking the other way. These last few months I've been way too busy to dwell on how sad my life is, and now I come to think of it again, I'm not that broken person any more. Somewhere down the line, the fragments of my life have glued themselves back together again. Yes, the result is a completely different life, in new places, doing things I never imagined I was capable of. But to be honest, as I am now, with all the weddings, and making the cakes I love, and filling in at the shop which is super busy, I doubt I'd have time to fit in a boyfriend, even if I did want one.

Thinking back, going out with Brett was always pretty time consuming. When I first moved in with him, he was always the one who decided what we did. I went along with that, because I was the one who'd parachuted into his life. What's more I'm not sure he'd have had it any other way. He was one of those guys who functioned best when he was in charge. Then as the years went by, and he got promotions at work, there were lots of functions where he needed a plus one. Admittedly the dresses I got to wear were great, but my main role was to smile and stay silent. Believe me, being bored out of my skull, whilst appearing to be totally engrossed, was something I nailed for Brett.

Then when he was away with work, which was more and more,

I used to run around at home on his behalf. At the time, I didn't think about it. It was natural for me to sort out his dry cleaning, take his car to be valeted after I'd run him to the airport, and buy him presents for his PA. There were hundreds of jobs that he was too busy to do, because his work was so important. But because I was 'only making cakes', as he always put it, everything else was down to me. On the rare occasions when we had free time together, he'd fill the diary months ahead with things he wanted to do, and I'd tag along. It was all down to him, because he was the important person, with the important job, and the important salary, and the important future. Looking back, I'm not sure I mattered at all.

At the time I assumed I was happy. I suppose having been brought up by my mum on her own after my dad died, getting my very own partner seemed like an important step towards creating the family unit I never had. Having my own guy was a way of providing security, not just for me, but for my mum too. And then there was everything else that came with Brett. I mean who wouldn't be happy with floor to ceiling sea views, shiny cars, a walk in wardrobe, flowers for special days and jewellery for birthdays? It took me years to work out the Interflora orders came automatically via a phone app. And when it was all taken away from me over night, I was so shocked, that I still didn't stop to ask the question about whether that life was the one I wanted. As for how good it was, I'm beginning to wonder. Because I might be on my own now, but I've got time for my friends. I'm really busy, life's full of things that I decide to do, and what's more, I'm good. And I'm damned pleased it's finally hit me.

'Great to hear you're happy as you are Poppy,' Jess's voice cuts through my pondering with the subtlety of someone wielding an axe. 'But don't come crying to me when someone else snaps Rafe up, because they will,' She snaps that last bit with a certainty I'd rather not hear.

Now she's brought it up, I hate the idea of Rafe getting snapped up. He's perfectly fine as he is. It's also highly unlikely he'd attract anyone, given he goes out of his way to be disagreeable at every turn, which seems to be a crucial factor Jess is overlooking here.

'I'm glad we're on own at last,' she says, in a way that makes my heart sink. 'I've been wanting a word all week.'

Shit. I've carefully avoided being alone with Jess since Josie's wedding, and it's only today's excitement that's made me drop my guard. She's going to talk about my dress. I know it.

Making a big thing of picking up the shoes Cate borrowed, from the fitting room floor, I rack my brains for a distraction. This will have to be good.

'Can you think of any other eligible guys in the area I could go out with then, Jess? Definitely not farmers though.' It's an attempt to divert her from where I know she's hell bent on going. 'Anyone single and sexy at Jaggers? The ones who you don't want, obviously.' Asking for introductions to Jess's rejects is a measure of how desperate I am not to get onto Jess's chosen subject.

Jess doesn't falter. She completely bypasses the juicy decoy I've tossed her, sticks to her guns, and comes straight out with it. 'You need to sell your wedding dress Poppy.'

'Fuck,' I mutter. 'I knew you were going to say that.'

She's straight back at me, with the speed of a top rank squash player. 'And do you have a problem with the idea?'

The diamanté stilettos I just picked up clatter onto the floor boards as I sink onto the sofa. 'No, I know you're right,' I sigh, wishing Jess would plonk a tumbler of neat gin in my hand. But she doesn't.

'Any other dress than this, I wouldn't give a damn, you could keep it in the dress store forever.' Jess stabs the air with that bloody Swarovski crystal pen of hers. 'But thanks to the current media circus surrounding Josie and her wedding, your dress would fetch at least ten times its value if you sell it now. Possibly more.' She narrows her eyes at me. 'You're never ever going to wear that dress yourself. Keeping it is a way of clinging onto the past that's not there any more. You need to move on. Now's the time to let go.'

'I know,' I say, pulling hard on my stump of a pony tail. This is the first week I've been able to scrape my hair into a scrunchy since I chopped it all off. That dress belongs to the girl with the long blonde ponytail who spent at least three hours of every day working out how she could get Brett King to marry her, and I'm not that person any more.

'It would be completely unprofessional of me to let you dither,' Jess says. 'If you don't sell immediately, you'll miss the opportunity. Basically, it's now or never.'

If she doesn't stop chomping on that sparkly biro, she's going to end up with a mouthful of diamonds.

Stretching upwards, I pull out my scrunchy, and recapture my pony tail. 'It's just hard. I bought that dress with the money my mum left me, which pretty much amounted to everything she'd ever saved in her life. Somehow selling it seems like a betrayal, even though she never knew I'd bought it.'

Jess backs up against the desk, and pushes herself up onto it. 'Try it another way then.' She crosses her legs, and takes a breath so deep, I suspect that whatever bend I'm driving her around, she's pretty close to reaching the end. 'Is there anything really important you can think of to spend the money on, something you especially want? A new car, maybe?' The smile she gives me is the one she reserves for brides who are being bloody impossible, but I'm past caring.

I stare at her blankly. Brett was so proud of splashing his cash around, but the weird thing is, since Brett and I split up, I haven't missed the material things at all. I gladly shoved all my evening dresses off to the Cat Rescue shop, without as much as a whimper. Even my little yellow car is part of who I am now.

'Something that will really make a difference?' Jess is pushing me. 'This is lucky money. Try to think of a way to spend it that would make you happy, to spur you on to sell.' She purses her lips. 'Think of it as a windfall profit – if you don't cash it in right now, later it won't be there at all.'

Something that will make a difference…to someone I care about…

I hammer my knuckles on my head. When it hits me, it's like the clatter of bridesmaids running down the street. It's like divine symmetry. Once it's hit me, I can't imagine what took me so long. This lucky profit from the wedding dress I don't need can help Cate and Liam with the shortfall for their wedding. Perfect. My mum loved Cate. And selling for someone else's benefit makes the whole sordid unworn dress part feel better. Something good coming out of something bad and all that.

'Okay, I'll go for it. I'll sell the dress.' My voice is so squeaky, it sounds like it belongs to someone else. What's more, I'm already talking as if the dress doesn't belong to me any more. That's progress in itself. 'How am I going to do it?'

Jess leaps off the desk, and the next moment she engulfs me in the bear hug of the decade. I might have been about to turn tearful, but the heady cloud of scent Jess brings with her saves me.

'You need to sell the dress on eBay,' she goes on seamlessly. 'Seven day listing, finishing next Friday, at one. That way all the brides can do their final bidding in their lunch hours.' She's on her feet again. 'Come on, bring your phone, we'll do the pictures now.'

41

In the old house at Daisy Hill Farm: Identical chicks

'So which playlist do you want…*No Cupcakes 'Til The Cleaning's Done–The Fast Mix*, or *Falling In Love…At A Hundred Miles an Hour*?' I ask Rafe. I'm eager to get to work, and giving him this choice might be a way of easing him in.

We're marching through cobweb central, a.k.a. the orangerie, towards the drawing room, and as this morning's task is to clear both, a zippy sound track is non-negotiable.

'Let me guess. They both begin with *Don't Stop Me Now*?' he asks, as he saunters through into the dimly lit room, and begins to undo the shutters. He doesn't need to wrinkle his nose. I already know that's his most hated track in the world ever.

'All my playlists start with that,' I say. Don't ask me why, it just seems like a suitably up-beat way to begin. No surprise that down-beat Rafe can't stand it.

'How about neither?' he says, as shafts of sunlight flood across the floor, illuminating large shapes, covered in dust sheets.

I stick out my chin. 'Not an option.'

'There's news…' He raises an eyebrow. 'I can't give you the gossip *and* compete with Mr Mercury.'

'Gossip?' It isn't a word I'd associate with Rafe, but I'm a sucker for it. 'Go on then. Spill and we'll leave the soundtrack until later.' If I'm forfeiting my mood enhancing music, this better be good.

'That woman came round again yesterday.' He looks exceptionally pleased with himself considering he's told me absolutely nothing.

'Which one? I need more clues than that.'

He scratches his head. 'Bad tempered, grumpy, unreasonable…'

I purse my lips to nip in my smile, because he could be describing himself here. 'Keep going.'

'Bag the size of a feed sack, boyfriend tearing his hair out…'

Got it. 'That has to be Nicole. And husband-to-be, Chas.'

'Bloody hell.' Rafe shudders. 'That's one brave man.'

'He's very much in love.' I add, attempting to explain. 'They're the camping half of our double booking. What did they want?'

Rafe frowns. 'I never got to find out. They got out of the car in the middle of a blazing row, so I hid in the feed store to give them some space, and the next thing I knew they were driving away.'

Rafe pulls a face. 'My mum drummed it into me to stick up for women every time, but seriously, this one's bad news. When Jet wandered up to say hello, she tried to bash him with her bag.'

Worse and worse. 'I'll give them a ring later, and check everything's okay,' I say. 'Nicole gets over-wrought, not that that's any excuse for lashing out at Jet.' Poor Jet's such a gentle dog. 'When I explained to Chas about the double booking he was fine. Originally they'd only booked the field but not the cottages, so they weren't expecting exclusive use.'

'It's a good thing the other couple are the ones using the garden,' Rafe says, putting my thoughts into words.

'Very true.' For one rare time, I agree with him, but I'm not going to let it go to his head. As I lift the corner of one of the dust sheets to see what we're about to deal with I get plenty of ammunition to bring him back into line. 'Rafe, what exactly are you hiding under these sheets?' More fool me for expecting furniture. I look more closely. 'Is this the tractor engine you had in the kitchen?'

He gives me a withering look. 'How can you possibly think that? This one's completely different.'

'Excuse me for not being able to tell two engines apart.' I'm spluttering with indignation.

His sniff is dismissive. 'You're the same with the cows. But give you a bit of lace or anything with icing on, and it's another story.'

He's so serious, it's hard to keep a straight face. 'Actually I've got the cow thing sorted now. I used to think they were all black and white or brown, with slobbery noses, but lately I can tell them apart.' Much to my own astonishment, not that I'll be admitting this in town any time soon. The ability to recognise cows is never going to figure large on my CV. 'And I know every one of Henrietta's children by name,' I add, happy to take credit here. Despite the fact they spend a large part of every day trying to sit on my desk it was damned hard learning to recognise thirteen identical chicks, just from the differences in their beaks and claws and sprouting feathers.

'They're not children, Poppy.' From the way he's shaking his head and closing his eyes, he's definitely talking down to me here.

I sigh, and give in. 'Okay, offspring,' I say. On balance I'd rather appease than set off yet another of our recurring arguments. To hide the climb down I go back to looking under sheets, and now I'm the one shaking my head. 'This is such a man cave Rafe, have you got anything in here other than bits of rotting tractor? And why the hell aren't they in a barn for chrissakes?'

His loud squawk of protest is predictable as he whips the sheets off enough stacks of metal and cogs and chaos to fill a large garage. 'These are all valuable vintage parts you're talking about.' At least he has the decency to look vaguely sheepish. 'Now they're all uncovered, there do seem to be lot of them. As it happens, there is something else in here that might make up for these.'

As Rafe crosses to the far end of the room, and his boots clatter on the scuffed floor, my optimism takes a nose dive. Whatever I'd envisaged this morning, it wasn't moving a scrap yard. I'm starting to doubt that the filthy windows will ever come clean again. As for the peeling walls, they're looking so much worse than they ever did on that afternoon in winter. In the full glare of summer sun, the task is looking more hopeless by the second.

'Okay, here we go.' Rafe begins to tug at the faded fabric that's covering the biggest pile yet.

Before I came here to help with the weddings, the worst problem I faced at work was trying to make a seven tier cake stand up. And I know it might have been hard keeping all the domestic balls in the air at home to keep Brett happy. I probably only realised how much of a strain that was once I didn't have to do it any more. Even when I was in London, all I had to do was design food that was nutritious and attractive. Okay, the clients were prestigious and demanding, but nothing that came before was anything compared to the challenges we face here.

We've already had double bookings, water-logged weddings, a bride giving birth, and the season's barely begun. Admittedly, the buzz I get from making things work is huge, but let's face it, things working out were largely accidental. Deep down, I'm not sure I'm up to the job. And I've got a horrible feeling I'm going to fall flat on my face by imagining I can make these rooms anywhere near wedding-ready.

Meanwhile, Rafe is carrying on like some kind of conjurer, about to produce something jaw-droppingly astonishing. Whereas I've given up all hope there might be furniture under this sheet, and I'm braced for more horrors. So when a corner of polished wood emerges, it's a pleasant surprise. I'm preparing myself for a sideboard, but as the cover slides back and the wood stretches further, my eyes widen.

'Is that a piano?' If I'm stating the obvious, it's only because it's the last thing I expected. 'It's massive.' That's an understatement rather than an exaggeration. I'm thanking my lucky stars it's not yet more pieces of tractor.

Rafe is buffing up the crackled varnish of the top with what looks like a candlewick bedspread. 'It's a Steinway grand. My grandmother's.' His eyes are strangely dreamy as he turns the lock, and lifts the lid. 'Luckily for me it thrives in the same atmosphere as bits of old tractor.' The grin he sends me is half defiance, half mischief.

'It's fabulous, people love pianos, it'll add so much atmosphere.' This room's going to need all the help it can get, and stage setting doesn't get much better than a grand piano.

'It hasn't been tuned for six months.' He taps one note, and screws up his face as the sound resonates around the walls. As he spreads his fingers wide and brings his hands down onto the keys, he's hitting black note as well as white ones. He tilts his head, narrowing his eyes as he listens to the chord as it echoes. 'If it's not too badly off key, maybe we'll try a tune.'

'What, you play?' If my voice has gone all high, it's because I'm so taken aback. The last thing I expected was that the piano was going to be used. Not that Rafe shouldn't be able to play, it's just I don't know anyone else who can. And somehow it's so much at odds with the whole rough farmer-in-a-tractor image.

'A little.' He shrugs, but the way he brings his outstretched fingers down and hits a whole lot more chords, he's obviously understating things. Big time.

Shit. I jump as my phone beeps in the pocket of my denim jacket. It's a whole fifteen minutes since I last looked at it, and that has to be a record. Since my wedding dress listing went up last weekend, it's barely been out of my hand. The bid that caused the beep has pushed the figure so high, I have to gulp for air, because my head is spinning.

'Everything okay, Red?' Rafe's voice comes from behind the piano, where he's already settled onto a stool. 'Come over here.'

'Why R-red?' What the hell is he calling me that for.

'Your name and your dress for starters…' He begins. 'The ends of your hair…I know you're really a blue Poppy, but for a minute back there the general impression was red.'

Walking into that was my own silly fault. I shouldn't have teamed my red daisy skirt with a scarlet T-shirt, and then gone puce in the face.

'I can substitute it for Blue if you'd rather?' he offers, suddenly all laid back and languid.

If he carries on like this I'll take refuge on my phone. 'Do what the hell you want, are we going to get on?' I snap.

'One song, and then we'll be straight back to work, I promise.' Sitting down, one foot in front of him on the piano pedal, his long legs bent, hands resting on the keys, he's suddenly all chilled.

I lean my elbows on the silky wood of the piano edge. 'Great idea, except you don't have any music.' Not that I'm trying to spoil the party, but someone needs to point out the obvious.

The corners of Rafe's eyes crinkle as he laughs. 'Not a problem.' And then he begins to play.

The notes are small at first, then they expand to fill the room. As the warm wood of the piano top vibrates under my wrists, goosebumps ripple up my spine. I'm torn between watching Rafe's hands travelling up and down the keyboard, and watching his face. All dark lashes and cheekbones, the stubble shading his chin, and the lines that slice down his cheeks. *I can't help…*Even as the tingling spreads across my scalp, I'm lip syncing, silently mouthing the words I somehow know as well as if they'd been inscribed on my mind's eye. *…falling in love with you…*

If I stopped to think about it, I'd curse him for his dangerous choice of song, but I don't. Instead I close my eyes and sway into the crescendos, leaning closer when the music fades, half opening my eyes to watch a broad tanned wrist coming towards me, as he stretches to hit the high notes. My chest is whirling like there's a tornado passing through, and I know it's all horribly mixed up, but just for a minute I'm Lizzie Bennet, seeing Pemberley for the first time, and tumbling head over heels in love with Colin Firth, striding out of the lake, soaking wet. Except round here that would be a duck pond. And just when I think I can't bear to listen any more, because my heart is so wrung out, the music changes tempo.

Next thing he's crashing into Bohemian Rhapsody, and those dark brown eyes have locked fast onto mine. I'm grinning at him for all I'm worth, and laughing, and he's grinning right back at me, daring me to look away. All the way through, right up until the last tiny notes fade to nothing.

42

In my flat at Brides by the Sea: Early birds and parcel tape

You know those times when you make fresh coffee for breakfast, and you're aching for a caffeine hit, but there are so many butterflies battering in your chest you give up after one sip?

That's me. It's five past seven on the morning my dress auction is ending. The current highest bid is already huge. I'm in my tiny living room, perching in a splash of sun on the sofa edge, staring at my cup full of number five strength Italian blend, watching it go cold beside an untouched croissant. How I'm going to make it through until the auction ends at lunchtime without chewing my hands right off, I've no idea.

The good news is: I have a plan. I'm going to lock my phone in my desk as soon as I reach the farm office. First I've got to go over some final details with next Wednesday's bride. Then I'm going to grab the scrubbing machine Rafe appeared with late yesterday afternoon, and attack the floor in the orangerie.

Right now I have twenty minutes before I need to leave. My dress – it still is mine, if only for the next few moments – is hanging in its cover. There's a box, bags and parcel tape all waiting. Plenty of time to say my last goodbyes and pack up the parcel, so it's ready to post as soon as payment comes through after the auction.

I fill my lungs and hold my breath as I slide back the cover for the last time. My tummy clenches as I run a finger over the soft tulle, and my head is starting to spin when a clatter of feet on the stairs yanks me back to earth.

'Poppy, are you there?'

As I turn Cate's already in the doorway.

Without bothering to say hello, she launches straight in. 'Liam found my secret stash of credit card statements and he's going ape.'

'Shit, that's not good.' As I make my understatement I turn and inch towards her, making myself as large as I can in an effort to hide the dress behind me. With any luck she won't see beyond the crazy flower print of my jumpsuit.

'We've never argued this badly.' If she tugs the belt of her lightweight mac any tighter, she'll cut herself in two. 'Not even when he cleaned his bike with my two hundred quid Nicole...' Her wail subsides midsentence.

Liam's buffing blunder is memorable enough for every detail to be etched on my brain. 'Liam polishing chrome with your Nicole Farhi cami was partly your fault,' I say, picking up the thread. 'You were the one who put it next to his dusters in the laundry pile.' I mean, who, apart from Cate, irons bike cloths? It was hardly Liam's fault that he couldn't tell the difference. For my money, most guys would have made the same mistake.

But Cate's not listening, because her distracted gaze has somehow locked on a point somewhere beyond my left ear.

'Is that Josie's dress?' she asks.

With the wall to wall coverage downstairs, it's an obvious get-out I'd overlooked.

'Josie's?' As I open and close my mouth like a guppy, I consider where lying has landed Cate, and decide to come clean. 'Nope,

238

this one's mine.' In response to Cate opening and closing her mouth back at me, I stick my chin in the air, and carry on. 'I'm selling it because I don't need it any more. And I'm donating the proceeds to your wedding fund.'

'You and Brett were…?' Cate grimaces, and as she comes towards me it's obvious she's completely missed the bit about the money going towards her wedding. 'Oh shit, I had no idea…my poor lamb…why on earth didn't you say?' Before I reply she's squeezed me into the bear-hug of the decade. When she finally releases her grip I'm dizzy all over again.

Glancing at my watch, I move across and slip the cover back over the dress, pull up the zip, and it's gone. 'Actually I need to pack it up before I go.' I'll have to tell her about the wedding donation again a bit later, as she's obviously missed it. So much for my heartfelt goodbye-to-the-dress ceremony, although it's probably better this way.

'Here, let me help.' Cate picks up the packaging and puts it on the sofa. 'Mind that coffee, I'm so damned pleased I came round,' she says, bustling across to where the dress is hanging. 'Imagine if you'd had to do this on your own.'

She likes to take charge, and this morning I'm not going to stop her.

Ten minutes later as I throw the dress onto the back seat of the car it's nothing more than a cardboard box swathed in a hundred metres of parcel tape.

43

In the office at Daisy Hill Farm: Ragged jeans and late bids

The dress looks amazing on the laptop screen.

Beautiful Seraphina East Wedding Dress, size 14, as worn by Josie Redman

'Auction ending soon' the banner says. If my eyes are pricking as I read it, it's probably down to tiredness. However much I threw my sheet around and punched the pillow last night, I never made the transition into sleep. As the seconds tick away on the eBay clock, and I flick through the pictures one last time, my hand quivers over the track pad on my laptop.

Ivory lace, silk and tulle, soft vintage style wedding dress

There are sixteen photos, views from every possible angle, yet none of them quite capture the fabulous cut. The whispering way it will transform a woman to a bride. Shut away in the office, the door is firmly closed on the heat of the day, the breeze, and the world outside. The last thing I want is an interruption, although I'm pretty safe, as Rafe's gone off with a rep, and Immie's in town. After seven days of build up, I can barely believe this ending is about to happen.

Seventy bids and counting. It's already five times the price I paid for it, but that's the rub. eBay is where items find their true value, where the strongest will wins. And there are some gritty buyers here. Each time the price flips higher I hitch in my breath, thinking of how I can help Cate and Liam, and know I must go through with this.

Purchased from the designer's sample sale. Unworn, with original tags.

Unworn. If you only knew how much Jess and I agonised over that word. Whether it implied bad luck. But then there's the clincher that over rides the rest.

Rare sample. As worn by Josie Redman.

Enough said. The picture of Josie in her version is the whole reason this auction is going wild.

'What's going on Pops?' Immie's husky shout precedes her as the office door bursts open. 'Cate just rang me, I'd had my phone off all morning.'

I should have known Cate would tell her. And if I'd wanted to be on my own, I should have locked the door. Finding the door ajar, Henrietta struts across the tiles, complete with a procession of her now adolescent and much less fluffy chicks. Then Jet follows, and flops on the floor, with a loud grunt.

'Definitely no hens on the desk.' I nudge the first flapping mountaineer onto the floor, because you have to make a stand about these things early on. 'It's no big deal Immie.' I make my croak as casual as I can. 'I'm just selling a wedding dress I bought a while ago.'

'Bloody hell, let me see.' She's already butted between me and the screen. 'Jeez, have you seen the price of it? That's ridiculous.'

'That's the idea.' I say. I don't often roll my eyes but I do now, as I push away another hen, nudge Immie out of the way, and muscle my way back to the trackpad.

'And it's ending right now,' she says, helpfully.

'What's ending?'

Fuck, it's Rafe. That's all we need. The ragged jeans, and beaten up boots I catch out of the corner of my eye tell me he's come in too, to hover. This wasn't meant to be a show.

'That's the wedding dress you've been watching all week.' He's right behind me now, his voice rising anxiously. And who knew he'd even noticed? 'Bloody hell, it's not for you is it?'

'Poppy's *selling* a dress.' Immie says. She's really surpassing herself today. 'On eBay.'

Rafe turns on Immie. 'I can see it's eBay, I'm not…'

'For someone else,' I add in the loudest voice I can, giving Immie a sharp prod in the ribs.

'Okay, Pop's is selling a dress *for someone*,' Immie glares at me. 'And the auction's ending, like, any minute.'

'Great, well that's all good then.' Despite Rafe's dismissive laugh, he's leaning in for a closer look.

My heart is banging as I see thirty seconds flash up on the screen. I may possibly have stopped breathing sometime back when Immie came in. The price is changing, going up, and up. And suddenly, out of nowhere, I'm gripped by the will to hang on. The flash of a feeling that, actually, I don't want to sell at all. That the last seven days has just been me going through the motions. And then my hands are flying across the keys, and I'm typing numbers in the offer box. A monster figure. A line of noughts so long it will blast every other bid out of the park.

'Pops, why the hell are you bidding?' Immie's voice is coming through a haze. 'Are you crazy?'

Five seconds are never longer than at the end of an eBay auction. My pulse is hammering in my ears, as I slide the cursor over the Submit Bid button. One click will save my dress. One tiny click will put me back where I started. My finger freezes…

In the last moments a frenzy of final bids hit the mix, and the price jerks up. Up. Up. And then it's finished, and I breathe again.

'Auction over.'

As Immie reads the prompt, the dress disappears from the screen, and I sag back in my chair.

I didn't bid. The only chance I have of keeping my dress now is if the buyer doesn't pay.

'Jeez, how tense was that?' Immie's wiping the sweat off her brow with her wrist.

There's a ping as an email lands in my inbox, then another. As I open the first my tummy lurches as I see the final price of the sale, then as I open the next, and take in a PayPal payment, my chest deflates.

'Shit,' I murmur. 'They've paid already. How fast was that?'

'Well done, Pops.' Immie drags me to my feet. 'Upwards and onwards.'

As she flings her arms around me, over her shoulder I see Jess and Cate dashing towards us across the yard. A second later Jess's loafers are clattering on the floor tiles.

'I can't believe we missed it.' Running flat out from her car has left Jess gasping. 'There were cows all over the road at Juniper Bottom.'

'Come here, sweets, you're so brave.' Cate takes over as Immie's hug ends.

Jess is beaming. 'That's what I call a result. I saw the final figure on my phone.' She winks at me. 'Who's bought it?'

After unwinding Cate's arms, then pausing for an air kiss with Jess, I go back to the desk, where the address labels are waiting. 'The lucky bride's called glitterknickers28,' I say, scrolling through the email and grabbing a pen. Although I try hard to stop my hand shaking, as I write the address my caps are coming out very wobbly. 'She's from Slough.'

'Great, is this the dress?' Jess scoops the parcel from the side of the filing cabinet, slides it onto the desk, and a moment later, she's taped the labels into place. 'Cate's brought you a picnic lunch, so I'll leave you all to it. Don't worry, I'll get this dispatched for you right away.' Two air kisses later she's off across the yard, package in her outstretched arms.

Cate blinks at me, with a bemused smile. 'What a powerhouse. If you weren't careful she could take over.'

I'm too busy smiling about the irony of Cate's observation to dwell on my dress heading in the direction of St Aidan on the back seat of Jess's car.

Immie's already moved on too. 'Did Jess say something about lunch?' She pats her stomach. 'All this excitement, I'm starving.'

Rafe swings out into the sunshine. 'Feel free to use the garden at the farmhouse for lunch, ladies.' He sends a parting grin over his shoulder. 'Sorry for crashing the eBay party, I only dropped in to say I'm off for a tractor part. See you later.'

44

In the garden at Daisy Hill Farm:
Party food and pained frowns

'Sparkling elderflower and raspberry?' The jewel pink liquid fizzes as Immie splashes it into glasses.

Okay, the champagne flutes are plastic. And we're sitting on a checked quilt cover from the boot of Cate's car. But we've thrown it out on the lawn in the shade of the apple tree, and the scent of the roses rambling up the garden wall is wafting in the warm air.

'There you go.' Immie passes me my drink. 'Bottoms up.'

'Cheers.' I take a sip, desperate for a sugar hit. 'Actually, I haven't been hungry all week, and now I'm starving.'

Immie looks at me, with what I call her professor expression. 'Hypoglycaemia, low blood sugar, very common after stress,' she mutters. 'Don't worry, when we've had our picnic nibbles and Cate's gone back to work, we'll get you a double chip butty from the pub.'

Cate strides across the terrace, clutching a stack of party food. As the adrenalin of the auction drains away, the lazy buzz of bees is making my eyes droop. Although the sun is dappled under the leaf canopy, Immie and I are melting to a collective grease spot. She's kicked off her sneakers and has sweat patches on her T-shirt, and I've slipped off my flip flops and rolled up the legs of my jump suit. Whereas Cate, as ever, is cool and unruffled in her cream courts and pistachio linen dress. At least she's lost the mac she was wearing earlier.

'Hope you don't mind alcohol-free fizz?' Cate hands us the boxes of food, then smoothes her skirt, and slides out of her heels, as she prepares to sit down. 'I need a clear head for this afternoon's finance meeting. I've screwed up so badly with my own calculations, I can't do the same at work.'

Cate managing the county budget when she let her own run so far out of control makes the mind boggle. In financial terms, her wedding is the equivalent of Cornwall Council sending their own astronaut into outer space.

'Don't worry, you're still going to have a fab day. We promise we'll still come even if you've cancelled the spa tent.' I'm making a joke of it, but that was only one of the later wild and expansive items we crossed off her list. 'Rafe's offered to put the friendliest calves and sheep in pens too, so the kids can have their fluffy animal fix.'

'Rafe's such a lamb these days.' Cate's narrow eyed glance is too searching for my liking, but luckily it softens to a grateful smile. 'And Liam says he can't thank you enough for offering to help with your windfall. I rang him at break, and we're good again.' She bends to squeeze my hand. 'I can't believe how far apart Liam and I were on this. I mean, when is the right moment to tell someone your wedding dreams?'

'Don't sweat it,' Immie says, 'but I bet if he'd had a whiff of your wedding wish list when you first met him at rugby coaching, he'd have started running and he wouldn't have stopped.'

'Maybe you should've shared your wedding vision that first

246

time you jumped him behind the changing rooms?' I'm teasing, but Cate's taking me seriously.

'We were too busy hiding from my kids,' she says, then catches sight of my grin. 'We'll pay you back, I promise. '

'No problem, I'm happy to do it,' I say, because I mean it. 'And I know my mum would be happy too. She saw you so often she loved you almost as much as if you'd been hers.' I add quickly, 'you too, Immie.'

Immie laughs her loud guffaw. 'At least she got paid for looking after you, Cate. My nan just used to shove me at her over the garden fence, then leg it to the Goose and Duck.'

Although my mum never minded that. Somehow Cate and Immie filling the cottage with noise made up for it just being me and my mum on our own.

Cate gazes at the climbing roses. 'I know it's much bigger, but this place reminds me a lot of your mum's garden.'

'True.' Immie nods in agreement. 'Without the downside of having my gran next door, singing her way back from the pub every night.' Her grin is rueful.

'You two have always been here for me in a way Brett never was,' I say.

Immie butts in. 'Dickhead of the Decade you mean? Proposing, and then snogging the face off some slag? It's way worse than we thought.'

Not that I'm defending him, but I need to explain, at least a bit. 'He never actually went down on one knee – one day he suddenly started saying we shouldn't put off getting married, and I saw the dress and grabbed it.'

Cate shakes her head. 'No-one can blame you for being enthusiastic, you'd been desperate for him to ask you for years.'

Nothing like best friends for home truths. I wasn't aware I'd been quite that obvious. 'Brett was under the impression the Chamber of Commerce wanted their top brass to have wives on their arms. It was nothing more than that.' That sounds cynical,

247

I know, but sadly, it's true. 'Getting married was a necessary evil for Brett. He couldn't reach the dizzy heights he was destined for as a single guy.'

Cate's face wrinkles into a pained frown. 'Then when reality kicked in, he cheated on you to get out of the wedding?'

'Something like that,' I shrug. There's no point dragging up the worst details. 'I mentioned I'd been looking at dresses, and the next thing I knew he was *in flagrante* all over Facebook. I guess he wasn't ready to commit.'

'Low life.' Immie spits.

The sigh I give is resigned. 'Now I've got some distance, I can see that Brett liked having someone to be in awe of him, and run round after him, but it was never two way traffic. You two were my support. To be honest, I could never rely on Brett.'

'That's right…' Cate says. 'If ever you had a crisis, he was always spectacularly absent. Like when your mum died.'

'Exactly.' I stare at the bubbles rising in my drink. 'In many ways, I'm no more alone now than when I was with Brett. And the dress was all part of me believing I had something I didn't. It's best that it's gone.'

As Cate kneels down beside me, I catch the gloss of nylon stretched across her knees. Of all of us, only Cate could fulfil the requirement for a senior female executive, and still be wearing tights when it's baking hot.

Immie grabs a pack of canapés from the pile of boxes, smacking her lips as she tears off the wrapper. 'Oooo, thanks Cate, my favourite. Saint Michael, patron saint of yummy food.'

As I pick up the next pack to open, the signage is achingly familiar. 'They're still doing these same Luxury Bite-size Open Sandwiches then?' I squint more closely at the contents, and sure enough, they're the ones I worked on, when I was in London. 'I helped design these.' I've probably claimed the credit for this a thousand times before. 'The grape garnishes on the brie and cranberry ones were down to me, and the chopped chives on the smoked salmon and cream cheese ones.' It's ridiculous that I still feel proud.

Immie pops one into her mouth. 'Take it from me, still truly delish,' she says, licking her fingers and reaching for another.

Funny, it seems like light years ago. 'Back then I had such a battle to include pastrami, because people didn't know what it was.' Given Immie's blank look, she still hasn't got a clue, even though she just downed three in succession. But that's rural living for you.

'If they have any jobs for tasters, or psychological assessors, I'm in.' Immie laughs.

I catch my breath, because there's an unexpected opportunity to say what I've been trying to get around to for a few days now. 'Actually, I emailed my old boss last week.' Instead of the roar of protest I'd anticipated there's a big silent space, so I rush on. 'Just to see if there might be any openings.'

Cate's eyebrows descend into a worried frown. 'Why do that when there's so much going for you here?'

That's a question I've been asking myself too, especially this last week when I've been too wound up to sleep. But I need to face reality. 'Yours is almost the last Daisy Hill Farm wedding, Cate – and that's only a few weeks away, in case you'd forgotten.' Even if it's slipped Cate's notice, I'm very aware that once she's married I'll be back to existing from the cakes I bake. Baking cakes is what I love doing, but I'm not sure I've built up enough business to survive in the long term. 'A new start might be good for me.' I'm saying it tentatively, because moving back to a job in the food industry would terrify the pants off me. But in another way, it might put me back to where I started before I made the mistake of moving in with Brett, and I'll only have lost seven years of my life. 'I doubt there'll be anything though, all I've had so far is out of office replies.'

Cate raises her eyebrows. 'In that case, we'll talk about this again if there are any developments.' She sighs. 'And make sure you let us know the minute you hear anything. We don't want another...'

Another hidden wedding dress scenario? That's what we all know she isn't saying.

Cate purses her lips. 'Secrets aren't always helpful.'

Of all of us, Cate knows that from experience. And Immie is horribly silent too.

'Okay,' I'm racking my brain for a way to move this on. I need some kind of metaphorical hatchet to break the ice, because this bright happy afternoon has frozen right over. 'We're in this lovely garden, probably for the first and last time, we need to mark the day. Come on,' I grab my phone and hold it up. 'Selfie anyone?'

When I look at the photo later, Cate and I are putting in the effort, with grins only a little less insane than usual, but Immie's scowl is as deep and unforgiving as they come.

AUGUST

45

In the house at Daisy Hill Farm:
Complications and ice cream cones

'Made any good cakes lately then?'

If Rafe's question was designed to take my mind off my note-book, it worked. For a nanosecond, I look up from the ten page long To Do list we're checking off.

'Why are you asking, you don't even like cake?' I say, chewing the end of my pen, pausing to glance around what are now manicured lawns and weed-free borders in the garden behind the farmhouse. So far every job highlighted has been ticked.

Rafe rubs a tanned hand across his forehead. 'Light relief before we move inside?' Nice try. 'You're a bit of a slave driver when you've got a list on board.'

Being called a slave driver by a workaholic is definitely an insult. It's true, I've barely had time to breathe the last few days, what with weddings, record numbers of cake orders, and the shop being packed out. And life is so much more complicated when the town is rammed with holiday makers wandering round eating ice creams. Some days the streets are so jam packed with cars, I need a tin opener just to get home. If I've taken to doing tasks at double speed, with intense concentration, it might be down to a recent article I read in the Huffington Post.

'Apparently best way to be productive is to forget multitasking, and concentrate on the job in hand,' I say. It's only thanks to this mantra that I've survived the last week's workload.

'Which is what we guys knew all along.' Rafe says with that satisfied gloat he does that's so annoying. 'You look like you could do with a drink. If you agree to take a breather, I've got Red Bull in the fridge?'

His questioning gaze lasts long enough for me to count every one of his eyelashes. It's hard to stay cross with someone who reads your mind before you do. What's more, there's something so absurd about being offered Red Bull by a farmer that I can't help smiling. 'A coke would be fab please, it's thirsty work.' That's the biggest caffeine input I can risk in my hyped-up state.

Rafe disappears into the house, comes back with two ice cold cans, and sits down on the wall as he hands me mine. 'Note, I'm only perching here while we consider the next move.'

'Red Velvet.' I begin, as I join him on the warm stone, then realise how random I sound. 'That's one of the cakes I did. Dark red sponge, vanilla cream cheese icing, and burgundy sugar roses. This high…' I take a swig of coke, and estimate three feet six tall with my hand. 'Then there was a four tier, covered in edible gold leaf.' I watch Rafe's eyes grow round over the top of his coke can. 'And then there was a diamond anniversary, where I had to make an exact copy of the original cake from the photos in the wedding album…to name a few…' I spare him the pictures. The poor guy was only making conversation. He doesn't want to sit through my entire back catalogue.

'Blimey.' He rolls his can round in his hands. 'You've been busy.'

Given that good managers shouldn't stint on praise when it's due, I need to dish some out myself. 'I'm not the only one. If the garden and terrace are anything to go by, you guys have been blasting through my list.'

He gives a low laugh. 'The guys pretty much nailed it. All your fault, once the playlist was going, there was no stopping them.'

'They went for *Breaking My Heart (the loud way)* then?' I'm amazed, but pleased at the same time.

'Not exactly.' Rafe pulls a face. 'It's been wall to wall heavy metal and Jeremy Clarkson's Driving Rock. If I hear one more Iron Maiden track, I may hide in a haystack and never come out again. But if the work's finished, who cares?'

'What, you've done everything on my list?' This isn't what I was expecting at all, hence my voice shooting up by two octaves.

Rafe's shrug is nonchalant. 'Pretty much.'

Rafe motivated, Rafe driving the work forward, Rafe focussed on making the house wedding-ready? This I have to see. 'Shall we go in then?'

The tingle of excitement that ripples through me is dulled by an inexplicable after taste of disappointment, because I had no idea they were going to get on so fast and finish without any more of my help. Although as soon as the thought pops into my head, I toss it away as ridiculous. Scraping walls and scrubbing floors and polishing windows can be satisfying. But add in doing it with Rafe hanging round, and it loses all its attraction. Obviously. So why I'm feeling like I lost a tenner and found ten pence, I have no idea.

As for the way my stomach flips when I follow him into the orangerie and he turns to me with a grin wider than I've seen, all stubbly jaw and cheekbones with the teensiest flash of tanned abs under his T-shirt hem as he stretches, well that's inexplicable too. When I've heard people use the term panty wetting, I've always cringed. Right now, I'm entirely ashamed to say I now know exactly what they mean. Too much information? Very sorry. I'm completely with you on that, and no-one could be more disgusted than me.

If this is happening because my grief for my lost relationship is waning, let me say, for the record, I'm definitely not a) happy about it, or b) up for acting on it. And, what's more, it's totally perturbing. I feel like I've been turned upside down and shaken. I'm single and staying that way. End of.

Back in the orangerie, my tummy's gone into free fall all over again. But this time it's because the place is looking so spectacular – so long as shabby chic's your thing. Somehow the guys have made it exactly the right amount of spotless. It's clean enough not to rub dirt on your clothes, yet there's still enough of that most elusive of things, patina.

'The tiles have come up beautifully,' I say, running my toe over the black and blue and white chequerboard pattern. 'And the colours of the garden look wonderful through those wobbly panes of glass.'

'Morgan helped in here,' Rafe says, his smile reigniting all over again. 'That lad's a grafter, just like his mum.'

It's the same story as we move on to check out the bride's changing room. This has been transformed simply with a wash of vintage blue paint. But if the other spaces were impressive the drawing room is breathtaking. The walls have been scraped back to reveal a mixture of muted lime washes and scuffs, which complement the bare scrubbed floorboards, and the tall, small paned sash windows splash light across the room. At one end of the room, there's the huge fireplace, which is balanced at the other by the enormous grand piano.

'You've done so well to finish,' I say. If anything deserves a congratulatory pat on the shoulder, it's this, even if I have to get too close for comfort to give it. If I let my hand linger for a second too long, it's only because I'm taken aback by the heat of the muscle beneath the soft cotton.

From the way his grin widens, I reckon he couldn't be more pleased or proud. 'Most fun I've had in years.' So damned typical of Rafe to go all ironic.

'Yeah, right,' I say. Sometimes the only way to deal with his sarcastic comments is to join in.

'Really. I'm not joking.'

For a moment our eyes lock, and he catches hold of my fingers and squeezes so tight all the breath leaks out of me. For a minute the room is spinning, but then I snatch my hand away, and take refuge in my notebook.

'Oh my days, so many ticks. Two weeks from now Tia and Sam are going to have the most perfect day.' I say, in a fluttery way that sounds nothing like me. 'Once their marquee's up, it's going to be dreamy.' At least that got over that awkward moment. Sometimes it's hard to handle Rafe taking the piss. Okay, and to change the subject to something more concrete, I'll also admit to a twinge of sadness that this wedding isn't mine. Although there would have been no chance of a country wedding with Brett. He'd have been set on the Yacht Club, or, on his more ambitious days, some seriously formal civic venue. End of discussion. This garden is special because it reminds me of my mum. It's true, the tent alongside the gorgeous summer flowers, mixed with the vintage interiors, are going to be amazing.

Rafe's arms are folded, as if he's making damned sure his hands don't get accidentally tangled up with mine again. 'So long as weddings keep the bank at bay, I'm not grumbling.' He gives a half shake of his head, then carries on. 'Anyway, all that's left to take away are the smaller pictures you thought we should take down. Remember page eight, instruction fourteen, remove all family paintings?' He nods at the large pile of frames by the hall door. 'They'll be fine in the bedroom at the top of the stairs, it's full of junk anyway.'

'I'll take those.' I jump forwards and pick up the first two. It's the least I can do, after all the work I've missed out on. Then it hits me. Do I want to look this desperate to dash into a bedroom at Rafe's place? I feel my cheeks warming.

Rafe's low laugh is husky. 'Okay Red, there's no rush, we'll do it together.'

That offer turns the heat up enough to make me feel like Jess in a full blown midlife flush. He's taken to using that nickname more and more since we've been cleaning, but right now it has to be because I'm scarlet. I'm dying here, aching for the floor to open up and swallow me, when Rafe's phone rings, and saves me in another way.

As Rafe puts his phone to his ear, he mouths at me, waving me through the wide door out into the hall. 'Carry on up, I'll be with you in a second.'

A second? I don't think so. That's the thing with these farm guys. Once they start nattering about corn and cows and cogs etcetera, they can talk for England.

The hall is dim, and the staircase wide and creaky, as I tiptoe my way to the top. When I reach the landing, I'm faced with two doors, so I go for the one that's slightly ajar. Sure enough, when I shoulder my way through, I find a room full of boxes and dismantled furniture. With a flood of relief that I got it right first time and don't have to open the other door, I prop the pictures against the wall, and skip down for some more. Five trips on, Rafe's still deep in conversation about gear boxes of all things, and I'm running out of floor space to stack pictures. Stepping back, I scan the jumble to see if I can make any minor adjustments to gain more room. By putting a box on top of a chest, and swinging round a loose bed head and a cardboard box, I should be able to fit in the rest. I'm just congratulating myself on my three dimensional vision, and swinging round the large flat box, when I hear the stairs groan. 'Just making a bit more space,' I call.

To say the door flew open would be an understatement. It was more like Rafe ripping the door of its hinges, and bursting into the room like a bloody tornado, face dark as a storm cloud about to burst.

'What the fuck are you doing in here?' He couldn't have been yelling any louder if he'd been at a World Cup footie match, and England had scored.

The sheer force of his roar makes my insides wither. There's no point even trying to stammer that I'm putting pictures away, because that should be pretty damned obvious, and my voice has gone entirely A.W.O.L.

'And who gave you permission to touch that?'

The violence of his entry has left the lampshade swinging over our heads. As I stare down at the box I'm balancing, I screw round my eyes to read the vertical writing.

Drop Side Nursery Cot.

I'm no wiser. Rafe's miserable, he's grouchy, he can be the ultimate downer. But I've never seen him blow before. On balance it's probably best to get the hell out of here. I push the box at Rafe, but as I take a blind step backwards to make my escape, my hip bangs on the corner of the chest. The pain jabs through me and as I whirl round to make a run for the door, my elbow catches on a box. For a minute Rafe and I both watch helpless as it teeters on the edge. Then, as it tumbles down to the floor, it tips onto its side, and carefully folded garments spill out in a heap. Tiny garments.

Even though my mouth is dry I try to swallow. I'm blinking as I stare down at the pile, but still I can't make sense of it. 'Baby clothes?' The words are out before I know I can even speak. Even though it's only a whisper, if my voice was going to reappear, it couldn't have kicked back in at a worse moment. When my eyes roll upwards to search Rafe's face for some clue, his anguished scowl says it all.

'Just get out.' He's rigid, glaring at me. 'Now.' His fury has given way to an eerie flatness.

Good thinking. I was actually on my way already. My heart is doing bird wing flaps in my chest, as I flatten myself against the wall to get past him. Somehow, as I reach the door, I wring out a murmur. 'Sorry…I didn't…'

His arctic stare propels me out of the room, chilling my blood so fast I shiver.

As I pad past Jet, hovering on the landing, and steal down the stairs, my rings rattle on the bannister because my hand is shaking so much. I hurry back through the drawing room, run across the orangerie, burst into the bright sun, and come to a halt, gasping on the terrace by the wall. However deeply I breathe in, there doesn't seem to be enough oxygen. If I'd known this was coming I'd definitely have gone for the Red Bull earlier. As I grab my abandoned coke can, I'm throwing back my head to drain the dregs, when I hear a string of gruff expletives coming over the garden wall.

'Immie?'

She's the only person I know who says 'ass hat' *and* 'toad bollocks'. And I'm guessing from the Mr Muscle bathroom spray she's clutching, as much as from her third best holey shirt, that she's been disturbed whilst cottage cleaning.

'Crap, Pops, am I glad you're here.' She grabs at the spikes of hair sticking up beyond her sweat band, then she breaks off midsentence, and leans forward to scrutinise me. 'What the hell happened, you look green enough to have morning sickness… you haven't…you're not…are you?'

At least that thought is random enough to takes my mind off what just happened. 'How exactly would I be pregnant?' I ask indignantly. 'Immaculate conception with Cornish fairies?' I shake my head and lower my voice. 'It's nothing, I had a bit of a run in with Rafe, that's all.' If I'm playing it down it's because I'm not up for a post mortem right here, right now, when the man himself might walk out of the house at any moment.

'Fuck, thank jeez it's not the other. It must be a day for melt-downs.' Immie's hopping from foot to foot. 'You've got to come, Chas is here saying he needs to see you. Immediately.' She makes her eyes big for emphasis.

'Great.' I let out a long, low whistle. Right now I feel wobbly enough to collapse into a deckchair. Or to crawl under the duvet and hide for a fortnight. As for fielding more of Nicole's unending demands? Not so much.

'It's urgent and confidential.' Immie's voice drops to a hoarse whisper, as she gives an omigod grimace. 'He's in the office, I told him we'll see him straight away.'

'We? Both of us?' I query, knowing I'm too weary to object.

'Believe me.' She purses her lips, and waggles her Mr Muscle at me. 'Something tells me you're going to need back up with this one.'

46

In the office at Daisy Hill Farm: One-off hugs

'Lovely to see you again, Chas,' I say, as I hurry behind the desk, and make a hopeless attempt to steady my shakes with a bright smile. I decide to ignore that there are three chickens pecking at Chas's trainer, as he obviously has. 'How can I help?'

Constructing a replica of Buckingham Palace in the farmyard for Nicole's exclusive use perhaps? Booking The Ritz to serve Royal Appointment burgers from the back of a vintage Rolls? Persuading Jimmy Choo to do personal pedicures in a Spa Tent? Any of the above would be completely in line with Nicole's recent requests.

I ignore that Immie is doing a kind of soft close thing with the door behind Chas's back. The way she charged up the yard to get to him and left me trailing miles behind was a bit blatant, even for Immie. As for being so desperate she's locking the guy in the room, someone needs to remind her that in two weeks Chas will be married. And no-one on Daisy Hill Farm staff is going to be responsible for trying to persuade Chas otherwise. If Immie is hoping to snog some sense into him, as I suspect she'd like to, she can damn well forget it.

'I'm not sure anyone *can* help,' Chas says, absently brushing a chicken off his cargo shorts.

If I needed an explanation for why Immie's stopped to perch on Chas's side of the desk, I get it as he extends one tanned leg. I send a silent prayer to the god of swooning women, asking that Immie isn't perving on his muscly calves. Given that the opportunity has cropped up right under my nose, in the interests of my own personal single-thirty-something research, I focus on his foot, and check for fizzing hormones. Despite his ankle being particularly attractive, my pulse doesn't start to race at all. So I put that result down as inconclusive.

'We're here for you, Chas,' Immie says, obviously jumping the gun here. The way she pats his arm, well that's all wrong too.

Swallowing back my shriek of horror, I try to prepare my reaction by flicking through the likely scenarios of what the hell might have happened. Nicole finally pushing Chas over the edge with outlandish requirements comes top. Chas recognising Nicole for the grasping user she is, comes a close second.

'What's wrong, Chas?' I might sound insensitive coming out with it, but someone has to ask.

The breath he draws in before he speaks is never ending. 'It's Nicole,' he says, at last.

There you go, what did I tell you? I give myself full marks for insight.

Chas puts his head in his hands for a moment, then he looks up and goes on. 'She's called off the wedding.'

'She did what?' I take a second to check I've heard right. 'Surely not?' I manage to say at last. At least this way round my squeal of disbelief is genuine. 'It has to be pre-wedding nerves. Last minute cold feet are very common.' Now I'm adding couples counselling to my list of Event Planner duties. 'She's probably stressed.' If I'm gabbling at a hundred miles an hour, it's only because I can't help it. 'Give her a couple of days, it'll all be back on again.'

Chas shakes his head. 'No, she's thought it all through. Apparently she's with me for all the wrong reasons.' The imploring look he sends us is crippling. 'She wanted a wedding, and security, and a home, and I can give her all those things, but in the end she doesn't think we're compatible.' He gives a tragic shrug. 'Not in the long term.'

I'm frowning, because this sounds so unlike the Nicole we've seen. 'Oh my days.'

'She says if we carry on, we'll only be condemning each other to a lifetime of unhappiness.'

'Shit,' I say, trying to pick my jaw off the floor. 'That's pretty final.' And very well thought out too. There were times when their tastes seemed miles apart. The fact we'd always blamed it on Nicole being a super selfish bitch makes me squirm with guilt.

'It's true we've had a lot of arguments lately. The wedding seemed to highlight all the ways we're different.' Chas gives a deep sigh. 'I thought as long as I truly loved her that would be enough. But it's not enough for Nicole.'

'It's better to call it off than go through with something you'll both regret.' I say. If I sound very grave, it's because I've put my professional hat on again in an attempt to lose my hyena shriek. I dig deep to find something positive to say. 'Nicole has a lot of integrity to admit this, it must have taken a lot of guts.'

'Maybe you rushed things, because you loved her so much.' Immie chimes in, sounding very unlike herself.

'But at least it shows you made a good choice in the first place,' I add. 'Nicole's obviously a very honest person. She's setting you free because she loves you.' Even as I'm talking, I can hear how trite I sound, but what the hell can you say? Nothing actually equips you to deal with a guy being left two weeks before his wedding. It makes what I went through with Brett look like a picnic.

'At least she hasn't left me for anyone else,' he says. 'Although it might be easier if she had. This way it just means I'm not good enough for a relationship.'

'Rubbish.' Immie and I chorus, although I suspect we're coming at this from very different viewpoints.

'Nicole was so damned stunning, it was like going out with a young Jerry Hall.' Chas's quiet moan is wistful. 'I should have known I was punching above my weight.'

I catch Immie's despairing grimace. 'It isn't all about looks,' I say. 'Personality plays a big part too.' However much I disapprove, I still throw that one in on Immie's behalf. Although if Chas is hooked on tall and polished, as a five foot nothing who doesn't believe in wasting money on moisturiser or make up, Immie needs to prepare herself for disappointment.

I'm silently racing ahead now, wishing I'd taken more notice of the cancellation part of the contracts in the filing cabinet. My heart's sinking too. I suspect Rafe's comment about weddings keeping the bank at bay might have been less throwaway than he implied. Then it hits me like a thunderbolt. Rafe's dire finances must be why he's suddenly so enthusiastic to get the house ready. That's the obvious explanation for that mystery. He probably can't afford to lose the fees. Chas and Nicole made their final payment ages ago. In all probability, Rafe's probably already spent it. I'm wincing, bracing myself to bring up the money side, when Chas does it for me.

'Everything's paid for.' He shakes his head, as he folds his arms. 'It's too late to cancel now.' Seemingly picking up on my twitchiness, he smiles at me. 'Don't worry, we won't be asking for any refunds. I'm not here for that.'

I hope my sympathetic smile covers up that I'm also letting out a massive sigh of relief.

'So what are you going to do?' Immie leans towards Chas, inclining her head with the same beady eyed look Henrietta has when she thinks there's some corn coming her way.

'For fuck's sake, Immie, give the guy a break,' I hiss. 'He's cancelled his wedding, now back the hell off.' Yes, I hold my hands up, I know it's not how an Event Organiser should carry on, but sometimes Immie goes way off limits.

Chas gives a sniff. 'Thanks Poppy, I appreciate your concern, but don't stop her, it's a valid question.' This time his shrug is guilty rather than distraught. 'I've talked to all my mates, and everyone's in favour. We're going to carry on and have a phenomenal tipi camping weekend. With all the food and drink we've bought, and the bands, it'll be the party of the decade. Jules is even dropping in to take some pictures too.' He hesitates, then turns to me. 'That's if it's alright with you, obviously?'

I'm on my feet, across the office, and before I know it I've thrown my arms around Chas's neck. 'Of course, Chas, it's a brilliant idea.' I'm hugging him for his sheer determination to survive. For taking this so well. But also for letting me off the hook, and making my job so easy.

'You're all invited too,' he says. 'Obviously.'

Out of the corner of my eye, I catch Immie punching the air. On the plus side she manages to stop short of shouting out 'Result!'

The frown I shoot at her is supposed to convey that this is a one off management hug, which I'm having for professional reasons, not a bloody free for all. But she takes shit all notice, and the next minute she's practically whirling Chas around the office herself.

As I stand and watch them, I do a mental check of my entire body. Inch by inch. For single women thirty something research purposes. Searching for after-hug hot areas. Or tingles.

But to my complete disgust, there aren't any. Another inconclusive result then. As it is, I categorically refuse to believe Rafe is the only guy causing a reaction, because if that's the case, it blows my theory out of the water. In the worst way possible.

47

In the courtyard at Daisy Hill Farm: Cornish beer

'What's going on?'

It's another valid question. This time from Rafe, who is in the office three hours later, as Chas, Immie and I arrive – or more accurately, roll – back from the Goose and Duck.

If we look like fugitives from a pub crawl in St Aidan, it's entirely accidental. But it's the kind of lucky accident that also offers the perfect cover for what would have otherwise have been a very awkward meeting with Rafe, given what happened earlier.

As a story it's not long. When Immie made an inappropriate grab for Chas as we hit the road to walk back to the farm, I neutralised it by moving in from the other side. Simple as that. Anyone glancing at our shambling threesome might easily assume that Chas is helping us helpless women along, holding us up on our non-existent heels. But in reality, Chas has been firing pints down as fast as they could pull them. He's not so much been drowning his sorrows, as burying them beneath an ocean of Tintagel Harbour Special. And Immie has been drinking Cornish Knockers, pint for pint, in sympathy. So from where I'm standing, it feels like I'm definitely the one supporting him, and probably Immie too.

'We took Chas for lunch and corporate commiseration.' I explain to Rafe, without making eye contact, as I guide our human chain through the doorway. 'He had…err…news.' I hesitate over the explanation. The truth sounds so harsh. As I let go, and Immie and Chas peel off to stagger across the office, it's obvious they're legless.

'His wedding's off.' Immie comes straight out with it, slurring as she grabs her Mr Muscle from the desk where she left it earlier. 'And I've got a cottage to clean.'

'You remember Chas?' I say to Rafe, keeping my tone clipped and professional. 'He's opted for the party of the decade instead of the wedding.' My beam stays bright, even though I groan inwardly as Immie collapses into my chair, and starts spinning around. 'I'll call a couple of cabs. These two need to get home.' I pull my phone out of my pocket and scroll down my numbers. If I send Immie off in the same cab as Chas, who knows where they'll end up.

'No need.' Rafe's hand lands lightly on my upturned forearm. 'Give me a minute, I'll get one of the guys to take them. Then there's somewhere I want to take you.'

He takes his hand back, and he's off down the yard before I can say tingle.

A few seconds later, Rafe is back. It's only when you see a sober person dashing around that you appreciate how ratted Chas and Immie are. Rafe wastes no time, as he leans in around the doorframe.

'Immie, Chas – Bob will take you two wherever you want to go. Poppy,' He nods his head towards the open topped Land Rover parked outside. 'Grab your jacket and come with me.'

Immie gives me a sozzled wave as I go. Hopefully she'll get home and sleep it off. As for Rafe and I, we make it into the Land Rover, and a long way up the lane without another word.

48

On the way to Daisy Hill: Shouting in the wind

'What colour is your hair anyway?'

When Rafe finally breaks the silence, it's only because I'm wrestling madly against the bluster of the breeze, trying to capture my wildly blowing split ends in a scrunchy.

'Well once it was pillar box, and then it was vermillion, now it's streaky orange growing out.' I might as well give him the full catalogue of dying disasters, even if I have to yell over the roar of the engine, as this heap of metal bounces over the ruts and potholes.

'No, I mean what colour is it really?' This is Rafe for you. He's so intense. Three answers, and he still digs for another.

'It used to be long and blonde.' I'm shouting as loud as I can but the wind's snatching my words away so I doubt he can hear. 'I chopped it and dyed it because I wanted to change who I was.'

His tanned hands are gripping the wheel. When he looks away from the dusty windscreen for a moment, I will him to look back at the lane instead of at me. I really don't want to end up in a ditch here.

I begin to yell again. 'The colour doesn't matter any more – I couldn't be that blonde person again, even if I tried.'

I couldn't be that blonde person again, even if I tried.

Yelling those random, yet significant, words at the top of my voice where no-one's listening makes me a glow inside. You know those times when you stand still for months, or even worse, slide backwards, then suddenly out of nowhere, you make a massive leap forwards? That's what I'm talking about here. I'm still smiling when Rafe pulls into a gateway a hundred yards further along the track.

'Here we are.' He jumps to the ground and slams the door.

I follow, and meet him by the gate, squinting up at the impossibly fluffy clouds scudding across a sky blue enough to have come off Shutterstock. 'Where exactly are we then?'

'Daisy Hill.' He pushes the gate open for me with a rueful grin.

'I didn't know that was a real place.' There's a crazy kind of flutter I my stomach as I brush past him and catch a blast of his scent. Don't ask me how he can still smell of delicious waxed jackets, when he hasn't been near one all summer.

'It's my favourite place on the farm. It's a good place to come.' His smile fades. 'I wanted to talk about this morning upstairs – the way I reacted was unforgivable. I'm not making excuses, but there's so much pain closed up in that damned room.'

I ram my hands in my pockets, and drag my jacket around me to suppress a shudder. 'I'm so sorry for whatever I did to upset you. Let's leave it there.' I'd rather not hear any more.

'The baby things are there because Helen had a stillborn child.' His voice is horribly low as we walk. 'It's a long time ago now, and I was so wrong to shout, but you caught me off guard.'

Crap, crap, crap. I'm kicking myself, because I should have known. 'You don't need to tell me this Rafe.'

'It's been hidden for too long, talking might be good.' He's striding beside me, working his way up the hill, his legs so much longer than mine that I'm stumbling over the grassy ridges to keep up.

He spins round to face me, walking backwards as he speaks. 'Helen was five months pregnant when we found out she was having a baby.' The words are coming out in bursts between gulps as he climbs. 'We hadn't been living together very long, it was a shock, and to be honest we were ambivalent. We'd got as far as telling the family, and my brother gave us a load of stuff – the stuff you came across this morning.'

'Oh, no.' I'm screwing up my face, because I just know what's coming. When he pauses, mid stride, I know what he's going to say.

'At twenty eight weeks, they couldn't find a heartbeat. They induced labour, but the baby was born dead.'

His voice is so desolate I feel like there's a hole in my chest. I jerk to a halt next to him, bumping into his elbow. 'So awful,' I gasp, wishing my lungs would hold more oxygen. 'And Rafaella being born brought it all back, didn't it? Of course, it would. I knew there was something that night.' My throat is burning as I stand panting.

'When something goes wrong, you still have to go through the agony of the birth. But afterwards you're left with nothing.' His voice catches as he speaks. 'Delivering the baby that night in the cottage took me right back.'

My heart is aching for him. I swallow back a mouthful of sour saliva. I'm longing to throw my arms around him, but there's something so defiant and alone in the way he's hugging his chest, I decide to keep my distance.

'It was weird.' He's still motionless, staring down the steep grassy bank we've just climbed. 'Before, I hadn't been that bothered, but as soon as I saw my baby being born, all I could think of was how much I wanted one. I was desperate to try for another.' He turns, and begins to climb again. 'But Helen didn't feel the same. And putting pressure on her made it worse.'

It's as if once he's started talking, he doesn't want to stop. For a few strides he's quiet, and then we reach the summit, and he takes hold of my hand, to drag me up the last yard. As he lets go and sits down, legs bent in front of him, elbows resting on his splayed knees, I flop down next to him.

'This is where I scattered the ashes.' He rubs his nose with his fist. 'Helen couldn't face it.' He says it with a quiet resignation. 'But it's a good place.'

The abruptness takes me by surprise. All this is so far out of my experience. No wonder he looks so sad. 'It's an amazing place. I love the way the wind comes rushing up the hill. And how you can see all the fields laid out down below.' It's strange to think that Rafe has been living through all this, and all the time, I was in Brett's penthouse.

'In the end Helen decided I wasn't the right person for her to have kids with. She didn't think we were good together.' Rafe props his chin on his hand.

If my eyes are widening, it's because it's the second time today I've heard this line. 'It's a lot harder to make things work when you face difficulties than when everything's going well.' Not that I learned that with Brett. If there were difficulties in our life, Brett's way of coping was to find a pressing engagement a plane ride away. 'So why weren't you a good match?' I'm thinking of Chas and Nicole here.

Rafe gives a shrug. 'Helen thought we were too alike, and she was probably right. We both had a tendency to see the black side, and sink.'

'Maybe not the best combination,' I admit. Rafe's bad enough on his own, without someone reinforcing the problem. 'You've got grumpy off to a fine art some days.' I laugh, mainly so he doesn't take it to heart, and go grumpy again. Although I must say, he's been noticeably happier since summer arrived.

'Daisy Hill Farm's been way lighter since you came,' he says, his face breaking into a sudden grin.

I'm not taking that in silence. 'Are you implying I'm shallow?' However much he might deny it, he definitely is.

He raises one eyebrow. 'You have to admit, you're big on smiles and cakes.' He rubs his chin. 'You go for the fun stuff that doesn't matter, rather than the serious side of life.'

Thanks a bunch for that. 'Putting on weddings has been more of a challenge than I ever thought possible, believe me.' Whoever thinks wedding planning is about wafting round with flowers and lace and sugar icing hasn't got a clue.

His brow furrows in a thoughtful frown. 'What I'm trying to say is it's good to have you around. Hearts on the office door, music blasting out loud enough to shred my ear drums, photos of brides and daisy chains all over the office walls, the forest of Thank You cards obliterating the kettle…it's all very…'

'Enough. Stop it there. I get the message.' This guy is so damned cutting at times. Who else would list their top five hates?

'Farming isn't all fluffy lambs you know, it's a lot of hard work for no return.' He's raising one eyebrow. 'You're like a summer breeze wafting through.'

Nice to know. Not. 'For fuck's sake, Rafe, first you call me shallow, then you say I'm full of hot air. I can't help it, that's how I am.' I snap off a buttercup, and let the golden shadow reflect on my palm. 'Give me a break.'

'What, and go back to talking about my past?' He juts out his jaw.

'Anything's better than being told I'm frivolous.' I give a sniff.

'Not exactly frivolous, more…kind of laid back yet lively? In a good way?' He picks up that I'm raising my eyes to the clouds, and gives a sigh. 'As for me, there's not much more to tell. My best mate was helping Helen through the bad times, and he turned out to be everything I wasn't. It makes sense really. Helen and I were very similar. He was as good for her as he was for me.'

'And that's how she ended up at the next farm?'

'Yep.' Rafe nods. 'She didn't lose any time with him, they've got four kids now.'

'That must have been hard.' Talk about a kick in the teeth, not that I'd say that to Rafe.

'I can't say it wasn't tough, losing both of them. The funny thing was, no-one knew the real reason we split up. That made it easier in a way. Local legend has it that she left because I refused to get married.'

'Actually, I did hear that.' I give a guilty grin, but I have to come clean. 'That's supposed to be why you hate the weddings so much.'

'Who says I hate them?' The look he flashes me is inscrutable, considering what we've been through the last few months.

'You used to think they were a whole load of trouble.' I'm not going to push him too much on this, in case he does a U-turn.

'They are a lot of trouble. But as you've told me so often, maybe the trouble's worth it in the end, once you consider the return.' He says, pausing. 'Have you thought of kids then?'

Wow. What next? But somehow, given how much he's just shared, I don't feel like I can skip over this one.

'I did think about kids a while back.' I can't lie about all those fantasies of curly haired, blonde children – mine and Brett's – running around, mainly on the beach. They usually followed on seamlessly from the ones where I was walking down the aisle towards him. Jeez knows what happened to the bit in between. 'But not now I'm on my own.' Kids are something else that won't be featuring in my future on my own, but given what Rafe's been through I'm not about to moan.

Something tells me, now might be a good time to make a run for home, because there surely can't be anything else left to discuss up here. As I scramble to my feet, the startle in his eye tells me if I go fast, I'll get a great head start. 'Race you back down,' I say. 'Last one to the bottom buys pasties tomorrow.'

And as I'm bumping and lurching down the hillocks, I can't

help thinking about the guy who climbed up a hill but came back down a mountain. Because somehow that's how I feel about what happened this afternoon.

49

In the courtyard at Daisy Hill Farm: Talking of photographers

'In a way it's a shame Nicole and Chas didn't go through with it,' I say to Immie two weeks later, on the day when Chas and Nicole should have been getting married. I immediately pick up that she's looking daggers at me for that. 'It's like tipi city down there, the ceremony photos would have been awesome.'

Bringing you up to speed, in case you'd forgotten, it's the day that should have been the double wedding, so we've split the staff between the house and the field. This is the first time I've seen Immie all day, and there's something different about her, although I can't put my finger on what it is. She volunteered to be our woman on the ground in the party field – no surprise there then – while I've been tiptoeing around the house and garden reception, holding my breath, willing that we don't have any disasters.

She flips the subject deftly away from Nicole and Chas. 'So how's it going in the garden?'

'The ring bearer's a French Bulldog, and he gave Henrietta a run for her money when he first arrived,' I say. Dogs as ring bearers? They have a special little box dangling from their collars apparently. He was only letting off steam after his big moment in church, and it ended happily with Henrietta taking refuge on the back of the open topped wedding car as Tia and Sam got out. 'In the end no-one minded, because a chicken pecking at the gypsophila in the bridal crown made for some great unscheduled pictures.'

'Talking of photographers, Jules is still down by the tipis, snapping away for all he's worth.' Immie says with a secret smirk. 'He's been asking me all day if he's still in with a chance.'

Who said men were like buses? None for ages, then lots come along at once, all lining up in front of Immie. 'Wow, if it comes down to a choice, who would you go for then, Chas with his hunky fireman looks or suave and stylish Jules?' I'm dying to hear.

Immie gives a grunt of disgust. 'Jules was asking if he's in with a chance with *you*, not with me.'

'Ahhh…' I say.

'You're the only reason Jules is hanging around, still fulfilling his booking duties at eight thirty in the evening.' She gives a disgusted snort. 'I mean, how many pictures of a party can you take? Once you've seen one shot of drunk people falling over guy ropes, you've pretty much seen them all.'

I wince. 'Bad as that already?'

Immie grins. 'Afraid so. No-one's holding back – apart from Jules and me, because obviously we're working.' She gives me a wink. 'So any message for love-sick Jules then? He's been waiting for you like a faithful dog for months, don't forget.'

Closing my eyes, I screw up my face. 'He knows I'm not in the market.'

'He's still convinced Rafe's the main obstacle.' Immie drops that one in with a wicked grin.

'Rafe?' I let out a shriek of horror. 'That's so wrong, it doesn't even deserve an answer.' I shake my head and blow out a long

277

breath. 'That's a typical male reaction. Everything's about rivalry, rather than about what the woman wants…or doesn't in this case.'

'So I say that to Jules?' She's pushing me here, still amused.

'No, definitely not.' I need to work out how to put this in a kind way. 'Tell him he'll always have a place close to my heart. That's the best *any* guy's going to do, believe me.'

Talking of racing hearts, I did the hormone-rush test when Jules dashed in and swung me round first thing this morning. Despite three spins without my feet touching the floor, once I was firmly back on the ground I wasn't the least bit dizzy. Or fluttery.

'You should come and have a peep in the garden now you're here,' I say, leading the way towards the house. 'It's gorgeous with the fairy lights around the open sided tent, and the scent of honeysuckle and roses.' If I'm going on, it's only because it's so dreamy. Quietly we make our way through the gate in the garden wall.

'How far through are they?' Immie whispers, as we pad across the grass.

'They just had their first dance.'

'And?' Immie cocks her head expectantly. Despite being totally disinterested in ever having a wedding herself, she's always fascinated by couples' choices of songs for their significant moments.

'Nina Simone, *My Baby Just Cares For Me*, played on the grand piano by Sam's brother. We moved the piano into the orangerie. Sam and Tia met at ballroom dance classes, so their dancing was fab.'

'Nice.' She gives a nod of approval as she watches the couples, moving together in time to the music out on the terrace now. 'And is Rafe playing for them later?'

No-one's more surprised about this than I am. 'He played during the wedding breakfast, and apparently he's said he'll take over again at the end of the evening.'

'It's a shame I'll miss that.' Immie wrinkles her nose, and glances at her phone. 'I'd better be getting back down to the field. I only came up to put a bit more slap on.'

And then it hits me. That's why she looks different. 'Are you wearing lippy, Immie?' Now she mentions it, it's obvious. Well, blow me down. She must be keen.

An embarrassed grin spreads across Immie's face. 'Only a bit. Cate lent me it.'

I widen my eyes, as my voice goes high with surprise. 'So Cate's in on this too?'

Immie gives a shrug. 'She did me a very minor make over. I've been doing running repairs all bloody day. One swig of real ale, and my pout's gone. What kind of a mess about is that?'

I bite back my smile, and keep a straight face. 'I thought you weren't drinking?'

'I'm not,' she says. 'Anyway, I'd better be off, who knows what disasters might be happening in the field. Wish me luck.'

And then she's gone. And although she wasn't specific, we both know exactly what my lucky wishes are supposed to be for.

50

By the car at Daisy Hill Farm: Camp fires and late nights

It's half past two by the time I finally get to leave to drive home. I'm just about to unlock my car, when a noise behind me makes me jump so hard I drop my keys.

'So you didn't come for a song request then?'

It's Rafe, his voice low in the moonlight. Someone should tell him not to pad around the farm at night scaring people, making their pulses race fast enough to give them heart attacks. And I know I'm wide awake, thanks to my after-wedding adrenalin, but now's hardly the time to talk piano tunes.

'Sorry.' It's probably best not to admit I was at all disappointed to miss Rafe playing at the reception. Hoping I'd have time to sneak in and hover in the shadows was a pretty unrealistic ask, and hearing it from a distance wasn't the same. 'First there was a lost handbag which turned out to have been in the car all along. Then I was hunting down a missing fluffy bunny. Then I was out directing taxis.'

I'm absolutely not going to say how a tiny part of me was hoping I'd bump into Rafe when I was rushing round in the dark after the caterers had done their final clear up, checking the garden, and locking up the house, because there's no rational reason for why I felt that. Unless it was because the white shirt and dark trousers he'd put on to play made him look pretty edible. Note here that I wasn't the only one thinking that, all the women were commenting.

Rafe stoops to pick up my car keys from where they're lying on the cobbles. 'You dropped these.' He sounds suddenly doubtful as I take them from him. 'You aren't leaving now are you?'

My stomach sinks. 'I was about to head home, yes.' As I hear a flurry of shouts from the party field, suddenly I'm aware that maybe I'm going too early. 'I know they've got a camp fire down in the field, but I thought as every second guy's a fireman, it would be okay.'

'That depends if they're trained to operate when rat arsed.' His grin is wry. 'They're old enough to look after themselves, but you'll be coming back again early. Why aren't you staying over in the cottage?'

Ooops. Now he's got me. 'Actually Immie's let it out. With two parties going on, there was a lot of demand.'

Rafe gives a disgusted snort. 'Well that's hardly the idea is it? Come on, you'd better stay at mine.'

'I…I don't know…' Even while I'm racking my brains for an excuse, part of me is hoping I don't find one. 'Actually I'm not tired, I'm still buzzing.' That should get me off the hook.

'Me too,' he says. 'These long days get you like that don't they? We could always have a debrief? Wind down with a glass of wine? The spare bed's made up.' Typical Rafe. Quietly covering every aspect.

Something about the way he's turned it into work makes it easier to agree. Also something about the halflight accentuating the shadows of his stubble, coupled with that soft white shirt, means my legs have pretty much set off to walk in the direction of the house all on their own. 'Wine might be nice,' I say, as I fall into step beside him, making what could pass for the under-statement of the century. As for the rush of butterflies in my chest, that's equivalent to a whole summer's worth of small blues, all arriving at once.

51

In the kitchen at Daisy Hill Farm: A debriefing with Rafe

'I'll see if I can find you a witty T-shirt to sleep in,' Rafe says, as he pushes the house door open, and leads the way through to his kitchen, which never gets any less fabulous. 'So, what shall we crack open – red or white, vintage or new, sparkling or not? Or there's a cool beer if you'd prefer it?' Three strides, and he's already opened the fridge, and he's holding a bottle of Stella in one hand and some wine in the other.

'Fizzy white would be brill thanks.' It comes out without thinking, despite the fact I'd usually drink red late at night. 'Nothing vintage though, I tend to throw it down.' If my sub conscious is planning for us to stay up long enough to finish the bottle – we all know fizz won't keep – it must have lightening quick reactions.

If we're talking fast moves, in seconds Rafe has popped the cork, and is handing me a very full glass.

'Cheers.' I follow him across the room, kick off my ballet flats, and feel comfortable enough curl up on the corner of the sofa.

He takes the chair next to me, snaps open the bag of snacks

he's carrying, tips them into a bowl, and puts it on the small table between us.

'Pretzel?' he says, as he takes a handful. 'So what's your verdict?'

I watch his Adam's apple bob behind the opening of his shirt collar. Catch sight of the bump of his collar bone. How dark his eye lashes are when he's looking down. On balance, my verdict is a big fat yes. 'Sorry?'

'About today?' His lips twist into a smile. Almost perfect teeth. 'Did it work having the wedding in the garden?'

If I'm about to think how it would feel to run my tongue over those teeth, I put the brakes on that thought, before it is even formed. A large glug of wine goes a long way to putting my mind back on track, although the bubbles backfire and sting my nose. We're talking about today. Right.

'Given Tia and her mum and dad were all crying buckets as they left, I'd say it worked very well.' I grin at Rafe's sudden look of horror. 'Weddings are emotional – those tears told me it couldn't have been any more wonderful. You can't get better praise than that.'

'Well that's good to know.' Rafe leans over and refills my glass.

The label on the bottle is familiar. 'That's the same prosecco we serve in the shop,' I say.

'Immie told me, only because I asked her what you drank.' He gives a guilty sniff. 'Not that I'm stalking you or anything, obviously.'

Rafe getting wine in specially? Settling back into the sofa, the wool throw is soft against the skin of my calves. As I wave my glass in the air, I try to subdue the ripples of pleasure that has kicked off. 'As Jess says, you can't beat a bit of fizz.' I nibble on a pretzel, because firing down wine at the rate I am on an empty stomach isn't the best idea. What Jess believes about fizz having the power to enhance the mood isn't something I'm going to go into here, when every bubble I'm consuming is making a beeline for one particular place.

'Very true.' He laughs that very low laugh of his that makes me shiver, empties his glass in one go, and gives us both refills.

Maybe I need to make the most of this opportunity of Rafe being stationary, in quite a good mood and mellowed by alcohol. Come to think of it, I haven't ever seen him drinking before. Given that the ideas that have been buzzing around my head for ages really crystallised today, I'd be stupid not to. Let's face it, anything that takes my mind off what's going on under those dark trousers of his, might be a damned good thing. I take another glug of wine, to bolster my courage, and go for it before I lose my nerve.

'Have you ever thought, it might be a fab idea to use the house and have a few indoor weddings?' Nicole and her aspirations have got a lot to answer for here.

From Rafe's puzzled frown I take it that's a 'no'.

'It would extend your season. You could do smaller, more intimate weddings, all year round. And it would be the higher end of the market, so it would bring in cash, and would be great for cottage lettings too.' It comes out in a rush, and I kick myself for gabbling when I should be sounding cool and businesslike.

'Right.' Putting down his wine, he brings his fingertips together. 'You could be onto something there.' A smile spreads slowly across his face. 'Nice one, Red.'

That's all the encouragement I need. 'There's a lot of potential to take some of the cottages a lot more upmarket too.' I hesitate, because I don't want to tread on his mum's toes. 'What I'm really saying is if you lose the hideous pig pictures and invest in some decent furniture, you'd soon see a return.'

'God, those awful pigs.' He appears to be suppressing a grin. 'I can see you've been working overtime on my business plan.' He takes a deep breath and becomes more serious. 'Let's face it someone needs to. It takes your flair to see what's been staring me in the face for years.' He rests his chin on his hand. 'The way you put it, it sounds easy. Go on. What else? I can tell from the way your nose is all wrinkled up, there's definitely more.'

'How the hell do you know about my nose wrinkling?' Cate and Immie used to tease me about it nonstop. And my mum of course.

He laughs. 'Six months sharing an office, I'm bound to have learned something.'

What other secrets have I inadvertently given away? Hot desking has so many more pitfalls than you'd think.

'So, go on, what else?' He's resting his chin on his elbow again, smiling that laid back smile, as if he's waiting for me to amuse him.

I might as well go for it. 'If you split the lets into two, and did a midweek let, and a weekend one, you'd up the income, as well as fitting in with the weddings better.'

He takes another drink of wine. 'Why didn't I think of that?'

'Maybe because you're a busy farmer, always dashing round looking after your animals.' I say. 'Whereas I only have myself to look after, and hours to think about things when I'm doing fiddly bits of cake icing.'

He shakes his head at me. 'There you go again…making what you do sound trivial, talking yourself down.'

'You were the one who pointed out I was a lightweight.' I remember distinctly, that day on Daisy Hill.

'These are all great ideas of yours, but aren't you overlooking something?' The corners of his eyes wrinkle as a smile lilts around his lips. 'If you take over the whole of the house for weddings, where will I put all the children I'm going to have?'

That came out of nowhere, and for a second I blink, swallowing down the bitter taste that fills my mouth. Rafe wanting kids and a relationship had never occurred to me. That I'm biting back the jealousy for some, as yet, faceless woman is bizarre. But right now, the idea of anyone getting their hands on Rafe makes me gnash my teeth.

'Kids?' The word comes out as a high pitched croak, so I down most of my wine before I carry on. No idea why it came out like that. 'Sorry, I didn't know you were planning a big family.' Hopefully that comes out as less panicked.

His cheeks crease. 'Gotcha. Joking about that, obviously.' His low laugh ends in a grimace. 'At least for the time being, anyway.' He tips the last dribble of wine into my glass.

That's the trouble with fizzy wine, sometimes it goes down without touching the sides. And it's gone straight to my bladder.

'Fancy another bottle?' he asks, getting to his feet. 'There's plenty more to discuss. Unless you're too tired?'

'I'm not tired.' Actually I couldn't be more wide awake. As for another bottle, I know I shouldn't, but what the hell. I ease myself up, and head for the hall. 'I'll just nip to the loo.'

'Fine.'

If my reflection looks vaguely bleary in the cloakroom mirror, it's probably down to the long day. There's something unreal about it just being Rafe and me, in his kitchen, in the heavy quiet of the night. It's highly unlikely this will ever happen again. And it's strange that I'm aching for it not to end. Part of me wants to spin it out, and sit there with Rafe until the morning, just because it feels so comfortable.

As I pad back into the kitchen, I steady myself on the door-frame as I catch sight of him by the fridge. I walk over, and rest my hip against the granite work surface. And you know those times when all the alcohol heads for one place? Mine has gone straight to the triangle at the top of my legs, and it's sending waves of hot ripples, radiating outwards.

The bottle Rafe holds up is damp with condensation. 'So, shall I open this? Or would you rather come to bed?'

The double flip of my tummy almost makes me sick on the spot. As I sink against the hewn wood of the kitchen unit, the warm pulse in my panties becomes an ache. The way I'm arching my back, and pushing my boobs at Rafe, I have to look like I'm desperate.

'Come here.' As the bottle clanks onto the granite, his hot

mouth connects with mine, sweet and velvety. As his stubble grazes my chin, his body presses into me. Fuck. Two things flash through my brain.

'It's so long since I did this.' I murmur out loud. That aching need driving me on never felt this big before.

His laugh reverberates in my ear. 'Me too.' He brushes my hair off my forehead, then gently drives me wild as he casually grazes my nipple with his finger, where it's poking through the cotton of my dress. 'Though I've been wanting to for a while...'

And as he leads me by the hand, and the stripey carpet on the stairs scrunches under my toes, I realise I'm finally about to see inside Rafe's bedroom.

52

Upstairs at Daisy Hill Farm: Waking up in Rafe's room

'Oh shit.' I groan and roll over, as I feel the bed lurch. As I open my eyes a crack I take in the sunlight seeping across the white painted floorboards. 'It can't be morning already, we only just went to sleep.'

'Sorry, I didn't mean to wake you.' Rafe is dragging a T-shirt over his head, sounding as croaky as I feel. 'It's six, and Sunday, which means I'm milking.' His eye roll turns into a grimace as he pulls on his jeans. Then he leans over me, and rubs his thumb down my cheek. 'And you're right, you've been properly asleep for all of half an hour.'

When his mouth finds mine, he tastes just as delicious as before. The deep snog he gives me practically spins me off the bed, and leaves me wanting a lot more of what I've already had three lots of already. However many times I've imagined this room, the bed was never this comfy. As for the rest, what can I say? I'm struggling to find words. Think symphony orchestras, exploding rainbows, and erupting volcanos, and you still won't be close. I need to go and Google *sex after abstinence* to check if this is a phenomenon. I suspect it's something Immie might know, but there's no way I can share this with her to ask. All I know is, it's galaxies away from anything I ever experienced before, and there has to be an explanation. Why would two strangers set each other on fire like this? And when was I ever a one night stand person? What's worse, from what I remember, even if Rafe was very willing, I was the one who practically knocked him into bed, and took what I had to have. The shudder of shame that runs through me as I think of it shakes the bed.

'So if you're feeling guilty, there's no need.' He's smiling down at me, reading my mind. 'There's no way this counts as sleeping together.'

In case you're wondering – don't lie, I know you are – the sheets are petrol blue Egyptian cotton, with grey cashmere throws. And from the light dreamy warmth, I'm guessing the duvet has to be goose down. Rafe tugs it back into place, then leans over me, to reach for his phone from the bedside table.

'So what was it then?' I snuggle into the pillows.

'Fucking phenomenal,' he says, his face breaking into a grin, 'for me anyway.'

I can't let this pass without admitting it. 'And me too.' Although I'm suddenly worried that given my enthusiasm, he might get the wrong impression. 'Actually, I don't do this very often.' I never do it, but I don't want to sound like a prude. 'And definitely not with random people.' I'm panicking at my lack of morning-after etiquette. 'And I definitely won't be doing it again.'

'Don't go beating yourself up about it.'

Knowing I'm blabbering, I make a super-human effort to put the brakes on. 'I'm just not sure how this fits in with my plans to be single forever.' I really should have thought this through before. Before I drank all that wine and threw myself at him.

'It's no big deal.' He rubs a thumb over his jaw. 'You're fresh from your break-up. If it makes you feel better, look upon it as a one-off. A happy accident. End of.'

It's sweet that Rafe picked up my wobbles, and I should be punching the air because he's putting this in context so sensibly, in a way that totally lets me off the hook. So why my tummy is deflating with disappointment, I have no idea.

I glance at my watch, which is stupid, because I know exactly what time it is. 'So by the time you get back from the cows,' I say, 'I'll probably be gone.' There's a busy morning ahead. Dismantling a wedding is almost as much work as putting one together. What's more, he's made it perfectly clear I need to get the hell out of the bedroom part of his life, a.s.a.p.

He gives a shrug. 'I can cook you breakfast later if you like?'

Staring at the guy who just delivered the orgasms of my life, over grilled tomatoes and sausages might not be the best thing, especially when he's assured me it won't be happening again. 'Thanks, but I'll probably have eaten by then.' Not that I'd want it to happen again, obviously.

'I could make you hash browns?' He's really going the extra mile here, hopping as he pulls on his boots.

I shake my head. 'Thanks, but it's still a no.' Even if his hash browns are to die for, I need to quit while I'm ahead here. It's hard enough to turn my back on it as it is.

We both have every reason in the book to steer clear here. I might not be a country girl, but I can spot a metaphorical dead horse when it stares me in the face. And it doesn't need a fried field mushroom garnish.

'In that case, I'll catch you later then.' Rafe hesitates, leaning his back on the wardrobe.

If I didn't know better, I'd think he was reluctant to leave. As for the T-shirt he's wearing, it's so torn there's little point him wearing it.

I squint at the faded lettering. 'So what's your slogan for today?'

He looks down to check. 'Young Farmer on the Pull…' He gives it the grimace it deserves. 'Let me put that into context.' With a rueful grin, he spins around.

'Tug of War, 1995?' As I prop myself up on my pillows, I do the maths. 'Crap Rafe, that T-shirt's over twenty one years old.' I'm surprised his mother didn't take it for dusters a decade ago.

'As for this farmer…' Rafe turns, and heads for the door. 'I'm definitely not young any more either, but apparently I can still pull.' His laugh is low, and I'm almost certain that's a slow wink he sends me. 'Thanks for that Red, see you soon.'

But I don't get a second chance to check, because he's already gone and closed the door.

53

Outside at Daisy Hill Farm: The morning after

'Where the hell have you been Immie?'

Given she's walking out of Buttercup Cottage, doing up her shirt, at seven in the morning, I already know the answer.

'I just spent the non-wedding night in the bridal suite with Chas. Is there a problem?'

I'm guessing by the way she's chosen the word problem that she's picking up my disbelieving head shakes. On the plus side, it's taken my mind right off confessions about where I slept – or didn't.

'For fuck's sake Immie, shagging the poor guy on what should have been his wedding night? That's a bit much, even for you.' If I'm going in strongly here, it's because I'm shocked. Even as my words are bouncing back off the cobbles, I'm cringing at how hypocritical I sound.

'Who said anything about shagging?' The hard stare she gives me is a double reminder that I'm the one who's out of line here.

'You didn't?' This has to be a first.

'Pops, the guy is heartbroken, he's light years away from having sex. Yes, we went to bed in the four poster together, but we kept our tops and pants on, and mainly we laughed. And he cried quite a bit too. That's all.'

'Really?' It never occurred to me that Immie would hold back if she ever got her hands on Chas.

'It was great for Chas, and his ego, to leave the party with a woman, especially someone like me. Everyone will assume he got his nooky. I just hope word gets back to Nicole, because she's left the poor guy in bits. It'll be months before he recovers.' She's dropped her predator act, and come over all protective.

She turns to me. 'So what are you doing here anyway?'

I'm not ready for Immie to flip the interrogation onto me. It's ironic that we've swapped places. For once, Immie's the chaste one, breezing around fresh as a daffodil, and I'm the one creeping away from the one night stand with a thumping head and what feels like the hangover to end all hangovers. But it's probably down to lack of sleep.

I decide to brazen it out. 'It was very late when we finished, I blagged Rafe's spare room for the night.' If I do a Jules, say it like it couldn't be any other way, I might get away with it. I look at my watch pointedly. 'I wanted to make an early start.' Hopefully that's reason enough.

'Great.'

I give a huge sigh of relief, as Immie takes it on board without question. 'So given you could be lazing around the wedding suite until lunch time, why are you out and about this early?' Even as I ask, I see her crumple.

Her voice drops to a hiss. 'If you must know, Cate's coming to do me some emergency make-up, in the office.' She inclines her head in the direction of the courtyard. 'She's on her way up now.'

And with one wave of a mascara brush, the heat's right off me staying at Rafe's. I'm torn between falling about laughing at the absurdity of Immie having secret make-up assignments, and the realisation that if she's going to these lengths, she must be beyond desperate to make an impression on Chas. Luckily Cate and Immie are concentrating so hard on the task in hand, they have no time at all to think about me. Turning possibly the least groomed woman in Cornwall, into…Well, basically, when push comes to shove, and Immie's tilted back in my office chair, eyes closed, face to the ceiling, firing out instructions along with emphatic arm waves, it's plain to us all. She wants to become Nicole. End of.

I'm not sure how to begin, but I'm sure I need to make some kind of intervention. 'You do know Immie, when you're going into any relationship, it's best to be yourself?' If anyone knows this, it's me. Thinking back, since Morgan was born, Immie hasn't actually had anything resembling a relationship. And I'm not sure she had many before that.

Cate is currently dusting Immie's cheeks with bronzer

'What do you mean by that Pops?' Immie's grunt comes past the powder brush.

'It's dangerous to pretend you're something you're not, especially when you first meet someone.' I only have to look back to Brett and me to find a thousand examples. 'I regret letting Brett think I enjoyed sailing. If I'd come clean, and told him how much I hated it the first time we went out on a yacht, I'd have saved myself years of miserable weekends and holidays.' Not to mention the pain when our relationship finally fell apart. I suspect he'd have dropped me faster than a hot banana if he'd realised the truth about me and boats, which might have been no bad thing. We really weren't suited, but it was me pretending that kept those differences hidden. I take responsibility for that now. Having realised how wrong I was, I'd hate to see Immie make the same mistakes I did. She's wonderful as she is, and she needs a guy who appreciates her for herself. Not one who'd rather she was buffed and polished and in six inch stilettos. I suppose we should be thankful Immie isn't trying to totter round in high heels too.

Cate gently begins to work on Immie's eye-liner. 'It's true, it's important to be honest,' she says. 'If you begin something as someone you're not, it'll only unravel later.' She flashes the mascara over Immie's lashes. 'There, your eyes are popping now. So what colour shall we go for on your lips?'

As I watch, I can't help remembering Immie the day of the photo shoot. The way she was literally batting the make-up lady away. That was the first day Rafe began to loosen up. It was the first time I saw him properly laughing. That was before he'd even come round to the idea of weddings. When I stop to think about it, he's come so far since then. And now I've wrecked everything we'd built up, by letting lust get the better of me, and jumping into his bed. I mean what was I thinking? He's the boss. I have to work with him on a daily basis. I don't want a relationship. He doesn't want a relationship. How am I going to face him in the office now, when the last time I saw him he was...

'Maybe bright red again?' Immie says. 'That ruby whatsit you gave me yesterday was pretty close.' That would be close to a Nicole look-alike.

Cate and I exchange glances. Immie hasn't taken in any of what we've been saying.

'First rule of make-up – it's lips *or* eyes,' I say, hoping to help. 'Not both.'

Cate follows my lead. 'And your eyes are looking stunning.'

'What?' Immie gives a squawk of distress. 'What the hell are you on about?'

'Maybe something natural for your lips would work better than scarlet. Nicole always looked very expensive, so you don't want to look cheap.' Cate twists up a lippy. 'I've got *Just Nothing*, or *Crème de Beige*.'

'I have to say, what the hell's the point of putting on lippy the same colour as your lips, but what do I know?' Immie snorts.

I chip in. 'On the up side, it won't disappear every time you put your lips round a bottle.'

'Now that is good news. What's that one?' As Immie makes a grab for a lipstick, it rolls onto the floor.

Cate picks it up. '*Nude Hero*. How about that?'

'Whoa, now you're talking.' Immie says. 'Slap it on, and make it quick. Don't forget why we're here. I've got a man to catch.'

As she dashes across to Buttercup Cottage moments later, I decide there's only one way forward for me. I need to avoid Rafe, at least for a few days anyway. Let things blow over. And then maybe we can pick up at the point last night, before we left the kitchen. And pretend the rest never happened.

54

In the wedding field at Daisy Hill Farm: Dismantling Tipi City

Whereas some Daisy Hill weddings are gone without trace in hours, thanks to the summer holidays and the fire service shift pattern, the wedding that didn't happen is still hanging round three days later. Down in the field, as the main tipi is being dismantled, there's still a knot of die-hard revellers, relaxing under a gazebo by the last cluster of tents. As I get closer to the huddle round the Smokey Joe, Immie gives a wave.

'Fancy a sausage sarnie, Pops?' She's shouting through a mouthful. From the stains on the bread she's waving about, she's ignored all our advice about the importance of looking natural, and reverted to her *Ruby Rush*. What's more, I'm guessing from the haphazard edges, she's ditched her personal make-up artist, and is applying it herself. Possibly without help of a mirror. Of course I'm not surprised to see her, given she's practically taken up residence down here since the bridal suite rental ran out. What's more, red pout aside, she fits in like one of the guys. Seems that she and Blue Watch get on like a house on fire.

Chas wanders out of one of the tents and squats down by the cool box. 'Anyone for a beer?'

Despite the shade, he's looking decidedly rosy, probably where Immie's polish has rubbed off on him.

Shaking my head, I grin at him. 'No thanks.' Ten in the morning's a bit early for me, even when the sun's beating down. 'Has anyone seen Rafe? I've looked everywhere and I can't find him.' Given his telltale Land Rover is parked by the piles of poles and canvas that used to be the big tipi, he can't be far away.

Ideally, I'd have steered clear of him for at least a few more days, but the guy from the tipi company has a query that won't wait. At least if I see Rafe down here, we're on neutral ground. Well away from the house and all the echoes of what I'm silently calling my night of shame. Who'd have thought it would be so hard to drive those few hours out of my brain and pretend they didn't ever happen? No matter what I do, the flash backs keep coming. The truth is, I've spent more time reliving those two hours in the half light of dawn than I've spent concentrating on whatever I'm supposed to be doing. Whether it's wedding dresses, or websites, it doesn't matter – I can't keep my mind on the job. Thank Christmas I haven't got a big cake job on right now, because my mind is so upside down, I can barely tell my cupcakes from my chocolate soufflé.

'Uncle Rafie?' Immie gives an indulgent eye roll. 'Try the wood. He's found his new role in life – playing with the kids in the stream.' She peels away from the group. 'I'll take you.'

'Great.' This seriously doesn't sound like any incarnation of Rafe I've come across.

Once we're walking across the field, her voice drops. 'I don't know what you did to him the night you stayed, but he hasn't stopped bouncing since.'

My stomach goes into free fall. 'He loved playing the piano that evening.' It's not that I don't trust Immie to keep a secret, but no-one can know I had sex with Rafe. Even though I've been trying to get it out of my head ever since, what I can't quite get my head around is how damned incredible it was. And I'd somehow hoped I could put off seeing him for a bit longer.

Immie grunts. 'It must've been the music then.' She swings around a birch trunk, as we reach the trees. The sound of laughter and splashing nearby carries on the air. 'You don't always have to sleep on the sofa you know, he's got a lovely spare room.' She turns to me with a scolding smile. 'The cleaners went in, but they told me you'd slept downstairs. I *knew* you wouldn't have wanted to dirty the sheets.'

I swallow so hard, I almost choke on my tongue. 'Sometimes the sofa's less trouble.' I squeak. If I sound as if I'm about to expire, that's exactly how I feel. 'It was only for a couple of hours anyway.'

As we round the bend, the path opens into a clearing. I gulp again as I take in Rafe, in soaking wet cut off denims, bare legs planted in the broad stream. He's surrounded by a crowd of kids, and Jet's on the bank, watching patiently. For once Rafe's tattered Fat Willy's Surf Shop vest is entirely appropriate, even if it's a shock to see him wearing a shirt without a picture of a tractor.

He eases the rock he's manhandling into position. 'Red, hey.'

If a shaft of sunlight had fallen across his face it couldn't have lit up more, and my heart pounds so hard, it leaves me feeling queasy. At least we've broken the ice.

'We're building a dam,' he says, turning to his crew. 'Aren't we guys? Only for today though, then we'll take it down.'

Immie gives me a thumbs up as she slips away.

'Brill.' I shove my hands into the pocket of my skirt, and try to get a hold of my lurching breath. 'Have you got a minute to chat about an idea the tipi guy had?'

'Sure.' Rafe shakes back his hair and wipes his wrist across his brow. 'Building dams is very therapeutic, why not come in and help, we can chat while we're working.' He sounds suddenly doubtful. 'Unless you don't want to get mud on your clothes?' Okay, when I said I'd prefer not to be trapped in the confines of the office with Rafe, I wasn't thinking of trading it to meet thigh deep in water.

'It's only an old skirt.' That came out in an unexpected rush, before I thought it through. It's not that old, it's my second best work one, but I bought it because it's easy, washable, and hard wearing. When you share an office with thirteen hens, sad to say, some considerations count more than style.

I'm already kicking off my Converse. Next thing I know, I've hitched up my waistband, and I'm striding in. 'Shit it's freezing!' The icy water numbs my feet instantaneously, then sets up a serious ache in my legs. 'Whoahhh.' I throw up my arms, wobbling precariously as my bare feet slide on the slimy stones of the stream bed.

Rafe twists to watch me as I stagger across to him. 'So, we're taking rocks, and putting them in a pile across the stream.' The way his lips are twisting, he seems to be holding back his laughter.

As if to illustrate how easy it is, two small boys come across with rocks almost as big as themselves on their shoulders.

'Nice work, Chip, steady there, Tommy.' Rafe's encouragement is as easy as it is warm.

As they tip the rocks into the pool behind the dam, an arc of water leaps through the air and catches me broadsides. The chill smacks against the warm skin of my arms, and I gasp and jump backwards. Very bad move. My feet slither and as I fail to find a foothold I make a wild lunge. With each lurch I lose my balance more, and then there's an unholy splash, and the cold roars through my body, as I tumble sideways into the water.

The roar of sheer joy that comes from the delighted kids goes some way to soothing my dented ego. As my skin pricks to goosebumps, Rafe strides over, and his strong hands close around my wrists. With one yank, he hauls me to my feet.

'Beginner's error,' he says. 'If you're going to fall in, make sure you do it downstream of the dam, the water's much shallower there.'

'Great timing, telling me now.' I peel a piece of pond weed off my dripping skirt, and brush some mud off my leg. Even if I'm shivering, this is minor compared to winter soakings I've had on Brett's friends' ocean going yachts. Just to show the sea of waiting faces that I'm good, I take the stone the small girl nearby is holding out to me, and plonk it onto the dam wall.

Rafe's staring at me and my chattering teeth. 'Are you okay? Shall I run you back up to the house?'

I sniff, and push a soggy strand of hair out of my eye. 'No thanks, I'm fine.' Although I'm sticking my chin up in the air defiantly, it isn't that much of a lie. In response to Rafe's eyes sneaking towards my boobs, I peer down to check my pale grey T-shirt hasn't turned completely transparent. If ever there was a time I'm pleased I grabbed a solid, every day bra, it's today. I dread to think of the trouble I'd be in now if I'd put on the skimpy lace number from the shop that I blew Tia's wedding tip on yesterday. Again, that totally irrational purchase was in line with how things have been the last two days. I mean, I never intend to need lacy underwear again. Those few short hours with Rafe have completely dislocated my sensible brain from my actions. If you need proof, you only have to look at me now. Why the hell am I standing here arse deep in a bloody country stream, with a skirt like frozen cardboard?

There's what looks like a comfortable tree trunk lying midway across the stream, so I wobble across to it, and carefully edge my way to sitting. Then I bring my knees up, and hug them to my chest, solving the problem of any too-visible nipples.

'So.' If my hands were free, I'd be rubbing them now, but they're not, so instead, I just sniff loudly to get Rafe's attention, and it works. 'There's something I need to run by you.' I hesitate, only because I'm not sure how he'll take this.

Before I can carry on Rafe cuts in. 'Wait, don't tell me. You

302

want to bring brides to weddings by water?' Although his expression is dead pan, there's a smile lilting on his lips. 'Given the way you just made your entrance, I'd say it's a "no" to that one.' He grins over the head of one of the other small girls as she delivers a stone into his hands, then he carefully pushes it into place. 'Wouldn't you agree?'

Oh my days. I get what Immie means about Rafe acting like he's taken happy pills. Dismissing that with a head shake, I carry on with what I've come for.

'The tipi guys want to leave their big tipi up after the next midweek wedding they're doing. And have a mini wedding fair the weekend after.'

'Sorry?'

'It's the last weekend in September. They want an open day in the wedding field, to showcase the tipi range. The styling company and the caterers have said they'd exhibit in the main tipi, we can get Brides by the Sea to bring dresses and flowers, I can bring cakes, Jules will do a photo exhibition.'

'Fine, so long as it fits in with our other bookings, it sounds like a goer.' His shrug suggests he doesn't really know why I'm involving him at all.

'It's a great first point of contact for future brides and grooms.' I give it a moment for that thought to sink in, given I've no idea what Rafe's plans are after September. 'A wedding fair would be really good for you if you decide to carry on with weddings at Daisy Hill Farm next year.' No pressure at all either way from me here, but at least I've said it. 'That will be pretty much our last event of the season.' I've spent so long aching to get this whole job over, that I'm surprised by the pang in my chest as I say that. Somehow life won't ever be quite the same again without chickens perching on my desk, cows snuffling at me over the fence as I lock up my car, not to mention unscheduled dips in brooks.

Rafe's eyes widen, but a moment later his hands are on his

hips, and it's business as usual. 'Right, got that thanks.' The way he narrows his eyes gives no indication how much of that he's taken on board. 'So unless you're joining our dam building team for the day, I'd better run you back up to the house to change. Unless you can borrow something from Immie?'

The kids, wary they're about to lose their gang leader, raise their heads, and stop work to listen more carefully.

'Great idea, I'll scrounge something from the campers.' Even an already worn fireman's shirt would be preferable to ending up back in Rafe's kitchen. I ease myself off the tree trunk, and begin to slither towards the stream edge.

The grin Rafe sends me is wicked. 'We could wear matching Fat Willy vests?'

'Thanks, but no,' I say firmly, to close him down. I'm about to clamber onto the bank, but Rafe's already there, springing out of the water, arm extending down, ready to haul me out.

'Happy to drag you out of the mud. Again. You wouldn't let me take you home last time either.' His tone is rueful.

I'm not letting him get away with that. 'Like you even offered.' My voice is high with indignation. If he's harping back to that day in the ditch with Bolly and Brioche, it's so long ago, I'm surprised he can even remember. Although on second thoughts, given the way he's standing on the bank, all stubble shadows and tanned forearms, I'm so tempted to grab him, and snog his socks off, I'd better get a move on. Scrambling onto the drier ground, I grasp at a sapling to steady myself. 'Think about what I said about the wedding fair, and get back to me.' Snatching my converse from the ground, I hurry away. 'See you.' I shout that last phrase over my shoulder as I scurry away barefoot. Somehow it's very important to have the last word, and to get the hell out of here as fast as I can.

55

In my flat at Brides by the Sea: My own front door

The rest of August is wall to wall cakes and weddings, and our list of bridesmaid duties for Cate is expanding exponentially. It's all very well saying, 'Don't worry, we'll do the wedding flowers.' Ditto the favours for three hundred. Not to mention the hen night, which was supposed to be as last minute, low key, and low budget as they come, but still had to be organised. It's been hard pulling it all together when I've been working three other jobs at the same time. And on top of all that, Rafe took it into his head that he wanted to discuss ideas for the business. About 'taking weddings forward'. The down side is, I was up until the small hours preparing figures to persuade him it's a goer. But on the up-side, to save me time, he's coming into St Aidan so we can talk it through.

The trouble with not having my own front door is that I've no control over who Jess lets up to see me, or when. I'm getting ready to go and meet Rafe in town, when who should clatter up the stairs, but Jules. His excuse – he'd come to tell me how fab the Wedding Fair adverts are. They hit the local press today, and yes, I might have been jumping the gun, but they implied the farm is continuing as a venue. The real reason for his visit was to suggest we should join forces and launch a photography and wedding planning business together. And although I can see how the two services might complement each other nicely, I'm not sure I'm up for throwing myself into business with Jules. Although he was so enthusiastic and excited, I wasn't mean enough to tell him that straight. I'll have to let him down gently. But later.

Which brings is neatly onto the real business of the day, or evening. Cate's pre-wedding bash. Shoe horned in, at the last minute. So small it isn't even being referred to as a Hen Night, because officially she's decided not to have one of those, for reasons of economy. So instead it's Liam looking after the kids, while a few girlfriends go on a pub crawl in town.

Bearing all the above in mind, I'm not quite sure why a fairy costume just arrived by courier. But it did. If we'd had the opportunity to choose, I might have gone for a colour other than light mauve. So would Immie. She texted me a pic, saying how much she hates her pale yellow. So I'm all set to meet Rafe for an hour before, in my black wedding shop capri pants, topped off with an almost-sharp white shirt. Am I wearing the sexy bra? No. Of course I'm not. I've buried it deep in the drawer. Right at the bottom. So I don't have to undergo a personal interrogation, asking myself why the hell I bought it, every time I dip in for knickers.

My secret plan is to keep the capri pants on under the fairy dress. But just in case I don't, I'm ironing the lilac tulle, in the vain hope that smooth tulle will come further down my thighs than the scrunched up tulle, as delivered by Trans Global Express. I'm still staring at the tattered net despairingly, when there's yet another clatter on the stairs, and a very familiar low voice.

'Red, are you up there?'

It's Rafe. Good thing I had my mouth shut, because given the way my heart lurched, it might have bounced right out of the open window and landed on the beach. Ten minutes early too. And when did meeting outside The Surf Shack turn into arriving on my landing, and walking straight on into my kitchen? Unannounced, and uninvited. Giving me no time at all to get my head around how I'm going to act around him, when the last time we were properly together was in his bed.

'Hey, Rafe, I wasn't expecting you to traipse all the way up here. Come in,' I say, entirely unnecessarily, given he's already level with the kitchen table.

Drawn by the sea view, he moves forward to peer out of the window. 'You're on top of the world here. Wow, who knew the sea actually sparkled?' He's obviously spent too many years inland to have noticed before. 'And what a lot of baking tins.'

There's a pang in my chest, as he mentions the sparkle, and the tins. With my future after October not exactly settled, I'm not sure how long I'll be hanging onto my lovely porthole picture of the sea. Or be baking my cakes every day. 'I never get tired of looking at the sea, it's different every time,' I say.

As I lean to catch yet another glimpse, I accidentally nudge my laptop, sitting on the table. The screen bursts into life, open at the email I'd momentarily forgotten. My former colleague in London, who's been out-of-office all summer, is finally back at her desk. Not that she says anything other than good to hear from you, I'll keep you in mind if anything comes up. Which is a great way of saying 'you left, there's no coming back'. In a rush of guilt for emailing her at all, I slam the laptop shut. Too fast.

'Hiding something, Red?' Rafe's laugh is low and teasing.

I say the first thing that comes into my head. 'Only my Uniform Dating application.' And before anyone says, I'm not secretly wishing.

'You're joking?' His voice rises in shock. 'You want your own fireman? Shit, I did not see that coming.'

'Gotcha.' I laugh. 'It was an email from an old girlfriend in London.'

'Phew, right…Nice kitchen you've got here,' he says. If he's trying to take the heat off and change the subject, it worked. 'I like that it's colourful, with all your utensils and work tools on display. It's full of integrity, and very you.' Wonders never cease. Now he's giving feedback on interiors.

'I painted the cupboards myself.' I'm still pretty proud of the way the bright blue paint hides the hotch potch. 'Otherwise the colour's down to the tulips.' Red and purple and yellow. 'I couldn't resist them. They reminded me of the colours my mum had in our cottage when I was small.'

'Funny how nostalgia makes us feel safe.' As Rafe sticks his hands in his pockets, for the first time I notice he's wearing smart chinos. 'Actually I came early to give you a chance to change.'

Fashion criticism? 'Which bit of shirt and capri pants doesn't work for coffee?'

'I booked a table for early dinner at The Harbourside Hotel.'

What? Since when did agreeing to meet up for an hour at five thirty mean a commitment for a whole night out?

'I hope that's okay with you?'

I'm opening and closing my mouth like a guppy. 'Sorry, there isn't time, I'm going out…at 6.30.'

Before I get any more out his airy grin turns to a frown. 'Going out? When do you ever go out?'

'It's Cate's hen do, hence the dress.' I nod at the ironing board.

'That's a dress?' He screws up his eyes as he scrutinises. 'There's not much of it.' Then the furrows on his forehead melt away.

'Fairies don't wear many clothes.' More's the pity. 'Not the ones dressed by Cate's suppliers, anyway.'

'It can get a bit rough out on the streets late at night, are you sure you'll be okay? Out drinking in wings and not much else?'

'Safety in numbers, there are thirty four of us, we should be fine.' It's never occurred to me that we wouldn't be. 'Cate and Immie plan on getting off their faces, but I need to stay sober, because I've got a five tier wedding cake to put together tomorrow. But you know Immie, she won't take any shit.'

'Well, if you need rescuing, you can always ring me.' He's being over protective again.

I'd better humour him. 'We won't, but thanks, I appreciate the offer'

Rafe laughs. 'So how about coming to The Harbourside for a quick drink on the terrace then?'

'Or I could get you a drink here, then we can run through the figures on my laptop?' Not that I'd planned to entertain Rafe at my kitchen table, but it might save time. I open the fridge. 'Light beer? White wine spritzer? Elderflower fizz?' Out loud the options sound very girly.

'I didn't plan to burst in on you. So long as you don't mind?' He gives me a searching stare, before he decides. 'Thanks, in that case I'll go with the beer.'

But the soft smile he sends me as he puts the bottle to his lips is the last thing I need.

56

In my flat at Brides by the Sea: Sex with the boss

That's the problem with having sex with the boss. Afterwards it's impossible to look at them in the same way ever again.

'So, shall I run you through some numbers?' I say, as I re-open my laptop, desperate to pull off the meeting without crashing elbows – or anything worse – with Rafe. It might have been easier if we'd sat either side of the table, instead of being rammed together on our stools. The surprise is how comfortably he fits in. I guess we've spent so many hours trading insults across the farm office, we're relaxed with each other wherever we are.

'Great idea.' Rafe makes a point of angling his body towards the far end of the table to avoid ramming me up against the cupboard.

The one plus for me is knowing the sex was a one-off mistake for Rafe, in the same way it was for me. Despite my strict embargo on men, I'd find the situation a whole lot harder if Rafe was in the game. At least this way, I know any misplaced fantasies I might accidentally have can't ever be anything else. And that's helpful.

As for my figures, I'm damned proud of them. 'I've done a spreadsheet showing what the opposition are charging for venues similar to the farmhouse, at different times of year.' Whereas spreadsheets might be like falling off a log for some people, to me they're a whole new level of achievement. 'Although as an intimate venue, the farmhouse is pretty unique.'

Talking of difficult stuff, I've also underestimated how hard it was going to having Rafe's delicious scent pulsing through my kitchen, and wafting straight up my nose. At least on the terrace of The Harbourside, the sea breeze would have blown it away.

'Interesting.' He nods.

I flick onto the next page. 'This is what I reckon you could charge for the first year, but you could obviously go higher once the venue's established.'

He nods again, then sits back on his stool. 'Actually, there's a new idea I wanted to throw into the mix.'

I raise my eyebrows expectantly. 'And?'

'The house is good to use for smaller weddings for now. But in the long term, if we converted the group of old stone barns at the top of the courtyard, we could take all sizes of weddings, all year round.' His beam is as huge as his idea.

'Wow.' As U-turns go, this is more like a full blown tour of spaghetti junction.

'It obviously needs more investment than mowing a field, but the buildings are sound, and the stripped back, rustic style is what people are looking for right now.'

If I'm gawping in silence, it's because he's coming out with all the lines that should be mine.

'Subject to planning permission, of course.'

'Obviously.' There's one massive question bouncing around my head. 'Weddings in a barn complex sound totally fabulous. But why such a huge change?'

For a moment, as he deliberates, a flicker passes across his face. By the time he speaks, he's back in charge again. 'If we're going to do weddings at all, we might as well go for it, and do them properly.' He gives me a sideways glance. 'As you're always telling me, it makes good financial sense.'

There's something not a hundred percent convincing about what he's saying here, but I can't put my finger on exactly what it is. As for his hesitation, he almost looked guilty.

'But as you've said to me in the past, it's not only about the finances.' I scratch my head, because I can't completely believe this is what Rafe wants.

His grimace is the giveaway. 'There'll be an opening for an Events Manager.' He says, his lips slipping into a smile. 'But it'll have to be someone who loves weddings.'

My mind races. It's true, this could be my dream job. Permanent, full time, secure, satisfying. If this was on offer, life after October would take on a whole new shape, so different to the uncertain blur it is in my head at the moment. 'I'm sure you'd be able to find yourself one of those,' I say, not wanting to jump the gun. If I wasn't so desperate for him to give me the job, I'd find it easier to push myself forward. What's more, if I'd known this was coming up, I'd have made damned sure I stayed out of Rafe's bed.

'As it happens, there is someone I have in mind,' he grins, as he flips out his phone, to check the time. 'But right now, I'd better let you get on. Immie will never forgive me if I delay the hen party.' Easing himself up from the stool, he wriggles out from behind the table. Perfectly executed. Not one elbow clash. 'Unless you need help getting into your dress?'

'Haha, nice try.'

At the top of the stairs he hesitates. 'If for some reason your hens don't show up, give me a ring. I've never been out with a fairy before. If not we'll do dinner another time.'

'Great.' I give a cheery wave.

He's still hanging on. 'Take care, have a brilliant evening, and remember…any problems…' He does the 'phone me' hand signal.

'I've told you, we'll be fine.'

'I know, but in case you're not…'

I shake my head at him in despair.

And he's still waggling his hand doing the 'phone me' sign as he disappears from view, and clatters off down the stairs.

57

Out in St Aidan: Hens on tour

If I thought there'd be any chance of running Rafe's radical new wedding thoughts past Cate and Immie during the evening, I must have been mad. It might have been thrown together at the last minute, but the hen night is typical Cate, in that she's planned and printed out thirty five copies of the itinerary, and she's done her research meticulously. We're hitting Happy Hours around the town like clockwork. It's also typical that Cate waved away all our offers of help to organise, in order to stay in control. What's not so typical is the way she's throwing back the cocktails. At this rate she's going to lose her handle on the event pretty damn soon. Hopefully by that time she'll be past caring anyway.

As for the fairy outfits, they're certainly attracting attention, and not always the right sort.

'Sheesh, I wish I'd put my granny knickers on under here.' The fairy in the long yellow wig and purple glitter eye shadow is speaking for all of us, as she reels away from the latest wolf whistles, and tugs in vain at the transparent frills riding up her thighs.

'Have we met before?' I shout, as we rub bare shoulders together at the fifth bar we go to, waiting for the trays of cocktails which Cate pre-ordered earlier in the day. I'm hoping for some un-slurred conversation, given she's shared that her strategy for staying upright is to miss out every other drink.

'I know Cate from way back at the council, I'm in human resources.' She's yelling at the top of her voice so I can hear her over the noise. 'Could have done with more resources in this skirt if you ask me.'

'I thought I recognised you,' I holler back.

'Don't say that, I'll be dead meat at work if this gets out.' She gives a thumbs up to the barman as she grabs a tray loaded with lurid pink and green drinks in pint size jam jars. 'I'm in disguise,' she yells, as she tosses back a cascade of bleached Barbie hair braids. 'I'm brunette under here.'

'Better settle up for this lot,' I shout, bobbing up and down as I try to catch the barman's eye, regretting I came out in flats not heels. My hand's glued to a very un-fairy-like messenger bag full of cash that Cate's entrusted me with. My important brides- maid's job tonight is banker. I'm also in charge of the *Goodbye Miss, Hello Mrs* comments book, but so far everyone's been far too busy necking drinks to write anything. Whereas Immie opted to be in charge of first aid in case of collapses. From the way she's colliding with punters on her way to the loos, she might be the first one in need of her own services. She was supposed to be doing crowd control too, but trying to shepherd thirty odd hens around the streets of St Aidan would be a lost cause sober. Pissed, she's got no chance.

'How're you doing…I jusss want evvvryone to have a w-w- wonderful time…'

I can tell it's Cate, even before her arm flops over my shoulder. This has been her mantra for the evening. Her diamanté Bride-to-be glasses are at a jaunty angle as she grins at me. You'd have thought her long Cinderella gown would be a more modest option than the hen's barely-there dresses, but as the night progresses her plunging neckline is descending rapidly. That's the trouble with off-the-shoulder numbers – there's very little to hold them up. Right now she's got so much boob on show, she's verging on pornographic. If it wasn't for her *Last Fling Before The Ring* sash, she'd probably have lost the whole lot a few bars back.

By the time I've distributed the dayglow cocktails, Immie is staggering back from the ladies.

'Hey, Immie, how're you…I jusss want evvvryone to have…' Cate begins.

Immie wriggles away as I reach over to pull her skirt out of her knickers. At least one person thought to wear shorts rather than Brazilians, even if she hasn't learned the first rule about dresses is to check they're hanging down at the back before you leave the cubicle.

She nods at her drinks, accusingly. 'All good, b-b-but I l-lost my dick thing.'

Given she's got a full jam jar in each hand, I'd say losing her willy shaped straw is the least of her problems. On the up side, she hasn't hurled herself at any guys yet, so maybe she really has lost her heart to Chas.

'Come here Mrs…' Hitching up Cate's dress, I re-tie the sash around her ribs, re-adjust her veil and straighten her specs.

As she empties her glass, she grins at me. 'Jusss want evvvryone…to have a w-w-wonderful time…'

'They will,' I promise. 'They are.' Handing her a balloon to pacify her, I pull the itinerary out of my bag, and squint at my phone. 'Shit, it's ten o'clock.' We're late. As I'm sliding my phone away, bracing myself for the next leg, a text arrives. Why is Rafe texting me in the middle of the hen night?

How's it going? ;)

Come to think of it he's probably the only friend I've got who's as sober as I am right now. Although he's not exactly a friend. Whatever. In a weird way, it's good to talk.

Crazy as predicted…only four more hours ;) I type, then press send.

Then I raise my voice and yell across the bar. 'Okay fairies, time to move on.' I scour the sea of heads hoping to spot Immie, and haul her into action to sweep up the stragglers, but she's nowhere. I ball at the top of my voice. 'Next stop is Jaggers.'

Looks like from now on I'm on my own here.

58

Out in St Aidan: Taxis…!

You have to hand it to Cate. She might not be able to stand up after eight hours of solid drinking, but she certainly knows how to plan a great evening. And she's done us proud tonight, right down to the last detail. As we tumble out of The Beach Hut at two a.m., we find a line of waiting taxis, exactly as promised on my tattered instruction sheet.

'Why didnn I gerra blow up…hic…dick…' Cate's 'wonderful time' mantra changed about half an hour ago when we bumped into some hens with a six foot penis in tow. If there's one thing to be thankful for, it's that we didn't have to negotiate tonight and take one of those along for the ride.

I've got Immie on one side of me, and Cate on the other and somehow I'm propelling them forwards. As we lurch towards a red Mondeo with lights on top, I'm doing mental high fives because I'm within ten feet of the end of the evening. Then Cate stops moving her legs, digs her heels in, and pulls us to a halt.

'C'mon, almost there.' As I turn to encourage Cate, her smile is glassy, and she's moving her hand to her face. She opens her mouth slowly, and I'm expecting the blow up dick mantra, but instead she swallows a couple of times. I notice her cheeks have gone a weird shade of yellow under the neon lights. Then an arc of vomit flies through the air. I watch, open mouthed and help-less, as the rainbow of sick descends, reaches the pot of gold at the end, and splatters over Immie and me.

'Holy shit!' These are the first words Immie has uttered for hours. If getting covered in vomit has a plus side, it's Immie sobering up.

Meanwhile, there's one more heave from Cate, but this time we're out of the firing line, and the projectile force has all been used up. She completes the job, and spills puke straight down her Cinderella ruffles.

As I stand, with sick running down my legs, I can't believe the evening has ended like this.

In a nanosecond the taxi drivers are all out on the pavement, closing ranks, with a unanimous shout. 'No puke in the cars.'

Dammit that they've seen it unfold right in front of their windscreens. Although as I rub my face, trying to get the acid stench away from my nose, I can't say I blame them. One of them is already on his radio, spreading the word through taxi-world.

'No-one pick up Cinderella and the two ugly sisters, they're covered in puke.'

Indignant, I step forward to his open door to intervene. 'We're not ugly sisters, we're fairies,' I snap, then remember we're not in the best position. 'Please, we need to get home.'

'I don't care if you're the Queen of fucking Sheba love, you're not getting in any of our cars.' He's pretty damned decided.

That went well then. Not.

'Don't worry, you can stay at mine,' I say to Cate and Immie, loudly enough for the drivers to hear. Even as it comes out, I'm thinking of the four flights of stairs. Will I be able to get rid of the reek of vom in time for Jess's ten o'clock bride tomorrow?

Or will the smell drift down the stairs and permeate the shop for weeks? It might even cling to the lace and ruin the stock.

As a crowd of lairy guys shout their way down towards us, I try to bodily shove Cate and Immie out of their way. 'Get 'em off puke pants!' is the most imaginative insult they can manage as they jostle past, but I still give a sigh of relief when they've moved on.

'Come and sit on this bench, it looks comfy,' I say to Cate, trying to make the idea of concrete sound soft and appealing as I run through the possibilities in my head. By the time we've taken five minutes to reach the sanctuary of the bench, only a few feet away across a flat pavement, I've mentally crossed off all thoughts of four flights of stairs, regardless of the other considerations.

Liam's got the kids. Jules is nearby, but if he doesn't do childbirth, I doubt he'll be over the moon about Cinderella covered in sick. We could sit here until morning, go for a swim in the sea to wash off, then they could get the bus home.

Or I could ring Rafe. It's the last thing I want to do. But child birth, mud, cow dung, vomit – I already know he'll take this in his stride. I fumble with my phone for a moment of hesitation, and then I press call.

He might be asleep of course. As I listen to the ring tone I wonder how Brett would have reacted to this call, had we still been going out. Somehow I don't think he'd have been offering up his leather seats to rescue sick-covered hens. When Rafe picks up after only three rings, I want to hug him so hard I'd squeeze all the breath out of him.

'Rafe…'

'Red, how're you doing?'

'I've been better.'

'Where are you?'

'Outside The Beach Hut…we're covered in puke…'

'Stay where you are, I'll be there as soon as…twenty minutes max…'

How did I know he'd say that? As I slide my phone away, and sink back against the bench, I turn to Immie and Cate. 'It's all good, Rafe's coming to take us home.'

As Cate's head lands heavily on my shoulder, her damp veil sticks to my cheek. She mumbles as she takes my hand in hers. 'Jusss want evvvryone to have a w-w-wonderful time…'

* * *

Rafe's right about the twenty minutes. By the time the rest of the hens have negotiated their way into the line of taxis across the road, he's here, shouldering Immie and Cate up into the back of his Landy, making it look easy. Five minutes after, he's dropping me off at mine.

'Leave these two to me, I'll be fine,' he says, as he pulls up outside Brides by the Sea.

As go to open the car door I hesitate for a minute, staring out at a monster picture of Josie in the shadowy reflections of the display in the shop window. For the first time I feel very lucky that I didn't get to wear my version of the dress. Marrying Brett would have been a disaster. I'm not sure Rafe quite knows what he's letting himself in for, handling Cate and Immie solo, although there are deep snores coming from the back seats. 'Are you sure you don't want me to come?'

'No, you've got a big day tomorrow.' He grins at me, as he taps his fingers on the steering wheel. 'Five tiers will be hard enough without adding in sleep deprivation.'

I'm surprised he remembered the cake, given I've temporarily forgotten myself.

'They're supposed to be staying at Immie's.' I say doubtfully.

'I'd best take them back to mine, they can have a sofa and a bucket each in the kitchen. Don't worry, I'll make sure they're okay.'

And that's that. A moment later I'm on the pavement digging

in my bag for my key, listening to the sound of Rafe's exhaust echoing off the shop fronts as his Land Rover roars off into the night.

SEPTEMBER

59

At Daisy Hill Farm: Home truths and better offers

'Poppy, I need a word.'

Rafe's shoving his head around the office door, wanting attention. Again. Nothing new there then.

We've all recovered from our various hen night traumas. Immie's over the shock that she was out on the lash for eight hours and completely failed to pull. Everyone but her has worked out she wasn't actually trying. Cate's resigned herself to the fact she has a complete memory blank about most of her hen night. She refuses to believe she spent the last hour pursuing a giant blow up willy, but hopefully the pictures in her *Miss, Soon To Be Mrs* book might convince her, when she gets it on her wedding day. It should have occurred to us that a woman who once booked a fairground for her wedding would have wanted every hen accessory going, regardless of better judgement. Rafe has had pasties showered on him from my direction, and Immie gave his Landy the interior valet of its life. And I've vowed that's the last time I'll go out and stay sober, or wear wings of any description. So we're all good.

'Poppy, did you hear me?' Rafe's tapping a rolled up newspaper against his knee.

Impatient, and annoying. And why's he calling me Poppy when he always calls me Red?

So it's full speed ahead to Cate and Liam's wedding. We've got our final bridesmaid dress fittings tomorrow evening, and…

'Poppy…'

Given his growl is impossible to ignore, I look up with my helpful smile. 'Anything I can do?'

'You can damn well explain this for a start.' The paper slams down on the desk in front of me so hard it makes the filing cabinet vibrate.

I'm staring down at the advert for the Daisy Hill Farm Wedding Fair. I skim to check that the date's right. It is. 'We need to advertise, it's essential to get the word out there.'

He raps straight back. 'Yes, but the fair was supposed to be about suppliers. It clearly states in big letters that we're one of the most popular new venues around, which implies that we'll be taking bookings.'

'And we won't?' My voice has gone up an octave because I'm incredulous. What happened to barn conversions and weddings of all sizes, all year round?

His expression is as flat and noncommittal as his tone. 'Nothing's been finalised.'

Given the way I pulled out all the stops to get that ad out, something in his tight lipped response drives me a tiny bit wild. 'That advert simply states the current truth, nothing more.' This far I keep my voice level, but then it runs away to a shout. 'If you must know, I'm completely sick of everyone working their arses off on your behalf, and all we get in return is this "should-we-shouldn't-we" indecision.' As I flash my eyes upwards, I take in the hurt in his eyes, but I'm past caring. He's acting like a spoiled brat, and it's time someone told him. From where I'm standing he's back to the bad old guy who had so much handed to him on a plate, he's happy to throw it away.

'That's hardly fair…' He protests.

At the back of my mind there's a tiny voice reminding me I had so much on I didn't take the time to run the ad past Rafe, but frankly now's not the time to go back to that. Right now I'm rushed off my feet, and knackered, and it's all his fault. What's worse, the extra work has all been for the ideas that he's dumping, only days after he was jumping up and down with excitement about them. And what's worse, I was excited about them too. Excited enough to make me get to grips with spreadsheets, dammit. Excited enough to think I might even land a proper job, and secure my future, more fool me.

'We're having this wedding fair because the suppliers have carried you all year.' As the disappointment bites, my snarl escalates to a yell. 'But if you don't want to take any bloody bookings, don't take any bloody bookings. I doubt anyone will even give a shit, and frankly I'm past caring.'

I snatch up the paper and shove it into his hands as I storm past him, and stamp off towards my car. It's only when I get there, and I'm sitting in the driving seat thumping the steering wheel that I realise I've left my bag behind in the office. It's hanging on the back of my chair. I'm waiting, giving Rafe some time to leave the area, when I hear his Landy scream out of the yard and off up the lane. Typical. Still acting like a spoiled brat then. At least I can stalk back to rescue my bag without fear of meeting him.

I'm just unhooking it when Immie comes into the office with a file.

My heart's skittering. 'Shit, I thought you were Rafe coming back,' I say.

Immie narrows her eyes. 'And that's a bad thing?'

'I've just blown up at him.' I watch Immie raise one eyebrow. 'Weddings are off. Again.'

'Right,' Immie frowns. 'Any idea why that is?'

'Because he enjoys fucking with us?' I spit it out. From where I'm standing that's what it feels like.

She shakes her head. 'He might have changed his mind, but Rafe's really not like that.'

'Isn't he?' It comes out bitterly.

'You *know* he isn't.' Her voice is quiet, yet almost fierce. 'So it doesn't have anything to do with what Jules said to him?'

'When does Jules ever deliberately speak to Rafe?'

Immie's pulls down the corners of her mouth. 'Yesterday. Lord knows what he was doing here, but in passing, I overheard him telling Rafe you were wasted at Daisy Hill.'

I can't believe I'm hearing this. 'What?'

'Jules implied he was finalising better offers, which would let you express your full potential.'

I shake my head, not understanding any of it. 'The only offer I've had was Jules wanting me to go into business with him.' I say. 'Yesterday I finally plucked up the courage to tell him it wouldn't be happening.'

'Poor Jules is smitten with you.' Immie shrugs.

'It's not the big deal he's making it into. My finances are hardly in a place to set up a new business. Even if they were, much as I love him as a friend, I wouldn't lean on Jules.' Less than a month from now, I'm set to lose a big chunk of my income. Rafe whipped his potential job away as fast as it appeared. If I can't rely on that, I need to stay as flexible as I can. What's more, I've had a year of support from Jess. I'm not a wreck any more. I need to sort my life out.

Immie screws up her face as she thinks. 'I can't hope to second guess the workings of any male mind, but my guess is that Jules was lashing out when you rejected his offer. He wants to mess things up between you and Rafe.'

'Me and Rafe?' My squawk comes out so loud, it makes me jump. 'There's nothing between me and Rafe to wreck.'

'You must have seen the way he looks at you?' Immie frowns. 'Put it this way, if Rafe's smouldering glances were any hotter, you'd ignite.'

I dismiss that with a snort. 'Total bollocks.' Rafe doesn't like me. Not any more than anyone else. I'm certain of that. We both know the sex was a total mistake. He said so too. 'I think you've been hanging with too many fireman. It's making you imagine things. You're seeing things that aren't there.'

Immie rolls her eyes. 'Pops, you just balled Rafe out. He drove off at a hundred miles an hour. Something's not right.' She gives a big sigh and another of those searching stares of hers that turn you inside out. 'In your working relationship?'

The mention of work kicks me to a new place.

'Forget Jules. Find Rafe, and talk things through. Quietly and calmly, without yelling so loud the whole yard hears.'

'You heard?'

'Along with the rest of the world. Why else do you think I'm here?' She gives me a weird stare.

'Your files?'

'These are cottage instructions. I brought them in with me, I'm taking them away with me.' She heads for the door, waving the bogus file at me. 'You, find Rafe, right now, and talk to him.'

Easier said than done. 'I've no idea where he's gone.' It's not just an excuse. AWOL is a natural state for him.

'Come on Pops, think about it.' She's talking to me as if I'm being deliberately dense. 'Where does he go when he's upset?'

'The cow shed…the kitchen…the stream…the feed store?' I try, but Immie shakes her head to all of them. I rack my brains. 'I'm not sure I know anywhere else on the farm.'

She gives a huge snort. 'Sometimes you are *so* annoying. Think woman. I've given you enough, you have to get this bit on your own.'

And then it pops into my head. Scrambling up that grassy

bank that day. Rafe spilling all those secrets I'd rather not have known. 'Daisy Hill?'

'At last.' Immie's sigh is a mix of disgust and relief as she snatches a set of keys from the shelf. 'Jump in the pick-up, I'll run you as far as the gate.'

60

Up on Daisy Hill: Huffs and holding back

There have to be more accessible places to go off in a huff than the top of a hill. I'm lucky Immie brings me as far as the bottom. There have to be warmer places too, especially as I rushed off in a flimsy dress with a cropped cardi. To be brutally honest, my good friend Johnny Boden could have done with knitting a few more inches in all directions on this one. On anyone bigger than a seven year old, it's so skimpy it might as well not be there. What's more, a farmer scouring the sky before I set off would have known that the drizzle in the breeze was going to turn to blustering rain by the time I came to a halt half way to the top. Me? I had no idea.

Thirty seconds of rest here, taking in how far I've climbed, lets the burn in my throat subside. It's also enough time for me to kick myself for not grabbing a coat. Looking down, I can see the rain moving up the hill in waves. As for the wind, it's whipping around so fast it's freezing the bejesus out of me. I never thought I'd say it, but I'd give anything to wrap that damned tent of an old jacket of Rafe's round me now. As for the go-anywhere ballet

331

flats, they haven't lived up to their name. Wet grassy slopes like this one are definitely a challenge too far. A lot of the time my feet are sliding down faster than I can scramble up. Another day I might have cursed a tiny mark on the flowery canvas, but by the time I'm approaching the top of the hill, it's hard to make out a single bloom under the mud smears on my toes.

The weird part is, that by the time I reach the undulations near the summit, I'm gasping so hard the anger that powered me up here in the first place has faded. Worse still, I'm getting pricks of guilt because I rushed the publicity out without getting Rafe's approval. It's come back to bite me on the bum, so I might as well come clean and take responsibility.

Peering between the scrubby bushes as I put in a last surge of effort, I catch a glimpse of Rafe ahead of me, hunched over, back to the wind.

'Rafe, what are you doing up here?'

A gust all but whooshes my words away, but from the way he screws his head around, he must have heard.

'Red.' His tone gives away his surprise more than his impassive expression. 'I could ask you the same thing?'

Neither of us is giving anything away then. 'Where's Jet?' It's rare to see Rafe without him. I scour the hillside, in case he's off after rabbits.

'Jet wasn't fast enough, I left in a hurry.'

We all know he screamed off up the lane. The fact he didn't wait for Jet makes me feel even worse.

'I'm sorry,' I begin. Maybe I need to get straight to the point. 'I should have run the ad past you.'

Rafe sniffs. 'It wasn't so much about the ad. It's more about the future.'

Which tells me nothing. But I've made the first move. Given I practically expired getting up here, it would be good if he could offer me a bit more than that. 'You might want to apologise for storming off.'

It's a suggestion which he declines. 'You were the one who ran away.'

There's no way I've come this far to argue again. What's more, I've nothing to lose. Given how sullen he sounds, I decide to lay my cards on the table. He hadn't even offered me the damned job for next year, but I was still devastated when he whipped it away from me. 'I only ran off and yelled because I was upset that you'd just dumped a project I really believe in.' There, it's out there.

He rubs his thumb over his chin. 'The thing is, I really don't want to hold you back.'

I fail to see what this has to do with anything. 'I'd have thought you pulling the wedding business is going to do just that?'

Rafe's sigh is doubtful. 'I'll hold you back more giving you the opportunity to stay. I know we work well together.'

Don't ask me why that tiny throwaway phrase of his whisks me straight back to Rafe and I collapsing into a groaningly enormous simultaneous orgasm, but it does. I clear my throat while I rack my brain for a way to clarify the point. 'Professionally,' I say. I reckon that clears up any ambiguity, and blasts any misplaced orgasms out of the picture.

'Professionally, obviously,' Rafe adds his agreement before he settles back to what he was saying. 'But if developing the weddings here means you get stuck in a dead end place, where you're wasting your talents.' He gives me a knowing look. 'Well I don't want that to happen. I'd rather forget it before we begin.'

At least he knows the limitations. Although I have to admit, the middle of nowhere is less dead end than I once thought. Some days the farm is buzzing.

I bend down and ease myself onto the sodden ground next to Rafe.

'I'm not sure I'd do any better than this job elsewhere.' I say slowly, pulling my legs tight against my body for warmth. I can't pretend. I was literally *bursting* with excitement when I thought there might be work here next year.

He turns on me with unexpected force. 'There you go again. Why do you always undersell yourself?' He shakes his head in exasperation. 'You're hugely talented, but you never want to take the credit for anything. When exactly did you get this down on yourself?'

When my voice comes out it's so small it's embarrassing. 'Maybe when I was with Brett. He was never very complimentary, that's all.' He seemed to think if he criticised me, he'd make himself look better. But actually, he was better, at everything, so it probably worked.

Rafe's still huffing in exasperation. 'Critical is the last thing I want to be.' He blows out a sigh. 'But you need to learn to believe in yourself.'

That's the funny thing. I feel much more sure of my abilities, since they've been tested on an hourly basis here. And up to this point, I'd always thought I'd done well at holding my own with Rafe.

'I have got more confident since I've been here, so I'd say it's been good for my personal and professional development.' I might as well admit it. But I'm not going to hold back with him either. 'I could say the same to you. You have this fabulous business potential here, yet you're in constant denial, looking for every excuse not to succeed.'

He gives me a sideways glance. 'Why is it, whatever we're discussing, you always come out on top?'

Now it's my turn to give a shocked blink. The 'on top' stops me in my tracks. In my defence, I'd had a lot of fizz very fast that night. And I did come clean about it being all down to me.

His lips twitch into a grin. 'On top, in the professional sense, I mean.'

'Obviously.' I add, fast as I can.

Rafe's grin spreads. 'So all things considered, maybe we should make a joint decision.' He narrows his eyes at me. 'To push Daisy

Hill Farm Weddings forward.' He hesitates over the last word. 'Together.'

The sudden explosion of butterflies in my chest is definitely excitement about the job.

'I'm glad we've resolved our differences.' He's gone all understated and serious. 'As I said before Red, it's not about the bottom line. People are what matter.'

Definitely not going in for makeup sex then. *I did not just think that.*

'People like me already know that happiness doesn't come from things,' I say. My mum always taught me that.

'Why does that not surprise me?' he says, slapping his hand on my knee. 'Bloody hell, you're freezing.' He gives my knee a vigorous pat, then leaps to his feet.

A second later he's hauled me onto mine, and he's dragging me towards him. As his arms wrap around me, the heat of his body radiates through mine. Secure, delicious. I lean in, grateful for the enveloping warmth, but it's not just heat. There's another charge zinging between us. 'Come here.'

His low voice resonates against me. The arch in my back thrusting my boobs against his thumping chest has nothing to do with driving away the cold. It's an instinctive response to the urgent tug at the base of my stomach. As our eyes meet, his are smudgy behind his lashes. He scrapes the water off my cheek with his thumb, sending a thousand new shivers through my body. As I run my tongue across my lower lip, I'm willing him to kiss me. Somewhere in the seconds it takes his face to descend towards mine, I go rigid.

'Rafe, stop.' Pushing my palms against his chest, I twist out of his grasp.

What the hell am I thinking? It's taken weeks to live down what happened last time. I've battled up this damned hill because I'm desperate to persuade Rafe to carry on with weddings, so I can save my job. Not so we can have a fucking love fest. Snogging him is the fast way to blow our working relationship out of the water. Why the hell would I throw my professional future away on another clinch?

'Sorry, only trying to warm you up.' His face cracks into an awful wounded dog expression. 'Nothing more.'

'Right.' I believe him, thousands wouldn't.

I don't even like Rafe. Although that's not strictly true. I didn't used to like him. Nine months ago he was an arse. But credit where credit's due. Now not so much. Lately I've seen a whole different side.

'If you'd rather get hypothermia, that's up to you.' Stripping off his polo shirt with one easy movement, he hands it to me. 'At least put this on.'

'G-g-great.' I say again, although this time I'm being ironic. But once I've tussled my arms into the polo, I immediately feel the benefit. 'Thanks.' I grimace as my head pokes through the neck, and I take in a six pack, and low slung jeans. A feather of hair running down from his belly button and disappearing beneath his belt.

'Race you down?' His eyes are glinting.

Just this once, it makes sense to let him win. Which is how I end up slithering down Daisy Hill, watching a bare backed Rafe leaping ahead of me, arms outstretched, his tanned skin shiny in the rain. If I hadn't known better, I'd have sworn he was pretending to be an aeroplane.

By the time we reach the Landy we're red with cold.

'Feed sack?' Rafe drags a knife from his pocket, pulls a crumpled plastic bag from a pile in the back, and makes a few slits. 'The rural equivalent of the survival blanket. Some people round here wear them all the time in winter.' He hands it to me, as if it's the most natural thing in the world for me to put it on.

'Only for the ride back to the farm.' Okay, in style terms, a fluorescent yellow sack counts as such a huge disaster, it's probably edgy. But I care less than I should have because despite the crackling plastic, once I've slipped it on like a waistcoat, it's surprisingly warm.

'Binder twine belt?' He grins as he cuts me a length of rough string, and tosses it over. 'Essential to complete the outfit.'

Worse and worse. On balance I decide to manage without that final accessory.

'For the record…' I'm yelling over the roar of the engine, as we bounce back down the lane. 'Daisy Hill Farm Weddings would still be a good proposition, regardless of me.' Just saying. Because someone has to. Carrie messed up, but other people wouldn't.

'Good to know you'll be here though. It wouldn't be the same with anyone else.' He shoots me a sideways grin as he shouts back, his own sack flapping as he wrestles the Landy into the courtyard. 'Hey, we finally got our matching outfits. Lemon's big this season, did you know?'

Dammit. This man knows exactly which buttons to press.

'Rafe…' I wait until he negotiates the bend by the house, and looks me full in the face again. 'Fuck off.' As for not liking him, there are times, like now, when one glance is enough to turn my toes to syrup. When I kick myself for liking him way too much.

'Whatever.' He's laughing as he yanks on the handbrake. 'This is too good to miss, fancy a selfie?'

61

In my kitchen at Brides by the Sea: Fumbling and favours

What with preparations for Cate and Liam's wedding, and the small matter of their gigantic wedding cake, the next week passes in a blur, most of it spent up to my elbows in cake and biscuit mix, in my kitchen. As for Rafe, the most I see of him is a silhouette on a distant tractor.

'So here're the bags for the favours, with labels, and pink and red ribbons to tie them.'

We're closing in, and Cate's popped in to see me on her way back from work. She drops her soaking brolly into the sink, before dropping a damp carrier on the side.

'Hey, nice hair, Pops.'

I ruffle my fingers through, to make it as messy as it's supposed to be. 'I splashed out on a choppy bob for your big day.'

'It's fab, and the orange has finally gone too.'

'Orange was my break up colour.' I grimace at the memory. 'I'm not in pieces any more, so faded blonde's okay for now.' I laugh, as I reach for a plastic container. 'Here, have a peep at the favours, see what you think.' I prise the lid off, and Cate peers in at the pile of heart shaped biscuits, inhaling deeply.

'Wow, they're so pretty, and they smell delish.' Poor Cate's on a last minute diet of air, in a final attempt to get slender before the wedding in two days' time.

'That's the butter shortbread. They're only small, can you allow yourself one?'

Cate hesitates for a second, then dives straight in, wiping the crumbs from her lips as she crunches hungrily. Then she goes straight back for a second. 'And how many have you made?' She's mumbling with her mouth full. Her third disappears in one swallow. If she keeps this up, I'll be needing another batch.

'Six for each guest, so that's one thousand eight hundred biscuits altogether. I've got hearts imprinted on my retinas, after that, believe me.' I'm only teasing, I'm used to industrial quantities. 'I'll bag them up later tonight. Here, I'll show you one of the cakes.' I reach for a container from another stack. 'Have you decided what kind of butter cream you'd like yet?' I can see her salivating on the spot at the mention of icing.

'Well Liam's favourite is chocolate, but I'd set my heart on raspberry jam and vanilla.' She peeps in at the giant sponge, nodding. 'Gorgeous, how many are there?'

'There'll be sixteen altogether.' I've still got a couple more to bake. 'Four cakes, stuck together with icing for each tier. I'll make the tiers here, then stack them up and do the final touches in the marquee.' A dusting of icing sugar, and a scattering of fruit and flowers will complete the job. If it sounds massive, it's only because it's in scale with everything else about Cate's wedding. Right now the poor woman looks hungry enough to eat it single handed. 'Then we'll have some cupcake towers too.'

Cate swallows loudly. 'So what do you think for the icing?' She's agonising as she asks. 'With the red and pink theme, maybe Liam can get his chocolate fix with the cupcakes?'

Given their history, I reckon she needs to bend on her colours, just this once. 'The sponge is vanilla, so how about chocolate icing in two of the tiers, and vanilla and jam in the others.' I'm not sure I've swung her yet. 'Lots of people love chocolate,' I add, hastily. 'It'll be great with raspberries and strawberries.'

She licks her lips, then takes a deep breath. 'Sounds fab, we'll go with that.' Fumbling in her bag, she brings out another packet. 'I almost forgot, the bride and groom for the top.' She pulls off the tissue paper. 'Ta-dah. What do you think?'

The pottery groom dressed in a rugby kit cracks my face into a smile. As I take in the bride in her long white dress tackling the groom, my beam widens. 'I love that the bride's going in for a horizontal tackle, with her arms round his hips.' I'm laughing now, not only at the humour, but with relief that Cate is so in tune with Liam after all. 'It's perfect, Liam's going to love it.'

'So it's all settled that Rafe's coming too?' Cate asks, going straight in for a low tackle of her own.

After the hen night rescue he's guest of honour, obviously. In my absence, Rafe and Immie got together and decided that we'll all manage any problems jointly, in our wedding clothes. Although frankly, I could have done without spending an entire day with the scrubbed up version of Rafe.

'As far as I know he's coming,' I say, 'not that I've seen him.'

'We'll soon put that right.' Cate beams. 'Liam and I are doing the seating plan later, Immie's asked for you all to be together. Chas has volunteered to help, so he'll be there too.'

Immie's recent surgical attachment to Chas is getting worse, not better. 'Chas volunteered as what? Gigolo for bridesmaid two?'

Cate shakes her head. 'I think it was for traffic management. Or maybe crowd control?' Poor girl, wedding stress is giving her a sense of humour bypass. 'And then they've arranged for you to stay over in Rafe's spare room.'

Oh, shit. My stomach's plummeting like a lift in a twenty storey building. 'You're joking?' Even as my wail is bouncing off the sloping ceiling, I know she's not.

'No, the cottages are full, so Rafe's insisting you sleep at his.'

Dammit. Definitely no drinking allowed for me, then. There's no way I want to end up where I did last time. In his bed, begging is such a bad look. Something about the rugby tackling bride bringing down the groom is horribly reminiscent of my night in Rafe's bedroom.

'Great.' If I sound ten times too grateful, it's only to mask how appalled I am.

'Okay, well I think that's everything.' Cate peers out of the porthole as she goes for her umbrella. 'Except the bloody weather, of course. Have you seen it out here? It's been throwing it down all day.'

'All week actually.' Ever since that day up on Daisy Hill. And for the first time in months, the view from the porthole has been wall to wall grey, without a hint of glitter on the sea.

'But I *so* want a sunny wedding.' Cate's groan is heartfelt.

'I know, I want sun for you too, but England's a rainy place. At least you've ordered a load of umbrellas.' A load being a hundred. White to match the wedding. What else can I say? 'Jules will get some fab shots, whatever. His stormy shots are legendary.' I guess it's good if Cate can come to terms with rain before it ruins her day.

'Pops, what's this?' As she moves to pick up her bag, her voice takes on a quiet urgency. 'You didn't say anything about a job?'

Cate stumbling over the job description I just printed out wasn't in my master plan for this afternoon. 'That's because there wasn't any job until ten minutes before you got here. And probably there still isn't.'

'Tell me to butt out if you like.' She nods towards the pile of papers on the draining board next to her bag. 'But I'm here if you want to share?'

'I told you I'd emailed the place I used to work in London ages ago. They didn't have any openings, but now someone's gone off sick, and it might be long-term. Nothing's certain, but they sent the job details through anyway.'

'And?'

I shrug. 'No idea, I haven't read it yet.' That's how new it is. And given I'm pretty sorted here now, I can pretty much dismiss it. 'It won't come to anything. I've been away from the industry for so long, I'm probably unemployable.'

'Not from where I stand.' Cate sniffs, as if to say she's an employment expert. Which admittedly, she possibly is. 'But I thought Immie said you and Rafe are taking the weddings forward? As a team? Did she say you had a uniform?'

Oh my days. I knew those matching feed bags would come back to haunt me. And however reluctant I was to start back in February, I'm really excited to be to staying on now. Three damp pages outlining a job that hasn't come vacant isn't worth either of us bothering about.

'I'm really looking forward to next year at the farm.' I'm being truthful there. 'But first things first, we need to get you married.'

'Good thinking,' she says. 'You're always so sensible. Let me give you a huge thank you hug, and then I'll go.' The way she flings her arms around me and draws me into that Diorissimo-infused warmth is achingly familiar.

'Thank you, and not just for the cake.' She's mumbling into my neck now. 'We wouldn't even have needed a cake if you hadn't bailed us out with your dress money…and you working at the farm saved the wedding in the first place…if it wasn't for you there wouldn't even be a wedding, Pops.'

There have been so many times over the last few years when Cate's hugs are the only thing that have got me through. Every time Brett wasn't there for me, she was. When my mum died she couldn't have done more. And when Brett screwed up big time, she was here, mopping up my tears. It's good that I've finally got to a place where I'm the one who's come through for her.

'Right.' She finally stands back with a sniff. 'I'll go now.' Wiping her nose with the back of her hand is not what Cate would usually do.

As we stare at each other, I swallow back the huge lump in my throat. My eyes are blurry with tears, simply because it's taken so much for Cate to get here. 'Off you go, Mrs,' I bustle her towards the stairs. 'I'll be at yours first thing to help with the flowers,' I call, as she sets off down the stairs. 'Two days from now you'll be Mrs Williams.'

As her footfalls fade as she winds her way down, I go back to my kitchen to make the last batch of sponges and worry about how I'm going to cope with spending the whole of the wedding day with Rafe.

62

At Daisy Hill Farm: Missing bits and willing helpers

Hair and make-up for a bride and eight bridesmaids, in time for a wedding at twelve? When you do the maths, you pretty much have to start before you go to bed. As it is, we're in the marquee until late the day before, ignoring the depressing patter of the rain, doing the final touches like flowers and bunting and fairy lights. I dash home for a couple of hours sleep, then there's a hundred trips up and down the stairs at Brides by the Sea to load up my car. I'm back at the farm by seven, dodging the showers in my rain coat, to unload into Rafe's kitchen. Then I head over for my bridesmaid beautification.

Despite feeling like the crack of dawn to me, albeit a dismal one, Rafe's already up and out when I reach the farm. As I drop my overnight bag next to his sofa, the delicious scent of grilled bacon hanging in the air makes me wish I'd found time to squeeze in a breakfast of my own. Given how scared the bridesmaids are of bloating, there's no chance of finding any food in the cottage that's become Bridesmaid HQ for the morning. But I grab my dress and shoes from the car, and head straight over there anyway.

We've agreed I'll be first in, so I can dip out and build the cake, before we put the dresses on for a photo call with Jules at eleven. Even so, by the time I arrive, the long living room is buzzing with women in dressing gowns and rollers, all waving 'hello' with their flutes of buck's fizz. Everyone's clearly avoiding mentioning the rain, although I can't help thinking it would all be so much more relaxed if the sun was out. Someone's already put on their music, and Adele's competing with the background chat and laughter.

'Cate…' There's barely time for me to bend in for a kiss, before she's whisked off by Jules for some pics with her mum in the bedroom. Jules must have his mind fully on the job, because he scales back his full on hug greeting, and offers me an eyebrow wiggle instead. A second later a full glass lands in my hand, the next I'm being guided to a chair, by three women, intent on transforming me.

There are times when bridesmaid hair and make-up feels sticky and awful and you end up looking more like a drag artist who got on the wrong end of a builder's trowel. Then there are other times when the person who gets out of the chair afterwards is you, but a thousand times prettier. Which is what happens today. But hey, this is Cate we're talking about here. It was always going to be the beautiful outcome. Let's just say, if I was rich enough to employ these women to do their thing on me on a daily basis, believe me, I'd consider it. Even if I worked on a farm.

'Hi, Red.' Rafe squints at me from where he's standing by the island unit, as I arrive in his kitchen quite a lot later. 'You look different this morning.' He narrows his eyes. 'Are you wearing make-up?'

Great start. My look took so long to achieve, and he seems to have entirely overlooked that despite my hair still being short, the hairdresser has managed to twist it into gorgeousness. I consider telling him to fuck off, but I hold it in. There's a very long day ahead. We don't want to get off on the wrong foot.

'Maybe a bit of lippy,' I concede.

'I thought so.' He gives a satisfied smile. 'Different, but nice. Bacon cob? There's one ready.'

Honestly, I could hurl my arms around his neck for that. The cob that is, not the compliment. 'Yes please, I was already ravenous, but the bucks fizz made it worse.'

'You've been drinking already?' His lips are twitching as he hands me the cob.

I know drinking was not in the plan for today at all, but hopefully one glass will have worn off by tonight. Or was it two?

'First and last of the day.' I'm promising myself more than him. As I add a dollop of ketchup, and bite into the sandwich, I'm hungry enough to inhale it. But bearing in mind bridesmaid's bloat and the up-coming tight waist, after the first wolf sized chomp I try to nibble it.

'So what's next?' he asks.

'I'm heading down to the marquee with the cake, then coming back to change for photos.'

'It's great to get an insider view of a Daisy Hill wedding.' He rubs his thumb across the stubble on his chin, the way he does when he's thinking a lot. 'Today's like a dry run for us too.'

'Sorry?' I stop in mid chew. What the hell is he talking about?

There's another proud smile. 'I've decided to be much more hands on with the wedding side, so we'll be spending a lot more time together next year.'

'What?' As my gasp of shock drags cob crumbs straight down my windpipe, I begin to cough uncontrollably.

'Whenever there's a wedding, obviously.' He pours tea from the pot and slides the mug in front of me. 'Here, a drink might help, sorry, I should have offered before.'

It's hard to choke, drink tea, and have a nervous breakdown all at the same time. Especially when you're trying to keep your hair and makeup flawless. 'Thanks,' I croak, as I move straight into a massive sneeze.

'Farming can get quite lonely. Working with you – and the guests – will give me a new perspective.' He grins. 'It's exciting when a new project gives you a whole new lease of life.' He gives a rueful shrug. 'I'm really looking forward to it.' His voice takes on an edge of concern. 'Are you okay there?'

'Great.' I'm still hoarse, panting, and trying not to lose all my foundation on my tissue, as I blow my nose. 'Change can be very positive.'

I'm just not sure why I'm so floored by it. If Rafe wants to help with his own weddings, it shouldn't be a problem for me. I know I've taken to trying to avoid him lately, but I'll have to get my grown up knickers on, and man up. It shouldn't be that hard. If he can pull off spending time together, I'm damned sure I can. I stuff the last of my cob into my mouth, and slide my plate into the sink, crossing my fingers there's no more nasty shocks on the way.

I rub my hands together, in a businesslike way. That's the answer to this. So long as we stay professional, we'll be fine.

'Okay.' I bolster myself with a deep breath. 'Time for the cake.' As I check the piles of boxes that are arranged at one end of the work surface, my heart misses a beat. I look up at Rafe. 'Is this everything? There should be another box.'

'That's all you brought in.' His shrug and his tone are laid back. 'Did you leave any in the car?'

'Good point.' As I race across the yard, and hurl the car door open, I'm praying to the god of rustic sponges that he's right. But he's not. The boot and back seat are empty. Crap, crap, crap. If my hair wasn't twisted into tiny Greek style braids and curls, I'd be tearing it out. I bolt back into the kitchen, slam the boxes around, and check them again, in case it's bucks fizz confusion. 'Oh my giddy aunt…'

'Is something wrong?' Rafe's helpful smile partly makes up for his complete failure to realise this is a major crisis.

'Somehow,' and I can't quite believe how, 'I've lost the top tier of the effing wedding cake.' My voice is trembling, as I thump my fist on the granite work surface.

'Think about it calmly.' Rafe frowns. 'Cake's don't just disappear. If it's not here, and it's not in the car, where else might it be?'

I try to ignore how soothing and reassuring his voice is.

'On my kitchen table.' I can't believe I've been so stupid. I can't believe I didn't go back up for one last check. Except I can, because I'd been up and down so many times, and my main worry was not forgetting my dress, or my shoes. Can I race back to town, and still be ready for eleven? There are so many thoughts buzzing through my head, it feels like it's about to explode.

'Give me your keys.' He's sticking his hand out.

'What?'

'You carry on with cake building, or whatever it is you're supposed to be doing, I'll pick up the missing tier.'

For a moment I stare at his fingers. His broad thumb, roughened by the farm work. Something about the traces of veins on the inside of his wrist makes my tummy clench. And not in a good way. It's going to be so damned hard being this close to him on a daily basis. Except now's not the time. Shaking that thought away, I make a huge effort to drag myself together.

'If you're sure?' Unclipping a key from the bunch I drop it into his hand. 'This unlocks the door at the bottom of my stairs.' The smallest brush as he closes his fingers around my key sends a seismic shiver up my arm.

'I'll be back before you know it,' he says, as he springs across the kitchen. 'I'll send one of the guys to run you and the cakes that are here down to the marquee. It's looking pretty wet out there.'

'Ahh, the rain.' There are a hundred other problems to concentrate on. Stamping on a misplaced hormone rush comes low on the list, but I try to strangle it anyway. 'Thanks, Rafe, I owe you.'

'No problem.' As he reaches the door, he turns. 'By the way,

I took your bag up to your room.' His smile is lazy and unnervingly soft. 'I take it you decided not to risk borrowing any of my spectacular T-shirts to sleep in. Make yourself at home, it's straight ahead at the top of the stairs.'

63

In the wedding marquee at Daisy Hill Farm:
Ready and waiting

There's nothing quite like a marquee on the morning of the wedding day. The muted light, extra dim today due to the grey sky, the twinkle of fairy lights overhead, which, admittedly, are more like a galaxy this time around. Nothing less would have done for Cate. Ditto the crisscrossing bunting forest. And where Liam and his mates have worked wonders at high level, us women have worked our magic lower down. The round tables look amazing with their clusters of single flowers in bottles. The roses and daisies, in pinks and whites and reds and yellows are like the bridesmaid's dresses come alive. And the top table is fab, with the *Mr and Mrs* signs at the ready.

After the frenzy of the bridesmaids' cottage, and the panic in Rafe's kitchen, the warm quiet of the tent is deliciously calming. Rafe even saw to it that I had my own team of muscle, to bring the cake boxes into the marquee. Heaving the hewn wooden platter onto the waiting cake table, I finally set to work to construct the wedding cake. Once I get going with my sponges, fruit, flowers and icing, the rest of the world melts into soft focus around me.

'Could you do with another tier there?'

Rafe makes it as far as my shoulder before I notice he's arrived.

'Perfect timing, you're such a star,' I say. I feel like a huge weight has lifted as I take the container from him. A second later after a final dusting of icing sugar, the cake's complete.

He stands back, nodding at the towering creation. 'Amazing. That's pretty damned spectacular. From a non-expert view, obviously.'

Grabbing my phone, I take a few snaps, just for the record. Then I dive into the bag to find serviettes, and the cake knife Cate's had specially engraved. 'Oops, mustn't forget the Bride and Groom for the top.'

As I balance the figures on the cake, from the corner of my eye I see Rafe's face splitting into a grin.

'Good, aren't they?' I say.

As he slides closer to murmur in my ear, he gives a low laugh. 'Remind you of anything?'

Let's get this straight here. It's disturbing enough for me to remember wrestling Rafe onto the bed, and seeing the awful similarity playing out on top of Cate and Liam's cake. Rafe recognising it too is bad enough. But flagging it up to me? That's plain mean. I'm thanking my lucky stars I'm wearing cover all foundation, because without it I'd be bright red to the tips of my ears.

From the way he's biting his lip, and that slow half wink he does, he knows he's pushing it.

I heave a huge mental sigh. 'I thought we were…'

'What?'

If he's trying to look inscrutable, his dimples are getting in the way, big time.

Keeping it professional? '…it doesn't matter.' Dragging it up again will only make it more than it is. And given it's nothing anyway, and is over and done with and left in the past, there's really no point.

He glances at his watch. 'I don't want to rush you, but it might be time for us to scrub up?'

There he goes again. 'Us'. It slides out unnervingly naturally, even if he's only talking about his team. Hopefully when I get used to hearing him say it on an hourly basis, it'll jar less.

'Good thinking.'

Between us we pick up the bags and boxes, and wind our way between the chairs with their smart silk covers and chiffon bows, towards the entrance.

'So what are you wearing then?'

It's a casual enough, throwaway question from him. There's no need to read anything into it.

'Red flowery dresses, eight of us all the same, you'll be hard pressed to tell us apart.' I wince at my choice of words, although happily, he's oblivious.

'Easy enough, I'll just look for the red hair then.' He pushes back the entrance flap, holding it up as I bob through. A second later he's opened an umbrella and is holding it over me, sounding perplexed. 'Red, what happened to your hair? It's not red any more.'

As the dark clouds part, and there's a burst of sun, I squint into the light. My cropped hair has grown long enough for me to see it, and I pull at a strand now. 'It hasn't been red for months. Even the orange ends have gone now.' But if that's how much notice he's taking, I might be off the hook after all. I'm crossing my fingers that when he's done this scrubbing up he's talking about, it doesn't have the same end result it did last time.

64

In the wedding field at Daisy Hill Farm:
Power drills and chocolate flakes

There are times when it stops raining, and you're so pleased you
don't care that it's still blowing a gale and chilly. As we make
our way down to the open barn for Cate and Liam's ceremony,
the sun breaking through is like a gift. None of the rest matters.
Rafe has transported the registrars to the field by Landy, to make
sure they didn't get stuck in the mud on the way, and the ceremony guests are all in position, sitting patiently in the open
wedding barn.

We bridesmaids are squishing across the wet grass, and apart
from swapping our Spanx horror stories, we're mainly talking
about how pleased we are Cate went for the floor length version
of the dresses in the end, because they're great for keeping our
legs warm, and hiding our boots.

'Remember my festival wellies?' I give Immie a wink as I give
her a flash of my purple flowery boots under my skirt. 'I loved
them so much, I kept them for best.'

'I knew you'd thank me for raiding Brett's flat in the end.'

She gives a grimace, as she rubs her forehead with her posy, and clears a swathe through her foundation. 'Bloody ironic that my bridesmaid shoes are the first high heels I've ever owned, and I've had to take them off.'

I laugh as I lean across to blend her streaky make up. 'Five inch wedges too. Don't worry, you can put them on as soon as we go into the marquee.' Poor Immie has no idea what agony heels can be. I guarantee she'll be begging for her flats within minutes.

'Lovely that Bolly and Brioche are here.' I grin at Immie. 'Dragging a groomsman towards the wedding barn as we speak. Rather him than me.'

Immie snorts. 'When you and Rafe have kids, you'll be able to tell them you met when he pulled you out of a ditch after being dragged in by those two hounds.'

'What?' Just because she's met Mr Nearly Right, there's no need for her to assume everyone else is heading for coupledom too.

'Only joking.' She says. 'But seriously, you have to be close to argue the way you two do.'

'We both care a lot about out work.' I sniff.

'Sure.' She grins at me. 'So why are you thinking about taking another job then?' She turns on me with one of her power drill stares. 'And before you go ape, Cate told me, but only because she's worried about you.'

Immie certainly chooses her moments. 'It won't come to anything.' Whatever you do when you try to shout under your breath, but only be heard by one person, that's what I'm doing here.

'It better bloody not come to anything.' Immie's half hissing, half growling between her teeth but I'm saved from anything worse by Cate arriving.

'Wow, it's the coolest idea of Cate's to arrive in the ice cream van.' The office bridesmaids are in their own cluster next to us, chirruping as we wait for Cate and her dad to be ready.

Immie gives me a sideways look. 'Well done for that at least, Pops, you saved her a packet with that doubling up suggestion, especially as we were having the ice cream van all day anyway.'

'Tight waistband or not, I could murder a ninety nine.' I say, in an attempt to break the ice that just froze over between us because of the job. I thought I was still muttering, but the chorus of 'me too's suggests everyone heard me.

'You'll have to wait,' Immie says, grudgingly. 'But they're here now, so it won't be long. What's that tune the ice cream van's playing?'

'Greensleeves?' We wait as Cate and her dad clamber out of the van, and Jules leaps forward to take what seems like a whole album of photos. Immie's eyes go dreamy. 'That tune always makes me think of chocolate flakes, and now I'll always think of weddings when I hear it.' The fact she hasn't lost her dreamy look says a lot for how her and Chas are getting on.

There's another chorus of agreement, but we're being bustled into a crocodile by a groomsman. There's a sudden gasp as Cate appears from behind the van. Straight out of the cliché book I know, but with her lace billowing in the wind, and her blonde waves gently caught up in the simplest tiara, she looks like a princess. As she flutters along our line, we're all dipping into our hanky pockets. Even Immie is blowing her nose.

Cate stands in front of me so I can check she's perfect.

'Ready?' I ask, as I tweak a strand of hair into her tiara, and straighten a tiny twist in the lace of her strap. 'You're beautiful.'

'Is George okay?' she asks.

'Fine, he's with your mum and the boys.' I say.

'Thank you, Pops, for everything,' she says, giving my hand a last squeeze, and then the rest of the bridesmaids are walking ahead, then I follow, and Cate and her dad walk behind.

* * *

The moment when Liam finally sees Cate in her dress is wonderful. The way his face simply lights up with love has me diving for my hanky pocket again. I bet Cate didn't plan to have the noise of eight bridesmaids snivelling beside her as she got married. I've pretty much got my face in a tissue all the way through the repeat after me bits, and the *I do* part. By the time my emotion has subsided enough to put my hanky down, Liam's getting the crumpled piece of paper out of his top pocket to make his special promises. He must have run them past Cate a dozen times, and she always batted them back, and wrote something better for him herself. But he really wanted to do his own. So in the aftermath of their argument, he told her to butt out. So who knows what he's about to say, but for all our sakes, I just hope it hits the mark for Cate.

'Ahem…' As Liam clears his throat a gasp of nervous anticipation ripples through the guests. Running his fingers through his tousled curls in the silence, he shoots one more grimace at his best man, then he begins.

'Cate, the first time we met. When I saw you running onto the rugby pitch…in your office shoes and tight skirt…waving your hand bag…yelling like a banshee…I knew you were the one for me.' His voice is ringing out clear and strong, and then everyone laughs. Even Cate.

'You were hot – in the best possible way…' He pauses and gives Cate an extra grin. 'You were passionate…it was obvious you'd move heaven and earth to defend your kids…'

There's a lump in my throat as Liam's voice cracks slightly. As I glance behind me, through the blur of my tears, I can see people dabbing their noses. Cate's worst fear was that he was going to refer to her as Milf, but I think we've got over that one nicely.

'I knew I had to make you mine, whatever it took…and every day since then, you've showed me a thousand different reasons to admire you…and to love you…'

Oh my god, straight from the heart. Even though my mouth

is turning inside out from the effort of holding in my balling, I turn to share a grimace with Immie. But somehow I miss Immie, and instead, half a barn away, I lock eyes with Rafe.

'But more than that, you've loved me back…and cared for me…and touched me in a way no one ever did before.' Liam's absolutely nailing it here.

Rafe's leaning against the wall, smiling that soft smile of his with those crinkles at the corners of his eyes, and out of nowhere, I'm suddenly wishing he was saying these words to me.

'You trusted me with your wonderful children, and it's been my privilege to share their lives,' Liam goes on.

When I finally wrench my gaze away from Rafe's, it feels like there's a hole in my chest the size of Dartmoor. And if my hand wasn't clamped hard over my mouth, I think I might throw up.

'And today you're making me the happiest man in the world by marrying me.' Liam's face breaks into a beam. 'Cate, if I said thank you a million times for being my wife, it still wouldn't be enough…I promise to love you forever.'

As the clapping erupts around the barn, Cate's scraping the tears from under her lower lashes, frantically biting her lip. And I'm hugging my arms around myself, hanging on as hard as I can, as the aftershocks from Rafe's smile thunder through my body.

Eventually, the applause dies down, and Cate collects herself. She pulls a perfectly folded paper from somewhere in her bra, draws herself up, and looks deep into Liam's eyes. If I know Cate she'll have no need for her paper, she'll have memorised this weeks ago.

But I can't tell you what she says, because I don't hear a word of it. There's only one phrase hammering round in my head, and it's jangling loud enough to block out every other sound and thought.

I'm in big trouble here.

I'm in love with Rafe Barker.

65

In Rafe's kitchen at Daisy Hill Farm:
Empty glasses and office speak

The fab thing about working on weddings is that it really builds your stamina. By the time Rafe and I finally head for his kitchen sofas at three in the morning the rest of the farm is quiet.

'So, my high points of the day.' I'm listing them more for myself than for Rafe. 'That the sun shone. And the dresses, obviously.' Jess and Sera should be so proud. 'Immie and Chas dancing a little salsa number.' I'm ticking them off on my fingers as I go. Who'd have thought anyone would persuade Immie to go to dance classes? As if that wasn't enough, Immie keeping her heels on *all* day was yet another mark of her dedication to Chas. 'The animal area went down a storm, especially the tame chickens. The ninety nines were every bit as yummy as I'd anticipated. Was it too piggy of me to eat three?'

Rafe's face breaks into a smile. 'I know better than to answer that one. Wine?' Twisting the cork, he pours out the fizz.

'Please.'

'One glass, to wind down.'

The wink he gives me makes my tummy flip, even though I'm still in my Spanks.

'Are you staying in your dress?'

I take it that's not an invitation to strip. 'Might as well keep it on and get my money's worth. They were very practical and comfy in the end.' I brush my hands over the full skirt, noting how the muddy tide mark at the bottom is camouflaged by the bright print. 'Immie spilled half a bottle of red over hers, and it barely showed.' I'd say we well and truly road tested the brides-maid range.

'Great to know.'

'That was defo my best wedding ever.' I say. 'It used to be the one where I got together with Brett, but that lost its sparkle when we broke up.' My voice is rueful.

Rafe sinks into a chair, and stretches out his legs, his rolled up sleeves exposing a dangerous amount of forearm. There's something mesmerising about those wrists of his. That rare combination of strength and vulnerability. The flesh and the bone.

'Isn't it a bit of a cliché, hooking up at a wedding?'

That comment of his has me laughing. 'The first wedding Brett and I met up at, he went off with another bridesmaid. My cliché moment happened at the next one. Talk about second best, he used to joke my dress were prettier second time around.' No idea why I'm hanging this dirty linen out now, other than to try and remind both of us – okay, especially me – why I'm single and staying that way. Regardless of any heart fluttering, or nausea brought on by proximity to you know who.

'I've learned so much since I worked here.' There's no trace of the girl who had a stack of bridal magazines before she even found a steady boyfriend. The same one who hung on Brett's every word for years, in case it turned into a proposal. 'Before, I was so desperate to have a wedding of my own, but since I've helped with so many, I realise the wedding's hardly important.

It's more about the partnership the couple have. What matters is the strength of the relationship.'

'The wedding dress you sold that day in the office…' His searching stare turns me inside out. 'It was yours, wasn't it?'

I nod, chewing my lip in silence. I give a sigh, if only for how stupid and naive I used to be. 'Weddings are so stressful, you need to be really strong as a couple to get through one. Brett and I fell at the first hurdle. Whereas Cate and Liam made it all the way.' If I'm grinning wildly, it's only because I'm so proud.

'He really does love her doesn't he?' Rafe says.

'Totally and utterly,' I nod. 'Liam's promises to Cate were another high point of my day. He literally had everyone in pieces.'

Rafe's lips twitch. 'Actually, I helped him with those.'

So maybe that's what that smile was all about, at the ceremony in the barn? I take a second to pick my jaw up off the floor. 'How did you do that?' I had no idea Rafe had a way with words. Although on second thoughts, maybe I did. When he's not yelling, he's very eloquent. And thinking about it, he's pretty damned succinct when he is yelling too.

He shrugs. 'Liam was in the marquee, really struggling, so I chipped in.'

'Bloody hell.'

'We did them in no time.' Rafe's acting like it's no big deal. 'As soon as I took the pen, he unblocked. I asked him what he thought the first time he met Cate, then for the rest I thought of what it feels like when you really love someone, and it was easy.'

Rafe settles back in his chair, while I let his words sink in. 'So you're thinking of another job?'

If my glass hadn't been empty, I'd have hurled the wine down my throat so fast I'd have choked. As it is, my hand lurches so hard, I practically bite the glass.

He's gone quietly apologetic, almost embarrassed. 'I couldn't help but see the paperwork, at yours. The cake box was on it.'

So much for discretion. Blame myself for forgetting the cake. But sometimes I think it's a shame there isn't a town crier in the village. That way people could find out everything about every-body, straight away, and we'd all know where we stood.

I shrug. 'An enquiry I made months back…it's nothing really… still up in the air…'

'A bit like your kitchen then.' He sniffs. 'If you feel you have to go, it's fine.' The words come out in a rush. A bit like when he was writing wedding promises then. Except instead of being all squishy and adoring, this time round he's all matter of fact, and snippy. Like he's dismissing me. Pushing me away.

'Right.' It's all I can offer, and it's close to a whisper.

Talk about bad timing. My completely irrational self falling head over heels, for a guy who isn't on the market, but who I've got to spend a big part of every day with, for as far as we can see into the future. So why aren't I happier he's letting me off the hook?

'Where is it?' Now he's effectively pulled up the draw bridge to keep me out, he's moving onto polite conversation.

'London.'

'Better and better.' He gives a grimace. 'It's really important you do what you have to do, Red. Don't worry about the farm, we'll muddle through here.'

'You don't understand, that job was only a safety net, in case I couldn't get a job round here. Which is why I hadn't told you about it.' When the hell did this get so complicated? 'Shall we have more wine?' Suddenly it feels like a whole bottle wouldn't begin to be enough.

Rafe gets to his feet, and next thing he pops a stopper into the top, and the bottle's back in the fridge. 'No, you'll only regret it later if you have too much.'

'Please play me something on the piano…just before I go to bed…' I'm wincing at the whine in my voice, and really I'm bluffing. Where I'd put myself if I had to look at those fingers spreading over the chords, I don't know. But tiny part of me wants to see if it's possible to push him. And how far.

'It's three thirty in the morning.' He's almost as whiney as me. 'Bed. Now. Please.'

It was worth a try. And I have my answer. He's entirely unmoved. And unmovable. End of. 'Okay, I'm off.' Alone. Sober. A not quite perfect end to a perfect day.

Later, when I'm up in the guest room – grey and white sheets, broad stripes, impossibly high thread count, for anyone who needs to know – as I'm peeling off my high-line super-power panties, I can't help thinking it's a good thing I'm on my own tonight. If I'd tried the same moves as last time while wearing these, I might have catapulted Rafe as far as the coast.

Later still, I hear the clunk of his bedroom door closing. As I kick the sheets, aching to be somewhere other than in this very empty king sized bed, I know whatever lies ahead, it's not going to be easy.

66

In the big tipi at Daisy Hill Farm:
String quartets and butterflies

The last Daisy Hill Farm wedding of the season might have been sad. As it is, we barely mention the landmark, because we move seamlessly into the wedding fair. And instead of being filled with wedding guests, two days later the mammoth tipi is thronging with wedding suppliers. And seeing as many of them are people we've been working with all season, there's a real party atmosphere. And Immie's making the most of it.

'Bloody hell, those filo and spinach tartlets are to die for. Have you tried them, Pops? Oh, and by the way, Jess says "Hi".'

Immie's been stomping round the wedding breakfast section of the tent, on a one woman quality control mission. In other words, she's been lunching on the freebies. Big time. And Jess is here too, with some taster dresses and shoes. Sera is in charge back at the shop.

'You don't have to try one of everything, Immie.' I give an inward groan. 'Just make sure you leave some for the real customers.'

'Who says I'm not one?' she laughs.

Stomping? That would be because Immie's currently embracing a neat half-way-to-high-heel compromise – the wedge trainer. Hunters with heels, for winter, are speeding their way from Amazon as we speak. True enough, if she's up for changing her life-long Converse habit, it's entirely possible she's only a ring away from lifting her husband-ban too. Which goes to show the power of firemen. Except in his case he's been lighting fires, not putting them out.

'Are they going to be making that racket all day then?' She cocks her head in the direction of three girls with music stands and floor length low cut dresses, playing violins and tossing their hair like they're Vanessa Mae.

'You'll have to ask Jules,' I say. 'He's been talking about "his" string quartet for weeks. And it's not a racket, it's Vivaldi. And Bach.' Whether they need to do quite so much bending and stretching is questionable. They're certainly getting plenty of attention. Along with the Wedding Day Camper Van and the stall with personalised beer labels, they've completely sidelined the groom audience.

Immie's straight back at me. 'So where's the fourth one then? Got her bow caught in her cleavage?'

'Ouch, that's a bit harsh.' Although I'm telling her off, I send her a grin too. 'What's the matter with you, lipstick envy?' It definitely won't be boob envy. As we saw the day of Cate's wedding, when it comes to cleavage, once Immie is surgically detached from her hoodie, she's not short of bootie. Sometimes the best way to deal with Immie in this mood is to ignore her. Maybe if I tidy my card piles, and tweak my cake area she'll calm down. Moving along, I concentrate very hard on dusting the array of champagne bottles on the venue 'Welcome' display.

'Free champers to any couple who sign up for a wedding, who thought of that?' she says, as she descends on my sponge samples.

'That's Rafe's idea,' I say, whisking my plate of mini cupcakes out of reach before she hoovers the lot. I grin at her as she mouths 'wow' through a mouthful of popcorn and buttercream. 'He's really thrown himself into the wedding business lately.' So much so, we've barely been apart for the last two weeks.

And how am I finding it? If I'm honest, it's absolute hell. If Rafe being obstinate was difficult, Rafe being pro-active is totally bloody impossible. As for him being considerate – or even worse, meltingly kind – by the end of the day, I'm reduced to a grease spot. At night I'm so excited I can't sleep.

Immie gives a snort. 'A couple over there were having a full blown domestic over whether they need *Save the Date* cards. I doubt you'll be picking up a booking from them today.'

'Have you seen the new season booking files?' They're so pretty, I can't help rearranging them at every opportunity.

'Only about a thousand times,' Immie grins, 'but seeing it's you, I'll look again.'

'There are different colours for different years, one design for the field venue, and another for the house bookings, and then there's the Holy Grail, the email contact sheet.' There you go, once I get started, I can't stop.

'Very nice too…'

Rafe arrives, peering over Immie's shoulder.

'So have you given much champagne away?' His smile is laid back.

'There's serious interest,' I hesitate for a second, forcing myself to meet Rafe's gaze. 'But I just wanted to have a final, final check that you were going ahead, before I let anyone put pen to paper.' I couldn't bear for anyone to be in Cate's shoes again next year, and find their wedding venue was being pulled.

Before Rafe can reply, Immie cuts in. 'It's fine, Rafe and I had a serious talk. He's definitely a hundred percent committed.' She's nodding her head with a beam is as broad as the tipi.

'Hundred per cent,' Rafe echoes.

I'm smiling, even though Immie's input is vaguely perplexing.

I just can't put my finger on why. 'In that case let's give away some champagne.'

* * *

It's dusk by the time everyone has packed away, and the procession of vans have wound their way back to the main road.

'Last in the tipi, again?' Rafe saunters in, hands deep in the pockets of his Barbour jacket.

Immie grins. 'You know me, I never go home until the last free snack is packed away.'

'And as long as there's a bride and groom, I'll be hanging on in there.' I flick through my files one by one as I slide them into their box. 'The good news is, I've taken so many firm bookings, we ran out of champers.' As my phone beeps, I slide it out of my pocket, expecting it to be another confirmation text from a couple. But as I scan the text my tummy plummets. 'Oh my…' For a minute it feels like my knees are about to collapse.

'Pops, what's wrong, you've gone all green round the gills?' Immie's giving me one of her intense stares.

Oh crap. I'm not even sure I can speak. 'It's that London job… they're asking if I can start straight away.'

'Fucking hell,' Immie turns on me. 'I thought you told them you weren't interested?'

'I kind of thought I had.' I sigh. I'd got as far as writing the email saying I definitely wasn't available, then after one very long and excruciating day with Rafe last week, I deleted it. But in reality, I didn't actually think it would come to anything.

'Daisy Hill Farm or London?' Rafe cuts in brusquely.

'B-but I'm not sure I want to go.' My voice comes out as a squeak.

Rafe rubs a thumb across his chin. 'You've said how much you love London. If it hadn't been for that tosser Brett, you'd never have left. You can't let this one go, Red. Once you get there, you won't look back.'

I'm opening and closing my mouth like a gold fish. Not just because of the shock of the job, but because Rafe's intervention has the force of a hurricane. 'But what about the farm?'

He stares at me as if I'm an imbecile. 'With the bookings you've taken today, we'll have wedding coordinators queuing up to work here. I'm sure Jess will help find someone.' Although he's breezing through this, his voice sounds strangely strangled. 'We were chatting as she packed up.'

Rafe begins to back away. 'I take it Immie will run you back to your car?' He turns as he walks out into the field. 'Take tomorrow off, we'll manage here. Thanks a lot for today. I'll catch you both later.' And then he's gone.

I'm left quaking. 'What the hell happened there?'

Immie rounds on me. 'Sometimes I'd like to wring your bloody neck.'

'What?' The sheer force of her fury leaves me blinking.

'You are so damned stupid.' Immie's growling, her forehead furrowed by a zig zag of fury. 'That talk Rafe and I had. He only went ahead with wedding bookings because I told him you'd definitely be staying. If you leave now you'll be letting all of us down. Rafe, me, not to mention yourself.'

'But he just told me to go.' My voice is unnervingly firm and quiet. God knows, a huge part of me was aching for him to ask me to stay. Even if it's hard working with him, it's going to be a hundred times harder to walk away.

'For fuck's sake, Pops, you've really got no idea have you?' She's shaking her head. 'He's said that because he wants what he thinks is best for you.' Her growl turns to a snort. 'Because he loves you.'

It takes a second for her words to sink in. 'That's just bollocks.' And in the wholeheartedly unlikely event it was true, it's even more reason to go. Here's me saying I've learned so much, and how strong I am. How I've learned to rely on myself, because I know that's the way I need to be. I wouldn't be thinking about a relationship for a second, if I wasn't being weak. Going back to relying on anyone would be such a backwards step.

'You've turned this place around Pops, think of what you've achieved. You never found it hard to stand up to Rafe before, tell him you want to stay.'

'No, I can't.' However hard I've worked, his rejection has taken every bit of fight out of me.

Immie's frown is indignant. 'But you can't just leave.'

'Can't I? Just watch me.' Picking up my box, I step out into the halflight, where the outline of the giant tipi is like a series of spires against the darkening sky. I can't believe that things have spun around so fast. When it first came up, I was desperate to have the permanent job here. I admit I had no idea how hard it was going to be, working beside Rafe. Fighting an attraction when I don't want a relationship makes every day into a battle. And whatever Immie says, she's got Rafe wrong. He's practically ordered me off the property. He wouldn't do that if he saw me as any part of the future here. There's no way I'm going to beg him to let me stay. What's more, begging is too reminiscent of how I was with Brett. Now I've finally found myself, I need to stand on my own.

'I think I'll walk back to the farm thanks,' I call to Immie, as she turns out the lights and heads for the pick-up.

Immie jumps in her truck, revs the engine, and yells at me out of the open window. 'I can't wait to hear what Cate says about this.'

But in the end there's no intervention. Nor do I see Rafe again. And when I leave for London on Monday, Jess is the one who takes me down to the station and waves me off.

OCTOBER

67

London: Wall to wall pedicures

Although I've been away from London for so long, as soon as I'm back it's less of a new start, more like picking up. It's almost as if by returning, I've closed the circle I broke when I left to return to Cornwall to live with Brett. Okay, there's a lot more denim in the office, some women have popped out whole families in my absence, people are drinking weird coloured juices. And biker boots have replaced pumps. But apart from that, the last eight years in Cornwall might not have happened. Career wise, I'm miles behind where I might have been, but the relief is I can do what they're asking. And within hours of arriving I get the offer of a tiny bedroom near King's Cross, in a flat belonging to someone who works in accounts.

The best thing about being in London is not having to look at Rafe every day. But in the end that's also the worst thing too. When I walked away from Brett, it felt like my whole world fell apart, and so did I. Whereas now I have work and a solid, structured routine, in the place I always assumed I wanted to be. There are shops and bars and galleries and people. I can even afford to

371

treat myself to pedicures. But the ache inside me makes every day heavy and desperately long. And somehow I can't believe that the pictures that run through my head before I go to sleep every night, are the cows and fields at Daisy Hill.

As for Rafe, I try not to go there. But if I go to the Daisy Hill website, we're all there. Cate and Rafe dressed as a bride and groom. Immie and I in our bridesmaids' frocks. All laughing out from the home page. But that sun filled day of Jules' photo shoot seems like it belongs to a different world. Which of course it does.

And I can't get away from the thought that although I've got my shiny new life, and the job I always should have had, somehow I've managed to drive everyone I care about away.

NOVEMBER

68

London: Shopaholics crossing the road

**Red, are you around tomorrow? I'm in London, if you fancy
lunch?**

11.30 Regents Park? We can grab a pasty and have a walk?

Rafe? In London? Yes, I was picking my jaw up off the floor too.
It's all a bit last minute. But when a text makes the bottom drop
out of your stomach like that one did, it's better not to have too
much thinking time. I managed to get away from work early, so
we can grab an early lunch. Not that I could face the confines of
a restaurant, but for an outdoor guy like Rafe an al fresco sandwich should work. I need to be back in the office by two for a
client presentation, which is good. It's always best to have a time
limit on these things.

'So what's in your parcels?' I ask Rafe. We've got as far as
compromising on paninis instead of pasties, and finding an empty
park bench so we can eat them. It wasn't hard. Although it's
lunchtime, the drizzle and the blustering wind mean there aren't

many takers. As for Rafe, striding along the pavement to meet me, his best Barbour billowing, looking like he's visited every Department Store on the London Top 10 list. This is a whole new side of the man for me. Once the initial rush of excitement is over, and I'm brushing crumbs off my meet-the-clients stretchy black skirt, I steal a sideways glance, he's looking a lot leaner and way older. 'Hey, have you lost weight then? ' Something about the deep hollows in his cheeks turns my insides to mush. 'You look pale. Are you okay?'

'So many questions.' He shrugs, staring down at his charcoal jumper. 'Maybe my tan faded. It's winter in Cornwall,' he laughs. 'And I'm shopping for England, because my mum's coming home. After a year away, she'll expect a decent Christmas gift.'

'Really?' I blink at all the bags. 'You've got some serious bling there.'

'That's the idea.' He gives a grimace. 'So how's the job going?'

'Fabulous.' If that's not quite the truth yet, I'm hoping it soon will be. 'Developing an innovative range of ice cream sweets, making ready meals look good on photos. It's a piece of cake after brides and grooms.'

'Can't be bad if you can blag lunchtimes this long.' He gives a derisive snort.

'Actually, I don't normally take a lunch break.' Working through keeps the doubts at bay.

He nods slowly.

'So you don't miss Daisy Hill Farm at all then?'

The question takes me by surprise. I stare into the distance and puzzle. We're in a park, there's grass, and shrubs and amazing trees, yet somehow it's not the same. It doesn't feel like home. 'Actually…' Of course I ache for the farm. It's what puts me to sleep at night. I just never quite thought of it as missing it before.

A smile creeps across Rafe's face as he watches me. 'You've gone all dreamy. Who'd have thought? So you do miss it?'

'Maybe.'

'I'm sorry, I should have given you longer to settle. But I had to come and ask, is London everything you'd hoped?'

'Actually it's horrible, but it's nothing to do with London, it's because I miss you so damned much.' The words come out in a rush.

Rafe takes a deep breath, and turns to look at me. 'When Helen left, I didn't want another relationship. But she left because we weren't compatible, and it's only now I've met someone I've truly fallen in love with that I realise what she meant.'

Something inside me feels as if it's breaking. I let my panini drop.

Rafe is shaking his head. 'Shit Red, I'm talking about you. You're the one I'm in love with. Head over heels, nothing I can do about it.' He rakes his fingers through his hair. 'I'm not shopping, I don't shop, I hate shopping. I've come to tell you it's awful being without you.'

Completely overlooking that the pile of bags that completely contradict everything Rafe's saying about shopping, I let out a wail. 'But you're the one person who was supposed to understand why I'm scared to be with anyone again.'

He purses his lips. 'You can't just shut down and give up on love just because of one bad guy. It's easy to close down when you're hurt. Brett hurt you, but you deserve so much better. If you're lucky enough to find love, you have to open up again.'

'But I can't.'

'Have I ever let you down?'

I rack my brains to find an instance. Because time and again he's come through for me in so many different ways. Those taxis stuck in the mud. Rafaella's arrival. The hen night. The day he brought me roses from the garden. Then suddenly it hits me. 'For fuck's sake Rafe, you were the one who sent me away.' My voice is sullen. 'If that wasn't letting me down, I don't know what is.' The stabbing pain of rejection from that day is still as fresh as if it happened yesterday.

'Red, I had to make you come to London. If you hadn't you'd always have wondered "what if". That's the only reason I didn't ask you to stay. At least now you've tried it, you know.'

'I see.' So what Immie said is right after all.

'I also knew if you were sure you wanted to stay at the farm, you'd just have come out and said it.' He grins at me. 'That's one of the things I love about you most, Red. You always come straight out with what you think.'

'Except I didn't this time.' I give an inward groan. 'In the end it was too hard to stay and see you every day when I was in love with you.'

His smile widens, and his voice is soft. 'So you do love me. You don't know how good that makes me feel.' He bites his lip, and hesitates. 'When you first came to the farm, I was miserable. You helped me see I didn't have to be like that. I admit having you there pushed me out of my comfort zone at first, but you've become such an important part of my life. I don't want to live it without you.'

I give a sigh. 'The last few months changed me too.'

'You've learned to be strong. But now you need to learn that you can trust me.'

I sink down on the bench. 'So what are you saying?'

'We could take things at your pace.' His smile is as soft and reassuring as his voice. 'I was hoping you'd consider coming back. Your job's still there, but I don't want to rush you. Maybe we could start with Christmas?'

Put like that, it sounds a lot less scary. Trust Rafe for finding a way to make me comfortable. 'Christmas sounds good.' I chew on my thumb. What am I letting myself in for?

'Immie might not be talking to you, but she's still saved you a holiday cottage.' He grins. 'She and Chas are so loved up, you really wouldn't want to crash with them. Jess has got your living room full of dresses. And with four kids and two dogs, Cate's would be mayhem.' He's ticking off the alternatives on his fingers as he rubbishes them. 'Or you can always stay at mine of course.'

Something about that last grating throwaway line makes my lips twitch into a smile. 'In the guest room, I presume?'

He ignores that comment. 'I promise we'll have a gigantic tree in the kitchen. And I'll play *Silent Night* on the piano…'

There you go. He knows how to get me every time. 'Now you're talking,' I laugh, 'Carry on like that, I might just be persuaded.'

Getting up, he takes my hand, and pulls me to my feet. 'Come on, let's go somewhere less cold, get a coffee to warm you up.'

But first I let him pull me into his Barbour, for a full blown heat-up hug. And if I keep tight hold of his hand after that, it's only because he's a guy from the country, who really has no idea how to cross roads in London. And at one fifty nine, when he leaves me outside work, the snog he gives me is long and achingly sweet. I know I'm supposed to be holding back, but it's enough to make my body explode on the spot. How the hell he thinks that's enough to get a girl the whole way through the next four weeks, I have no idea.

DECEMBER

69

In St Aidan: Snowflakes and sequins

Although Rafe is desperate to come to London to pick me up, in the end I decide to come back by train. It's not about the distance, or the threat of snow, or the nightmare holiday traffic on the A303. It's more that there's something fitting about coming back in the same way I left. Also I'm banking on six hours solitary travel to give me time to get my head around how I feel about everything. Not to mention a gentle adjustment to the culture shock of leaving London.

More fool me. In reality, it's the week before Christmas, and the trains are rammed. I'm squished between some very drunk geology students, and an extended family, fighting over their iPads, spilling coke and flicking popcorn. Who'd have thought a popcorn bucket could really be *that* bottomless. Or that sticky. By the time I drag myself out of my seat in St Aidan, the only thing I'm wiser about is Angry Birds Star Wars, and mining opportunities in South America. As for myself, I haven't even got to the questions, let alone found the answers.

'Red…'

When I finally fight my way through the barrier, and bury myself in Rafe's huge hug, his smell is exactly as I've imagined every second since he left me a month ago. Wax jacket. Soap. Soft wool. Warm skin. And a big dash of what I suspect Immie would call pure pheromones. My scalp tingles as he runs his fingers through my hair, and tugs.

He mumbles as he tilts my chin upwards. 'Did you know you have toffee in your hair?'

'Actually, yes.' But before I get to the bit about the bottomless popcorn, his mouth is smoothing over mine. Then I go dizzy, as the world begins to spin, and we only get dragged back to reality when a suitcase-on-wheels the size of a sideboard crashes into us.

Okay, I grew up with my mum's eighties music videos. Everyone's allowed one cheesy Christmas reunion moment. But maybe a snog that finishes in almost falling over, where you end up being hauled back onto to your feet by your hunky boyfriend isn't the best look. Although when I say boyfriend, we all know I didn't really mean it personally. For me. Obviously. Because he isn't really.

'So where are we going?' I ask, as Rafe tosses my cases into the back and we escape the biting wind in the shelter of his best Landy.

He raises an eyebrow, as he glances at his watch. 'First stop is Brides by the Sea. You're just in time for Jess's Christmas drinks.'

Oh crap. I pull out my best client smile in the dark. 'Brilliant.' Although I pull off sounding enthusiastic, part of me is shy and horribly embarrassed to be coming back. 'Actually, I'm really worried everyone's still pissed off with me for leaving.' Even from three hundred miles away, I could feel the chill at the way I rushed off. I'm hoping the ton of Sanctuary gift products I have with me will help to break the ice, even if it can't fully make amends.

Rafe's laugh is low. 'I think they'll be pleased to see you.'

As we turn into the mews, and the shop building looms, excitement flutters through my chest. 'Look at the windows.' I'm clenching my fists, because Jess has nailed it, yet again. 'They're *so* pretty.'

The white tulle dresses are set off by garlands of frosted ivy, and suspended white and silver baubles. Strands of starry lights, shimmer against hanging snowflakes, flecked with a thousand tiny sequins. But the best thing of all for me, there isn't a single picture of Josie, or our dress. It's as if the world has moved on, and I can too. It's also lovely to see lace and tulle again. Up until the moment I saw the amazing windows, I hadn't realised quite how much I've missed weddings.

We hurry from the car, pushing through the door into the warmth of the shop, and head for the noise in the White Room bridal area. Our hollow footsteps on the broad boards sound comfortingly familiar. It's as if I've never been away.

'Poppy…' As we peep around the corner into the party, Jess swishes towards us, jug in hand, and there's a surge of greetings as everyone turns to smile and wave. 'Rafe.' We each get two kisses, although Rafe's are seriously more lingering than mine, but whatever.

'Come here Mr Farmer, let me tidy you up,' Jess says.

As I watch Jess stretch up, and tweak the tiniest piece of hay from Rafe's temple, a feral growl rises in my throat. I grit my teeth, and swallow back the most violent pang of jealousy I've ever had. Not that I'm possessive, but for a second there I could have happily clawed her face off.

'Hands off Jess, this one's definitely mine.' Hopefully my laugh is light and sparkly, rather than the snarl it could have been. I sense Rafe's warmth extending around my back, as he closes his arm around me. As I look up into his face, his grin tells me he's ecstatic he's been claimed.

A voice comes through the crowd. 'And finally. Jeez, Pops, am I glad to hear that.'

That voice can only be one person. 'Immie?' She's so short, that even in heels she still disappears in a crowd. As I scan the heads, I can see Jules and Chas, but not her.

Next thing I know I'm knocked so hard backwards I practically end up wearing the line of Alexandra Pettigrew dresses hanging in front of the window. It's Immie, hurling herself at me with the force of a full rugby team, closely followed by Cate, who gives me a much calmer kiss on the cheek, and a small, but meaningful squeeze.

Jess is powering towards us again, as we slip out of our coats. 'Help yourselves, there's Christmas punch, or Ruby Duchess.' She drops a couple of cocktail glasses into our hands. 'And in honour of Christmas we're floating frozen red fruit in the drinks.' She gives a grimace. 'I only hope I don't live to regret it.'

'In other words, for chrissakes keep the raspberry ice cubes away from the dresses.' I translate for Rafe's benefit as she breezes off. 'Jess only ever serves prosecco, dressed up to match whatever season. She gets a killer rate from the wholesaler.'

Rafe nods. 'I called in to see the wine merchants last week, I'm hoping we might be able to move into wine for the weddings soon.'

I have a sudden rush of realisation that everything has moved on without me, even though I've got no right to feel left out. Realistically, Rafe was hardly going to put the whole business on hold because I'd gone.

He goes on. 'I'm looking into T-shirts too. "We got hitched at Daisy Hill Farm" and stuff like that.'

'Brilliant.' Yet so typical. 'Why didn't I think of that?' I groan.

He gives a shrug. 'I guess we each have our own areas of expertise.' The king of the T-shirt slogan sends me a meaningful stare. 'Which is why it's best when we work together.'

But before I have time to react to that, Cate returns dragging Liam behind her.

'So how's our city girl getting on?' he asks.

'All good thanks.' I smile. 'How's married life, Mister?'

'Ditto.' He laughs and slides his arm around Cate's waist.

Immie butts in. 'For god's sake, get real Pops. If city life was suiting you, you wouldn't be looking so peaky and ill.' She snorts, and rolls her eyes. 'You'll be over producing adrenalin. It's a common problem in London. People who live there feel constantly stressed.'

Cate gives Immie a sharp kick on the ankle, which she might have felt more if she hadn't been in biker boots.

'Don't take any notice, you're looking fab Pops.' Cate gives me another squeeze. 'She's still furious with you for leaving. She's even worse than she was the first time, when you went off to uni.'

And that's when it hits me. The difference between here and London. Immie bringing up the stress is like a light bulb moment. Because for the first time since I left here three months ago, I'm completely relaxed. How the hell had I not noticed? Even if Immie is balling me out, I'm warm and safe and secure, with the friends I've known forever. Whereas all I have in London is a career. But that's a career for someone I used to be, not the person I am now. Trying to pick up the pieces with that is like the square peg and round hole metaphor. Which is why the fit is so uncomfortable.

As I stare around the familiar bridal room, and take in the faces of all the people I love, it finally sinks in. What I have here isn't just a job, it's a life. And I'm surrounded by friends, and a whole extended network of wedding professionals. And with all that support, and with the amazing opportunities at Daisy Hill Farm, my whole future is poised to take off. Six hours of agonising on the train didn't get me anywhere. But one mouthful from Immie, and I'm right on track.

'So talking of prosecco and pomegranate, how's life in the food industry?' Cate sips her pink cocktail. 'Made it onto the board yet?' She gives me a wink.

I drag in a breath. 'Actually, they've offered me a permanent position.' That's the surprise they sprung on me a couple of days ago. 'Based on the work I've done in the last couple of months.' The shocked intake of breath beside me is from Rafe, as he visibly shrinks at my side.

Cate's eyes are wide, but she keeps her voice light. 'Well… wow…that's fabulous…obviously…You've done really well to pick it up again.'

The last few months, I've thrown myself into the work, desperately trying to make up for those lost years. And yet the offer of a full time forever job didn't thrill me as much as I'd imagined it would.

I give a grimace. 'I don't think it was eight years of cake baking that swung it. It was working up at the farm that gave me my confidence back.' I smile at Rafe.

'Holy crap Pops, do not ruin my Christmas by accepting this.' Immie growls.

Rafe's breath is warm on my cheek as he sighs. 'Last time I suggested you took the job, but this time I can't pretend any more.' As he stops to clear his throat, everyone stops talking and turns to watch him. 'Every bit of me wants you to come back here, Red, because I don't want to be without you.' He's biting his lip as he looks down at me. 'You've already made the most amazing changes at Daisy Hill, and you've only just begun. There's a great partnership waiting for you up at the farm, and I think that's where you belong.'

'Awesome.' Sera's hanging onto the dress rail, one foot on top of the other. 'That has to be the best welcome home ever.'

And she's right. 'Thanks Rafe.' What can I say? 'I know some of you thought I was running away.' I narrow my eyes at Immie here. 'But I'm so pleased I went back to London. This way I'm lucky enough to be able to make a choice, knowing it's the right one for me.' As I smile up at Rafe, his face is drawn and pale. 'I'd always regretted leaving London. Going away helped me realise what I really value. But coming back to you all made me realise even more, that this is where I want to be. So I won't be taking the London job.' Talk about making it up as I go along. But there's no doubt about it, I know now this is what I want. And now I've decided I can't think what took me so long. 'And I'll be coming back here again, as soon as I can.'

There are whoops from all around the room, and Immie thumps me so hard on the back that I almost have a soft fruit disaster.

Rafe's face relaxes into a happy smile again, although the colour doesn't come back to his cheeks for quite a while. After all the hugs and congratulations have finally subsided, he leans closer, murmuring in my ear. 'The good news is the permission's are going through for the indoor weddings in the house and the barn too. Just saying, if you were ready, there would be plenty to get your teeth into by January.'

Later, as we leave for the car, and pull our collars up against the cold, I swallow back a big lump in my throat.

Rafe's breath is warm in my ear. 'Are you okay?'

I wipe a tear away from the corner of my eye. 'It's lovely to be back.' I sniff back at him, praying my smudged eyeliner's not giving me panda eyes. 'Sometimes you have to leave and come back, to find out where you truly belong.'

'Very true.' He squeezes my hand tightly, and the kiss he bends to give me is incredibly sweet.

When it's over, his voice is husky in my ear. 'Thanks for choosing Daisy Hill, Red.'

'You taste of raspberries.' I laugh. 'And it wasn't only Daisy Hill you know, I chose you too.'

'That makes two of us.' He holds out his car keys. 'Ready to go home?'

70

In the drawing room at Daisy Hill Farm: P.S.

Rafe's as good as his word. His Christmas tree is huge and the decorations around the kitchen – garlands, and enough hearts and hessian bows for a whole house, not just one room – are to die for. His excuse – by next Christmas we might have expanded into the rest of the house, and if not, they'll always come in for weddings. Eye rolls to that one. Since his spontaneous trip to London, he's developed a serious shopping habit. Talking of sheets – and I know you'll want the bedroom details – they're new too. White with tiny silver stars on. Bought in London, the day he left me at the office. In a way I'm pleased he was certain enough to do that. And one of my presents from him, among many, is a Barbour jacket. Who'd have thought I'd ever become a country person with my very own Barbour, but somehow I almost have.

His present from me is a London T-shirt – not a six hundred pound Versace one, just a normal boy one, with a photo collage of the Shard, to add to his tractor-wear collection. And an I Heart London mug for the office. Just so he'll always be reminded of that day he came to bring me back home again.

And on Christmas night he fills the empty drawing room with candles, and Jet and I stand in the flickering light, listening to Rafe playing the piano. The first thing he plays is *I Can't Help Falling In Love With You*, and by the end we're both crying. Because neither of us can help it. Or could help it. Or whatever.

After we've both blown our noses a few times, he leans his chin on his fist, and looks up at me, as I lean on the piano. 'You do know we'll be lambing soon, Red.'

Okay. He's a farmer. He can't help having a one track mind. And these days I can hold my own talking animals anyway.

'I thought lamb was a noun, not a verb.' I frown.

He raises one eyebrow. 'So there will be lambs in the kitchen. For a few weeks.'

I feel my eyes go wide. 'What, all of them?'

That seems to amuse him. 'No, just the ill ones…and the orphans…and the ones who need extra care.'

Which in the end sounds like it could be quite a few. 'Right…' Where's he going with this?

'And sometimes we have to put them in the oven to warm up.'

What the hell? 'Great,' I say, even though it's mind boggling. Although when I think about it more, it's really not that different from cooking. 'And your point is?'

'They're very cute. There's nothing like a baby lamb wiggling its tail as it drinks from the bottle. You'll love it. But I'm just flagging it up…in advance…so you have time to get used to the idea.'

And then I get it. We're parading worst moments here. Before they happen. So we can get them out of the way.

'I'm guessing I can live with that.' I say. 'Which just goes to show how much I love you.'

He bites his lip, thoughtfully. 'You know I think I started loving you that day with Cate's dogs, when I hauled you out of the mud.'

'Love at first bite?' I laugh. 'I remember thinking if you were mine, I wouldn't have let you out of bed so early, so you definitely made an impression. So long as you remember, don't volunteer for too many dawn starts for milking.'

Rafe turns and grins up at me, his stubble etching the shadows of his cheek bones. 'Just think, Red, years from now, we'll be able to tell our grandkids we met in a ditch.'

Actually, I've heard that somewhere before – thank you Immie – so I don't react. Instead Jet and I stay silent, and arch an eye brow at each other. Because we both know, he's winding me up. Not that I'd ever envisaged that my future would contain so much mud. But if that what it takes to be with Rafe, I'm happy to work with that.

'So what shall I play next? Silent Night? Life on Mars?' Rafe narrows his eyes. 'Or there is this other one I've been practising an awful lot while you've been away. Because it reminded me so much of you.'

The four chords he plays resonate through me. I recognise it immediately. 'Don't Stop Me Now?'

'It's pretty much your signature tune. But it's got to be played really, really loud.' His mouth is bunched up as he tries to hold back a grin. 'And obviously, you'll have to do that air punching thing where you run around the room.'

Shit. 'You know about the actions?' My insides are withering, as I let out a squeak of panic. 'But how?'

'Two small words.' His cheeks are bursting. 'Office window.' Then he lets his grin go.

'Oh crap, surely not?' To say I'm dying of embarrassment is an understatement.

'Used to be the highlight of my day. Everyone else's too. It's for stuff like this I love you so much.' It takes a few seconds for his laugh to subside. 'So what do you say?' He slides me a wink. 'As you said once before, that track seems like a suitably up-beat way for us to begin?'

And finally, he's come round to my way of thinking. 'I can't argue with that.' I grin, and swoop in for a kiss, because at this moment, we have to be the happiest people in Cornwall.

A moment later, Rafe's hands come crashing down on the piano keys, and as the opening bars of *Don't Stop Me Now* thunder around the empty drawing room, I reach up and punch the air.

Acknowledgements

A big thank you…

To my hugely talented editor Charlotte Ledger, who works tirelessly with amazing flair, and somehow distils the chaos of ideas, and the mess of a manuscript into a finished book. This series is as much hers as it is mine. To Kimberley Young and the team at HarperCollins, for a wonderful cover, and all round expertise and support.

To Debbie Johnson and Zara Stoneley, and my writing friends across the world for sharing and caring. To my friends, the fabulous bloggers, who spread the word.

To Samantha Birch for her awesome wedding tips. A special shout out for Emily Bridal of Sheffield, and Alexandra Anne Bridal Boutique at Chatsworth. Those beautiful shops provided so much inspiration for Brides by the Sea. And thanks to Caroline Tranter for baking Poppy's cakes, and providing photos.

Big hugs to India and Richard, for their wonderful wedding. The wedding shops we visited were where this series began. I wish we could do it all over again. And to Anna and Jamie for carrying on where they left off. To all my family, for constantly cheering me on. To Max for the techy stuff, for reminding me it's time for tea, that the garage needs tidying, and that we need a new shed. And big love to my own hero, Phil…for never letting me give up, and for always being there.

Favourite Prosecco Cocktails
from Brides by the Sea

In case you'd like to try a taste of Brides by the Sea at home, here's how to make some of the fab cocktails featured in Cupcakes and Confetti. Don't stress too much about the quantities. At Brides by the Sea it's much more about sloshing it in and having a good time. As Jess would say, 'let the fun begin…'

ENGLISH GARDEN

This is a summery mix, perfect for cooling off in the shade on a warm afternoon, or for enjoying on a lovely summer's evening.

Ingredients

20ml elderflower cordial
20ml gin
Prosecco
A sprig of mint

Pour the elderflower cordial and the gin into your flute, and top up with prosecco. Then add a sprig of mint to garnish.

Jess would always use Hendricks gin, of course. For a variation use elderflower liqueur, or add apple juice, and a squeeze of lime. Cucumber garnish also works well.

RUBY DUCHESS

This great Christmas cocktail will bring rosy colour to your celebrations. Purists sometimes make it with champagne, but at Brides by the Sea it's prosecco all the way.

Ingredients

A bottle of prosecco
500ml pomegranate juice

Mix together in a jug, or alternatively splash pomegranate juice into a cocktail flute, and top up with prosecco.

Floating raspberries are a gorgeous addition. Freezing the raspberries before floating is a nice touch.

If you want to "up" the Christmas spirit add 125ml Chambord (raspberry liqueur) to the jug.

JESS'S SPECIAL CHRISTMAS PUNCH

Ingredients

A bottle of prosecco
Half a litre of ginger ale
A litre of white grape juice

Half a litre of pomegranate juice
Frozen raspberries and pomegranate seeds to float

Put the grape juice and pomegranate juice in a jug and chill. Just before serving, add the ginger ale and the prosecco. Float frozen raspberries and pomegranate seeds, or alternatively add frozen red summer fruits to float.

ELDERFLOWER LEMONADE WITH FROZEN BERRIES
(non alcoholic)

So here's a little treat for the designated drivers and non drinkers....

Ingredients

1 lemon
2 tbsp caster sugar
35ml elderflower cordial
Frozen berries (summer fruits from the freezer section work well)
Sparkling water to top up

Squeeze the lemon and add the juice to a jug. Add the sugar and elderflower cordial and mix until the sugar dissolves. Pour into the glasses, on top of ice cubes, and a handful of berries. Top up with sparkling water. Throw a slice of lemon into each glass for extra zest

Cheers!

Love, Jane xx